'So what do you th
you be happy here?'

'Aye, if you are here to share it with me,' she
said, and although her tone was light, the words
were heavy with meaning.

He studied the small earnest face that looked up
into his. 'You deserve to be happy,' he said
simply.

'And you, Luke,' said Alison. 'Mayhap –' She
broke off and averted her eyes but he put a
finger under her chin and turned the blue eyes
once more to meet his.

'Mayhap –' he prompted.

'– we can have a fresh start,' she said.

The Heron Saga 2
This Ravished Land

PAMELA OLDFIELD

SPHERE BOOKS LIMITED

SPHERE BOOKS LTD

Penguin Books Ltd, 27 Wrights Lane, London W8 5TZ (Publishing and Editorial)
and Harmondsworth, Middlesex, England (Distribution and Warehouse)
Viking Penguin Inc., 40 West 23rd Street, New York, New York 10010, USA
Penguin Books Australia Ltd, Ringwood, Victoria, Australia
Penguin Books Canada Ltd, 2801 John Street, Markham, Ontario, Canada L3R 1B
Penguin Books (NZ) Ltd, 182–190 Wairau Road, Auckland 10, New Zealand

First published in Great Britain by Macdonald Futura Publishers Ltd 1981
This paperback edition published by Sphere Books Ltd 1986
Reprinted 1987

Printed and bound in Great Britain by
Cox & Wyman Ltd, Reading

For Joseph

While researching this novel I read many fine books. My thanks to the staffs of the County Library, Maidstone, and Westcountry Studies Library, Exeter, for helping me to find them.

PROLOGUE
1501 *Plymouth, Devon*

Below the tall masts and fluttering pennants of her ship the Princess Catharine of Aragon, being tugged into dry clothes by her maids, could not be persuaded to 'take a look at England' – that cold, dour land of which she had heard such tales and which she would one day rule as queen. She was weak from seasickness, weary with fright and chilled from the soaking they had all received during the nightmare crossing. Doña Elvira fussed round her, reminding her of the speech they had rehearsed in English and the various aspects of protocol which must be observed. Outside the blue sky was pierced by countless masts and standards of the rest of the fleet, for a Spanish princess could not meet her English prince without the most impressive entourage Spain could afford. There were maids of honour, gentlemen-in-waiting, four equerries, a marshal, a butler and a steward. She had a chamberlain, her confessor and her major-domo. Doña Elvira Manuel, the major-domo's wife, accompanied the Princess as her duenna. Even her personal cup-bearer, cook and baker were on board. She brought her own physicians and was in the personal care of the Abbot of Compostella himself. The Archbishop, Bishop and the Count of Cabra completed her 'court'. A large number of Spanish nobles accompanied her and their ships, too, were crammed with staff and servants. And everyone of this

7

vast assemblage was now making frantic preparations for the disembarkation.

Below them the quayside was bright with colour as the people of Plymouth and many nearby towns crowded to the water's edge for a glimpse of the young woman who would one day be their queen. Although unsure when the fleet would arrive, the town councillors had long since made contingency plans and these had now been put into operation. Musicians struck up a lively tune, the Mayor and a delegation of aldermen in the city barge were afloat between the foremost Spanish ship and English soil. On royal instructions, all Devon's nobility and many more from Cornwall were there to provide a fitting escort for the Spanish court as they travelled slowly towards London. Somewhere along the way they would be met by the King's royal representative – Lord Willoughby de Broke, Richmond King at Arms and Somerset and Rougedragon Heralds. For the present the flower of the West Country must suffice.

Joseph and Elizabeth were at the back of the crowd with three-year-old Luke riding on his stepfather's shoulders.

'Oh, wouldn't little Sophie have loved this,' said Elizabeth, 'If we had known, we could have sent word to London and Matthew could have brought them down.'

Joseph shrugged. 'No one knew when they would make landfall,' he said. 'They were turned back once and might never have made it without Brett's help. 'Twas folly to attempt it without a pilot. Hi – keep those feet still, young monkey!' he said to Luke. 'This is no horse you're riding but a man. I count myself lucky you aren't wearing spurs!'

At that moment a cheer went up from the waiting crowd as the first visitors appeared on deck and at a given signal all the bells in the town pealed out in a clamorous

8

welcome as the slim form of the Princess was seen moving gracefully towards the waist of the ship. She stood looking out over the water at the thriving harbour below, and the towering red cliffs. The Mayor of Plymouth began his speech of greeting in Spanish and then in Latin.

'Just see how the rigging is torn,' said Joseph. ''Tis a wonder the poor child reached England at all.'

'And no one here from the King to greet her!' said Elizabeth ''tis strange don't you think?'

'I dare say the King himself will be hotfoot to meet her,' said Joseph, 'and the Prince of Wales with him.'

'Poor little girl,' said Elizabeth. 'Only fifteen and in a strange land. 'Tis to be hoped Prince Arthur can speak Spanish.'

'They have been betrothed for long enough,' he laughed. 'There is no excuse for him if he cannot!'

Elizabeth thought of her own first wedding night and sighed. But Catharine was at least marrying a young man and not an elderly widower. The speeches over, there was more cheering as the Spanish visitors began slowly and carefully to disembark. They had had one soaking and nobody wanted to risk another. Elizabeth, watching the momentous occasion, sighed deeply, with an unconscious sense of prophecy. She could not know that the slight, serious girl stepping on to English soil would be widowed within four months of her marriage, and as queen to Henry VIII would indirectly change the lives of all her subjects, and cast a shadow over that of Luke Kendal who now rode so joyfully on his step-father's shoulders.

CHAPTER ONE
April 1518

As she made her way down the cliff path cold needles of
rain pricked her bare face and arms and the wind tugged
at the coarse woollen shawl thrown carelessly round her
shoulders. Slipping on the loose scree, she clutched at
the cliff wall to steady herself, then glanced at the newly
broken nail on her right hand, cursing angrily. She had
tried so hard with her hands, rubbing them with stolen
pig's grease and sweetening them with lavender. And
her chestnut hair, combed free of tangles, now clung
damply around her face, its glory hidden by the faded
shawl. She scrambled further down, muttering to herself that her wretched state would soon be at an end and
she, Isobel Gillis, would be a fine lady. Below her on the
beach the sea rolled to and fro, endlessly hurling itself
against the rocks in an explosion of spray and drawing
back with a deceptive smoothness that scoured the
pebbles from the sand.

'Mistress of Maudesley I'll be,' she told herself, 'and
eating at a table board and drinking from silver! And I'll
go upstairs to sleep and there'll be sheets made of linen,
aye, and feathers in the mattress instead of straw!'
Reaching the beach at last, she rested a moment, huddled against the cliff, and let her mind dwell on the
glorious future which she did not doubt would be hers.
'There'll be no more shrieding brambles for me,' she
said 'nor bundling birch twigs. I'll not make another

broom as long as I live! I'll be done with dirty nails and sore thumbs. Sweet oils for my skin, that's what I'll have, and silks to my back – and mayhap a ring. Aye, a ring for my finger. Why not?' She sighed with pleasure at this rosy picture and the warmth gave her renewed energy to continue her journey.

Pushing herself away from the protection of the cliff, she drew her shawl closer and strode forward into the teeth of the wind. One day she would wear shoes on her feet and a warm cloak and hood. And that day was not so far away. A smile lifted the corners of the ripe mouth and creased the corners of her eyes – light brown animal eyes flecked with black and set too wide apart. With the smile her face softened and became almost beautiful, losing its fierceness and taking on a gentle expression. Isobel Kendal . . . Isobel Kendal . . . She repeated the name like an incantation, as though by repetition she could conjure the reality. As well she might! For wasn't she Isobel Gillis, daughter of Marion? She laughed suddenly, tonelessly, and with the laugh her features resumed their harshness. 'Isobel Kendal! Isobel Kendal!' She shouted it triumphantly at the top of her voice but the wind seized the words and scattered them across the empty beach robbing her of breath so that she came to a halt, coughing, and was aware once more of the cold wet sand beneath her bare feet.

Above her on the cliff Luke Kendal reined in his horse as the sound of her voice reached his ears and made his heart leap. He did not catch the words but recognized the voice. Often, waiting for him, she sat on a rock if it was fine and sang like a siren, luring him on. Her outlandish ways had intrigued him and her untamed spirit had challenged his own. His love for her had been a consuming passion and their stolen meetings all that he lived for. But now . . . he sighed wearily and slithered from his horse's back, tossing the reins over the branch of a stunted hawthorn. Despising the path which Isobel had used, he climbed down the face of the cliff using foot and hand holds which were by now familiar to him. Isobel, sheltering in the lee of the rocks, heard the rattle of a dislodged stone and darted out to greet him. She ran to him and they clung frantically, whispering endearments until he held her at arm's length repeating her name soundlessly with his lips. 'Did you miss me?' she asked as usual but for answer he pulled her close again and kissed the unruly hair that now fell free of the protective shawl. 'You didn't come Sunday,' she said. 'I waited but you didn't come.'

'I couldn't. I didn't promise.'

'But I hoped so that you would. I hate the Sabbath, for then I don't see you.'

'Hush! Don't say such a thing,' he protested.

'But I do. If the seventh day means I can't see you and can't hold you in my arms, then I hate the Sabbath! I hate it, hate it!' She raised her voice and once more the wind carried the words to the top of the cliff where Luke's horse whinnied at the thin human sound. To silence her, he put a restraining hand over her mouth but she bit him fiercely, then held his hand against her mouth while she licked at the pain she had created. The feel of her warm moist tongue and the soft breath contrasted with the iron grip of her fingers round his hand and the sharpness of her fingernails as they bit into the back of his hand. His body sprang into immediate awareness and he withdrew his hand with a suddenness that pulled her off balance. Letting herself fall, she slid down on to her knees. Her face was against him and her arms twined round his legs, tugging him down beside her. Looking down at her, his resolve weakened. He would tell her after the loving. He would take her once more.

'Let me please you,' she begged.

'You always please me.'

But will I today, she wondered, when I tell you my news? Or will it frighten you? Weren't most men feared of the results of their bodies' work? And should this one be any different? She was wise for her years and doubted it.

'Come down beside me,' she said.

'Here in the rain?'

'Why not?'

She flung herself down on to the hard wet sand laughing as the rain beat into her face, licking it from her lips with the tip of her tongue. Then Luke was beside her, tugging the bodice from her breasts, her arms pinioned to her sides by the tightness of the cloth. Bending his head he kissed the dark nipples which stood stiffly from the pale skin. As his hand slid down over her thighs he threw up the woollen skirt and turned to watch the rain falling on the long bare legs.

'I love you,' she cried. 'I love you, Luke. Speak to me. Tell it to me the way you do, how much you love me.'

But he was silent, for today was the last day. Slowly he shook his head and his fingers traced a path round her nipples; the flesh was cold and slippery to his touch, a new sensation, but it gave him no joy. Leaning over he kissed the full mouth which hungered for him, but his ears were deaf to her pleadings. This long wild woman could no longer be his. After today he must deny his passionate nature, put aside her eager body. Alison was to be his wife.

Even as he thought of her his hands flowed along Isobel's legs and her mouth opened in a moan. There was a low crackle of distant thunder and on the cliff top his horse whinnied restlessly. Above them the storm broke, beside them the sea pounded against the rocks, below them the beach could not cool the heat of their bodies. He would take her once more – and then he would tell her.

'Luke! Oh Luke! Oh, my dearest Luke . . .' As he came into her she thought of his child that slept there, and could not wait to tell him. 'Luke –' she began.

His mouth came down on hers, effectively silencing her, and his tongue put everything else out of her mind. 'Afterwards,' she told herself. 'I will tell him afterwards . . ' and gave herself voluptuously to his urgent rhythm.

The clouds had passed but their own private storm was now breaking. Their energies spent, they faced each other wretchedly, as slowly they realized the measure of their predicament and could no longer look to each other for succour for she was the cause of his as he was hers. All memory of their recent delight had now faded and they stared at each other through eyes cold with dismay and fear.

'Mayhap you are wrong,' said Luke. 'You may be late or even –'

'Late!' she whispered. 'Five months late? Do you think I don't know the workings of my own body? Here, give me your hand. Give it, I say, and feel this.' She snatched his reluctant hand and placed it on her scarcely swollen belly. 'That is your child,' she told him. 'A son, I'm told.'

'You are told?' he said. 'Who tells you that it is a son? No one can know.'

'My mother knows,' said Isobel. 'The needle swung from east to west and that is a sure sign.'

'A sure sign of a credulous mind,' said Luke angrily. 'I don't believe such folly.'

''Tis no folly, but the truth,' she said. 'Would you deny your own son?'

He looked at her, disconcerted by the change in her. Minutes earlier she had been passionate to the point of violence, her body arching and writhing beneath him, her eyes a dark brown, liquid with desire. She stood now apart from him, her shoulders bowed with the burden of her disaster, her eyes pale, her expression hard.

'I can't wed you,' he repeated and his voice sounded strange.

'You must,' she cried flatly, but he shook his head.

'I have told you it must be Alison,' he said. ''Tis all settled and the banns due in four weeks. We have been betrothed for two years now and she has lived with us since April.'

''Tis strange you did not speak of it to me,' said Isobel.

'There was no need. We did not plan to wed.'

''Tis news to me that we didn't,' she said, her voice ominously calm as she studied intently the expression on his face. 'I think this Alison had best go home and look elsewhere for a husband – Luke Kendal is to wed another.'

He shook his head but made no answer as he tried to hold down the panic that rose within him.

''Tis no use to shake your head,' she said, and her downcast eyes hid her growing hostility. 'This is your child, Luke. Your son. Would you have me lose him before he can draw breath? Or shall he live? Oh, let us be wed, Luke. I swear I will make you a good wife.'

'A good wife!' His eyes travelled down the dishevelled clothes to the bare feet, toes curled against the cold. Isobel Gillis, his wife! The thought was monstrous. Her father was a maker of brooms and her mother a strange creature who some called 'witch', though never to her face. How they had bred such a girl he dared not imagine but she stood before him, and he

16

seemed to see her properly for the first time. Uncouth, untamed, a wild creature, prey to her needs and passions like a vixen on heat. Beautiful, desirable, yes. But his wife, no, that she could never be. His sweet Alison would be Mistress of Maudesley. He saw her in his mind's eye, small and fragile like porcelain, remembering the soft voice and delicate movements of her hands as she spun. Such dainty hands, and smooth to his lips. Of the rest of her body he could not know for she remained chaste and would do so until they were man and wife.

Suddenly Isobel's work-roughened hand struck the side of his face and the blow surprised and shocked him. 'You dare think on her!' hissed Isobel, her face distorted. 'I see it in the curl of your lips. You dare to think on her!' She spat her anger and he felt a sudden prickle of unease at the back of his neck as he glimpsed the fury in her eyes. 'You dare think on her when I am here,' she cried. 'I carry your child and yet you'd choose her. You have used me again and again, taken your fill of me, and now your mind turns to her. Don't try to cheat me, Luke, for I won't be cheated.'

The colour rushed into his own face and with difficulty he restrained his own hand from returning the blow. What he had said was true. He had never promised her a wedding. They had never spoken of it. Surely she had never dreamed that a Gillis could wed a Kendal. It was unthinkable. They had loved each other, satisfied each other, nothing more. But now she was with child and he trembled. At eighteen Luke Kendal was the image of his father with the same long slim body, blue eyes and blond hair. The features were there too, the straight nose and high cheekbones. Only the arrogance was missing. Where John had been confident Luke was unsure of himself and at eighteen had none of John's strength of purpose. He had never seen his father but

17

had known love from his mother and friendship from his stepfather. Neither had enabled him to deal with his own insecurities. It had taken Isobel to make him feel the first thrill of manhood and their secret meetings had sweetened his life. Now he must lose her. Already the Isobel he knew was slipping away from him. The passionate girl he had loved was turning shrew. But even as he opened his mouth to speak, her expression changed – from anger to grief as the tears sprang to her eyes and she fell to her knees beseeching him to care for her and the child. He looked down on the tangled wetted hair with pity. No longer a proud woman, she had become a whimpering child and his heart softened, as she had known it would.

'Wed me, Luke. Oh wed me, my dearest Luke,' she begged and heavy tears coursed down her cheeks. Luke was moved with a desperate pity for the girl he had loved. He knelt beside her and heard himself speak the words she longed to hear. She, Isobel Gillis, would be his wife. But even as he spoke he was seized with a great sense of foreboding and a voice within him cried out fearfully that she had bewitched him.

As he went into the house Alison hurried to meet him, arms outstretched, her grey eyes lighting up as usual at the sight of him. 'Oh, there you are, Luke,' she said. 'You are so late. I feared you had been thrown by your horse or met with some other disaster.' She held up her face for his kiss but he merely brushed her cheek with his mouth, reluctant to kiss her with lips that had so recently been Isobel's. 'You are so wet!' she cried. 'Why, your hair is dripping – and where is your hat?'

'The wind has taken it,' he told her. 'I rode down to the beach and –'

'In this weather? Are you mad, Luke? You will take a chill –'

'You know how I enjoy the seashore,' he said, guilty at the deception. ''Tis a fine sight in a storm if the tide is in with the long rolling waves breaking against the cliff.'

'I'll take your word on it,' she laughed, 'for wild horses would not drag me down to the sea unless the sun is shining and I can gather seashells and skim stones across placid water. You are besotted with your seashore and I am jealous for the many times it steals you away from me. But I prattle on so. You make your peace with your Mama, for she too is worried at your lateness. I'll fetch you a hot lemon drink and a slice of the saffron cake which I made myself under Izzie's watchful eye.'

She turned to go but he caught hold of her arm, restraining her. 'Haven't you forgot something?' he asked lightly and she coloured faintly.

'Oh, Luke, you must not,' she murmured. 'Every time you ride out 'tis too generous.'

'You thought I had forgotten.'

'Aye, but –'

'I spent the morning in Honiton,' he said 'and have brought you some –' he drew it from the pocket of his coat ' – lace. The very best that money can buy.' Her genuine pleasure at the small gift was like a reproach. Dear Alison, so unassuming, so quickly moved to joy, so easily moved to sorrow. Like a small creature that responds only to love and gentleness and is driven away by a harsh word or thoughtless action. Alison, his little mouse.

''Tis so beautiful, Luke,' she cried, draping it along the demure neckline of her gown. 'I shall edge my new collar with it – or perhaps trim my velvet head-dress. My thanks, dearest. You are too good to me.'

'And you are too good,' he said, suddenly serious. 'Too good for me. I don't deserve you, Alison, and I love you.'

She was instantly sobered by his earnest tone. ''Twas not always so,' she said simply. 'When I first came to Maudesley you – you felt nothing for me I could tell. Not that you intended me disrespect,' she added hastily for fear he took her remark as reproof, 'but you couldn't hide your true feelings. I read them in your eyes but I prayed most passionately and see – my prayers are answered and you do love me, Luke.' She faltered into silence as the familiar guarded look came into his eyes.

'Aye,' he said almost roughly, 'I love you, and you must remember that always. Always!'

'I will, Luke.'

'Whatever happens 'twill not alter the fact – the fact that I love you.'

'Luke – ?' She was alarmed and he cursed his stupidity. 'What is going to happen?' she cried.

With an effort he smiled. 'Why nothing, to the best of my knowledge. Whatever should happen? Don't frown so, little one. There's nothing to fear, I promise you. Now what of that saffron cake you made for my delight? A slice of that would go down well and would keep me going until supper.' Relieved, he saw the anxiety fade from her eyes. She lifted his hand to her lips and kissed it then ran from the room, calling to Elizabeth that her son was home safe and sound.

In the Priory kitchen, Henry shouted for the boy and, receiving no answer, shouted again. 'Where is that dratted boy,' he grumbled to himself, sweeping the day's peelings into the bucket and giving the table a cursory wipe with the edge of his hand. 'Gawping over the pups, I'll wager.'

He shouted again until Tom finally rushed in, his peaky face flushed with running, a wary look in his eyes. 'Do I have to shout myself hoarse to fetch you?' demanded Henry. 'Hollering fit to burst and you come strolling in as if you've got all day.'

'I ran all the way,' Tom protested, but the old man was not so easily mollified.

'Where was you, then?' he asked. 'Other side of the town I should reckon, the time it took you. Why, at your age, I could have run rings round the likes of you *and* with one leg shorter than t'other!'

The boy listened sulkily to the familiar tirade, waiting for his chance. As soon as Henry drew breath he said, 'There's two with their eyes open this morning but the others is still little slits –' He screwed up his eyes to demonstrate but Henry dumped the bucket of peelings into his arms and snorted.

'There's nowt you can tell me about pups,' he said. 'I was coursing with dogs afore you was thought on and I've seen it all. But when I first came here as a lad there was no dogs – nor pigs, neither, wandering free as air. Shoo! Out!' he yelled, stamping his feet as a large sow appeared at the kitchen doorway. 'There was a place for pigs, then, and that's how it ought to be.'

Tom glanced round anxiously for fear this disloyal outburst should be overheard by the wrong ears. It was well known that the monks relaxed the rules here and there, and the Prior turned a blind eye, but Tom liked it that way. ''Tis doing no harm,' he protested mildly, the bucket of scraps still clutched in his arms.

'You wouldn't say no harm if you slept where I do, with a leaking roof over your head and a damp bed whenever it rains,' grumbled the old servant. 'I warrant you'd moan a bit then.'

''Tis no one's fault,' said Tom recklessly but Henry's fist came down on the table with a surprising force which denied his frail appearance.

'Course 'tis someone's fault,' he said. 'Where's the money for fires in the Prior's rooms all year round and fancy hangings for the walls? There's money for that, well enough. Aye, and hospitality for his sister and her son – and her son's son! You ask me where the money's gone for my roof and whose fault 'tis? I'm telling you. Oh, I keep my eyes open and don't you doubt it. There'll be a bit of explaining to do when the Bishop comes next or I'm a monkey on a stick.'

Tom grinned but Henry had no intention of being jollied out of his ill humour. 'Don't stand there grinning,' he said. 'Get off about your work. I've Brother Eustace coming shortly and no doubt he'll have some dratted errand for me, though he makes such a secret of it I can scarce tell what he's on about. Are you still there? I thought I told you to feed the pigs.'

Still the boy hesitated. 'Shall I feed the merlins after?' he asked hopefully but as usual received a sharp 'no'. The man was inordinately proud of the three birds entrusted to his care and would let no one else near them. The sulky look returned to the boy's face. 'Mayhap the Bishop will have something to say about them too,' he suggested, 'mayhap the merlins'll have to go.'

'Any more of your sauce and 'twill be *you* that goes,' snapped Henry, touched on a raw spot by the idea of such a loss. 'If I have any more of your dratted "mayhaps". Ah, here's Brother Eustace so you get along – and after the pigs there's wood to chop so don't let me find you idle when I get back. The devil finds work for useless lads like you.'

Brother Eustace hurried in. His beady eyes looked shiftier than usual and he was decidedly ill at ease. He waited until the boy had departed then said, 'Come along then, come along,' in a tone which suggested that the servant had kept him waiting. Henry limped after him as he led the way down the steps into the crypt. Above them the monks' voices hummed in chorus as they observed the offices of Prime. It was a few moments before Henry's eyes grew accustomed to the dim interior but when they did he was surprised to see a young man and a girl standing close together, the man's arm protectively round the girl's shoulder.

'Candles, man. Light the candles,' said Brother Eustace and he indicated a candle and two stubs which lay in an alcove where one burned already. Henry did as he was bid and in the better light his surprise increased. For the young man was undoubtedly Brother Andrew's youngest nephew, Luke. The young woman's face was vaguely familiar but as yet he could not put a name to it.

The old monk produced a small rolled parchment from the sleeve of his habit and unrolled it nervously.

'Watch the steps, man!' he told Henry. 'We want no one near. If you hear footsteps or voices tell me. Anything you hear, you tell me. Now we must hurry . . . let me see . . .'

Henry stood as look-out at the foot of the steps and heard the old monk's mumbling voice and the occasional crackle of the parchment. The young man's voice was too low and hesitant for him to catch the words but when the girl spoke he rolled his eyes heavenward in an expression of despair. He was witnessing a clandestine wedding!

'I, Isobel Gillis . . .'

'Not so loud,' hissed the old monk.

'Take thee, Luke Kendal, to my wedded husband, to have and to hold, for fairer for fouler, for better for worse, for richer for poorer, in sickness and in health to be meek and obedient 'til death us do part if holy church it will order . . .'

Isobel Gillis, thought Henry. No wonder he had thought her face familiar. The child of Marion Gillis whose name was a byword for miles around and her fool of a husband who made brooms for a living – when he did anything at all, which wasn't often. So Luke Kendal was wedding the Gillis girl! There could only be one reason for that, Henry reflected, and, stealing a quick look at her, noted with satisfaction the girl's rounded belly. Wait until his folk got to hear of it. There'd be sparks flying then, he had no doubt, and that Brother Eustace might look to his prayers if he wished to save his soul from eternal damnation. Aye, there'd be trouble if this was known – and he, Henry Bell, knew of it! No doubt his silence would be worth a coin or two. But now the ceremony was coming to an end and the ring was slid on to Isobel's finger. She held up her hand to admire it, and the look of triumph on her face was evident to the two older men although Luke was too agitated to see it. She flung her arms round his neck but he tugged himself free of the embrace as he hurriedly paid the monk for his services. Henry heard the clink of coins and coughed and Luke crossed to him to slip a half sovereign into his hand.

'Thank you, kindly sir.'

'And you've seen nothing,' Luke whispered.

'No, sir. Not a thing, nor heard nothing.'

'Well said.'

The old monk was now in a great hurry to be rid of his guests but at that moment the bell began to toll and feet shuffled on the stone floor over their heads. 'I must go or I'll be missed,' cried Brother Eustace, a note of panic in his voice. 'And you, Henry. You must go. But not you two,' he said. ''Tis too late and you'll be seen. You must stay here until all the brethren are at their midday meal, then slip away the way you came.'

The newly married couple agreed reluctantly.

'But how shall they know when 'tis safe?' said Henry. 'Shall I return for them?' Brother Eustace hesitated but

Luke received the idea enthusiastically so he was forced to agree. The old monk and his servant hastily withdrew to the sunlit world above, leaving Luke and Isobel on their own.

One of the candle stubs flickered and went out.

'I shouldn't care to spend a night here,' said Luke but Isobel was still admiring her hand and made no answer.

'Mistress Kendal,' she said. 'No longer Isobel Gillis but Isobel Kendal. Does it suit me, Luke?' She swirled round, her arms flung wide and the cheap skirt, which was her best, swung out and back again, wrapping itself round her legs, accentuating the shape of her swollen body. 'You have not kissed me,' she went on. 'Surely 'tis done to kiss the new bride.' She threw herself into his arms and he forced a smile and kissed her lightly on the lips.

'You smile with your mouth but not your eyes,' she told him, her voice sharpening. 'We are wed and you don't tell me that you are pleased. Say it, Luke. Say that you're pleased we are wed. Say that you love me!'

'I love you,' he said. 'I'm pleased we are wed. Indeed I am.'

But his heart was heavy with fear and the knowledge that he lied. His fierce infatuation had finally cooled and his presence in the crypt and their wedding held the qualities of nightmare. Nothing in his short life had prepared him for such happenings. At home Alison waited demurely to become his wife and now that his passion for Isobel had faded, he saw that the small fair girl loved him also in her gentle unassuming way, so different from Isobel's tempestuous demands. But the realization had come too late. Already Isobel's body was quickening with the child he had given her and he was lost. The stubborn pride which he inherited from his father would not let him seek advice. He had made the mistake and he would right it as best he could. With a cold, sick feeling in the pit of his stomach he watched his new wife pacing up and down. She was impatient to be outside in the world again. No longer a thing to be pitied and shunned, she would soon be a woman to be envied. She stopped abruptly.

'And when shall we tell your parents?' she asked. 'You will not name a day.'

'Before too long,' he said. 'I have told you my mother is unwell at present. When she is recovered we will tell her, I swear it.'

'And when will that be?'

He shrugged. 'I can't say. No one can say. But the physician says she will recover as soon as her stars are in conjunction.'

'I doubt your stepfather will welcome me as a daughter!' she said. 'He'll recall our last meeting when I traipsed to the door in thick snow and he would not buy a broom. No, nor spare me as much as a farthing.'

'You have spoke of it before,' said Luke. 'You dwell on it as though the idea pleases you.'

'Mayhap it does – ah, there goes another candle! We shall be in darkness soon if they do not make haste to rescue us. I do not care to be buried here.' Isobel was alone in her reluctance. To Luke, frightened and at a loss how to proceed, the idea was almost welcome.

CHAPTER TWO
June 1518

Alison sat quietly, her head bent, hands busy with the delicate beadwork of the head-dress she would wear for the wedding. Elizabeth watched the slim fingers guiding the needle in and out, tugging at the silk thread, smoothing the creamy white linen. She looked at the round childish face and saw the slight frown which puckered the forehead. The little mouth drooped miserably. Sun through the open windows lit the fair hair so that it gleamed white against the dark panelled wall behind her. She sighed as she reached for the scissors and snipped the thread carefully close to the cloth.

'What ails you, child?' Elizabeth asked and the girl looked up guiltily.

'Ails me? Why, nothing ails me,' she said.

'You look troubled and you sigh over your work.'

'Do I?' said Alison. 'I don't mean to.' She wore a gown of dark blue silk which by contrast made her face pale.

'Are you troubled?' Elizabeth persisted. 'I'll help you if you'll tell me what is wrong.'

Alison shook her head and lowered her eyes to hide the tears that sprang into them at the older woman's kindness. She measured a fresh length of silk, cut it from the reel and rethreaded the needle.

'Is it Luke?' asked Elizabeth.

A rebellious tear splashed on to her trembling

fingers. Elizabeth leaned forward and gently removed the head-dress for fear it should be spoiled.

'What is it, child?' she asked again. 'You are to be wed in one more week to a man who loves you –'

'Does he?' whispered Alison, and covering her face began to sob.

'But of course he does,' said Elizabeth. 'You know that he does. You have been here at Maudesley for five months now and never a cross word. Everyone says how well suited you are and you told me yourself you adore him. Why are you grieving so? I don't understand.'

'Neither do I,' whispered Alison. 'That's the trouble. Suddenly Luke has changed towards me and he will not say why. I asked him but he denies it and speaks of other matters, telling me 'tis my imagination.'

'And most likely 'tis just as he says. All young girls –'

Alison shook her head. 'It is what he doesn't say,' she said wiping her eyes with a small handkerchief. 'Not what he says. He used to call me Alice to tease me – and "little mouse". Now always Alison . . . He doesn't walk with me in the garden but always finds something else that he must do. And will not catch my eye.' She shook her head miserably, twisting the handkerchief in her fingers. 'If I have done aught to displease him I would ask his forgiveness most willingly but what have I done? I search my mind again and again but –' She broke off in alarm as footsteps sounded in the passage outside and Luke came into the room carrying a birch broom and with a thunderous expression on his face. Elizabeth looked at him in surprise but Alison had snatched up her sewing and her head was once more bent over her work.

'Where did this come from?' Luke demanded. 'I found it in the stable yard as I came through and 'tis quite new. How did it come there? I must know.'

'Must?' said Elizabeth coldly. 'I think you forget your

manners, Luke. There is no "must" about it. 'Tis merely a broom, I would think, and hardly worth such an outburst.'

'I must know where it came from!'

'Then you will be disappointed,' said Elizabeth 'for I have no idea. I have never set eyes on it before now. Perhaps the stable lad –'

'I asked him and he doesn't know. Yet someone has bought it, and recently.'

His face was white, his voice harsh and Elizabeth's concern grew. Such a ridiculous fuss over such a poor object!

'I bought it,' said Alison, her voice no more than a whisper.

'Dear God!'

'I meant no wrong,' she cried. 'The woman insisted –'

Elizabeth put out a comforting hand. 'You have done no wrong, child,' she said.

But Luke's face had paled. 'Which woman?' he asked, and Elizabeth fancied that his voice shook.

'From a woman – in the birch wood beyond the river.'

'Damnation! Look at me, Alison,' he said, 'and tell me what she was like, this woman you speak of?'

Alison lifted her head. He made no comment on her tearstained face but waited intently as she explained.

'I was out hawking yesterday,' she said 'and the merlin went for cover into a large sycamore in the copse. I went in after her but there was no sign. I knew she must be in there but she's a wilful bird and –'

'The woman, Alison, for God's sake!'

'I – I lost my way and met the woman. She was bundling up birch twigs and I asked her if she'd seen a merlin and she said "no" but –'

'What sort of woman? Describe her to me. A young woman?'

'Aye, about my age but big with child. A pretty woman.'

Luke sucked in his breath sharply but let her continue.

'She promised to look out for the bird if I would buy a broom. I said I had no use for one but she persisted. I had no money with me but she would not be denied. I felt sorry for her. Her home was so dirty and there were –'

'You went to her home?'

''Twas close by. A mean little cottage. She thrust the broom into my hand and said –' She broke off suddenly.

'Said what?'

'That I owed her more than I think. I didn't understand. Oh Luke. I meant no harm. Please believe me. On the way here I found the bird. I left the broom in the stable yard so that you wouldn't see it.'

'And why shouldn't he see it?' asked Elizabeth sharply.

'The woman was so strange,' said Alison. 'She frightened me – and she said "Show it to your betrothed" – and the old woman there, she laughed. I think she was crazed. I'm sorry, Luke, if I did wrong. Indeed I am.'

There was a long silence while the two women stared at him anxiously.

''Tis nothing,' he said at last, convincing no one. 'The old woman is quite mad. They are both mad and bear me a grudge. They wanted to frighten you, that is all.'

'A grudge?' said Elizabeth.

'Aye. I once quarrelled with the old woman's husband. He was poaching.'

And you are lying, thought Elizabeth. But why?

'Think no more on it,' said Luke, and he strode from the room without another word.

Alison covered her face with trembling fingers. 'He is so changed,' she whispered. 'Do you not see?'

But to her surprise Elizabeth smiled brightly. 'Do as he says, child, and think no more on it. You'll soon be wed and a bride must wear a happy face! A loving wife makes a happy husband, you'll see. The Kendal men bark but they rarely bite! So no more fears.' She finally coaxed a timid smile from her future daughter-in-law so that she went down to 'four hours' in a more cheerful frame of mind. But Elizabeth's smile was only skin-deep. She was extremely disturbed by what she had heard and a growing suspicion dominated her thoughts. She determined to make inquiries of her own but for the present would say no more to anyone. As for Alison – Elizabeth sighed deeply. She was still no more than a child and yet would be a bride within the week. Luke's name for her was an apt one. She was indeed a 'little mouse'.

It took a moment or two for Elizabeth's eyes to accustom themselves to the gloom of the cottage. While they did so an ill-tempered mongrel dog snapped and growled at her feet until a kick from Marion Gillis sent it howling outside. Looking about her Elizabeth saw that the strange smell came from a large pot over the open fire from which a bundle of birch twigs protruded. A young woman in an advanced stage of pregnancy sat on a stool in the light from the doorway and scraped the outer skins from a tangle of bramble beside her. The girl had a vagueness about her eyes and her lips moved soundlessly as she worked. She paid no attention to Elizabeth.

'Well!' said Marion. 'We are honoured, aren't we, Isobel. See who's come to visit us. The great lady herself, from Maudesley. Come to meet your new daughter-in-law, have you? Or inquire of your new

grandson? Or didn't you know that that swollen belly of
hers is the work of –'

'That's enough!' said Elizabeth, but the woman was
not so easily silenced.

'Any day now she'll be brought to bed and your precious son will be able to see his first born – if he dares so
much as show his face, that is. Not that we've seen
him –'

'That's enough I said!'

' – since the wedding day. Oh yes, they are wed, you
see. My girl's not a –'

'I don't believe it,' cried Elizabeth. 'Not wed.'

'Oh aye, they're wed,' said the old woman triumphantly. 'Show the lady your ring, Bel . . . Bel!'

The girl ignored her, seeming absorbed in her task,
her fingers endlessly fumbling with the strands of
bramble. Her mother snatched up the girl's hand and
held it up. Elizabeth's heart sank at the sight of the
narrow gold band. It was far worse than she expected.
But she was not so easily defeated.

'A ring proves nothing,' she said sharply. 'There was
no ceremony and my son is not the father of your
daughter's child. If you try to say 'tis so, I shall –'

'I do say so!' said Marion. ''Tis most certain so and
hasn't she a ring to prove it? Gold rings don't grow on
trees.'

'Then 'tis stolen and the girl's in trouble.'

'And the baby – is that stolen, too, then? Is she lying
about what kicks inside her? Or would you pretend that
there is no child? A litter of pups, mayhap?'

'She bears a child but 'tis no Kendal child.'

'And I say 'tis!' screamed the old woman, in a sudden
rage as she saw the drift of the exchange between them.
'I say she's wed to your fine son and big with his child
and none can deny it.'

'I deny it,' said Elizabeth with a great deal more conviction than she felt, 'and my son will, also.'

'But will the holy man deny it?' snapped Marion, 'or will you call him liar, too? Oh yes, they was wed by a holy man and in a holy place. Bel! Leave what you're doing and tell of your wedding. Tell this lady how 'twas. Tell her I say!' She shook the girl angrily but Isobel drew back, huddling against the wall, arms raised as though to protect herself from attack. Elizabeth, seeing the girl's pitiful condition, felt a pang of conscience about what she was doing.

'Why doesn't she speak?' she asked. 'Is she sick in her mind?'

The girl's mother hesitated, reluctant to agree to any suggestion that Isobel was not a fit person to be wife to Luke Kendal. 'She was fit enough before this,' she said cautiously, 'but the shock and grief have turned her brain seemingly. She mopes and won't speak. You might beat her but she won't answer.'

'Is she dumb, then?'

'Not dumb, no, for she'll scream at the dog – aye, and croon to the birds if she's a mind. But to her own flesh and blood, not a word.'

Elizabeth turned away, a hand thrown despairingly across her face. Sweet Mother of God, the girl's state was tragic. What was to be done? Her thoughts raced. If the girl's mind was indeed addled, then she was fit for no man. But even if she was of sound mind the alliance was impossible and Elizabeth had no intention of allowing Luke to honour his commitment to her. Isobel's silence was heaven-sent, for if the girl herself could not give evidence, then a match could not be proved. 'And I will see to it that no whisper of this folly is ever heard,' she vowed silently. Luke was betrothed to Alison and they had negotiated for nearly a year to win this match which was deemed a highly satisfactory one. She would see to it that Luke's future and the family honour would never be at risk from the Gillis woman's crazy daughter. Elizabeth hardened her heart. If the girl had hoped to ensnare a rich husband for herself, then she would be disappointed.

There was a sudden hissing from the fire as the water in the pot boiled over and Isobel crossed quickly to it. She lifted out the twigs and clutched them, steaming, in her arms.

'Outside with them, girl!' shouted her mother and obediently Isobel took them to the doorway and threw them on to the ground. Then she took up another armful from a pile inside the door and thrust them into the boiling water. Elizabeth made up her mind. She took some gold coins from the purse at her waist.

'Take these,' she said, thrusting them into Marion's outstretched hand. 'I will bring more tomorrow. The child must be fed until I can make provision, then it must go away.'

'And if I won't agree?'

'You will agree,' said Elizabeth, 'for if we quarrel then I will tell how you bewitched my son with your daughter's charms, then cuckolded him with another man's child. You will have to prove it otherwise. You have many enemies and none will support you. Believe me, you had best take the money and be thankful.'

Marion gave her a look of pure hatred but still played with the gold, letting the coins pass from one hand to the other, revelling in the sound. 'And there'll be more?' she asked.

'Aye.'

'And you'll take the brat?'

'I shall find a family. It shall be well cared for, I promise. Do you agree?'

'I dare say.'

'And the matter is most secret.'

The woman shrugged and turned away and Elizabeth

stepped outside thankful for the fresh air. Isobel now sat against the wall of the house, binding a bundle of damp twigs with a length of bramble. The dog sprang forward, hoping for a game, and snapped at the twigs barking excitedly. Isobel's apathy suddenly vanished. She hurled the half-finished broom at the dog and began to scream, a wild desperate sound which rang in Elizabeth's ears as she rode away and stayed with her all that night and many more.

'With this ring I thee wed, and with gold and silver I thee serve, and with my body I thee worship and with all my worldly chattels I thee honour.'

All eyes save Alison's were on the ring as Luke slipped it on to her finger. Hers were on his face which still wore the haunted expression she saw so frequently. She glanced past him to his mother and fancied that her face, too, was guarded. A slight pressure on her fingers brought her eyes to Luke and she saw that now he smiled.

'Luke,' she whispered and the shadow vanished from his eyes, to be replaced by a look of affection. A deep sigh welled up, shaking her slight body. He did not love her. Elizabeth said that he did but her own instincts told her otherwise. He was fond of her, nothing more. But she loved him devotedly, without reserve, and she would make him happy.

The vicar pronounced them man and wife and amid cheers and laughter they moved into the church, followed by all the guests. Luke and Alison knelt at the high altar. As the performance of High Mass proceeded the Latin words flowed over them and their thoughts wandered, Luke's to his private nightmare in the Priory crypt and Alison's to her strange meeting with the young woman in the wood. But once in the Lady Chapel all other thoughts fled before the determined merry-making of the guests. The bride cakes were broken and dipped into the wine by bride and groom alike. Then the sacred sign was made over the cup and it was passed round.

'Heaven bless you both!' said Elizabeth when her turn came and the words were echoed again and again. Gradually Alison's mood lightened as she was swept along on the wave of gaiety, infecting those around them, and even Luke joked a little with the bride knights as they made their way out of the church to the lane.

'Are you happy, Luke?' Alison asked him. Looking down into her sweet face he longed to say the words that would please her. Instead he nodded and gently drew her close, so that her face was pressed against his chest and she could hear the beating of his heart. Even as his hands encircled her narrow shoulders the small voice of conscience reminded him that this girl was not his wife nor ever could be while Isobel lived.

In the lane a small cart pulled by a small white pony awaited them. Flowers and ribbons decorated the wheels; and bells and streamers hung from the pony's harness.

'Into the cart! Into the cart!' chanted the crowd and Alison, abashed by so much attention, blushed as the smiling Luke lifted her up and deposited her on the fresh straw. He climbed up beside her amid cheers and ribald comments which deepened the colour in Alison's cheeks. Elizabeth, watching her son, marvelled at his composure and Joseph, beside her, squeezed her arm reassuringly.

''Tis nearly over,' he said 'and all gone without hindrance.'

'Aye, thank the Lord!' she answered and waved as the pony was urged forward and the minstrels struck up a lively tune. The answer was more heartfelt than Joseph knew for she had told him nothing. She took on her own shoulders the burden of her discovery and she alone accepted responsibility for her subsequent decisions. The fewer people who knew the truth the less likely it was to ever be revealed. Already she had found a foster home for the child in a neighbouring hamlet and waited daily for a message of the birth. Brother Eustace would say nothing, she was sure of that, for the direst penalties would follow if news of his unscrupulous actions came to the ears of the Bishop.

The servant, merely an accomplice, had been well paid for his silence for Elizabeth had added to the sum which Luke had already given him. As she watched the bridal cart moving away she sighed heavily. Her own conscience troubled her and she was under no misapprehension about her own soul. She had condoned the deed and knew that she risked damnation. But she did so willingly. Luke was the only surviving child that John had given her and she could not stand by and see his life ruined by this one folly. Youth was a wild and heady time. She would gladly suffer retribution after death if by doing so she could save her son from the consequences of his mistake.

'Shall we follow them?' asked Joseph. Hand in hand they joined the wedding procession as the young couple set off towards Maudesley under a veritable shower of corn thrown by well-wishers along the way.

The wedding cart bearing Luke and Alison had almost reached Maudesley when ahead of them Luke recognized a bowed figure walking towards them. It was Isobel, a bundle of brooms fastened to her back, a black mongrel dog running at her heels. Luke hoped they might pass her without incident but Alison had seen her, too. 'Look, there's that woman,' she began. 'The one that sold me the –'

'Give me the reins!'

She looked at him in surprise as, his face suddenly grim, he snatched the bridle from the leading minstrel and looping it into a whip, urged the surprised pony into a trot and then a canter.

'Luke!'

The wooden wheels of the cart zig-zagged wildly across the rutted road, now baked rock-hard by weeks of sunshine. Alison clung desperately to the side of the cart as they raced on, swaying and jolting, until Isobel was left far behind, out of sight. Only then did Luke bring the pony to a halt. As it stood panting, its flanks heaving, Alison burst into tears. 'I don't understand,' she sobbed. 'I don't understand.'

Luke pulled her fiercely into his arms. 'Hush now. 'Tis all over, I promise,' he told her, but his voice shook. He knew intuitively that far from being over it was only just beginning.

In the darkening Hall the scanty remains of the wedding feast confirmed that the guests had done it justice. On the table board the carcass of a goose had been picked clean and the back-bone was all that remained of a large salmon. Of the venison pasties only crumbs, and the hound foraging hopefully among the rushes on the floor found little to excite him. Here a discarded crust, there a broken biscuit or a scrap of saffron cake, but he gulped them down gratefully, ears pricked all the while for the sound of Izzie's approaching footsteps which would mean his immediate return to the kitchen. But it was Beth, the little maid, who came cautiously into the Hall, casting nervous glances over her shoulders for fear of detection. 'You bad dog!' she scolded. 'She'll have your guts if she catches you here!' Finding herself a spoon, she wiped it on her apron and made her way along the length of the board, sampling the various remains – a mouthful of lemon custard and the scrapings of the syllabub. 'But no marchpane,' she muttered. 'Not so much as a crumb! The greedy pigs have eaten it all – and the plum tart, seemingly, or someone has been here before me . . . Ah! Nigh on a whole slice!' She seized the apple flan, stuffed it into her mouth and frowned. No doubt too tough for some wobbly old teeth, she thought, and grinned.

The dregs of wine, apple flan and half a mug of ale went down her throat and a warm feeling spread through her bringing with it a strange recklessness. She spotted another flagon and to her delight saw that it was almost full. A sip told her it was cider, and with a sigh of contentment she settled down to enjoy herself.

Upstairs Alison stood surrounded by the bridesmaids who had finally finished preparing her for the coming nuptials. Her long blonde hair gleamed, a daisy chain formed a circlet round her head and her body was scented with lavender oil. 'You look beautiful,' they told her. 'See for yourself.'

She looked into the mirror and nodded, reassured by the sight.

'Now turn around –' Three pairs of eyes examined her critically.

'Perfect.'

'So into bed!'

There was an outburst of giggling as Alison slipped between the sheets of the four-poster and watched as her bridesmaids smoothed the bedspread and scattered rose petals.

'Don't lie down, Alison. You'll spoil the daisy chain.'

'Sit up and he will see you the moment he comes in.'

'Don't look so nervous. He won't eat you!'

'Smile, Alison.'

'Pull a strand of your hair forward – there.'

'Look happy . . . it's not so terrible.'

'She knows that.'

'She doesn't!'

'Don't you, Alison? Don't you know?'

Alison shook her head and they giggled again.

'Oh, you should have tried it. No wonder you look nervous.'

Alison longed for them all to go away. If only they would leave her in peace but no, they would flutter round her like starlings, until the men brought Luke in.

There was a tap at the door and the men rushed in, pushing Luke ahead of them. He looked different in his white shirt, almost foolish, and she wished she needn't look at him.

'Give her the posy, then!'

'Go on, man. Dear Heavens, don't gawp at her like that. You've seen a woman before.'

'Not in bed, he hasn't.'

'I'll wager he has!'

Luke held out a small posy of sadly wilted flowers and she took them awkwardly, silently, her eyes downcast.

Someone cried, 'The flowers are drooping but nothing else is!' More laughter. They were all enjoying themselves so much, thought Alison, so why did she feel so wretched? And Luke too, when she stole a glance at his face, looked ill at ease. He had drunk too much wine, she knew, and eaten little. Now he stood pale and tongue-tied.

'Into bed with her. Go on, Luke!' They pulled back the bedspread, in a spray of petals, and urged him in beside her.

'That looks very cosy.'

'Isn't she beautiful!'

'Lucky man, Luke. I fancy a bite of that myself.'

'Treat her kindly.'

'Remember, don't canter before you can trot!' Reeling

with merriment at this last sally, the men allowed themselves to be dragged out of the room by the bridesmaids. Luke and Alison sat side by side and listened to their voices as they made their way, laughing and shouting, their footsteps clattering on the stone steps. A tear trickled down Alison's cheek.

'Don't cry,' said Luke. 'Please don't cry.'

'I don't mean to.' Her fingers played with stems of the posy and another tear followed the first. 'They've gone now,' he said. 'What nonsense it all is!'

'I'm glad they've gone.'

'So am I . . . Are you weary?'

'A little,' she said. 'I woke very early this morning and couldn't sleep again.' He took the flowers from her and, reaching down, laid them on the chest at the foot of the bed.

'I should put them in water,' said Alison.

'Not now. 'Tis no matter.'

'Luke –' He looked at her woebegone face and felt a surge of pity for the waif-like girl who sat beside him. 'What is it, little mouse?'

A sudden smile lit her face. 'Oh, Luke, you said it. You called me –'

'Little mouse? Do you like me to call you that?'

'Aye.'

He relaxed a little and smiled also. 'Come here,' he told her. 'I don't think a wife should sit so far from her new husband. There are at least eight inches between us!'

'So much?'

She laughed. Below them they heard the bride knights mounting their horses in a confusion of farewells as they repaired to the nearest inn where they had taken lodgings overnight. When all was quiet once more Alison said, 'I love you, Luke, with all my heart.'

'I know and I love you. Shall I put out the candle?'

She nodded. In the darkness he slid further into the bed, pulling her with him until she lay encircled by his arms. She was aware of the contour of his body though separated from it by the silk of his shirt and her own nightgown.

'You smell sweet,' he whispered.

''Tis oil of lavender . . . Luke –'

'What is it?'

'All that jesting –'

'They meant no harm,' he said. 'Forget them. They have gone.'

'But should we have – lain together? Before today?'

'There was no need. Now is time enough.'

'I know so little of love,' she whispered. 'Almost nothing.'

''Tis no matter. I shall teach you.'

They lay silently together. He wondered about Alison's slim virginal body and the image of Isobel floated into his mind, sprawled on the sand, wild and sensuous, as the rain fell on to her long legs. Then he saw her as he had glimpsed her earlier in the day, her back bowed under her load, her movements aimless and vague. With a cry he buried his face against the soft breast and felt Alison's hands timidly stroking his head.

Later he tried to initiate the girl who was now his 'wife' but her lack of passion dismayed him and her frailty unmanned him. Alison woke to the pale light of morning no wiser than before.

Isobel lay on a pile of straw in the corner of the hut, her eyes fixed on a crack in the wall through which she could see the last glimmerings of daylight. Her face and body ran with sweat, her breath was painful and uneven. Beside her Marion sat in silent disapproval, her fingers busy with the shrieding that was rightly her daughter's work.

'Is he come yet, Ma?' Isobel asked again. 'Is Luke come?'

Before her mother could answer another contraction seized her and she doubled up, moaning, her eyes rolling wildly and her hands clenched until the knuckles gleamed. She remained, tight, until the pain passed, then fell to gasping and cursing while Marion reached for another bramble without comment.

'Luke, Ma – is he come, I say?'

'Not yet.'

'But is he coming? Does he know about the babe? Will he come and see it?'

'There's nowt to see so far.'

'But 'twill be here shortly, I can tell,' she insisted, wiping the sweat from her face with the corner of her apron. 'The pain's that bad it must be soon.'

'Those pains is nothing,' said Marion. 'You're not half-way there yet, believe me. Such a pother over a birthing, you should be ashamed. Get up and walk about a bit, 'twould ease you to move about.'

'I can't, Ma. I've tried, honest I have but – Ah!' Another contraction silenced her and Marion watched dispassionately as she curled up, tensing herself against the searing pain which gripped her body as her womb prepared to rid itself of Luke's unwanted child. As the pain faded once more Isobel began to weep and hot tears mingled with sweat on her face. It was nearly dark and she lay miserable and exhausted, listening to the small sounds of her mother's busy fingers.

'I wish I'd never set eyes on him,' she sobbed. 'I wish I'd kept him at arm's length for all his sweet talking –'

'They can all sweet-talk,' said Marion. 'Your father could charm the birds out of the trees when he were a lad and look at him now. Never here when he's wanted and in his cups when he *is* here, useless swine. They're all the same! Oh, quit that bawling. 'Twill do no good and I can't stand to listen to it. You let him take you so you've none but yourself to blame.'

'I loved him –'

'Then more fool you!' Marion snapped, 'for I've yet to set eyes on a decent man. Oh, my fingers are that sore! It can wait till morning.' She threw the offending brambles back into a large basket and heaving it on to her hip, carried it outside. Isobel screamed again in the midst of her sobbing so that she almost choked and even Marion's hard heart was touched. She poured some goat's milk into a bowl and crossed to Isobel who now lay whispering to herself. 'Stop that, Bel!' said Marion sharply. 'I've told you of it before. Sit up, and drink this.'

'I can't. I want Luke. Is he come, Ma? Does he know about the babe? Will he come now?'

'I don't know and I care less,' said Marion. 'He'll do you no good if he does come. Now sit up, I say. I've no time to be playing nurse to you. If you don't want it, I'll drink it meself.'

Slowly Isobel pulled herself upright and sat leaning against the wall, her legs spreadeagled, her skirt twisted uncomfortably across the huge belly. She drank greedily, tilting the bowl with trembling hands so that some of it spilled over and ran down her neck, pleasantly cool to her flesh.

'That's better,' said Marion. 'Now give it here and up you get. Oh yes, you're going to get up, my lady, and walk a bit. Don't tell me you can't 'cause I know better. Put your arm round my shoulder – round my shoulder, I say. That's it. Now up you come –'

Isobel protested but was finally dragged to her feet. Almost immediately another contraction racked her but when it was over she managed to stumble round, leaning heavily on her mother, grunting with the effort but surprised to find herself somewhat eased. The movement distracted her attention and she even smiled faintly at the dog who pranced alongside, curious and uneasy.

'Get away, you stupid animal,' Marion cursed, 'you'll have my feet from under me!' She lashed out wildly with her foot and sent it howling outside. 'The cur makes more noise than you,' she said, 'and with less reason!' She walked Isobel up and down until at last the girl's weight proved too much for her and she was once more lowered on to the straw. She slumped against the wall and again began her whispering, punctuated by her pains which grew rapidly more frequent. Marion lit the small rush lamp and scratched up a fire over which she set an iron pot full of water. When she could stand Isobel's whisperings no more, she cried, 'Stop that whispering. You know I can't bear it!' and the girl fell silent and stared fixedly into the fire. Suddenly she began again.

'Is he coming, Ma?' she asked. 'Is Luke coming to see the babe? Does he know it's – Ah!'

Her mother's hand struck her across the side of her face. 'Will you stop it?' cried Marion angrily. 'I've told you already I don't know. He's been sent word and there's no more I can do. If he comes, he comes. If he doesn't, you must lump it! 'Twill do you no good if he does come so forget the lad. He's paid well for his fun – or his mother has – so forget him. I doubt his lordship'll set foot in here tonight.'

She was wrong. Luke arrived less than an hour later in time to see his son still shiny from the birth before he was hastily wrapped in a woollen cloth. Isobel, her mind weakened by the delivery, barely recognized the man she had longed to see and it was left to Marion to ask him for a name. He called the boy Simon and held the small bundle in his arms for a few moments while Marion made Isobel as comfortable as she could. When Marion's back was turned Luke kissed the tiny wrinkled face of his first-born and for a moment held it close to his own. 'I'm sorry!' he whispered, 'Indeed I am.' Then, laying the child on the straw beside Isobel, he stumbled from the room, half blinded by his tears.

Seven months later Alison woke to find Luke's side of the bed empty. So he had gone hawking after all, no doubt with his stepfather and Joseph's son by his first wife who was on one of his rare visits from London. It was a pity Jo lived so far away, for he and Luke got on well despite the difference in their ages. She lay for a moment imagining them riding together through the early morning countryside and the vision thus conjured pleased her. It always pleased her when Luke shared the company of others for he was a very private, almost solitary man, and the knowledge troubled her vaguely although she could not discover why it should. She turned sideways and put a hand to her back, which ached abominably and had done for the past two days. It was the weight of the child, they told her, and nothing to be afraid of. At the thought of her child – hers and Luke's – her eyes softened and she moved her hand to her swollen abdomen feeling the small flutter of tiny movements and the fierce, more painful kicks. For the past week she had felt lethargic and had sat for hours stitching, reading or singing to herself. She had shunned company as politely as she could, listening to the inner workings of her body. The child was due any day now – a day late already but that was nothing to be concerned about or so they said. Everyone, it seemed, knew more about childbirth than she did. She sighed. Well, before long she would know more than any of them. She would have her first child. A son, she had promised Luke. Your first son, she had said and had wondered at the shadow that crossed his face.

She called for Beth, who helped her to dress, and then sent her downstairs again. Tidying the bed, she crossed to the window to look out over the garden and tried to imagine her children playing there. Their sons would chase with the dogs and shout and wrestle with their father. They'd haunt the stable pestering to feed the horses. She smiled faintly. And their daughters? They would dance and make daisy chains and maybe tease the boys. Or would sit under a tree out of the sunlight and work samplers or stand beside her at the virginal and sing in sweet piping voices . . . A pain shot through her and she stiffened in alarm. But it was not repeated and she relaxed again. Straightening up, she realized with pleasure that her lethargy had passed to be replaced by a refreshing feeling of well-being. She felt a new energy and decided suddenly to organize the spring cleaning. Elizabeth now spent most of her time at Heron involved with the mine and Alison had taken over the household management. Now that May was half over, the weather was warmer and the winter fires belching smoke would soon be over for another year. The walls of the Hall must be whitewashed and the tapestry on the wall should go down to the orchard for a good beating. The rushes must be replaced. She hurried downstairs before her new-found energy should wane and burst into the kitchen where Izzie and Beth listened in amazement as she described her plans. Over the past weeks they had slipped into a delightful indolence and were now being rudely awakened.

'All the bed hangings can come down for an airing,' said Alison, 'and the sheets and blankets can be washed. I hope we've plenty of soap. The stable lad can help you fetch water from the well. I want all the windows opened and Beth, you run out and fetch some herbs to sweeten the air. 'Tis always foul after the winter. We'll burn them in pans of hot ash –' She paused for breath.

'Is that all ma'am?' asked Izzie.

Alison thought for a moment. 'I want the walls whitewashed in the Hall,' she said 'and the hinges on the shutters oiled. Er – have I spoke of the rushes?'

'You have ma'am,' said Izzie evenly while Beth struggled with a desire to giggle.

'Then I think that's all,' said Alison. 'Shall we make a start, then?'

'There's only one thing ma'am,' said Izzie humorously. 'What shall we do this afternoon?'

There was a moment's silence, then Beth erupted into uncontrolled giggles. Alison, taken aback, looked at Izzie and saw the large grin. Her first instinct was to retain her dignity at all costs but then she relaxed and laughed with them.

'There's enough work there for ten pairs of hands,' said Izzie 'but don't you fret. We'll make a start on it but the mistress always hired a few girls from the village and it'll take a day or two to find someone suitable. You leave it to me –'

'Oh no, I want to help!' cried Alison.

'Help?' protested Izzie. 'In your state? Oh ma'am, do you think that's wise? 'Tis heavy work.'

'Nonsense!' said Alison firmly. 'I shall make a start in the Hall. Hand me a broom, Beth.'

The girl threw an anxious glance in Izzie's direction but Izzie nodded and Beth hurried to find the broom. Satisfied, Alison carried it into the Hall and began to sweep up the winter's rushes. They lay an inch thick on the floor and months of dirt and grease had matted them together. Undeterred, Alison set to work, humming cheerfully to herself. As she swept, the dust rose thickly in the air and made her sneeze. At the third sneeze, she felt the pain again and put a hand to her back inquiringly. The pain passed and she began to sweep again. The pain returned more sharply. The next one took her breath away but stubbornly Alison persevered, sweeping between the pains. Now that the time had arrived she resisted it, refusing to admit the significance of the pains. At last, beaten, she threw down the broom, bent double by a fierce cramp which made her gasp with fear. As soon as it passed, she hurried through the doorway to call Izzie but another savage cramp seized her and she was speechless until it faded. She had never experienced such pains before. Hardly knew such pain existed. She stumbled on and reached the kitchen and was starkly aware of two faces turned towards her, surprised at her return. She opened her mouth to explain but was seized again and this time her agony found a voice and she screamed.

'I thought so,' cried Izzie as they ran to help her. 'Spring cleaning, indeed. Her time's well and truly come!'

The following day Alison gave birth to Luke's second son. They laid him between the linen sheets of the large four-poster bed at Maudesley and called him Jeffery.

CHAPTER THREE
1522

Alison laid down the quill with a sigh and wished the chore done with, but she had written so little. 'From your loving daughter Alison in good health and spirits this fourteenth day of January. I wonder how you are faring in this inclement weather which Jeffery delights in but I confess I do not. The child I carry kicks me and I tire easily. With God's will another month will see it over and I have hopes of a sister for Jeffery but dare not tell Luke so.'

She rubbed at a smudge of ink on her forefinger then sucked it clean, frowning at the unpleasant taste. Her back ached and she straightened up wearily. Outside she could hear Jeffery, his voice shrill with excitement as Jack, the gardener's lad, threw snowballs at the dogs to amuse him. She began again. 'We have a new steward by name Thomas Benet, most highly recommended by friends in London. He joined us yesterday but Luke is still in Cornwall on business so Elizabeth is instructing him in household matters since Joseph is smitten with a persistent fever but is bled daily and we pray for his recovery.' She re-read the letter critically and made several alterations to the spelling, then laid down the pen once more and crossed to the window. Jeffery had fallen over and she smiled as Jack ran to him and set him on his feet, brushing the snow from his clothes. The dogs leapt excitedly, sinking deep into the snow, and the little boy scolded them which made them worse. Jack glanced up at the window and saw Alison. 'His little nose is cold and glows like a beacon!' he shouted. 'Shall I bring him indoors and thaw him out?'

She nodded and he swung Jeffery, kicking and protesting, over his shoulder and strode back towards the house. Alison laughed. She had chosen Jack from several applicants for the job and the small responsibility had pleased her. Jeffery had taken an immediate liking to the wiry lad and he in turn showed remarkable patience with his young admirer and since the onset of the snow spent more time than he should playing with him. She heard a door bang as they went into the kitchen and knew that Izzie would soon warm them with bread and hot milk with a spoonful of honey. Outside the land lay silent, muffled by the snow, until the priory bells rang out reminding her that Andrew, Elizabeth's brother, would be visiting them for supper that evening. Footsteps approached and she looked up as Elizabeth came into the room followed by Thomas Benet. He was much taller than Elizabeth and trimly built with tight curls growing close to his head like a golden cap. His grey eyes surveyed Alison with evident approval and she felt herself blushing as she instinctively folded her hands across her stomach in a vain effort to conceal her size. 'Good news for you,' said Elizabeth. 'Thomas is already experienced with hawks and has offered to exercise your merlin for you.'

'You're very kind,' said Alison.

He smiled. ''Twas scarcely a generous offer,' he admitted. 'I shall enjoy the task. The bird and I have been formally introduced and I hope I shall quickly earn her trust.'

'Be warned,' said Alison. 'She is a very self-willed creature.'

'Then we are well matched!'

Elizabeth laughed. 'We shall see who trains whom! If we see Master Benet perched in a tree we shall know the bird won!'

'Such little faith!' cried Thomas. 'I shall fly her shortly – with your approval – and we shall see.'

Alison nodded and Elizabeth glanced at the letter. 'I see you have finally put pen to paper,' she said. 'We must not keep you from your labours. Your mother and father will wonder, else, what has become of their beloved daughter.' Laughing at Alison's rueful expression, she withdrew and Thomas, with a smile and a brief nod, followed her out. Alison sat down again and waited for inspiration. She had a chilblain, but that was hardly news. Jeffery had had one or two nightmares in the past weeks but that would merely worry them. She must make an effort to rise above such trivialities.

'The mine at Maudesley continues to yield good tin,' she wrote, 'and Stephen says Heron has a new horizontal shaft in progress.' She sighed, wishing that she liked Stephen better than she did. Luke's older half-brother was John's son by his first wife, Bet.

'Poor Stephen,' Elizabeth said but Alison could not share her sympathy with him. She found him brusque to the point of rudeness, and wondered how his wife tolerated his sullen moods and cold manner. There were tales of a misspent youth, gambling and roistering, and she knew Elizabeth had bought him out of prison on at least one occasion. Alison found it all rather shocking. She was almost afraid of him. She wondered what else she should say about Heron but her mind was a blank. That would have to suffice. She knew very little about the workings of the mines and did not choose to know more. Since Will Retter had died, Elizabeth had once more assumed responsibility while trying, unsuccessfully, to interest Stephen. He and Hester were also coming to supper. Elizabeth liked to have the family under one roof although Alison did not enjoy their visits for Stephen, moody and taciturn, with the years grew worse instead of better. She sighed again, then continued.

'Luke speaks of another war with France,' she wrote, 'and further troubles with the Scots. I grow weary of such tidings and pray St Katherine that soon we might be at peace. Your grandson grows mightily and I'm in hopes that you will see him at Easter if the roads are passable by then.'

She would wear the amber gown for supper since company was expected, even though it was a little too tight for comfort, and the new head-dress. She had taken the pearls from her wedding cap and stitched them at intervals along the braid and was enchanted with the effect. Hester might be slimmer than her at present, but she hunched her shoulders awkwardly and laughed too loudly. Instantly, she regretted her ungenerous thoughts. She must try to like Hester more but she was so overbearing and always managed to increase Alison's sense of inadequacy. All those airs and graces, thought Alison resentfully, because they lived at Heron, yet Luke was Elizabeth's only son and Heron had been hers. Surely Luke had just as much right to it. She would ask him one day.

At the thought of Luke, her expression softened. Her love for him bordered on adoration and her whole life centred round him. Even Jeffery could not replace Luke in her affections and she almost felt herself jealous of the time he spent with his son and envied her child the endearments he received from his father. Towards her Luke was gentle, loving and considerate. Buried deep in her memory she retained the picture of Isobel, bowed under the weight of her load, and heard again the clatter of the horses' hooves as Luke whipped them past. If it had surfaced it would have troubled her but she kept it locked away and was able to forget.

'I am learning to play the virginal and the tutor says I make good progress,' she wrote, 'but lately I neglect to practise and can expect a scolding on his next visit. We have a new hanging for the chamber wall in greens and gold and the gold threads shine in the light of the fire and look very fine.' She lost interest suddenly and brought the letter to a close. 'And so I bid you farewell and trust you will forgive the brevity of this letter and all our prayers go with you as ever.' She sanded it, folded it carefully and left it for Luke to read and approve.

The sound of fluttering wings drew her to the window and she saw Thomas about to exercise the merlin as he had promised. Minutes later, wearing a warm cloak and hood, Alison settled with Elizabeth and Jeffery on a stone bench to watch the proceedings. Thomas came over to them, the bird blinking on his wrist. 'The sun reflects off the snow,' he said 'and might dazzle her, but I'll try her with a spinning lure.' With a deft movement of his wrist, he tossed the merlin into the air and she immediately swooped upwards with rapid thrusts of her wings and perched in a nearby oak tree. Jeffery clapped his hands and shouted with delight.

'Hush, little man,' said Elizabeth. 'We must be very quiet and very still or Thomas will lose her.'

Thomas began to twirl the lure – a piece of wood covered in feathers on the end of a line. He let out the line, the lure swooping round in ever-increasing circles, and then he whistled. At the signal, the bird launched herself from the branch catching the lure as it spun and landing with her 'prey' in a flurry of snow.

'Quickly!' cried Elizabeth, forgetting her injunction to Jefferey, but the young steward needed no bidding. Already he had taken a scrap of meat from the pouch at his waist and offered it to the merlin in exchange for the lure and waited until she had eaten it. He repeated the exercise twice more before he was satisfied.

'What do you say?' he asked Alison. 'Shall I try her with the trailing lure?'

'Please do,' said Alison. ''Tis Mistress Tucker's favourite! She loves to watch it.'

Once more Thomas tossed the bird free of his wrist and it flew up, this time into a pine tree. The trailing lure was an imitation rabbit. Thomas, whistling, pulled it behind him and the merlin dived down but instead of pinning it to the ground she was confused by the soft snow and suddenly flew upwards, taking the lure with her. She settled herself in the oak tree from where she called down, as if in defiance.

The two women struggled to hide their amusement at the look of dismay on Thomas's face. He whistled and held out his wrist with an imperative gesture but the bird watched impassively, content with her neat manoeuvre. He whistled repeatedly but the bird declined to co-operate.

'You'll blow yourself short of breath,' Elizabeth teased. 'You'd best go up after her.' After a moment's hesitation he took her at her word and moved over to the foot of the oak, searching for a hand-hold.

'Oh dear,' said Alison nervously. 'He means to do it.'

Elizabeth laughed. 'Don't fret,' she said. 'It's been climbed before and will doubtless again. Why our young Jeffery himself will be climbing it in a few years' time.'

Thomas climbed rapidly, proving himself more adept than either of the women expected while little Jeffery watched open-mouthed. Reaching the branch on which the merlin was perched, he began to edge along it, talking reassuringly. The bird watched until he was almost within reach, then seized her 'rabbit' and flew to a higher branch.

'What a spectacle!' cried Elizabeth, delighted at the

young man's discomfiture. 'The bird is a natural actor and plays to the gallery. I swear we might sell tickets and make ourselves a fortune.'

Alison began to think she was right, for the merlin refused to co-operate. She rejected the tempting scraps of meat which Thomas offered and, as soon as he came within an arm's length, flew still higher. At last, crest-fallen and unable to hide his irritation, Thomas was forced to come down empty-handed and stood brushing the dust from his doublet.

'Well tried,' said Alison kindly. 'You did well to go so high and I apologize for my bird's wayward behaviour.'

He smiled briefly. 'You warned me,' he said, 'and she has proved you right. But I will try her again with the spinning lure. By now she should have grown bored with her unappetizing prey.'

Fortunately the ploy proved successful. The merlin abandoned the lure in favour of the spinning 'bird' and the women watched thankfully as the bird was persuaded once more on to Thomas's glove and the leash slipped into place. Thus secured she was brought to Alison for a good-natured rebuke before being returned to her quarters. They walked back to the house shivering a little, for the sun had dropped behind the trees and the crisp air turned chill with the approach of nightfall.

Alison's child, a girl, was born prematurely a few weeks later and they named her Melissa. She was under-weight and sickly and Alison doubted that she would rear her. The village girl who acted as wet-nurse had milk to spare but the child had no appetite. She would suck feebly for a few minutes and then fall asleep. If woken to take more nourishment she bawled lustily, making herself hot and miserable, but if left to herself she would sleep for hours showing no interest in the world around her. However as days passed into weeks, and Melissa did not die of starvation, Alison's alarm gradually subsided. 'She must be a fairy child,' she told Luke, 'for she can live on kind words and air!'

Luke smiled but his relief was relative. He had wanted another son. Perhaps next time they would be more fortunate.

Beth opened one eye, took a quick glance at the dark sky outside and closed it again. She pulled the blanket so closely round her ears that her toes were uncovered and, grumbling, she drew up her legs. The truckle bed creaked and she looked nervously across to see if Izzie had stirred. Faint snores told her that she was unobserved, so she slid out of bed and snatched up the old sheepskin that served as a rug between the two beds. She threw it across the lower half of her bed and then climbed carefully back into it. A blissful smile spread over her face at the extra warmth. Closing her eyes she relaxed, listening to the March wind in the trees outside and the spattering of rain against the shutters. The straw pallet on which she lay had been refilled at the end of the last summer and was comfortable with no sharp ends to scratch her skin. Somewhere in the dark corner a mouse scuttled in search of crumbs; Beth leaned out of bed and threw her shoe in the direction of the sound. The noise disturbed Izzie who mumbled restlessly but then dozed again. Beth sighed happily. She loved the few minutes before waking and rising even more than the time before going to bed and sleeping. The latter was so short. She fell into bed exhausted and there was rarely time to savour the luxury of being horizontal before her eyes closed. She fought against sleep for sleep was oblivion and she liked to prolong the precious time that was hers alone. No one to shout at her or ask her what she was about – or tell her not to dawdle when she wasn't.

Izzie mumbled again and Beth muttered, 'Oh stop gabbing!' Once Izzie had been 'loaned' to Heron for two days and she, Beth, had had the small bedchamber to herself. The silence and the privacy had been blissful. She still treasured the memory and hoped that Izzie might go again. Izzie spoke wistfully of Heron, where she had worked as a girl, but Beth was content to be at Maudesley. She liked the old lady well enough and Luke could do no wrong in Beth's eyes. As for Alison, she wouldn't say 'boo' to a goose and rarely chided the servants. Now at Heron it was a different kettle of fish. That Hester had a sharp tongue in her head, so they said, and Stephen was bad-tempered all day and every day. What a household! Not to mention little Hugo who was so spoilt and petted. When the new baby came it would put his nose out of joint, without a doubt. Not like the two little pets at Maudesley, young Jeffery and his new sister. Beth was inordinately proud of them both. She stretched luxuriously, wriggling her toes against the sheepskin, and wondered what the day would bring. Clean out the hearths, relay the fires, fetch in wood – unless maybe Jack was in a good mood and would do it for her. Collect the eggs, if any, and hang a fresh muslin for the cheese. Take up the old lady's breakfast of coddled eggs and warm ale, though she'd likely leave most of it. She hardly ate enough to keep a flea alive these last few months and everyone said she was wasting away. Bundle of dry old twigs was how Jack described her but Izzie had boxed her ears for his disrespect. Beth smiled at the memory. Jack was twice Izzie's size but had nevertheless gone hurriedly back to his work, a sheepish look on his face . . . Then help Elizabeth to dress and brush her hair for her. Beth hated that although she couldn't say why. Alison's long blonde hair was a joy to handle but Elizabeth's sparse grey locks made her cringe. Not that she let on for that would never do, poor old soul.

Izzie's bed creaked and Beth scowled.

'Beth!'

She pretended to be asleep but it was a vain hope.

'Beth! Wake up girl.'

'Mm?' Beth sounded convincingly drowsy.

'I say, wake up girl. 'Tis nearly light.'

'Nearly light? Is it?' She remembered the sheepskin and groaned inwardly. Too late now to put it back.

'Hark at that rain! Dratted winter, I hate it,' grumbled Izzie as she struggled to sit up in bed without over-turning it. Without looking, Beth knew what she would be doing – yawning, scratching her head, rubbing at her eyes.

'Beth! What have I told you about that sheepskin!' cried Izzie. 'Full of fleas that is and you laying it on your bed. On to the floor with it this minute and don't let me tell you again.'

'My feet were cold,' grumbled Beth, kicking it on to the floor with bad grace.

'Then keep your hose on.'

'I do!' cried Beth, 'but I'm still cold. I wish you'd ask the old lady for another blanket.'

'Wish away, then,' said Izzie 'because I shan't. Another blanket indeed. 'Tis March now and the worst of the winter's past. There's spring round the corner –'

'Sounds so!' cried Beth as a fresh gust of wind rattled the shutters.

'What did you say?' demanded Izzie.

''Twas nought,' grumbled Beth hastily. She put one leg out of bed and then the other and shivered loudly, making her teeth chatter pathetically, before dressing as quickly as she could. 'That kitchen'll be like ice,' she grumbled.

'Then the quicker you get the fire going the sooner 'twill warm up!' said Izzie. 'I'll be down in two shakes of a lamb's tail and I'll expect to see things happening down there. So get along with you.'

As Beth was going out of the door, Izzie called her again. 'And look in at the master's bedroom and blow up the fire. Put another log on but do it quietly so as not to waken them.'

'Nice for folks to have a fire all night,' said Beth enviously.

Izzie snorted. 'Mayhap you'll have a fire all night when you're as old as they are. Blood thins as you get older. Now get along.'

Beth pushed open the door of Elizabeth and Joseph's room and revelled in the warmth. The fire still smouldered and she knelt beside it, blowing carefully on the embers to bring them back to life. Ash flew into her face and made her cough but there was no sound from the four-poster bed behind her. Joseph wouldn't wake, she knew. It would take wild horses to drag him from his sleep. But the old lady might. Carefully she took a log from the basket and settled it on the glowing coals. She blew again until a small flame licked at the log, then sat back dizzy and out of breath. As she did so, she caught sight of Elizabeth's arm hanging limp, free of the blanket. There was no movement – no rise and fall of the bedclothes. No sound at all. As though hypnotized, she reached out and touched the hand, which was stiff and cold. An unreasoning terror seized her and she screamed. Behind Beth the fire flickered hungrily around the log but Elizabeth was dead and would never feel its warmth again.

The funeral service over, the mourners followed the coffin to the newly dug grave and stood in the freezing cold while Father Benedict paid his respects to Elizabeth's memory. He had written pages of nicely rounded prose and did not intend to let the weather rob him of its delivery. He had known Elizabeth for many years and liked and respected her. The family, friends and mourners, huddled in their black clothes, shivered as he unrolled the page and his own fingers were already blue with cold for the church had been unheated.

'Dearly beloved brethren,' he began, 'we are gathered here in the sight of God to witness the passing of His daughter Elizabeth into His safe keeping. 'Tis fitting at the time of her death to consider her life. We here today knew Elizabeth in many guises – wife, mother, sister, friend – for a woman in her lifetime plays many parts. We all play many parts, some well, some not so well. Indeed, we play some parts badly for we are all prone to afflictions of the mind and body and no one is blameless in the sight of God. Yet He is merciful, He forgives us our sins . . .'

Luke, listening, thought, 'Amen to that'. Did God forgive *all* sins? Was his sin too heinous for even God's forgiveness? He stood fearfully beside the open grave looking down at his mother's coffin, seeing through the wooden lid to the woman who lay within. She no longer felt the cold, nor would she enjoy the heat of summer when it came. He saw her again as he had seen her laid out all in white, her hands folded across her breast, a silver crucifix tucked between her fingers. Her face, tired and wrinkled, had been lightly dusted with white powder and a white bonnet enclosed her hair. In life she had seemed so strong, so tall, so wise. Now in death she looked smaller, vulnerable, and her wisdom would be buried with her. A feeling of panic seized him but he fought it down. He was alone with his sin and must bear the secret guilt without her support. Mama, he cried silently, what will I do without you?

'– she has played a part in the community in which we live – a very substantial part. She busied herself in the affairs of Heron as a good wife should and was able to continue with great success after the death of Daniel Heron, her first husband, may he rest in peace. But a young widow has a lonely path to tread and we rejoiced when she wed again, and John Kendal came from London to share the delights of Heron, bringing with him four children, Catherine, Stephen, William and Matthew . . .' Sophie glanced up at her father and Matthew smiled faintly. Beside him Blanche, his wife, wept silently for the woman who had loved her like a mother, taking her into her heart along with John's children. She had been 'the girl next door'. There were no children at Maudesley and she had gravitated daily to the welcome bustle that was Heron so that Elizabeth declared she had five children instead of four! But none of her own for so long. Poor Elizabeth, they had felt for her as she struggled to hide her despair. Until she was almost past child-bearing age and then she had given birth to Luke. The son that John longed for. The son who was born after he died.

'– to them she was a mother, loving and kind, caring for their needs and comforting them in their afflictions. Elizabeth was a woman with that rare gift – imagination – and this gift was reflected in the lives of all who knew her and were close to her . . . Andrew, her brother . . .' Head bowed, Andrew stood with his eyes closed not wishing to see the yawning grave in which his sister lay helpless and still. He did not care to think on the heavy soil that would soon cover her coffin and hide her away for ever. Except in the minds of those 'who knew her and were close to her'. The priest's voice droned on, rising and falling, but Andrew heard little of it. He had no need of an obituary to remind him of his sweet Elizabeth. He could see her now as Daniel's young bride, little more than a child, humouring the old man, apologizing for his mean ways, struggling to manage the household under the watchful and amused eyes of the servants. She had sent for her brother soon after they were wed and had found a place for him in nearby Harben Priory as soon as he was old enough. He had wanted desperately to take his vows and had never regretted it. Not even when Blanche – His gaze wavered irresolutely and he allowed himself a quick glance at her. He could not see her face under the dark veil but knew that she wept. Tender-hearted Blanche. He had wronged her grievously and Elizabeth had never quite forgiven him. The child, Sophie, was his but he had been sent away and she had wed Matthew. He sighed. It was all a long time ago. Now Elizabeth had carried the secret to her grave. He looked round at the mourners. Joseph Tucker, Elizabeth's third husband; Stephen and Hester and young Hugo in Stephen's arms; Jo Tucker, Joseph's son and his wife Louise and their children, Samuel, Gregory and Anne. Catherine, still childless, and her husband; Mark Lessor, John's friend from London and Ella, his wife; the servants from Heron and Maudesley and many friends. Elizabeth was dead but she would never be forgotten. She had brought them all together on this one occasion. Later they would separate once more and go their individual ways. Elizabeth was gone and there was no one to take her place in the centre of their universe.

The priest finished speaking and made the sign of the cross. The first spadeful of earth fell on the wooden lid with a terrible finality. She was gone. Gone.

'No! Mama!' All their heads jerked up as one. Luke had snatched the spade from the gravedigger's hands. His eyes blazed with an expression no one could interpret.

'But sir,' began the old gravedigger. ''Tis my job to –'

'No, I say!' He clutched the spade to his body defensively as they all stared at him with shocked faces.

'Not yet! Not so soon!'

Hurriedly, the priest made his way through the mourners to Luke's side. ''Tis only decent,' he whispered. 'It must be done. Give him the spade now, and let him finish.'

'Not yet,' whispered Luke, his eyes wild. 'I'll do it. She would like that. Aye, she'd like that.' He said it appealingly, looking to those nearest him for their agreement.

'But you can't, Luke,' said Alison, her face flushed with embarrassment. 'It is his job, not yours. Give him the spade, Luke, I beg you.'

But Luke thrust it into the mound of earth and tossed soil into the grave. 'Don't fret, Mama,' he muttered. ''Tis only me, Luke. I'll see it done right, never fear.' He sent a second spadeful into the hole as the startled mourners whispered among themselves. The old gravedigger shook his head and looked to the priest for advice. He, in turn, looked at Joseph.

'Let him be,' said Joseph after a moment's hesitation. ''Tis what he wants. The shock has been deeper than we imagined. Come, Alison.'

'No, I'll stay with him,' she said.

'I think you should come, dear,' said Catherine gently. 'He's distraught but if it comforts him to do her this one last service —'

Several groups of mourners were moving away, reluctant to watch him, unable to bear the look in his eyes as he bent over his dreary self-imposed task. 'Wait nearby,' the priest told the gravedigger. 'He'll likely tire before long and you can finish the job. Come, we have paid our last respects. Let us return to the house. The wind is bitter and 'twill soon be dark.' His going was a signal for the rest who had waited indecisively. Catherine took Alison's arm but she turned to wait for Joseph who stumbled through the long grass, his eyes blurred with tears. 'Poor Luke,' he said. 'Poor Elizabeth. Oh God –'

Alison put an arm round his bowed shoulders and fought to keep back the tears in her own eyes. 'We can't help them,' she said. 'Not either of them.'

They made their way back on to the road where a small group of local people waited to express their sympathies with the bereaved. 'Thank you . . . Thank you . . .' murmured Joseph, touched by the fact that they had waited so long in the cold.

'God rest her soul!' cried one of the women. 'May she rest in peace.' Alison turned at the church gate. Luke still worked feverishly, his back bent. 'What a dismal task,' she said, 'but if he must do it –' She shook her head and allowed Joseph to help her on to her horse for the ride back to Maudesley.

The fire was well stocked with logs and flames and sparks leaped into the chimney. A large tabby cat revelled in the heat, staring into it, ignoring the bustle and activity that went on around her. Izzie and Beth, with aprons over their black gowns, carried in mulled wine. All stood ready on the two long trestle tables which groaned under the weight of the funeral feast. There was a roasted goose, still hot from the spit, a pan of hot soused mackerel and two large iron pots full of stewed meat and vegetables. Beth carried in a large onion tart and a dish of brawn and the guests, after warming themselves at the fire, transferred to the benches alongside the table on which trenchers and forks and spoons were set in readiness. Outside the light faded but inside the warm food and comforting drink took the edge off their misery. Frozen hands and feet gradually thawed and the conversation began, haltingly at first, then more readily.

The children were seated on rugs by the fire, for there was no room at the tables and it was felt they would enjoy themselves all together while the adults' conversation could develop without the inhibiting knowledge that small ears were flapping. The tabby cat, objecting to the children's attentions, wandered off but the two dogs took its place and snapped up the many titbits offered to them.

'They seem happy enough, bless them,' said Sophie watching them, 'and the dogs believe themselves in heaven!'

Hester laughed. 'You should find yourself a husband and have some babes of your own,' she told her. 'I shall keep my eyes open for a likely man who'll make you a good husband.'

Jo winked at Sophie. 'Hester wishes you to share the worries and the sleepless nights!' he said and then called sharply to one of his sons, warning him to keep further back from the fire.

'I wish Luke would come,' said Alison. 'It troubles me to think of him –'

''Tis no use fretting,' Andrew told her gently. 'If he finds comfort in the deed, let him be. Say nothing when he returns. Now what will you eat, Alison. Shall I carve you some goose?'

'I have no appetite,' she said but he insisted, laying three thick slices of the brown flesh on her bread.

Stephen said little, answering briefly when spoken to but for the most part applying himself to the food. The youngest Tucker began to cry and Jo plucked him from the group by the fire to sit on his lap.

'You spoil him,' said Hester sharply, which set the child howling again and earned Hester a black look.

Father Benedict appeared in the doorway and there was an embarrassed hush because they had started the feast without benefit of a grace. In fact no one had noted

66

his absence, they were all so thankful for food and warmth after their vigil in the cold churchyard. Matthew recovered his wits first and jumped to his feet.

'Ah, there you are, Father Benedict,' he said. 'We thought you had lost your way. Now we can ask your blessing on the meal. Bring a goblet for Father Benedict, Izzie. We must warm him up without delay. 'Twas a fine speech, Father.'

There was a murmur of agreement and, mollified, the priest took his place at one of the tables and uttered the blessing. They all fell to once more and the prevailing mood mellowed from stark grief to a less painful sharing of memories and the recalling of happier times.

Still Luke did not appear and Alison's anxiety turned to apprehension.

'Something has happened to him!' she whispered to Andrew. 'I feel it. Someone must go in search of him for my mind will not be easy until he comes.'

'Then Jack shall go,' said Andrew soothingly. 'Let me see to it. 'Twill arouse less interest if he is missing for a few moments.'

'He has no horse,' said Alison 'and 'tis dark.'

'I'll send Jack with a spare mount,' said Andrew. 'Do not alarm Joseph.' And he slipped out quietly to find the groom and despatch him to the churchyard.

Jack arrived at the church gate and tied up the horses. Then he made his way by the light of a torch to Elizabeth's final resting place. The flickering light revealed Luke still kneeling beside the newly filled grave. The gravedigger had long since gone.

'Sir,' said Jack. 'It grows late. Won't you come home now?'

He watched with compassion as Luke lifted his stricken face towards him. 'Is that you, Jack?' he asked slowly.

'Aye, sir. Won't you come back to Maudesley, sir?'

'To Maudesley? Oh – Aye, I'll come.' He rubbed tiredly at his eyes and then struggled to his feet. His knees and coat were stained with mud. He followed Jack to the horses without a backward glance and swung himself on to his horse. 'You never speak of *your* mother, Jack,' he said suddenly.

'She died when I was born,' he said.

Luke nodded slowly. 'I almost envy you,' he said.

'But what you've lost, sir – I never had!'

'No. Then put like that, Jack, I pity you.'

After the funeral, Luke became even less communicative. Alison thought privately that he had the air of a haunted man, but not daring to probe the reason, busied herself with the children and management of the household which, on Elizabeth's death, had become her responsibility. She did not know, therefore, that he made frequent trips to the church to ask for forgiveness and to pray for peace of mind. Without Elizabeth's support he felt threatened by the knowledge of his sin and could not conceive of any penance that would salve his conscience and lighten his dark world. He brooded constantly on Isobel's condition and the fate of his first son and only legitimate heir. Finally, he determined to break his promise to Elizabeth. He would visit the Gillis family and ask news of him.

A rabbit simmered in the pot over the fire and Marion Gillis held an apron full of chopped onion. As she threw in a handful she met his inquiry after Isobel with a question of her own. 'D'you like rabbit stew?'

'Er – no.' He looked at her, startled.

'Oh don't fret, I'm not offering any. Though you look

68

as if a good meal wouldn't come amiss. You're all skin and bone!' And she began to laugh, a choked, grating sound that sent a shiver of unease down Luke's spine. A few herbs from her apron pocket went into the stew and she took up a spoonful which she tasted noisily. ''Twill do well enough,' she said. 'So you wonder where your son is, eh? Well, well, after all these years, you wonder where he is! Pah!' She spat.

Luke, trying not to show that he flinched, took refuge in formality. 'I merely wish to inquire if he is in good health,' he began but she rounded on him angrily.

'Don't bandy those grand words with me,' she cried. 'You merely wish to know nothing of the sort! You've only one son by her that's called wife and now a sickly girl. Ah, I've heard of it, don't you fear. What you mean is, how's your first-born and is he more handsome than the bastard up at Maud –' The word was never finished for, with an oath, Luke seized her by the shoulders and shook her half senseless. His fingers bit into her bony shoulders and his face, white with rage, was less than an inch from her own.

'Don't you ever dare,' he hissed, 'not ever again, to name my son a bastard. D'you hear me? Never again or I swear I'll kill you and by God's wound 'tis no idle threat. Try me and you shall see!' He flung her away and she stumbled and fell, cursing as she did so. Luke stood appalled at his own ferocity, his chest heaving as she slowly struggled to her feet. He expected retaliation but instead she ignored him momentarily, moving to the fire to give the contents of the pot a careful stir.

'You'll not kill me,' she said simply 'and I'll not kill you, though I could if I'd a mind to. I'm letting you live to rue the day you meddled with my daughter.' She glanced at him slyly. 'Don't you ever wonder why your own daughter's sickly? Or why your mother is under the ground? And you cannot eat so that the flesh begins to fall from your bones? Think on it quietly when you've a moment to spare and ask yourself why? Aye, ask yourself why! And I'm not finished with you yet.' She threw back her head and laughed again. An icy coldness seized Luke at her words and he clenched his jaw to silence the sudden chattering of his teeth. He wanted to speak but his thoughts were frozen. 'So don't come "inquiring" after your son,' she continued levelly. 'Chance is you'll never set eyes on him again. I don't know where he is – your mother thought it wisest.'

'But Isobel, does she know?' he stammered.

'If she did she couldn't tell, her mind's that clouded, but she doesn't know. The only one as knows where he is lies rotting in her grave, and she won't tell!' This time she laughed until she began to cough, racking her thin frame until she doubled up, leaning against the wall for support.

'If you've bewitched me,' Luke whispered, 'I'll see you hanged as a witch. If you've harmed a hair of my loved ones, I'll see you at the stake, aye, and light the first faggot myself.'

There was an expression of fiendish glee in her eyes as she looked at him mockingly. 'Did I say that?' she queried, her tone innocent. 'Did I say as how I'd done anything?'

'You said ask myself –'

'Ah, that's more like the truth,' she said. 'Think on it, I said, wonder about it. Nothing more. Not a word as will get me to the gallows. How am I to blame if your mother dies or your child pines? Think on it I said – but wait!' Her expression hardened as Luke abruptly turned to the doorway. 'I've something to show you before you go. Something you should see. Come.' Reluctantly he followed her to the rear of the hut.

'There!' said Marion and Luke winced at the malice in her voice. His eyes followed her outstretched hand and what he saw brought the bile up into his throat. Isobel sat on a circle of ground worn bare of grass, an empty bowl beside her. She was tethered to a post by a rope around her waist. 'Like an animal!' gasped Luke, his mind reeling from the shock, his stomach heaving with disgust.

Her hair was matted, her body, arms and legs, filthy. Her fingers toyed aimlessly tracing a small circle in the dust, round and round, ceaselessly, while she watched the small movement of her finger as though hypnotized by it.

'Bel! We've a visitor!'

'No!' cried Luke. 'Don't!'

He longed to look away but the terrible sight fascinated him. Isobel turned towards them at his cry with a vacant gaze and the brown eyes looked on him as though on a stranger. She stared unblinking at his face, her expression unchanging. Her mouth hung slightly open, the head was tilted slightly to the left as though to hear more acutely.

'Bel,' she repeated and her voice, too, was devoid of expression.

'That's all she knows,' said Marion. 'Just her own name. That's all she ever says. Bel!' She sighed heavily.

'But why the rope?' asked Luke. 'Surely there is no need to treat her like an animal.'

'She is an animal.'

'But not dangerous.'

'She wanders away,' said Marion 'and I must needs go searching for her. A week or more since and she wandered into the river and nigh drowned herself. 'Tis for her own sake, the rope.'

'I've seen enough,' he said.

'Aye, reckon you 'ave,' she told him bitterly. 'Reckon you've seen all you can stomach. Well I have to look at it every day. So think on that.'

Luke had scarcely reached his horse when his

71

stomach erupted and he vomited. Leaning against a tree, sick and trembling, he faced the knowledge, too awful to put into words, that Marion Gillis had most certainly put a curse on him and his. As long as she lived his innocent family would pay for his sins.

Stephen Kendal rode fast and furious. It was nearly dark and he was still nine miles from Heron. His head ached abominably and he cursed his own folly – too much wine with his midday meal as usual. He had slept for several hours in the hay loft over the stable and woke heavy and lethargic to find the rest of his party already departed, unable to find him and reluctant to waste time searching. It was his own fault but the admission did nothing to ease the throbbing in his temple, nor did it improve his temper.

He had left home three days earlier to attend a hiring fair in Tavistock where he had found a new shepherd for his small flock. He sighed. He would dearly love to dispense with a shepherd and do the work himself. Hacking tin, however lucrative, had no appeal for him and never had done. Since his mother's death he had neglected the workings, devoting himself almost entirely to the sheep and their pasturing. Will Retter had trained his successor well and the mine did not need Stephen – or so he argued.

The new shepherd was an experienced man. With his help Stephen planned to enlarge the flock and expand the acreage under pasture. In spite of the ache in his head, he felt more cheerful than of late. In his saddle-bag he carried a small carved horse for his son Hugo. For Hester there was an embroidered collar. And she should have her lessons on the virginal if her heart was set on it. He smiled, amused by the rivalry between the two women.

When the lantern swayed ahead of him it was a few seconds before he realized its significance. By that time it was too late. Two more lanterns appeared from the bushes at the side of the track and turning, he saw others closing in from behind. He had ridden into an ambush. Instinctively, he drew his sword and took the offensive. 'The first man within reach loses his head!' he cried, tugging his horse into constant movement so that its flying hooves might act as an extra deterrent to his attackers who were on foot. At a guess he thought them seven or eight in number.

'And yours'll follow!' cried one of them, thrusting his lantern at the horse's head so that the animal reared up in alarm and sent another man crashing and cursing into his fellows. A lantern fell and one light was extinguished.

'Out of my way!' urged Stephen angrily but they closed in a little. A man at the rear brought his stave down on to the horse's rump and Stephen was nearly thrown sideways as it lunged forward, its terror mounting. He felt only a consuming rage that this rabble dared interrupt his journey but experience warned him that such men were dangerous and not to be underestimated. If only he could see them! All he could make out was the dim glow of their lanterns and occasionally the whites of their eyes if they ventured close enough. On horseback he was probably safe. Un-horsed his chance of survival would be slight.

'Stand back, I tell you!' he shouted and, leaning down, cut a flashing circle with his sword. A cry of pain told him that someone had suffered its keen edge and there was a hasty move backwards. He found himself in a circle of hostile men. A dagger glinted on his right and a large stone was flung from the left, catching him painfully on the side of his neck so that he gritted his teeth and cursed. He would have to make a dash for it.

'Throw us your gold,' cried one.

'I'll see you damned first!' he answered and spurred his horse forward through the small knot of men ahead of him. Their lack of resistance should have warned him. Almost immediately, the road was blocked by a tree trunk which brought down the distressed animal, throwing Stephen heavily to the ground. The air was thick with derisive cheers and the sound of footsteps as his assailants crowded upon him; he lay defenceless, his sword knocked from his hand in the fall. A knife sliced into his shoulder, another between his ribs. Staves wielded with hate flailed his body and he heard the crack of his bones as they broke. A massive blow from a rock shattered his head and the last thing he knew was the warm taste of blood oozing up into his open mouth.

It took Alison, Izzie and the doctor three hours to make his body presentable before Hester could bear to look at it again. Her first glimpse, when they brought him in, showed a hideous bloody carcass and only the sodden clothes proclaimed it man instead of beast. She fainted and fell, striking her head against the edge of the door so that she had to be carried unconscious to her bed and the maid set to watch by her until she came round. It was a merciful interlude for her and when she did open her eyes again the maid had strict instructions to keep her in her bed. Little Hugo had been taken over to Maudesley where he played with Jeffery and Melissa under Beth's watchful eye.

Alison and Izzie worked feverishly, tears in their eyes. They cut away the clothing and sent it to be burnt. Then they washed the body as well as they could but the blood still flowed until the doctor arrived at last to close the wounds. The justices had been informed, he told them, and the murderers would be found. Ashen-faced,

Alison nodded but his words did little to reassure her. Such attacks were so common and the men concerned so rarely caught. This time it would be no different. Even if they were apprehended, it would make no difference. Stephen was dead, Hester a widow and Hugo fatherless. Stephen – poor moody Stephen – would never see the child that Hester carried in her womb. Alison wept for the mangled flesh and the broken bones that were all that remained of the once-beautiful body. What had been a man – thinking and feeling, loving, and perhaps hating – was now defiled by careless hands, something Alison found unforgivable.

They dressed him in a white robe and covered his feet. Tomorrow they would lay him in a coffin full of bran. For the present he was laid out on Hugo's bed. It was too short so they pushed an oak chest up to the foot of it to lengthen it then covered it all with a clean linen sheet. The priest came and gave the last rites – too late but it must be done. Before he left, he talked with Hester, meaningless words of consolation that did nothing to pierce the darkness that had overwhelmed her.

Alison and Izzie stood back and surveyed the result of their efforts. The face, badly swollen, lay under a fine gauze. The rest of the body was hidden by the burial gown. Only the hands showed, washed clean and neatly folded across his chest. It was possible to look at him without revulsion. They could do no more.

'Thank you, Izzie,' said Alison. 'I don't know how I would have managed without your help. We have done all we can for him and now I must see to poor Hester.'

'Poor Hester. Poor Stephen,' said Izzie dully and Alison saw that the shock which she had resisted so long was now making itself felt.

'Go back to Maudesley,' she told her, 'and make yourself a drink of hot wine. Add honey and spices. You're shivering and 'twill warm you. And again, my heartfelt thanks.'

'I was glad to be of service to the poor lad,' she began, but sobs choked her once more and she hurried away, anxious to get back to her familiar kitchen where, hopefully, the dreadful memories might blur a little.

When the priest had gone Alison went upstairs to the bedchamber where Hester now lay, propped up on the pillows, her face blotched and red, her eyelids puffy. She stared straight ahead and made no sign that she heard Alison enter. 'You may go now,' Alison told the maid, 'and send word to Thomas Benet at Maudesley to notify Luke when he comes home – and to prepare draft letters for the rest of the family. We must tell Blanche and Matthew in London, and Catherine – oh, and he must send word to the Priory to Brother Andrew.' The girl, impressed by the list of names and awed by the responsibility, began to count off the names on her fingers and Alison took pity on her. 'Tell Thomas Benet,' she told her. 'That will suffice. He will know what has to be done. Now, off with you and run all the way.'

The girl hurried away, thankful to be gone from the heavy, depressing atmosphere at Heron. Alison watched her with something amounting to envy, then turned her attention to Hester. The narrow shoulders were hunched forward in an attitude of abject despair and the eyes were blank with shock and grief. 'Dear Hester,' said Alison gently. ''Tis I, Alison. Take my hand – that's the way. Oh, what poor little cold hands. I'll rub them for you. Is that better?'

'Hugo?' said Hester. 'Where's Hugo?'

'Safe at Maudesley,' said Alison. 'Beth will take care of him. Do not fret. Now give me your other hand to rub. Two little slabs of ice, that's what they are. Not hands at all!'

'There was blood,' said Hester swallowing nervously, 'dripping from his hands. I saw it, I tell you. Blood dripping from his fingers –'

''Tis all gone now,' said Alison. 'We have washed him and dressed him in white. There's no blood now.'

'Ah . . . that's good.' She turned her head slowly to look at Alison. 'I'm so cold,' she whispered. 'Not just my hands but all of me – inside I am cold and dark and empty. Poor Stephen. My poor dear Stephen.' As a fresh storm of tears racked her she threw the sheet over her face to hide her grief. Alison put an arm round the shaking shoulders and stroked her hair which hung loose around her shoulders. 'What shall I do?' sobbed Hester. 'I can't stay at Heron without Stephen. He never wanted it and now he's dead. He never loved Heron the way the others did. He hated the mine, you know he did. Everyone knew. He wanted his sheep – poor dear Stephen – and now he has nothing. No one to love him.'

'Hush, don't speak like that!' Alison was shocked. 'He is on his way to God now. He has God's love.'

'I wish I were dead!' cried Hester passionately. 'I want to be with him, dead or alive! I cannot live without him. Oh Stephen, Stephen . . .'

'Hush now, dearest girl. You still have your beloved Hugo! He needs you now, more than before. He has no father now.'

'And what of this child?' cried Hester wildly, clasping her swollen body. 'Never to know his own father!'

'He'll survive, never fear,' said Alison. 'Why, Luke didn't know his father. John died before he was born. Luke has not suffered and neither will your babe.'

'Oh but he has!' cried Hester. 'Luke has suffered. Everyone says so. Why else is he so cold and – and strange?'

'Strange?' stammered Alison.

'Aye. Wrapped up in his thoughts. He broods inwardly and folk say 'tis because he lacked a father's love.'

'That's not true!' cried Alison. 'He had a father's love, from Joseph. A stepfather can be loving.'

But Hester, refusing to be comforted, wept afresh, unaware of the effect her careless words had had on Alison. So others, too, thought Luke strange and withdrawn. It was not her imagination. She looked at Hester and was ashamed to discover that her sympathy had waned a little. The girl had merely rekindled an old fear, but Alison resented it. It was an unkind reward for all she had done that day. Alison tried to look on the distraught widow with the same warmth as before but the damage was done. She was right, she thought. Hester was noticeably round-shouldered and she laughed too loudly. But not now. She would not laugh again for a long time. She still felt a deep compassion but her involvement had lessened. She could stand back. For a while longer she sat on the edge of the bed comforting, reassuring. Then she stood up. 'I must go home,' she told Hester, 'but I'll send the maid up with the sleeping draught the doctor prescribed. Tomorrow I'll come again.' And then she left Hester alone with her grief.

The pack horses stood with lowered heads as the last of the bundles were loaded on to their backs and fastened securely. Hugo clutched at his mother's skirts as she and Alison clung together in a last tearful embrace. 'And you will write to me,' said Hester. 'You promise?'

'I do,' said Alison 'although you know I'm no scribe, but I will try.'

'And you will visit. You will come to Sampford Courtenay.'

'Indeed I will.'

'And bring Jeffery and little Melissa. Oh, Alison, I shall miss you.'

'And I you, for who will I chatter to as I spin? But no more tears now. Poor little Hugo will wonder at all this weeping, won't you, little man.' She bent to give him a last hug and kiss. 'And you take care of your mama, for you are the big man now.'

He stared at her wide-eyed but said nothing.

'He's lost his tongue,' said Hester. 'Say "God bless you", Hugo, to your aunt Alison, and Jeffery and little Melissa.'

But the little boy remained silent. He was longing to climb into the wagon for the long ride he had been promised to visit his grandmother. 'Ah, here comes Thomas with the terriers,' said Alison. 'Now you are all set.'

She had loaned her new steward to Hester for the journey, not wishing the young widow to travel accompanied only by her servants. Apart from Thomas Benet, Hester's own gardener would ride with them and three strong men had been hired from Ashburton, all armed. There would be no repetition of the previous week's tragedy. The shock of her husband's death had affected Hester deeply and now that the funeral was over she was returning to her parents' home until after her confinement.

'Now don't fret, dearest,' Alison told her. 'Your journey is a short one, 'tis broad daylight and you are well protected. You will come to no harm.'

Hester climbed into the wagon with Hugo and Thomas Benet swung himself on to his horse. 'We'll delay no longer,' he said. 'We should make Sampford by late afternoon.'

'Say farewell to Luke for me,' cried Hester. With a clatter of hooves and a rumble of wheels, the little cavalcade began its way down the drive. 'I'm sorry I cannot thank him for all he has done.'

Luke had stayed away from the leave-taking, convinced that Marion Gillis had brought about Stephen's death. Alison waved until they were out of sight then, sighing, went in search of her unhappy husband.

CHAPTER FOUR
1524

The sun was comfortingly warm on the back of the monk's neck, the soil yielding beneath his sandalled feet as he moved carefully between the rows of beetroot. Gently and without haste, he pulled the hoe through the soft earth, marvelling at the deeper colour beneath the surface. From time to time he bent down and retrieved a pebble and put it into his pocket to be discarded when he reached the end of the row. It was quiet in the garden and he was alone except for a stray hen that scratched among the grass and innumerable butterflies which decorated the air like animated flowers.

Soon she would be here. He sighed deeply. Soon he would see Sophie and the thought pleased him. Sophie, now a grown woman past twenty, was a reminder of the only time in his life of which he was ashamed. And yet to see her and talk with her was a rare delight. A large clod of earth defied his hoe and clumsily he lowered himself to his knees. He took the offending soil in his clenched hands and pressed it, lips pursed in effort, until it crumbled suddenly and the red soil spurted between his fingers. 'So!' he said, satisfied with the small achievement, and was struggling upright again when Sophie appeared beside him, a hand outstretched to help him up.

'What!' she laughed. 'Do you pray to your saints in the middle of a beetroot patch! What strange religion is this?'

A broad smile lit his face at the sight of her and, laughing, he dusted the soil from his dark habit. 'A stubborn piece of Devon,' he told her. ''Tis hard soil but I flatter myself I can master it. How are you faring, Sophie? You look in good spirits as usual and there are roses in your cheeks.'

'Uncle Andrew!' she protested. 'You flatter me like a young gallant. Where do you learn such phrases?' She kissed him lightly on the cheek and then looked quickly away feigning ignorance of the tears that sprang into his eyes at this small gesture of affection.

'The beetroots thrive on your attention,' she said, 'but must you work? They told me you had been ill and yet I find you gardening.'

''Twas nothing,' he protested. 'The same fever which I brought home from Spain. It still recurs from time to time.'

'Uncle, will you sit with me awhile?' said Sophie.

'Sit with you?'

'Aye. I want to – talk with you.'

His expression grew suddenly anxious and he looked at her in alarm. 'Talk with me,' he stammered. 'Oh, I don't think I should. That is, I must finish my work.'

She tried to look into his face but he turned his head away.

'Please, Uncle,' she said gently. 'I must ask you something. I think you know what it is.'

'Aye,' he said, his voice a whisper. 'I knew one day – but not today, Sophie. I beg you.'

'Please,' she begged. 'I've made the journey from London especially to talk with you. Won't you please sit with me awhile?'

He looked helplessly at the hoe as though it might suddenly find a voice and offer him advice. 'Sit with you,' he repeated, and his lips trembled.

She took his arm and led him out of the vegetable plot

into the neat flower garden, guiding him to a wooden seat. He sat down, the hoe still clutched in his hands, and she took it from him and laid it beside them on the path. Then she took his hand in hers and smoothed it soothingly with her fingers. Carefully, she searched her mind for the right words. 'Mama is well,' she said at last, 'and sends greetings.'

'Ah, she does?'

'Aye. And Papa also. They both speak well of you always – yet never speak of the past. A week ago I asked Mama about that time.'

He looked at her and then away. The fingers of his other hand drummed nervously on the wooden arm of the seat. 'What did she say, your mother?' he asked.

Sophie sighed. 'She said 'twas over and done with but if I must know then I must ask you. She said 'twas *your* secret.'

He nodded. She waited for his comment but he made none.

'Will you take it to your grave, Uncle?' she asked at last.

He looked into her face, then, searching for a likeness as he always did. As a child she had been the image of her mother but now she was taller than Blanche and her face was longer. As was his own. Blanche did not have the high forehead but the eyes – they were her mother's without a doubt. In her voice Andrew always detected a likeness to his sister Elizabeth. No doubt a family trait in the Sheldyke women. She was no Kendal, that was certain. He drew a deep breath.

'Am I a Kendal?' she asked abruptly, as though reading his mind.

Slowly he shook his head. 'You're my daughter,' he said humbly and there was no surprise in her eyes when he looked at her.

'I thought so,' she said.

Abashed by her composure, he turned away, flicking a speck of soil from the skirt of his habit with a trembling finger.

'Will you tell me about it?' she asked.

'You ought to know,' he said slowly. 'Aye, 'tis right you should know . . . Blanche – Blanche Tucker as she was – was very young, a mere child, when I first knew her. Always over from Maudesley to play with Stephen, Cathy and the twins. They all adored her. Elizabeth used to say they had a family of five at Heron!' He laughed softly. 'Blanche loved me as the other children did until – until she began to grow into a woman. Then she changed towards me, almost overnight. I had no idea at first, being untutored in the ways of women –' He shrugged helplessly but Sophie said nothing, fearing to distract him from the story. ''Tis so long ago,' he said, 'and best forgotten.'

'No, Uncle – I think I must still call you Uncle.'

'Indeed you must . . . where was I?'

'My mother changed towards you.'

'She did, poor child. She was betrothed to William.'

'Uncle William? But he died.'

'That was later.' He sighed again at the memory. 'She wanted to wed me but of course . . .' He held out his hands in a helpless gesture. 'I am a monk and a monk does not wed. He is dedicated to Christ. She would not eat. Joseph locked her in her room. He was beside himself . . . Poor little Blanche. One day she climbed out of the window and we met quite by chance in the wood. I told her I could never marry her.'

'Poor Mama.'

'Aye. It was a most terrible time.'

'For you also.'

'A nightmare. I was young, inexperienced, afraid.'

'Did she wed Uncle William?'

'No. Something happened – between us. I did not

intend such a thing but – we had talked again and she knew I would never leave the Priory. I was fearful of the outside world. I still am.' Sophie squeezed his hand sympathetically and waited for him to continue. 'She agreed to the betrothal with William and then one day we met accidentally. I was swimming in the river . . . she swam with me,' He looked at Sophie earnestly. 'You must understand that your mother loved me.'

'And you?'

'For that hour beside the river. Aye, I think I loved her. I knew only that I deeply desired her.'

'You went on pilgrimage then. I know that much.'

'Aye. I confessed and was sent to Galicia. By the time I came back,' he shrugged again, 'you were born and she had wed Matthew.'

'But why Matthew?'

'William would not have her because of the child, you.'

She was staring at him, wide-eyed. 'Then Papa knew?'

'Aye. Your father is a fine man, Sophie. And then later for his sake – for all our sakes – it seemed better that you shouldn't know. I was to blame, my weakness brought about such miseries.'

'Oh do not look so sad, I beg you,' cried Sophie. ''Twas years since and no one blames you now.'

'Not even you?' he asked, his face haggard.

'Indeed no. I think myself fortunate.'

'Fortunate?'

'To have two fathers! You and Papa and both so dear to me.'

'Oh my child!' He turned to her with tears in his eyes and impulsively she threw her arms round his neck and held him close.

'Weep if you must,' she told him, 'for now 'tis all said and we love each other still. The terrible secret is out and it was not so terrible.'

'Sophie! Sophie!'

She kissed him and he wept anew and she held him in her arms until the shuddering stopped and he was calmer.

''Tis my turn to ask your forgiveness,' she said soberly. 'I didn't mean to distress you. Please believe me.'

'There's nothing to forgive, little one. I'm older now and weep for my youth. Things might have been very different.'

'You did what you thought best and none of us can do more than that. I thank you for telling me. I feel happy, and strangely at peace.' He nodded and smiled.

'So,' she said brightly, 'let us talk of other things. Your face looks thinner. Do you eat?'

'I eat enough, child,' he said. 'An old man does not expect a young man's appetite.'

'I wish you need not work,' she said again, the teasing gone from her voice.

'I work because I choose to,' he said. 'The work is light and I don't hurry myself. I believe the fresh air and the sunshine are good for me.'

She nodded, satisfied with his answer. 'And what other news?' she asked. 'I have come straight to you, you see, and will go to Maudesley when I leave you.' He leaned back and closed his eyes against the sun's brightness, pleasantly aware of the slight pressure of her hand in his.

'You know that Hester is not returning to Heron?' he asked.

'Because she lost the child?'

'No, the reason is elsewhere. They say she will be betrothed again.'

'So soon? Dear God! 'Tis most indecent.'

'Aye, as soon as her mourning is done, to a man from Crediton.'

86

'But what of Heron?'

'Luke and Alison will move in, when the trial is over.'

Her face darkened at these last words. 'Trial? Oh, sweet St Katherine! 'Tis not come to that!'

'I fear so,' he said. 'Indeed Luke is convinced of the woman's guilt. He blames her for the death of his mother as well as Stephen. It seems a black mongrel dog was seen near the body when they found it. The Gillis woman has such a dog, her familiar Luke calls it. He now claims he heard the same dog bark the night Elizabeth died.'

'I must talk to him,' said Sophie, greatly disturbed, but Andrew shook his head.

'Too late,' he said. ''Tis set for tomorrow, the place and method to be decided, though no doubt 'twill be the river.'

Sophie crossed herself despairingly and the old man did the same. Then, dismayed at the sombre turn of the conversation, he stood up. 'What am I about!' he said lightly. 'You have journeyed all this way and I offer you no refreshment. Come, we will ask Brother Eustace for ale and a slice of cake, and mayhap a dish of plums. I do believe my appetite is returning. See what a benefit your visits are to me!' He led her, laughing, out of the sunlit garden, through the cloisters and into the quiet shade of the refectory.

Later, as she made her farewells and left, the poor were already arriving.

Old William was first to arrive as usual. He hobbled up to the door, tapped on it to let them know he was there, then sat down on the near end of the wooden bench and leaned against the wall. It was warm to his back and he closed his eyes, relishing the moment. He had walked nearly two miles on legs swollen with rheumatism and every step had made him wince. Each day he thought he would never finish the journey and having reached the Priory he thought he would never reach home again. But if he didn't come he would starve. He prided himself on being first and it was always a good moment when he tapped on the stout wooden door of the kitchen to let the monks know there were folks outside waiting to be fed.

'Stir your stumps in there!' he muttered with pleasure. Hustle them a bit, he thought. Do them good. They had it too easy by far, these men of God. Fed and watered with a roof over their heads and a fire in the hearth in winter. Say a few Hail Marys, sing a few psalms and pray for the sins of the world. Servants to wait on them hand and foot and a nice warm habit and a pair of sandals – all free. Some folks had to work for what they wanted! He'd had a wife and seven babes to feed and every mouthful had been earned by the sweat of his brow: well, almost! He chuckled wheezily and fell to coughing. He hadn't been averse to poaching here and there – a rabbit or a hare and a fish or two from the river when backs were turned. Not to mention a young boar once. Ah! That had been a right old dance, that day. A real day's sport with him and his brothers chasing the boar and the keeper chasing them! He laughed again until the tears trickled down into the furrows in his mottled cheeks. Still, they'd outrun him – aye, and outwitted him! No trouble at all. He put up a trembling hand and wiped his cheeks.

Maybe the Brothers were too free and easy as folks said and not as dedicated as they might be. Maybe they did spend their money on the wrong things and gallivanted off to foreign parts on so-called pilgrimage. He for one cared not a jot. They fed him and humoured him and he'd no complaints. They paid a high price for it! He chuckled obscenely at the thought of what they had renounced and his chuckles turned into laughter which shook his skinny frame, stirring his thinning blood. Ah, it did him good to laugh. Oh aye, they paid a high price for their bed and board. Only that's what they lacked – a bawd! A bawd! He positively rocked with laughter at his pun. Bed and bawd! He must remember that when the others arrived. They'd like that . . .

Henry, one of the servants, put his head round the door and grinned at him. 'I thought 'twas you, you one-eyed old devil!' he said. 'One of these days you won't be first, d'you know that, eh?'

'That day I'll be dead, I reckon' said William.

'You've got an evil laugh, you have.'

'And a mind to match!'

They both laughed.

'What's it today then?' asked William hopefully. 'Nice slice of swan or is it heron Thursdays?'

'Swan or heron! That'll be your lucky day that will. Swan or heron indeed! No, 'tis porage and a handful of beans.'

The old man stopped laughing. 'Porage and beans?' he repeated, 'but you had visitors here last night. Travellers on their way to London. I saw them ride by with my own eyes.'

'So we did,' said Henry 'but they was hearty eaters and not a scrap left.'

'There's always scraps left,' said William indignantly. 'I'll wager you've eaten them yourselves, you greedy hogs!'

Henry grinned. 'I thought that'd hit the mark,' he said. 'Oh, the look on your face!'

The old man relaxed. 'So there are some scraps,' he said. 'I thought as much.'

'A few biscuits,' Henry admitted, 'and some apple pasties. Maybe a bite of saffron cake.'

'What d'you mean, maybe?'

'Why there's not enough to go round,' said Henry and the old man rose to the bait once more.

'Not enough to – what do you mean!' he demanded. 'I'm first, aren't I? First come, first served. That's the way of it.'

'Is that so then?' said Henry, tongue in cheek.

'Aye. 'Tis so, I'm telling so.'

'Then maybe you'll be lucky,' said Henry, withdrawing his head suddenly in answer to a shout from inside the kitchen.

Tired by this exchange of wits, the old man leant back once more against the kitchen wall. Lucky indeed, he thought crossly. He made it his business to be first and deserved any titbits that were going. Porage and beans – ah well. The porage was lumpy and carelessly made but the beans were tasty enough and filling. Emmie, his wife, had made good porage, smooth with a generous pinch of salt. And once she'd found a whole nutmeg in the market which was a real treat. Grated over the porage! Real tasty, that was. They were good days, he told himself.

A crunch of gravel told him that someone else had arrived and he opened his eyes. It was Mary from behind the ale house, drunk as a lord. He'd have no truck with her. He closed his eyes, ignoring her greeting, pretending to be dozing. He felt her weight settle at the other end of the bench and heard her struggling to regain her breath. She was scum. More footsteps and he squinted with his good eye as a group of unfortunates struggled up the path towards the kitchen. They greeted him cheerfully and he winked his blind eye in return. 'Porage and beans,' he told them, 'and maybe a few titbits.'

They gathered hungrily outside the door, tattered, thin, hopeful. One of them tapped on the door and

Henry shouted, ''Tis coming, 'tis coming!'

More appeared, stumbling and shuffling, some old, some young, some with youngsters. One woman with a child sucking at her breast. The crowd grew, eleven then fourteen. They stamped their feet jovially and clapped their hands and laughed at their plight.

Brother Andrew came to the door and they all stood still while he counted the heads. So there'd be a hunk of bread, too! A bowl of hot porage, a handful of beans and bread. And titbits which they fought over. There were seventeen poor at the door of the Priory that evening and they were all fed.

The sun slanted through the windows of the Hall, its rays falling across Melissa and Beth who sat on the floor. The hearth was empty and the sun's warmth very welcome. Outside, despite the sunshine, the wind blew strongly and made mournful sounds in the chimney. From time to time Melissa turned her head towards the sound but there was no curiosity in her face. A deerskin had been spread over the rushes and Melissa, Beth and the two hounds shared its comfort. Behind them at the table Jeffery practised his letters, working diligently with a stick of charcoal and casting envious glances at his young sister who claimed so much of Beth's attention. Reaching out a hand, he tried to snap his fingers the way his father did, hoping to entice one of the dogs from the magic circle on the deerskin. No sound came and he examined his small fingers critically to see where the fault lay. They were smudged from the charcoal. Maybe that spoilt his performance. Surreptitiously, he put his finger into his mouth to suck them clean.

'Jeffery!' cried the watchful Beth. 'Take your fingers out at once! How many times has your Mama told you.

Look at you now – with a mouth like a chimney. And that nasty charcoal will do you no good! Come to Beth and let me wipe your hand.'

Delighted, he slid from the bench and held out the offending fingers. 'Ugh!' said Beth with an expression of exaggerated disgust. 'See here, Melissa . . . What a pickle your brother is in!'

She rubbed at the offending fingers with her apron while Melissa watched, her face impassive. 'And all round his mouth! Dearie me. If the mistress could see you now, Jeffery, I don't know what she'd say.' She wiped his mouth and he grinned at Melissa but she made no comment. 'Show Jeffery the pomander,' Beth urged her. 'See all the cloves, Jeffery, that she has put in!'

'That's very well done, Lissa,' said the boy in a fair imitation of his father.

'Most certainly well done,' Beth agreed. The orange had seven cloves pressed into it and a pot full of cloves stood beside the little girl.

'Now,' said Beth. 'Jeffery must finish his letters and we will finish the pomander.' Reluctantly the boy seated himself at the table and picked up the charcoal. Beth handed a clove to Melissa and pointed to the orange. With endless patience, she persuaded Melissa to press more cloves into the orange while Jeffery scratched away as slowly as he dared. Suddenly he leaned on the charcoal and it snapped into two short pieces. 'Oh!' he said innocently. ''Tis broke!' He assumed an air of surprise mingled with regret but Beth was not deceived for a moment.

'You bad boy!' she scolded. 'You press too hard. You wanted it broke. Now you can't finish your letters. And don't smile like that. I know what you're about. You're a bad lad.'

'Shall I help Lissa?' he asked hopefully, sliding from

the bench once more. They both looked at her but she said nothing.

'Shall Jeffery help you?' asked Beth patiently. 'Give him the orange and he'll press some cloves in for you. What d'you think, eh? Nod your head.'

They waited but Melissa stared at her wonderingly. Beth sighed, took the orange gently from the girl's hand and gave it to Jeffery who began to add cloves with great enthusiasm. 'In goes one!' he chanted. 'In goes two! In goes –?'

'Three!' prompted Beth.

'Three,' said Melissa.

They looked at her and then at each other. A response was rare enough to be exciting. 'She said it!' cried Jeffery.

'So she did! Clever little pet!'

'We must tell Mama.'

Izzie put her head round the door in search of Beth. 'Oh there you are,' she said irritably. 'Larking about with the babes when there's work to do. I thought –'

'The mistress told me to give an eye to them,' Beth told her. 'She's ridden over to Maudesley and won't be gone long.'

'And Lissa spoke!' cried Jeffery. 'She did!'

'Aye,' said Beth proudly. 'She said "three".'

Izzie's wrath gave way to delight as she smiled at Melissa. 'There's a clever lass. Then you shall have a reward. Izzie shall give you a handful of currants. Come along.' She held out a hand but Melissa had once more relapsed into her usual lethargy. Izzie shook her head. 'Then Jeffery shall come with me and bring a handful for each of you,' she said. He for one needed no further invitation. He was up and out of the room ahead of her, roaring exultantly.

Izzie and Beth looked at the small girl and then at each other. 'Poor little soul!' said Izzie despairingly. 'What is to become of her?' It was the thought in all their minds.

Joseph Tucker sat in the high-backed chair, a woollen rug tucked warmly round his knees. At his feet one of the dogs twitched in his sleep. Opposite him, her features mellowed by the firelight, sat his beloved granddaughter. They had eaten well and now talked in a leisurely way as the glowing logs turned grey and fell to ashes and the hour grew late.

'So Mark Lessor is soon to be a grandfather!' chuckled Joseph. ''Tis a fate that comes to all of us. I see no reason why he should escape it!'

Sophie laughed with him. 'You know you enjoy it,' she said. 'Jo tells me you are besotted with young Gregory –'

'Who will shortly make me a great-grandfather! Oh Sophie, I am an old, old man and who bothers with me now but you?'

She looked at him fondly but her finger wagged in remonstrance. 'You know that is unjust,' she scolded. 'Since Elizabeth died you have insisted that you stay here alone. Jo was minded to move back to Maudesley – aye, and Louise also despite her condition. But you would have none of it. Jo's place is here. Maudesley is his. Why do you keep him away, grandfather?'

He made no answer but pushed the sleeping dog with his toe until the animal woke up and thumped the floor with his tail before lapsing once more into his dreams.

'You rattle round here like a lone pea in a pod,' she went on. 'With none but the servants for company. 'Tis not good for you. Why keep your son in London when he wants to be with you? And Louise is so fond of you. Will you not tell me, grandfather?'

'I'm a stubborn old man,' he said.

'No. 'Tis more than that.'

He sighed deeply. 'Then I'll tell you,' he said, 'but this must stay secret between the two of us.'

Sophie nodded and waited. A log slipped and the fire settled once more before he spoke.

'I hear Elizabeth,' he said quietly. 'I fancy she is not gone on but waits for me. I hear the rustle of her skirts across the rushes – and sometimes she lies beside me in the bed. No, no, I cannot touch or see her but the bed creaks when I am still. Once I heard her laughing, very faint across the garden. I fancy she holds out her hand for me and I want to join her, Sophie.'

'And you only hear these things because the house is quiet?'

'I think that's the way of it. Laugh if you will.'

'I don't laugh, grandfather,' she said.

'I am an old man and when the good Lord calls me –'

'Oh do not speak of it more, I beg you!' She knelt beside him and took his hands in hers, kissing them passionately. 'We will speak of other matters,' she urged. 'I will tell you of the latest news from London. Or will you go to your bed now? Are you tired?'

He shook his head. 'Talk on to me, child,' he said, 'but first make good the fire with one more log. That's well done. Now tell me of the court gossip and the latest fashions – and why you are not wed.'

She laughed, settling herself on the floor beside him, one arm thrown casually across his lap. 'Why then, the last question first. I am not wed because I cannot find a husband to my taste,' she said lightly. 'There was only one Lawrence and he, poor lad, is dead and buried.'

'That was six years ago,' he reminded her. 'A woman cannot mourn for ever. You will find another good man.'

'I daresay, grandfather,' she said. 'And when I do, why that's when I shall be wed. Now, what news of the court? They say the King tires of his Mary Boleyn and casts his eyes over her sister Anne.'

'Do they indeed? And what of the Queen?'

'Poor Catharine! She is grown dumpy and plain.'

'Plain? That beautiful girl plain? Oh, I can see her still when she first stepped on to English soil. We went down to Plymouth, Elizabeth and young Luke, to see her land. So slim, she was then, and so beautiful. Such large calm eyes. Such dignity, she had, for one so young. Catharine cannot be plain!'

'She grows older, grandfather,' Sophie told him, 'and the years have not been kind. Since Bessie Blount gave Henry a son, she has lived her life for the Princess Mary and a distance has grown between herself and the King.'

The old man shrugged. 'The eighth Henry is a hard man,' he said. 'A ruthless man.'

'But a strong king and growing stronger.'

'And richer on the taxes of men like me! He's too ambitious. His poor father would wring his hands, or his son's neck! – could he see the country's fortunes slipping like sand through his fingers!'

'I beg you keep such thoughts to yourself,' she urged him. 'The King does not take kindly to such talk but calls it treason. But what of the mine? They say in the city the tin yields are up again and the quality with it.'

'Aye. We have had an excellent year. Luke told me the exact figure but it escapes me yet. Maudesley and Heron together gave nigh on a ton of metal.'

'A ton!'

'Aye, and 'tis the same story everywhere.'

'And can it last?'

'Who knows?'

The dog barked in his sleep and his paws jerked as though running. They both laughed. 'He dreams of coneys,' said Sophie.

''Tis the only time he catches them!' said Joseph. 'He is old like his master.'

'What ails Melissa?' asked Sophie suddenly. 'I thought today she had a strange look in her eyes, and says so little while Abigail chatters like a flock of starlings!'

The old man looked surprised. 'She is a placid child,' he said 'and obedient.'

'Too placid by far,' said Sophie 'and too obedient. She sits and stares and will not share the fun. This afternoon we fed the ducks and Abigail was so excited she all but threw herself into the water along with the bread! Yet when we came back to the house Melissa still held her bread in her chubby little fist. She seems to stand apart from whatever is happening. And Alison says she has twice in the last month wandered away, once as far as the highway.'

'And is Alison alarmed by this?'

'She is uneasy,' said Sophie. 'She spoke of visiting a wise woman, and has already bidden Uncle Andrew burn candles for the child.'

'Luke knows of this?'

'No. Alison fears to speak on the subject. He is so obsessed by the Gillis woman, so disturbed by the curse, he will not interest himself in any other matter. Alison is waiting until after the trial, by which time 'tis to be hoped Luke will be himself again.'

'Amen to that!' said Joseph. 'The lad is haunted by the wretched woman. I cannot say whether she is truly witch or not but for the harm she has done Luke, I would gladly watch her execution.'

'Here they come! I see the witch.'

The crowd on the bridge stirred nervously as young Willy Samms arrived, breathless with his news, and was immediately snatched into safe keeping by his mother's side. 'Don't you let her hear you say so!' she warned fearfully, 'or you will be lying in your grave next! Such a loud mouth, this one,' she told a man beside her. ''Twill get him into trouble one of these days, I tell him but will he listen?'

'They don't,' he agreed. 'My sister's girl's no better and she's older than your lad by a couple of years. They don't listen to what's good for them and –'

'See!' the boy cried again. 'Here comes the witch – Ah!' His mother hit him across the mouth and shook him into silence but all eyes were on the small group riding towards them. Marion Gillis, her hands tied behind her back, sat astride an ancient pony. The animal was led by a constable and flanked by two other men, one a gaoler from the prison where the accused had been held since her arrest and one a young minister. A few paces behind them Luke rode alone, his face set, his expression grim. The people on the bridge flattened themselves against the rails as the horses passed between them and many crossed themselves as the arraigned witch drew near and averted their eyes lest any evil should be directed towards them. But once the group was on the far side of the river half a dozen braver spirits followed them, while others ran to the opposite bank to watch events from what they hoped was a position of safety.

Marion Gillis was pulled from her mount and the constable unrolled the charge and began to read it in a loud voice. 'This declaration be in regard to one Marion Gillis, broom-maker, of the town of Ashburton who does stand arraigned on the charge of witchcraft in the said town namely that she did, by means of sorcery, bewitch unto death one Elizabeth Maudesley and her son Stephen – the one in secret ways, the other by means of a black familiar in the form of a dog. The same

Marion Gillis does heartily deny all charges and –'

'He lies!' The shrill words cut abruptly into his speech, making his listeners jump nervously. The young minister held up a warning finger but she spat derisively and lashed out at him with her foot.

'Bind her legs!'

'She's a wild one, that Gillis woman!'

'Mad! They're all mad, the Gillises.'

Luke watched impassively as a rope was thrown round her ankles and pulled tightly so that she staggered and almost fell. No one wanted to support her so they brought up one of the horses and propped her against it.

'The bastard lies! Aye, and knows it. Ask him why he –' The constable's whip fell across her shoulder and cut into her flesh, bringing a thread of bright colour to her forearm. She closed her eyes, cursing silently, but when she opened them again those near enough to see remarked on the malevolence of her gaze as she turned towards Luke.

The constable cleared his throat and continued. 'The same Marion Gillis does heartily deny all charges of the said sorcery and witchcraft and at the King's pleasure and command shall be tried henceforth and if found guilty, sentenced in accordance with her crimes.'

On the far side of the river Willy Samms, his mother and the rest of the onlookers chattered excitedly among themselves as further ropes were taken from one of the saddles and the longest was tied round Marion's waist with equal lengths each side.

'They should tie her crossways,' muttered one of the men. 'That's how they do it up north, I'm told, and 'tis more certain.'

'How d'you mean, crossways?'

'Like I say. Right hand tied to left foot, left hand to right foot, and pulled tight.'

They considered his suggestion and Willy's mother nodded. 'Aye, you're right, there'd be no cheating then.'

They looked across to Marion who stood at the water's edge with a look of fear replacing her earlier defiance. Early autumn rains had swollen the river so that it flowed rapidly, bubbling against the boulders and combing the thick clumps of weed into long green strands. The gaoler now made his way over the bridge and down to the water's edge where one end of the rope was thrown across to him.

'She'll not survive a ducking in that water!'

'She won't that!'

'Mayhap 'twas her bewitched that young woman in labour that lost her child.'

'More than likely. Nothing would surprise me, with that look in her eyes.'

'Even her daughter is bewitched and lost her wits.'

'Poor soul! And her own daughter! What a thing, eh?'

''Tis terrible, terrible. Tied up like a dog, they say, though I daresn't go near enough to see for meself.'

'Such wickedness! It hardly bears thinking on – oh, she's going in. She's in!'

'The witch is in!'

A sharp tug from the gaoler had pulled Marion Gillis off her feet and into the water where she stumbled awkwardly and sprawled heavily across a boulder. Unable to protect herself, the next tug pulled her clear and into deeper water where her hands found nothing to clutch at and the water rose to her chest. She gave a shrill scream of fright which inspired the watching crowd to jeer and mock her desperate efforts to keep her head above water. The constable indicated one more tug, the gaoler obliged and at last the accursed woman found herself in the strongest part of the current, hopelessly out of her depth.

'She's going down! She sinks!'

'Aye, but then she's innocent!'

'She's never that, I'll wager. No, see, she's up again.'

'She'll drown most likely.'

'Not her. Guilty as the devil, she is. She'll float, you'll see.'

The constable watched fascinated as the luckless woman fought desperately against the downward pull of the current. The gaoler hurled abuse, even the minister cried, 'Drown, you old she-devil!' but minutes passed and still her head reappeared each time she went under.

'Let out the rope,' called the constable in the hope of greater sport and they did so. The extra length allowed Marion to be carried further downstream and she was thrown head first against a jagged boulder which cut her forehead. The sight of the blood oozing down her face drew cries of approval from the crowd.

'Mayhap she'll learn a lesson!'

'That'll teach the likes of her to meddle with honest folk.'

'Drown her!'

'Let go the ropes!'

Skilfully they jerked the ropes, driving her into the boulders so that she was soon battered into semi-consciousness and slipped below the water. A groan of disappointment went up. Was she drowned? Was she innocent after all?

''Tis trickery! She's a witch right enough.'

'She's guilty. Why doesn't she float?'

'She must float unless —'

All eyes were on the spot where Marion had disappeared. Briefly traces of blood stained the surface of the water to be immediately dispersed by the current. Silence fell. Luke watched anxiously, his heart beating uncomfortably at the unexpected outcome of the trial. She must surely be guilty for how else could he explain the tragic sequence of events that had so far blighted his life? The two men hauled on the rope and Marion Gillis was brought to the surface, gasping for breath but still cursing horribly.

'She floats! She *is* a witch!'

'She isn't drowned then.'

'Saved herself by magic, I reckon. She'd be drowned else. Oh, she's a certain witch! The signs are there for all to see.'

'She's proved it right enough.'

They dragged her from the water and dumped her on the grass where she lay retching and blaspheming, railing against her captors and struggling to break free from the ropes that still bound her. From her head wound the blood flowed freely, running down her neck and soaking into her sodden gown. It was an awesome sight and one which made the watchers thankful for the distance between them. The constable turned to Luke. 'Seems your suspicions were correct, sir,' he said. 'The woman is a witch right enough.'

'No shadow of doubt,' said the minister. 'Poor wanton creature. There is nothing I can do for her if the devil has her soul.'

Luke spoke for the first time. 'Then what next?' he asked.

'Oh, she'll hang, sir, soon as maybe. Will you wait to hear her confession?'

He shook his head, satisfied, and turning, gave her one last look before he spurred his horse into a canter and rode from the scene.

The following night a full moon between broken clouds shone on the dangling body of Marion Gillis, avowed witch, as she hung silhouetted against the tall framework of the town's gibbet.

'Holy Saints!' exclaimed Izzie. 'What a pickle. I shan't know where to start and that's a fact.' She stood, hands resting on her ample hips, and surveyed the kitchen with a jaundiced eye. The move from Maudesley to Heron was in progress and the Heron kitchen was cluttered with boxes and bundles which were being unloaded from the horses. Cooking pots were piled around the hearth which was grey with ash and charcoal from a fire long since dead. Hester had been gone for several months, taking her cook with her, and the room had a damp, neglected air which depressed Alison but inspired in Izzie a fierce desire to improve matters.

'Look at that hearth!' she said. 'Not even cleared the ashes. Would you believe it! Now I couldn't do that. Not move out and leave a messy hearth.'

'I expect their going was a hectic one,' said Alison, 'in view of Stephen's death.'

'Death or no death, there's no excuse for it – look at these pots!' She ran an indignant finger round one of the pots and held it up for Alison's inspection. 'And the dust on this shelf!' continued Izzie tartly.

Alison nodded. 'You'd best get another girl in from the village,' she suggested, 'for a few days, just to help out until you're straight.'

'Mmm, I reckon it might be for the best.'

Slightly mollified, Izzie began a more detailed inspection of the kitchen. She grumbled at everything but the process gave her a strange satisfaction for she had spent her youth in this same kitchen working under Martha's supervision. Now the wheel had turned full circle and she, Izzie, was in charge.

'"You're a dogsbody," she'd tell me,' Izzie told Alison with a grin. '"So you've no call to put on airs and call yourself a maid. A dogsbody, that's what you are and don't forget it."'

'I heard she had a sharp tongue.'

'Sharp tongue!' cried Izzie. 'I'll warrant she did. Sharper'n a knife blade, it was, and cut you down to size as easy as wink. Sharp? I never knew anyone get the better of Martha. And talk – why she'd argue the hind leg off a horse.'

Alison hid a smile, deciding that Izzie seemed likely to follow her predecessor's example, and picked up a bundle of sheets and pillow cases. 'I'll take these up,' she said, 'and make up the beds. Then I'll find the bed drapes and Jack can hang them for me.'

'If you can find the lad,' said Izzie. 'He's having a rare time riding to and fro with bits and bobs. Always "to" when he should be "fro" and none can find him when they want him. I've asked him for the last keg of young ale but "can't find it" he tells me. Then open your eyes, I tell him, for a keg of ale's large enough and can't go missing – and take a look at this pantry.' She waved a hand dramatically, ''Twill need more'n one good scrub before I put anything in it. Ah dear, if old Martha could see her kitchen now she'd weep tears of blood, I swear she would.'

Leaving her to her grumbles, Alison withdrew and quietly made her way upstairs. So Heron was to be her new home. Hers and Luke's. The low rambling house had never been home to him as it had to the others, because he was born after his father's death. But Luke was still a Kendal for Elizabeth had married Joseph Tucker after Luke's birth. And Heron was the family home. Slightly awed, Alison stood in the main bed-chamber and looked at the large four-poster bed, gaunt and unwelcoming without bedding or drapes. First Elizabeth and John, then Hester and poor Stephen. Now Alison and Luke would sleep there. Or not sleep, as the case might be. For months, maybe a year or more, Alison had lain silent while Luke tossed restlessly beside her, wide awake. Sometimes she feigned sleep but occasionally she asked him what troubled him, or begged him to share with her whatever it was that kept him from his slumbers. Always she received the same reply – that his conscience was clear but the chamber was too hot or too cold for comfort or an ache in his leg disturbed him.

Dumping the linen on the chest, she crossed to the window and looked out. Ahead of her sloped the lawn where three tethered goats cropped widening circles in the grass, and two dogs watched from a distance, reluctant to move too close. Immediately below Thomas Benet talked with the groom; from somewhere she caught the high sound of Jeffery's laughter and a smile lit her face. 'Little pet,' she whispered and thought that without him the world would be an empty place. Then she realized guiltily that Luke would arrive shortly and the bed was still unmade. Selecting a sheet, she shook it open, holding it against her cheek to check that it was aired. From the bed she removed the four bricks, now grown cold, and threw the sheet across. As she did so she heard Thomas's voice raised in greeting and knew Luke had arrived. He would come in search of her; hurriedly moving the rest of the linen, she found a mirror in the chest and looked at her reflection anxiously. It wouldn't do to look too dishevelled. The rest of the house might be in a depressing state of chaos but a wife should be serene and welcoming. She patted a little colour into her cheeks and smoothed back a wisp of hair, then bent hastily to her bed-making as footsteps sounded on the stairs.

She turned smiling to greet him and, as always, her heartbeat quickened at the sight of him and the familiar joy filled her heart that this man was her husband. Had she chosen freely she would have made no other choice. Luke put his arms round her and she stood on tiptoe for his kiss.

'So what think you of Heron?' he asked, 'will you be happy here?'

'Aye, if you are here to share it with me,' she said and although her tone was light, the words were heavy with meaning.

He studied the small earnest face that looked up into his. 'You deserve to be happy,' he said simply. 'I pray God that Heron will bring you such happiness.'

'And you, Luke,' said Alison. 'Mayhap –' She broke off and averted her eyes but he put a finger under her chin and turned the blue eyes once more to meet his.

'Mayhap –' he prompted.

'– we can have a fresh start,' she said. 'We have not always been –' she shrugged, afraid to express what she felt. 'Oh, Luke, there have been times when I couldn't get close to you. I knew you were unhappy and wanted to help you –' She shook her head helplessly and by way of answer he pulled her suddenly close and let his head fall so that his lips were brushing the triangle of silk which covered her hair.

'My poor little sparrow,' he said. 'You have tried so hard to please me. Oh, I know. I know it hasn't been easy for you.'

'But Luke,' she cried 'I wouldn't have any other but you. I love you so dearly that anything I do for you becomes a pleasure.'

'I believe you, Alison. You're too good for me.'

'Not so! Don't say such things, Luke. 'Tis you are good for me but just let me love you. Let me be near you, caring for you. The house doesn't matter. Nothing matters except that you love me, Luke, and I love you.' She clung to him despairingly and he led her gently to the bed and sat down, taking her on to his lap.

She leant against him, reassured by the warmth and hardness of his body and the steady beating of his heart. He stroked her hair and slowly she grew calm again.

'I do love you, Alison,' he said. 'Most truly. The past is done with. The evil gone forever.'

She straightened up. 'You mean the Gillis woman,' she said levelly.

'Aye. The witch. She cast a blight – I couldn't expect you to understand. But now she's dead, and Heron is ours. Fortune smiles on us.'

'A new house, a new life together!' she said and he saw with relief that the fear had left her eyes.

'A new life together,' he said. 'Amen to that!'

Later that night they lay long and straight in bed, hands clasped. Luke's chest rose and fell and he breathed deeply and regularly but the pressure on her fingers told Alison that he had not yet slipped into oblivion.

'Was it sweet for you?' she whispered.

'Very sweet.'

'I wanted it to be specially so, to celebrate.'

''Tis always sweet,' he said. Sensing that she needed more words, he struggled to emerge from the languor that enfolded him but no words came and his breathing changed slightly, a harsher note creeping into it. She turned towards him, straining her eyes to see the beloved face in the darkness.

'The air is heavy tonight,' she said. 'Shall I open the drapes now?'

A grunt was all he could manage by way of consent but she tugged back the brocade curtains that enclosed them. By the time she was once more beside him Luke was asleep. Tenderly she took the relaxed hand in hers and kissed it, restraining her passion so as not to disturb him. Then she nestled as close to him as she could and tucked the sheet around her shoulders. Somewhere in the darkness a dog howled, splitting the night with its mournful sound, and Alison groaned. Fortunately for her peace of mind she could not know that a black mongrel dog sat baying beside the gibbet and its lifeless burden.

CHAPTER FIVE
1525

The three men rode under a cloudless sky into a town thronged with people. It was the first day of the Michaelmas coinage and tinners from miles around had come into Ashburton to negotiate the sale of their tin to various dealers, Italian and French traders or the many London pewterers' factors who followed the progress of the Controller of the Coinage as he made his way round Dartmoor for the twice-yearly tin sales. The local inns, bakers and cookhouses did a roaring trade and foreign tongues mingled with the Devonshire dialect on every corner as sales were discussed prior to the official weighing and assaying which would begin promptly at noon.

Luke, riding between young Jack and Thomas Benet, looked fit and at ease. He even smiled and joked with his companions and had given Jack a handful of coins to spend in the town. Thomas, noting the change in him, marvelled to himself that the death of the witch had made so much difference to the man. Jack broke into cheerful but tuneless whistling and was not reprimanded! Luke had much to be thankful for and had considered these blessings as they journeyed from Heron. Marion Gillis was long since dead, the curse removed from his loved ones. Her husband, aware of the town's growing hostility, had hastily removed himself and Isobel to another locality and the shack that had been their home now stood open to the wind and rain. When Luke himself had visited the spot he found only a trampled circle in the grass to reproach him for the past. His little Alison adored him. His children so far survived the rigours of childhood. The tin yield was up on the previous year and the future looked bright. He had made a disastrous start to his life but fate had been kind. He had a second chance and meant to take it. Alison was with child again and this time it would be a boy. He was sure of it. A brother for Jeffery would make him the happiest man in all Dartmoor.

The Coinage Hall was a large building designed like a warehouse which stood near the market place. For weeks the tin ingots had been arriving at the Hall by cart and pack-horse to be stowed, awaiting the arrival of the Controller, Receiver, Weigher and Assay Master who would conduct the official inspection of the metal.

'You have the coinage bills?' Luke asked. Thomas nodded and patted his pocket in reply. 'Then if we are dealt with quickly we can be away by early afternoon. I have promised Alison a yard or two of lace for her new gown and fur for the girl's hoods.'

'And Master Jeffery?' asked Jack, ever the young man's champion.

'Oh, I shall take him a gift, never fear,' said Luke. 'The young scamp shan't be forgotten.'

'He would raise the roof else!' grinned Jack and Thomas smiled at the momentary picture of the six-year-old boy, his round face set in a fearsome scowl, his fists clenched, stamping with rage whenever he was thwarted.

'Alison is too lenient with him,' said Luke. 'The lad has a temper, right enough.'

'Yet he does not take after his mother!' said Thomas and Luke laughed aloud at the sly suggestion, making no attempt to deny it.

Outside the Coinage Hall a large square area had been marked off and already a crowd pressed up against the ropes. Luke and Thomas dismounted and left Jack to stable the three horses wherever he could. They pushed a way to the front of the crowd just in time to see the King's Beam carried out and set down by two porters. The day's business was about to begin.

'Tell me again which ingots we have,' said Luke and Thomas drew the receipts from his pocket and read them aloud.

'One at 487 lbs, one at 174 lbs, one at 169 lbs and two at 52.'

'And the total?' asked Luke.

'Nine hundred and thirty-four pounds,' said Thomas. 'Nigh on a thousand!'

'Very good indeed,' said Luke. 'And the largest two already spoken for.'

'Bewley & Sons?'

'Aye.'

The London pewterer was a regular buyer. 'And I've had a letter from a Signor Mancini, recently docked in Portsmouth from Italy, who hopes to be present. With luck we shall sell him the two smaller pieces.'

Now the Assay Master laid out his hammer and chisel. The official weights were unsealed and placed in position. The Steward, Controller and Receiver sat facing the King's Beam and a cry was made for silence. At a signal from the Controller, two porters brought out the first ingot and set it on the scales.

'Two seven seven pounds – Prideaux!' shouted the weigher and it was duly written down by one of the coinage officials.

'One eight three pounds – of the same name!'

'One one three pounds – of the same name!'

John Prideaux, a small fat man, pushed through the crowd to the ropes and had a brief word with one of the officials who nodded several times and made a note in his ledger.

'You have done well John,' said Luke as the man turned back.

'Aye, well enough,' said John Prideaux. ''Tis a fine year for all of us. The best yet, some say.'

'I don't doubt it,' said Luke. 'Have you met Thomas Benet, our steward? He's been with us several years now.'

The two men bowed.

'Will you join us for a tankard of ale later?' Luke asked but the man shook his head reluctantly.

'I've my wife waiting on my return,' he said. 'Left her at her sister's before nine and I'll wager their tongues have not been still since! And she'd have me believe there's no love lost between them. Then why visit her, I ask? To hear the news and see how the babes do, she says. Ah, women!' They all laughed.

'And are you wed?' John asked Thomas.

'That I'm not!' he retorted. 'Nor like to be for a while yet.'

'They serve to warm the bed on a frosty night,' said John, 'but for little else, God bless them!' And with a few more pleasantries, he made his farewells and left Luke and Thomas to return their attention to the day's work. At last it was their turn.

'One seven four pounds – Kendal!'

'Four eight seven pounds – Kendal!'

There was an appreciative murmur from the crowd. Four hundred and eighty-seven pounds was one of the largest ingots recorded. Luke and Thomas exchanged satisfied looks. 'That'll give them something to talk on while they sup tonight,' said Thomas proudly as they watched the Assay Master chisel off a corner from each ingot. It was found to be of high quality and the Duchy arms were duly stamped on each block. The rest of

Heron's tin was approved and registered and Luke and Thomas hurried round to the side of the building to await their buyers. James Bewley, wreathed in smiles, congratulated Luke on the metal, Thomas handed over the appropriate receipt and money exchanged hands – the previous price of fourpence per pound having held firm for another half-year. The ingot was loaded into Bewley's cart for carriage back to London and Luke looked round hopefully for signs of his prospective Italian buyers. Instead Jack appeared and was promptly sent off again to buy three venison pasties, 'The largest you can find!' which he did to the best of his ability, returning within minutes, the pies still warm from the oven. They bit into them hungrily as all around them bills of coinage were exchanged, money passed from hand to hand and the air was full of shouted instructions, the clatter of hooves and rumble of wheels on cobbles.

'Master Kendal?' A young Italian bowed to Thomas who laughingly shook his head and indicated Luke. 'Ah, Master Kendal. Greetings to you.'

'Signor Mancini?' asked Luke. 'Delighted to be of service. Master Benet, my steward.'

Greetings and due formalities were exchanged. The young man was strikingly handsome, with a sallow complexion, brown eyes and black hair that curled to his shoulders. He was instructed by his father, he said, to purchase five hundred pounds weight of tin. Could Master Kendal supply such an amount? Luke regretted that he could only offer four hundred and forty-seven. Would he take that and look elsewhere for a small ingot to redress the balance? The young man nodded. Jack, watching attentively, envied the young man his self-assured manner and the style and cut of his clothes. The slashed cream silk doublet was richly embroidered and the cuffs of his sleeves heavy with fine white lace.

Jack, hastily wiping crumbs from his face, was sent in search of Richard Mollison, an independent tinner who might have a small amount of tin for sale which would be suitable. Meanwhile, the three men repaired to a nearby tavern where the ale was never sour and where an old man sang bawdy ballads for the price of a tankard of ale. Thomas, scarlet, listened to the tale of a lusty dwarf and a short-sighted widow and hoped that their visitor's grasp of the English language was not as good as his own!

Eventually Richard Mollison arrived and the day's business was concluded to everyone's satisfaction. Luke purchased the lace which Alison had asked for, the piece of fur and a small carved horse for Jeffery. He rode home with his two companions under a rapidly darkening sky, at peace with the world. Almost, but not quite, at peace with himself.

As Luke led his mare into the stable he was astonished to see Izzie peering down at him from the stable loft. ''Tis young Melissa,' she cried, greatly agitated. 'She's been missing this last two hours and the mistress is nearly out of her wits, she's that worried. And where can she be, the poor little mite?'

'Come down from there Izzie and calm yourself,' said Luke, tossing the reins to Jack. 'You say Melissa is missing again?'

Before Izzie could answer, Alison herself came flying to meet him. She flung herself into his arms and burst into a torrent of tears and self-recrimination. 'It is my fault, Luke,' she sobbed. 'I thought she was with Jeffery and then, finding him alone, thought her to be with Izzie. You know what a one she is for the kitchen. She will be helping whenever Izzie will let her, mixing in currants or weighing the flour, and Izzie thought she was with me and –'

'Hush now, little mouse. Hush.'

'I've been so fearful, Luke, and have sent all and sundry in all directions but she's nowhere in the house nor the garden. I'm sure she's been stolen away by gypsies or the like. Oh Luke, Luke, what is to become of her? And her so quiet and will not speak. How will anyone know who she is or where she comes from?'

'Hush, Alison. You'll make yourself ill. I'm home now and she shall be found, so stop fretting and help me. You say she has been gone several hours?'

Alison nodded, dabbing her eyes and sniffing loudly until Luke offered her his own handkerchief. He sent Thomas down to the pond and Jack was despatched to the nearby woods with instructions to search and shout for the missing child. He took Alison back into the house and left her in Izzie's capable hands, urging her to give her mistress a draught of soothing syrup to settle her nerves.

He ran down to the pond where Thomas had found no sign of Melissa. 'There's no mark in the ground where a foot might have slipped,' he said, 'nor no disturbance in the water, though 'tis a long time since she disappeared if Izzie says an hour or more.'

'You are right,' said Luke, relieved. 'There are no signs here. We must comb the countryside. I'll go east, you go west. We must find her before nightfall.'

With heavy hearts they remounted and clattered out of the yard and Alison, hearing them go, wept afresh and wouldn't be comforted.

Luke restrained a natural desire to gallop and slowed his horse to a trot. Time was short and it would never do to pass the child in the dark. He wondered uneasily if gypsies had passed that way but inquiries at several cottages revealed they had not. He made his way to the Priory where the monks were at supper. He called to one of the servants as he hurried past with a tray of bread. 'I would speak with my uncle,' he told the lad. 'Tell Brother Andrew I'm here and beg him make haste.'

The old monk hurried out to greet him.

''Tis Melissa,' said Luke briefly. 'The child has disappeared. I beg you pray for her.'

'I will do so at once,' promised the old man. Without finishing his meal he made his way into the deserted chapel and knelt to plead for the little girl's safe return.

Luke hesitated as he left the Priory. An instinct drew his thoughts towards the broom-maker's hut and yet he was filled with a great loathing for the place and struggled against his better judgement. He would find his daughter dead. He was sure of it. An icy chill seized him and he shuddered violently. He feared to approach the dread clearing with its tumbledown shack. It was evil, haunted by evil memories, a bitter reminder of his own folly. He could not face it. And yet he must. Still he hesitated. The sun slipped suddenly below the rim of the hill and a coolness touched the air. Around him the trees creaked in the sudden breeze that swept the moor and blew damply against his face. Urging his horse slowly forward, he strained his eyes for a glimpse of his daughter. There was no sound as he rode abreast of the hut where Marion had once stood, her head thrown back in anger, her voice shrill with hate – with good reason, he thought wearily. But she was gone. They had all gone. He swung himself out of the saddle and, leading his horse, made his way round to the far side. In the half-light he saw something which made his heart pound: a small figure was moving round the post to which Isobel had once been tethered. It was Melissa. She had the rope in both hands and circled the post, staring at it as though hypnotized.

'Melissa!'

She obviously heard him but did not look up.

'Melissa! Little one!'

Slowly she turned towards him. Running forward he snatched the rope from her hand and lifted her up into his arms. 'Time to go home,' he whispered. 'Mama is wondering where you are and clucking like a mother hen who has lost her little chick!' He hugged her a little too tightly and she wriggled irritably. 'You shall ride home with Papa on the grey mare and we shall bring back a smile to your poor Mama's sad little face. Come.' He swung her into the saddle in front of him and rode home, his lips murmuring a prayer of thanks for the happy outcome of the adventure. Yet, later, as he watched the family reunion, a small fear persisted and troubled his sleep with uneasy dreams.

A week later Joseph Tucker's health began to cause concern and Alison insisted that he move into Heron with them so that they might care for him more easily. Another week saw him noticeably weaker and the doctor called daily. Friday night, as Luke went into the old man's bedchamber, Alison moved towards him.

'Don't let him talk for too long,' she urged. 'It tires him but he wouldn't rest until he had seen you. I doubt you will understand much that he says for he mumbles so, yet all day it has been "Luke, Luke" and I couldn't convince him you were away on business.' She turned back to Joseph who lay in the large four-poster looking frail and lonely. 'See, Luke is come now,' she told him brightly. 'And I have made him promise not to tire you. The doctor said you must rest and I shall bear the brunt of his displeasure if he finds you weary!'

Joseph smiled faintly and nodded. He knew himself to be closer to death than any of them realized, yet would not have it any other way. He had outstayed his welcome on earth and the separation from his beloved Elizabeth grew harder to bear. He would gladly surrender his soul into God's keeping to be with her again.

'So, Papa,' said Luke. 'Alison tells me you have taken a little mutton broth. She is well pleased.' He pulled the stool nearer to the bed and put his hand over Joseph's, feeling the bony fingers and swollen knuckles warm but insubstantial.

'Luke,' he whispered. 'I fear for you, son. Tell me, is all well with you?'

Luke tried to hide the surprise he felt at the old man's words.

'Aye, all is well,' he said hastily. 'You have no cause to fear. Indeed, I am in excellent health and spirits.'

'I have seen you,' said Joseph, 'I have seen you. Your body has been with us but your thoughts have been elsewhere. Your conscience troubles you, Luke.'

'No, in faith, it does not! What should trouble me? You speak in riddles.'

The old man shook his head with an effort. 'Let me help you,' he said. 'Tell me what troubles you, Luke. I am an old man but my mind is clear yet.'

'Papa!' said Luke. 'Believe me, you are mistaken! And do not speak this way to Alison. You will alarm her for no good reason.'

'Is it the Gillis woman, Luke? Has she bewitched you?'

For a moment Luke thought he referred to Isobel, then with heartfelt relief realized his error. 'The Gillis woman did bewitch me,' he said grimly. 'She bewitched us all. But I have put her aside where she can do no more harm. I watched her body swing from the gibbet and knew that we were safe. . . I beg you, think no more on such a dreary subject. A Kendal is a match for a Gillis as she found to her cost.'

Such a burst of coughing racked the old man's chest that he was momentarily silenced, and Luke cast around for some way to distract him. 'Will you have a sip of wine?' he asked.

'No, no –' Joseph coughed again and the fierce spasm shook the feeble body until Luke grew seriously alarmed. As it came to an end tears welled in the faded brown eyes and the old man put up his free hand to wipe them from his cheeks. 'Elizabeth,' he whispered. 'Your mother –'

'What of her, Papa?'

'I long to see her, Luke.'

Luke's dismay showed on his face. 'She is dead these last two months,' he began but Joseph smiled.

'She waits for me,' he confided. 'Last night I fancied I saw her at the window looking out though the shutters were closed. She was so beautiful, Elizabeth, so passionate in youth. Ah, you did not know her then –' He began to cough again until Luke feared he would choke and ran to call Alison. She came hurrying to the bedside.

'Oh Luke, what must we do?' she cried. 'His eyes are closed. Is he asleep? Oh Luke, not –'

'Not dead,' he whispered, 'but I am fearful. Send Jack for the doctor and Thomas for the priest.'

'Oh, sweet heaven! And Jo not home yet.'

'Go, Alison. I'll wait with him.'

He resumed his vigil as a clatter of hooves outside told him the messengers were on their way. Joseph's son, Jo, should arrive the following day. They had sent word earlier to London to warn him that his father's strength was failing rapidly. He would come immediately, Luke knew, but now he wondered if he would arrive in time.

'The children,' whispered Joseph, opening his eyes.

'They are abed, Papa. 'Tis nearly midnight.'

'I want to see them. I want . . .'

Luke patted the old hands comfortingly. 'They will be in at first light,' Luke assured him. ''Tis always their first thought – to see Grandfather.'

'I want to see them now, Luke!'

Luke hesitated. He was reluctant to disturb his young family at such a time but Joseph was growing restless. 'Let me see them, Luke.'

'You shall see them,' said Luke. 'I will summon them now. Will you rest while I fetch them?'

Joseph nodded and Luke hurried out of the room, his heart heavy. He was unprepared for the clamour of death. His mother had slipped her life so easily, falling asleep and never waking again. This anguished, visible parting tore at his emotions, making him vulnerable and afraid. He was back five minutes later with three of the four children. Paul, his new son, still slept with his wet-nurse in the village. Jeffery appeared, grumbling mournfully, disgruntled by the sudden awakening. Little Abigail laughed and gurgled, her sunny disposition never deserting her. She held out her arms towards Joseph and the old man's face lit up with pleasure at the sight of her. Only Melissa remained unmoved, as though unaware of the unusual circumstances. She clung to the hem of her father's coat, her large eyes expressionless, as her brother and sister were lifted on to the bed for a kiss from their grandfather.

'God bless you, Jeffery,' whispered Joseph 'and you, too, Abby. Be obedient children and learn your lessons – and poor little Melissa. Come to Grandfather. That's the way.'

She allowed herself to be kissed, indifferent to the tears on Joseph's face. 'God bless you, Melissa. Be a –' The voice faltered to a stop and Luke's heart pounded. He bustled the children out of the room, shouting to Beth to rouse herself. She came stumbling down the stairs, her eyes bleary, her hair dishevelled.

'Put them back to bed,' Luke told her, 'then wake Izzie and bid her prepare. The doctor will be here soon and the priest.'

'The priest! Oh Lordy!'

'Stop gawping, you ninny and do as I say.'

Joseph was still alive when the priest arrived, but only just. His lips moved but said nothing that anyone could understand. By the time the last rites were read, the doctor too had arrived, but his journey was wasted. The doleful tolling of the passing bell finally sped Joseph's soul on its way to join his beloved Elizabeth's.

The winter was a hard one and Dartmoor was as bleak and uncompromising as ever. Autumn rains gave way to heavy frosts which set the churned earth into icy ridges that horses and wagons could scarce manoeuvre. Later, snows blotted out most of the landmarks so that only the guide stones remained visible – a line of granite 'spears' a mile apart thrusting up out of the snow to guide the traveller from Ashburton across the moor to Tavistock. Heron was cut off from the town for weeks at a time but such isolation was nothing new in winter and was shared by Harben Priory and Maudesley, now tenanted by Jo Tucker, his wife Louise and their children Samuel, Gregory and Anne. Joseph's death had cast a gloom over them all and the dark cold days seemed never-ending but when at last winter gave way to an early spring creatures everywhere emerged to sample the sunshine and marvel in a land grown green again.

Luke rode out with Thomas Benet to inspect the furthermost corners of Heron land. Their autumn sown corn had suffered from the large herds of scavenging ponies that wandered freely across the moors but it was no worse than they had expected and with the promise of fine weather, they hoped, most of the losses would be made good.

Easter came, the fine weather continued. Alison decided they should celebrate with a picnic and woke the children with the good news. Jeffery hallooed his delight while Abigail clapped her hands. She, like Jeffery, was a tubby child but unlike him promised to be short. Only Melissa had Luke's blue eyes. Both Jeffery and Abigail inherited Alison's dainty features, clear grey eyes and soft, almost dove-brown, hair. The youngest, Paul, already had a fine sprinkling of tawny red hair, echoing back to Elizabeth and the Sheldykes.

'Run and tell your Papa,' said Alison, 'while I see what Izzie can find for us.'

The children departed in search of Luke while Alison hurried into the kitchen. Izzie threw up her hands in horror at the mention of a picnic. 'Why there's nought but salt beef and some dry old cheese,' she said dismayed. 'How can you picnic on such fare as that?'

'Of course we can,' said Alison, prepared for her reaction. 'We've a few eggs as'll make a custard tart, and half a rabbit pie – you know the master likes it cold. And what of the saffron cake? We never could have eaten it all.'

Izzie began to relent. 'I've a few dried plums,' she said 'and half a jar of currants. I could make some spicy currant tarts for the babes.'

'Then do your best, Izzie,' said Alison, 'for today the master cannot hide himself at the mine or take himself off to Cornwall. I'll send Beth to fetch baby Paul and we shall be all together.' And she bustled away, almost as excited as the children at the prospect of a family outing. She found Luke in the garden listening to Jeffery and Abigail who were telling him of the joys to come. Some distance away Melissa stood watching, her hands by her side. Only the tilt of her head betrayed that she too listened to them. Alison fought down her anxiety at the sight of her daughter. The doctor had said she would outgrow the condition by the age of four. Now she was nearly six and showed no sign of improvement. She did not speak nor did she communicate with those around her. She watched impassively as life passed her by – a spectator.

'Melissa! Come, my pet.' She held out her hands to the little girl who looked at her blankly but allowed herself to be led towards the others.

'And little Paul is to come too,' Abigail told Luke. 'Beth has been sent to fetch him. I shall teach him a new word today. Yes, today I shall teach him "Papa". Would that please you, eh?'

Luke laughed. 'Why it would please me enormously. You are a fine teacher, Abby. Little Paul is fortunate to have such a sister.'

The little girl looked at him anxiously and then glanced at Melissa. 'Lissa is a good sister, too,' she prompted.

'Oh indeed,' said Luke. 'Young Paul has two fine sisters – and a fine brother!' he added quickly forestalling his daughter's next comment.

'Don't kiss me, Papa,' said Jeffery sternly as his father embraced both his sisters. 'Kissing is for girls.'

''Tis for boys sometimes,' cried Alison. 'And if I should catch you –!' She sprang forward, arms outstretched, and his dignity forgotten, Jeffery ran laughing and screaming to hide behind the nearest oak while Alison gathered up her skirts to run after him.

By noon all was ready and, leaving Heron, they turned left over the bridge and made their way across the river bank in search of a picnic site. Alison carried Paul and Luke walked beside her, the girls on either side of him, holding his hands. Jeffery ran ahead with Thomas who carried the basket and the rugs; the dogs circled the party ecstatically, enjoying the novelty of so much attention. They found a spot and spread the sheepskins on the damp grass. Alison sat down with Paul on her lap and Jeffery and Abigail played with the dogs, throwing sticks for them and trying to coax them into the river.

'They are much too cunning for that,' laughed Luke. 'But watch they do not push you in! That water looks very cold and I have no mind to come in after you.'

Thomas unpacked the meal and everyone fell upon the food with healthy appetites; the dogs were rewarded with a variety of titbits.

'You won't get more than a snippet from me,' Alison told them. 'I'm far too greedy to spare anything. Go catch a coney if you are hungry.'

'Or a squirrel,' said Abby helpfully.

'A squirrel?' said Jeffery. 'Dogs can't climb trees, you ninny. Squirrels live in trees.'

'I'm not a ninny!' cried Abby.

'Now hush,' said Alison hurriedly. 'We mustn't let little Paul hear such wrangling. He will wonder what kind of family he is –' She stopped in mid-sentence. Beside her Melissa sat paralyzed with horror as a huge furry spider crawled slowly across the skirt of her gown. It was a female wolf spider and carried thousands of young on its back which doubled its normal size. Alison herself was terrified of spiders but before she could ask for help, Thomas saw what was happening and, leaning forward, flicked the creature with his thumb and forefinger in an attempt to remove it quickly. Disastrously, the force jerked the parent spider into the grass but also dislodged the young ones which scattered into the air and fell over Melissa's pale yellow gown in a sprinkling of fine brown dust.

'Oh sweet heaven!' cried Alison.

Appalled, Thomas began to brush clumsily at the offending brown specks but they smeared under his touch into a pattern of dark streaks against the pale woollen cloth.

Dumbly, Melissa scrambled to her feet and threw out

her arms in appeal. Suddenly she found her voice. 'No Thomas! No! Take them away!' she begged and began to scream. Thomas, helpless to undo the harm, caught her up in his arms and held her close against his shoulder, covering the small blonde head with awkward kisses and murmuring words of comfort.

'What ails Lissa?' asked Abigail, startled by the unexpected crisis.

'Nothing, little one,' said Alison, but her eyes were on her second child and her expression was anxious. Thomas caught her eye and shook his head.

'Forgive me,' he whispered.

'You couldn't have known,' said Luke. 'Don't reproach yourself.'

'I will take her,' said Alison but Melissa refused to be parted from Thomas. She clung to his shoulder and gradually, as he rocked her, her trembling eased and then stopped altogether.

''Tis all over,' he whispered.

'All over,' she repeated. 'All gone.'

He set her on her feet again and shook the remaining specks from her skirt. She inspected the spoilt gown with interest and then repeated: ''Tis all over.'

Jeffery stared at his sister, confused by her changed manner. 'Why is Lissa talking to us?' he asked.

Luke shook his head. 'I don't know,' he said 'but 'tis enough that she does!' He put out a hand for Alison's and clasped it gratefully.

They didn't realize until later that the incident was to prove the first step in Melissa's eventual recovery.

CHAPTER SIX
1526

Alison glanced at her husband who paced restlessly up
and down the Hall. There was something troubling him
and she had no idea what it might be. She knew, however, that he would tell her when he was ready and not
before. So she chatted idly about trivialities and he
answered with an 'Aye' and 'No' but little else. 'Jack's
finger is mending well,' she said cheerfully, 'I had fears
he might lose the top joint. The wound was deep and
slow to heal but now I feel easier in my mind about it.'

He nodded absent-mindedly and stopped pacing to
pick up a bone that lay among the rushes on the floor.
He flung it into the empty hearth muttering about the
dogs. 'Beth must go over this floor,' he said. 'These
rushes are filthy.'

'They are indeed,' she agreed mildly. 'Jack shall
gather more rushes and we'll change them. Did you
read Hester's letter? They seem well enough and the
grandparents dote on young Hugo. He'll miss his
father, poor little lad.'

'He'll soon have another, seemingly.'

'She cannot stay alone,' said Alison, springing to
Hester's defence. 'And we gain by her re-marriage. We
have Heron.'

''Twas all too hasty,' said Luke. 'It showed disrespect
to Stephen's memory – and now to talk of changing the
boy's name.'

'Poor Hester,' smiled Alison. 'You never did like her
and she can do nothing right in your eyes.'

'She is a greedy woman,' said Luke. 'This new husband, Bannerman, is a rich man so Hugo must become a Bannerman! Kendal is no longer good enough, nor Heron either.'

Alison was silent. Hester and Luke had never liked each other although neither had spoken of it directly. The letter and its contents had obviously annoyed Luke but was not the cause of his dour mood. The letter had only arrived the previous day but Luke had been ill at ease for several weeks.

Abruptly Luke came to a halt and sat down opposite Alison. 'I've been thinking,' he said. 'I wonder if Benet is the right steward for us.'

Alison had been prepared for almost anything but that. She could only stare for a moment, completely taken aback by the unlikely turn of the conversation. 'Thomas?' she said foolishly. 'You think Thomas –'

Her obvious amazement disconcerted him a little and he spoke more brusquely than he intended. 'Aye, Thomas. I think he is not entirely satisfactory. We might consider replacing him before the year is out.'

'Replace him? Luke, I don't understand. How can you suggest such a thing? He is entirely satisfactory. You have said so yourself.'

'I have revised my opinion of late,' he told her. Unable to meet her eyes, he stood up again and moved to stare into the hearth and kick at the remains of a fire. 'This hearth is not cleared,' he said irritably. 'Tell Beth I want to see it swept clean before the day's out. You must be stricter with the servants, Alison. They grow idle if you are too kind.'

Alison nodded but she didn't hear him. 'What has made you revise your opinion of Thomas?' she asked. 'To my mind he has always striven to please you in anything you ask and we have had no trouble with the household accounts. He is diligent too.'

'In your eyes he is obviously a paragon!' cried Luke. 'I don't complain of his work but his manner. He is too quiet. A steward should be a man of strong character, more forceful in his dealings with people. He must be respected by those who have dealings with him, as a force to be reckoned with.'

'He *is* respected,' protested Alison. 'Granted he is a quiet man but he is respected for his honesty and hard work and is pleasant with people.'

'He is *too* pleasant,' said Luke. 'That is what troubles me. What does he do? He doesn't hunt, he doesn't converse in the town with friends. He's too solitary.'

'But, Luke,' she said, 'the man must be allowed to live in his own way. We are all different people and can't easily change. He *is* a quiet man but he has been with us for four years and is almost part of the family. I can't agree that we should dismiss him on such slender grounds. And where would he go? He has no kinfolk of his own. He is always willing to be of service, the children are fond of him, the servants –'

'Aye, too fond!' cried Luke and suddenly Alison understood. Luke was jealous. The words sprang to her lips but she held them back. She would not confront him with the knowledge. She must be more subtle, more kind. 'Melissa dotes on him,' went on Luke, 'and 'tis not natural. The child should be with other children or with Beth or Izzie.'

Or you, thought Alison. 'But isn't it fortunate she dotes on anyone?' she asked. 'Over the last few months she has improved so much – she speaks more readily and laughs occasionally. After her early years, I thank God for it.'

'But she spends hours with him,' said Luke. 'She sits by him absorbed in all he does!'

'And he talks to her,' said Alison. 'He talks and makes her answer. He has infinite patience. Who else has time? Not Beth nor Izzie. And Jeffery must always be chasing with the dogs, or climbing trees or helping Jack with the horses. I confess I am sometimes jealous.'

'Jealous?'

'Aye, jealous,' said Alison shrewdly. 'I come upon them, heads bent together and see the adoring look in Lissa's eyes.'

'Aye,' said Luke. I've seen that look.'

'But I put aside my jealousy,' said Alison, 'knowing that she is in good hands and making good progress. I thank the Lord someone can reach into her little mind and coax out the Lissa who was hidden from us for so long.'

Luke was silent, wrestling with his feelings.

'If you are determined to get rid of him I won't fight you,' said Alison. 'But I pray you give it more thought. If we lose Thomas we might lose our new-found daughter for she would miss him desperately and all the good may be undone by his going.' She bent her head over her sewing and the silence lengthened. She heard Luke sigh as he resumed his pacing. Resisting the temptation to say more, she waited.

'You may be right,' he said at last. 'I confess I had not thought on it that way. We'll see. He may come out of his shell.'

'Why not take him hunting with you one day?' said Alison eagerly. 'He may enjoy it and will learn a lot from you. Give him another chance, Luke. Mayhap he lacks experience and you could instruct him.'

'I'll think on it,' said Luke. 'Mayhap he –' Before he could finish the sentence, the door opened and Jeffery hurtled into the room and flung himself at Luke, hugging his knees so that Luke nearly fell over.

'Hey whoa!' he cried. 'I'm not a tree to be felled, you know. Steady, Jeffery, steady!'

'But Papa!' he protested. 'You promised to take me

fishing. You did! You said we would go above the weir to the pool and we would catch hundreds of fish!'

'Why so I did,' said Luke beaming at his son. 'And so we shall, this very moment.'

Alison laughed. 'I never saw a boy dote so on his father!' she said. Luke smiled and kissed her while Jeffery tried to tug him bodily from the room.

'Bring me a big fish for my supper,' she told them and promising, they departed.

The room fell silent behind them and smiling tenderly, Alison picked up her linen and began to sew once more.

The July sun blazed down as Luke and Thomas Benet rode out on the long-awaited hunting trip. They were thankful for the breeze which moved the warm air against their faces and rode in single file until they came to the edge of the forest, then tethered the horses to a tree and continued on foot. It was the first time Thomas had been hunting and he was conscious of the bow across his shoulder and the arrows at his back. Luke, already experienced, took pleasure in initiating his companion.

'We must move into the wind,' he told Thomas. 'That way the beasts cannot smell our approach.'

'But might see us.'

'Not if we are cautious. Our sounds will not reach them – the breeze comes from them to us. No, it is movement that alerts them more readily than anything else. We must try to use any cover as well as we may.'

The two men moved steadily forward for nearly twenty minutes before suddenly they saw a small herd of deer ahead grazing on the open bracken-covered slopes beyond the trees. There were eight or nine stags and fewer hinds. The latter grazed fitfully, forever raising their heads to test the air and look about them. The stags ate steadily, rarely troubling themselves to look for danger – their hinds would do that for them. Occasionally one raised its head and the fine antlers gleamed palely in the bright sunshine, the velvet long since discarded, the polished horns tapered to a dangerous sharpness.

'They're beautiful,' whispered Thomas.

'Aye, and good to eat!'

Thomas blushed. He had almost forgotten the reason for their presence in the wood. Almost as he spoke, one of the hinds turned her head, suspicion in every line of the small neat head and finely arched neck. They could see the large soft eyes and flickering ears.

'Don't move!' whispered Luke and the two men froze into immobility. The hind appeared satisfied. Luke and Thomas were in the shadow of the trees. The herd grazed on the sunlit slope. Slowly, almost casually, the hind turned away and Thomas straightened up.

'Not yet!' hissed Luke but it was too late. The hind flicked her tail in alarm and moved forward. Immediately the whole herd abandoned their grazing and moved with her along the path down into the shelter of a small clump of trees. They flowed steadily in twos and threes, without panic, and were suddenly out of sight.

Guiltily, Thomas broke into a stammered apology but Luke patted his shoulder, laughing kindly. 'Oh, but they're crafty,' he said. 'The hinds are devious creatures, like all women. They seem to look away and yet they still see with the other eye.'

'They learn an early distrust of man,' said Thomas ruefully.

'Not so, in fact,' said Luke. 'They see us merely as a shape and colour that is out of place. Man is the unexpected so they take no chances.'

'And will we come up with them again?'

''Tis possible. But if not these then others like them. Come, we'll try again. They always graze with the wind so we can follow. We'll look for a stag with three or four years' flesh upon him, and seven or eight tines. You shall have the head as a keepsake!'

'If I kill one,' said Thomas. 'I confess I am not too hopeful of the outcome of this hunt. 'Tis many years since I last wielded a bow.'

'Such talk is treason!' cried Luke. 'The King will not be greatly pleased at such a confession! He likes his subjects to practise at the butts. Ah, we're in luck. See, they have stopped again – a mile or so ahead!'

But this time a woodcock rose suddenly to betray them, and the herd moved on once more, leaving them cursing.

Nearly an hour later they saw another herd, larger than the first. They grazed in open moorland, nibbling the fine deer grass with apparent unconcern while the females watched warily. The two men crept closer and at a signal from Luke, Thomas prepared his bow, his hand trembling as he fitted the arrow into place and sighted along it.

'Go for the beast nearest the leader,' whispered Luke. 'Aim at the shoulder and hope for the heart. When you are ready –'

Awkwardly, Thomas leaned on the bow until it was taut then released the arrow. It flew whining through the air and struck the stag full through the neck. 'Dear Lord!' he gasped and reached for the second arrow.

But already the herd were moving on, heads up, disturbed but dignified. Still they gave no sign of urgency. Even while Thomas's trembling fingers fitted the next arrow Luke's first sped on its way, straight behind the beast's shoulder through the rib and into the heart. To Thomas's horror it staggered on for several more yards, ignored by its companions. Then it faltered and fell sideways, rolling out of sight beneath the bracken which covered the slope. Thomas lowered his bow and a tight feeling of revulsion seized him. He felt no joy at the killing. Only a desperate pity for the animal which now lay dying or dead below the green stems that hid its last moments from the world. Unmoved, the rest of the herd trotted away and out of sight.

'Well done,' said Luke. 'We will make a marksman of you yet. King Henry need have no fear for the safety of his kingdom!' And pretending not to notice Thomas's emotion, he went forward to find their quarry. Thomas, ashamed, ran after him, snatching the dagger from his belt.

'Take care!' cried Luke. 'He's not quite dead. His antlers will tear you to pieces. Will you despatch him or will I?'

Thomas hesitated, then forced himself to look at the stag. It lay on its side, its body heaving, eyes rolling in pain and fright. Blood oozed from the two arrows protruding from its body and soaked into the smooth pelt. Thomas shook his head and pushed the dagger back into his sheath. Luke drew his own knife and averting his head from the jerking horns, slid the blade below the skull and pressed it home. One last frantic sigh and the stag lay dead. It was all over.

'I'm sorry,' said Thomas. 'I'm sorry.'

Luke tried to hide his disappointment. ''Tis no matter,' he said. 'And the deed is done. A well-covered frame – it will make good eating. Alison will be well pleased.' Kneeling, he tugged the arrows from the carcass and tossed them into the bracken. 'One of us must go back for the horses,' he said. 'The other stays here, or else we shall return and find it half-eaten and I've no mind to provide supper for half Dartmoor! Will you find your way back?'

Thomas hesitated. Much as he wanted to be gone, he

doubted he would find the way alone. It was decided Luke should go and he strode off back the way they had come leaving Thomas with the victim of their afternoon's sport. It seemed a long time before he heard the thud of approaching hoofbeats and welcomed Luke's return. Together they lifted the stag and tied it across Luke's horse, its slim delicate legs dangling carelessly on either side. They rode home silently, each busy with their own thoughts. For Thomas it was a time of self-realization. For Luke a time of triumph.

Tavistock market on a Thursday morning was a noisy, bustling place. The cobbles rang with the clatter of wooden pattens as the women tried to avoid the worst of the rubbish that lay around the stalls. Occasionally, a mounted rider would force a way through the indignant crowd but most of the shoppers were on foot, intent about their purchases and eager to be on their way home again. Women haggled over the price of fruit which filled the baskets set on the ground and proved a source of great temptation to the ragged children who slipped in and out, thieving with a professionalism born of long practice. A baker shouted his wares from a small wagon where his grim-faced wife stood guard with a stout stick in her hands to deter those without money from taking the warm, crisp loaves.

An old woman sat grinning. Beside her on a low bench stood three pots of honey, a basket of peas and a jug of mixed flowers. Behind her two men quarrelled noisily over the respective quality of their chickens which squawked their resentment in wicker baskets stacked untidily between them.

'Goat's milk! Fresh goat's milk!'

Alison watched as the young boy filled the customer's

jug from a large pitcher and stowed the coins in his purse. The nanny goat bleated pleasantly, its rope tied round the boy's waist for greater security.

'Fish for sale! Fish for sale!'

'Ripe currants! Come and buy!'

'Tallow! Tallow!'

'Duck eggs – fresh laid today!'

She wandered from stall to stall, passing an hour pleasantly until Luke's business should be completed. Her occasional outings to Tavistock and the ride across the moor were welcome breaks from household matters and the demands of the children. Here she had her husband to herself for a few hours and could put aside the cares of a growing family and renew the relationship with the man she adored.

> 'Lace for a pretty maid,
> Ribbons for a wife,
> Pins and fine needles
> To last all your life!'

In spite of her good intentions not to buy, she allowed herself a look at the old pedlar's tray as he dangled beads and trinkets from gnarled fingers and sang wheezily to attract more customers.

'Look here – the whitest lace this side of Honiton. 'Tis good enough for the Queen herself, God rest her gracious majesty. Why she'd be buying a yard or two, I'll warrant, if she was here. Oh yes! And these buckles! Solid gold or I'm a Dutchman – or a pearl on a silver chain. Fished for it myself, I did, and nigh on drowned fetching it up! No, don't mock, 'tis true, I tell you. Would I lie to a bonny lady like yourself? I have dainty feathers, all colours of the rainbow – and see these combs, my dears, all ivory and polished teeth, 'twould tease out the tangles in that pretty hair, my love.' He caught Alison's eye. 'Why, smile at me again and I'll be round in the morning to comb it for you. What time is your husband away about his business? Why now, I've made you blush. Shame on me for a rogue!'

Alison was indeed blushing to find herself the centre of attraction and withdrew, red-cheeked, to a quieter corner of the market. Here a cobbler patched a shoe while the owner, an elderly man, sat on a stool, one stockinged foot tapping a silent rhythm while he waited. Further over, under a tattered straw awning, a large woman fanned herself while her husband re-ground an assortment of knives and shears with the aid of a sharpening stone.

'Broom-oh! Broom-oh!'

Alison turned. A young woman sat huddled against the wall of a house, a stack of brooms beside her. An old black dog lay across her legs which were outstretched across the dirty cobbles, stiff and straight like the legs of a doll. Her arms hung loose by her side, the palms of her hands upturned, the fingers curled loosely. Her face had once been beautiful, her eyes were beautiful still, though dark and strangely haunted. At the sound of her voice Alison's joy vanished to be replaced by a cold dread. A nameless fear was suddenly recalled from the deep recesses of her mind. She looked at the woman and recognized her as the one she had met in the forest so many years earlier. The witch woman's daughter. So this was where they had hidden themselves.

'Broom-oh!' The voice was flat, like the expression on her face. The mad Isobel! Dear God! Alison fought down an urge to run away. Yet she was in no danger. Isobel did not see her. She watched a sparrow that pecked at a broken apple.

'Broom-oh.' It was more of a whisper than a cry. The dog looked up into her face, whining, and thumped its tail as though in sympathy. No one, it seemed, wished to buy a broom. There was no money in the wooden bowl. Alison watched, hypnotized by the woman's presence in this of all places. And after so many years. Pray God it wasn't an omen! Hurriedly she crossed herself, willing herself to turn and walk away yet unable to do so. A great pity filled her for the pathetic creature propped against the wall like a forgotten toy. Slowly Alison walked towards her, fumbling in the purse at her waist for a few coins. As she lowered them towards the bowl the dog whined again and scrambled to its feet barking. The staccato sound broke into Isobel's reverie and she turned her head suddenly. Seeing Alison, she snatched at the hem of her skirt as it swung against her bare arm. 'Oh no! Please!' cried Alison, fearing the woman's touch, but it was too late. Isobel held the smooth silk to her cheek and closed her eyes, a rapturous smile on her face. She crooned softly, holding the fabric to her lips and rubbing her matted head against the material in a kind of ecstasy.

'No, I beg you. Let me go!' cried Alison trying to free her skirt from the woman's grasp. The harder she tried, the more fiercely Isobel clung to it, and the dog, sensing friction, leaped about barking angrily so that passers by stopped to watch what was happening. Embarrassed by the attention and frightened by her predicament, Alison glanced through the crowd in the vain hope that Luke would appear to rescue her. There was no sign of him. Instead, however, a burly man elbowed his way through the crowd. It was Isobel's father. Taking in the situation, he grasped Isobel by the hair and jerked her roughly to her feet.

'Let her be!' he told her and when Isobel still clung to the handful of silk, he clouted her across the side of the head with the flat of his hand. The blow brought a cry of pain to Isobel's lips and she stumbled, loosing her hold on Alison's skirt. 'Now tell the fine lady you're sorry,' he roared. 'Tell her, I say, or you'll feel my hand again!'

Cowed, Isobel muttered something and the man pushed her violently against the wall so that she fell awkwardly. The dog's barking grew frenzied until he in turn received a kick which sent him squealing and whimpering to hide behind the cobbler who still stitched unconcernedly as though oblivious of the commotion.

'I thank you,' said Alison. She tried to avert her face in case the man recognized her, for he had been in the cottage when she called there. Fortunately for her, he was very drunk and not focusing too clearly. 'She meant no harm,' she told him. 'Please don't punish her.'

'She's got to learn manners,' he said thickly. 'If she's got to be beat, why then, I'll beat her.'

'Oh no, I beg you.' Alison's eyes filled with tears. 'She meant me no ill.'

'I'll beat her with one of my own brooms!' he promised, snatching one from the stack. 'But what a waste of a fine broom.' He became aware suddenly of the watching crowd and was not too drunk to seize his opportunity. 'You'll not find a finer broom this side of Dartmoor,' he bellowed. 'Best birch twigs, these are, and hand-bound with briar – and a handle that won't be loosed. Look at that, ladies and gentlemen.'

Thankfully Alison slipped away, her heart racing painfully, hot tears spilling down her cheeks. She gathered up her skirts and began to run; anywhere to be out of sight of Isobel who now cringed behind the stack of brooms, wide-eyed as a child with a finger in her mouth.

'Alison! My dearest girl!' Luke held out his arms and she ran into them, sobbing.

'Take me home, Luke,' she begged him, 'Take me home.'

'To Luke Kendal from your affectionate brother Matthew this last day of October fifteen hundred and twenty nine from Cheapside in London. Forgive me for my delay in answering your letter which came speedily to hand a month ago by Andrew on his way to pilgrimage at Westminster. A week after his visit Sophie was taken ill of a fever and has been near to death but is now whole again though much wasted in body and frail in spirit. The doctor has prescribed white meats and fish to make good her body and quiet rest for peace of mind. The fever ravages the neighbouring streets and two friends have died of it within the last month. As to your question, there is much talk of trouble for Queen Catharine since the King plans to marry Nan Bullen. 'Tis widely rumoured the latter lives now at Greenwich Palace in a great estate more fit for a queen and the King would put aside his wife, calling the little Princess Mary bastard. I know nought else of the matter but that shortly the Pope must make a decision on the divorce and risk the King's severe displeasure if it be no. Some say that Henry threatens to sever all ties with Rome if judgement goes against him and I doubt not he will do so – he is grown so set in his demands and will not be frustrated. Blanche and Sophie grieve for the Queen as many do. 'Tis said that Nan Bullen came near to a lynching by angry women – a most fearful death, you will agree!

'And now to news of a sad passing – 'tis that of Mark Lessor who was knocked down by a horse not fifty yards from his door and striking his head on the cobbles, did break his skull and was soon dead and now buried. His son John has fetched Ella to lodge with them for a week or more until the mourning is done. I would not fill my letter with sad items so ask now for news of the children and of Alison's progress with the virginal. Blanche perseveres with her tapestry but of late her fingers stiffen with rheumatism yet she persists. The shop flourishes and I am well pleased with my new prentice who has a delicate touch for the work. He greatly aspires to work with gold on silver as Father did before he wed Mama. And finally, what think you of the King's Navy for your young Paul when he is come of age? I lately watched the *Mary Rose* sail up the Thames and was moved by the sight of so fine a vessel and wished for a son that he might serve in her. They call her the flower of all Henry's ships and I can find no quarrel with that. A beamy ship, with nigh on seventy guns, her four masts fluttering with the King's own green and white pennants, her castles crowded with mariners and gunners, that cheered and waved so that all who watched cheered also and I among them.

'But night comes on and I must light the candles or away to bed. In hopes of a visit from you. Think on it, I beg you and God be with you all until such time and so I bid you farewell.'

Alison went into the kitchen holding her skirts carefully so that no speck of dirt or grease would soil her best blue damask. She wore her new satin shoes with the ivory buckles and her hair was smooth under the blue velvet cap decorated with beads and flowers. Izzie came out of the buttery to gasp with admiration at the sight of her mistress so bedecked in the middle of a Friday afternoon.

'Lordy, you look fairer than an angel!' she told Alison. 'Fit for a queen, no less. Turn around now and let's see it all. Aye, the Queen herself would be proud to wear such a bonny gown.'

Alison smiled modestly, a little embarrassed by the woman's fulsome praise. ''Twas the last sitting,' she confided. 'Master Treen has finished at last.'

'And not before time,' said Izzie. 'I thought the master's birthday would be come and gone before he should finish it. Real slow he's been, like an old snail.'

'He has been slow, I grant you,' said Alison. 'But to good purpose. The likeness is a fine one. You shall see it later and give me your opinion on it, but I'm well satisfied and Master Treen well paid. So all's well that ends well. Luke shall have his birthday gift.'

'He's a lucky man, though I says it as shouldn't and you might tell me to mind my manners, but he has you and the four bonny babes! What more can a man want?'

'I think he loves us,' Alison returned timidly, 'and we love him most dearly. But now where's Beth, for I need help with my undressing.'

Izzie looked embarrassed in her turn. 'Why ma'am, the truth is I don't know where she is. I've called her this past hour to no avail.'

'Then you must help me,' said Alison, 'and search for her after. 'Tis not the first time she's gone missing. The girl grows wayward and Luke will find me at fault if she falls into mischief.'

Izzie followed her mistress up to the bedchamber and helped unlace the beautiful blue dress, then hurried downstairs to seek out the errant Beth. She found her at last in the hay loft over the stable with Jack. As she went up the ladder, she heard Jack's voice. 'Quick. There's someone coming!'

And Beth's squawk of alarm: 'Why then, get off me, you dolt!'

Izzie put her head through the trapdoor and looked towards the voices, her mouth closed in a tight thin line of disapproval. Beth and Jack sat together in the hay, their hay tousled, their clothes dishevelled. Jack fumbled to fasten his jerkin but Beth, frozen with horror and their discovery, stared foolishly at Izzie, her skirt above her knees, the bodice of her dress partly unfastened.

'Why you baggage, you!' cried Izzie. 'You wanton young baggage! You come on out of there afore I set to and break every bone in your body. And you, Jack Briggs, let's be having you. Down this ladder in one minute flat or the pair of you will live to regret it!'

So saying, she made her way down again to wait at the bottom like Nemesis, hands on her hips, a fearsome scowl on her usually humorous features. Stumbling in their haste, the two young people complied. They stood in front of her as she drew herself up to her full height and Beth closed her eyes.

'*I* have had to unlace the mistress!' Izzie began. 'And *I* have had to make excuses for this young trollop's absence, I have had to come traipsing the gardens and hollering myself hoarse to find you on the mistress's bidding. And *what* do I find? Lord above but 'tis two young ninnies, hardly weaned of their mothers' milk, skylarking in the hay! And *now* I know, young Beth, where you was last time you went missing and the time before that! And 'twas "lost my way" and "forgot the hour" and so many excuses! So now what've you got to say for yourself, Beth – and it had best be good! Well, I'm waiting.'

Stricken, Beth looked at Jack who shrugged helplessly. The girl turned back to Izzie. 'I've given Jack my heart,' she said. 'I love him most truly, I do.'

It was definitely the wrong thing to say. Izzie seemed to inflate with rage at the mere idea. Her voice shook slightly as she roared. 'Give him your heart, d'you tell me? Lord, I hope that's all you've given him, you foolish slut. Love him most truly, do you? And I suppose he loves you.'

'He does! Oh Lord, he's been saying such sweet things to me!'

Izzie turned wrathfully towards the quaking Jack. 'Is this so?' she demanded. 'You most truly love her?'

Jack shook his head.

'What? You don't?'

'He does, I swear it!' cried Beth. 'He has told me so a dozen times.'

'I don't,' protested Jack. ''Twas only in jest, Beth.'

'Jest!' cried Beth. 'Oh Jack! Jack! 'Twas no jest and you – oh Jack!' And she burst into loud sobs.

Izzie's large arm swung out and her hand caught Jack a blow behind the ear which knocked him sideways on to the hay. 'I'll teach you to jest,' she shouted. 'Young girls have more to do with their time than be jested with by lads like you. There'll be no more of jesting, or I'll want to know why. And no more loving and saying sweet things.' She seized Beth by the hand and dragged her wailing towards the house. 'And you'll come with me, young baggage, and a good hiding's what you merit. But a good bath is what you'll get for you smell of horse dung. Give him your heart! I never heard such nonsense! I'll soon sort you out, my lady, you see if I don't.'

The kitchen was soon damp with steam as the large wooden tub was set in front of the fire and filled with hot water. Off came Beth's clothes and in she went, screaming and complaining that it was too hot and she would drown as like as not. Izzie was impervious to all her entreaties and proceeded to scrub the girl until her skin tingled painfully and stinging soap suds from her hair ran down into her eyes and made them smart. It was a subdued girl who stood out on the stone-flagged floor to be pummelled dry but underneath it all her emotions seethed. Jack should pay for his cowardly desertion in her hour of need. Tomorrow he would get a very large piece of her mind. Love indeed! She would waste no more time on the likes of him. Finally, her person clean and scrubbed to Izzie's satisfaction, her spirit outwardly subdued, she was sent to bed a sadder and wiser girl.

CHAPTER SEVEN

Luke woke next morning to find Alison standing beside the bed. Over her nightgown she wore a thick woollen shawl for the sun was barely visible over the hill and the fire had long since grown cold.

'Blessings on your birthday, my dearest Luke,' she said softly. 'I have something to show you – your gift from me – and I cannot wait another moment to see the look on your face. Oh Luke, I didn't waken you, did I? I waited until I saw you stir and thought you awake.'

'I was waking,' he lied. 'And I had forgot.'

'Forgot your birthday? Whatever next!' She knelt beside him to kiss him and stroked his hair with her hand. 'And have you forgot how old you are? Or do you pretend ignorance!'

Luke pulled her close and kissed her lightly. 'No, I recall most clearly I am twenty-five. You will not call a man liar on his birthday.'

'Twenty-five is it? Then you have lost six years and that's uncommon careless of you, Luke. But come. Up, up and out of bed and see what I have for you.'

Grumbling good humouredly, he allowed himself to be dragged from his bed and, barefoot and in his night-shirt, followed Alison downstairs into the Hall. He glanced around but saw nothing of note.

'On the wall!' she urged impatiently. 'Oh you cannot miss it!'

Beside the large fireplace, hung straight and square,

was Alison's portrait. Her small pale face stared out from the dark background in its ornate gold frame, the same soft, almost timid expression, the eyes gentle, the mouth small and defenceless.

'Like a little virgin,' he whispered, astonished at the likeness.

'A virgin?'

'Aye. Still soft and helpless as the day we wed. Oh my sweet girl.' Turning, he took her in his arms and held her while his eyes travelled from her face to the portrait and back again. Slowly he shook his head, amazed.

'He has captured your very soul,' he told her. I swear I have never seen such a likeness. 'Tis past belief. Who did this work?'

'One Leonard Treen from beyoned Honiton,' she said. 'He was well spoken of by the Courtenays and has painted Mistress Goddon – and much to her delight for she is painted so comely they say her own brother did not recognize her!'

'And did this Treen visit here? I did not see him.'

'You saw him once, Luke, although I begged him come secretly when you were away so that you could not guess at my gift. You passed him once on the road, a week since, d'you recall? You spoke with him and told me that his horse reared suddenly and nearly threw him off.'

Luke sighed. 'A portrait painter. So that was it. And I thought – but no matter.'

'You thought what, Luke?'

'I don't recall,' he said, reluctant to pursue the point. 'No that's not true. I do recall. I asked you who he was and thought you lied.'

'In faith I did, Luke, but I meant no harm. And were you angry with me? You did not speak of it to me.'

'No, I said nothing,' he said wretchedly.

Was he never to be free of a conscience that pricked

him night and day, tormenting him. He had misjudged this innocent wife of his. Had thought her capable of such a deceit! He sighed again. He had wronged her so grievously, so many years ago, and wronged her still! The woman deserved a better husband. 'Though God knows I have tried!' he said, then cursed his careless speech, for the delight had faded from her eyes and she looked at him fearfully.

'What troubles you, Luke? My dearest husband. Tell me, I beg you, that I can understand and help you.' She clung to him, the portrait forgotten. 'Luke! I know you grieve for something – or – someone – that is past. You mutter in your sleep and toss and turn.'

'What do I say?' he demanded. 'When I speak thus in my sleep. 'Tis no more than bad dreams. I swear it, Alison. You must believe me. What do I say in these dreams?'

'I cannot hear,' she said. 'The words are jumbled, some whispered low, some shouted . . . Once you cried "witch woman". Once you cried "forgive me" and "Simon".'

'God's truth!' He turned away from her, a hand to his eyes to hide the fear he felt at her words. What else did he say? How long would it be before she learned the truth?

'Is it the Gillis woman?' Alison asked. 'If so, then don't fear her, Luke. She is dead and gone where she can do no harm, and her daughter is no witch but a poor crazed creature.'

'Don't speak of her!' Luke shouted. 'She is nothing to you!' He seized her by the arms and shook her violently. 'Do you hear me, Alison. She is nothing to you nor ever will be.'

'Luke! You're hurting me. What ails you?'

'Ails me? Nothing ails me, I tell you. Will you not listen to me!'

'But you act so strangely, Luke, and you look so – so –'

Luke made a great effort to control himself. Breathing deeply, he managed to calm the wild pounding of his heart and fought down the panic which racked him. 'There now,' he stammered. 'I am myself again. I swear it.'

'Oh Luke! My dearest husband. I love you so much it hurts me even to think on it. Do you love me, Luke? Tell me truly, for if you do then I can bear anything. Can live with any fear'

'There is nothing to fear, little mouse,' said Luke. 'Nothing is going to hurt you, I swear it on my honour. I would die rather than see you hurt.'

'Don't speak of dying!' cried Alison, her fears redoubled by the intensity of his words. 'You must not die, Luke. I shan't let you die. Are you ill? Is that it? Tell me, I beg you.'

'Hush, hush, my little Alison. Husha. There is nothing to be afeared of. I still dream of the witch woman. That is all. Dreams cannot harm us, can they, except to spoil our sleeping. Why, if I start to mutter of such nonsense, then a prod with a wifely elbow will silence me. Alas, I have troubled you on this special day and all for no reason. We'll forget what has just passed and I will look again at the portrait.' He considered it gravely. 'Aye, 'tis well done and no man could ask a finer gift for his twenty-fifth birthday! A handsome portrait of my beautiful Alison.'

Alison smiled faintly. 'When I am old it will remind you that I was once beautiful.'

Luke looked into the sweet face, still shaken out of its usual composure, and his eyes were full of love. 'You will always be beautiful in my sight, Alison,' he said gently. 'And I will always love you dearer than life itself.'

Three mornings later, Alison awoke to find the rest of the bed empty. A letter from Luke lay folded on the pillow.

'My beloved Alison from your husband Luke. Trust me I beg you. There is a sad and urgent matter I must attend to. I should be with you again by Sunday next but if I am delayed do not fear for my safety, rather understand that my business is not finished. Light a candle for my success and pray for me in my endeavour which I swear shall be no secret to you on my return.'

Refolding it, Alison sighed deeply. She would be patient, and she would trust him! She could not guess the exact nature of his 'urgent matter' but intuition told her it concerned the unfortunate Isobel Gillis.

'Is she ready?' asked Luke without dismounting. 'Did you receive my message?' Old Gillis paused to sample the stew he was making before deigning to answer.

'Aye, and she's ready – Isobel! Come out here. Your husband wants to see you!'

'Don't say that!'

The old man laughed but Luke's eyes were on the door of the hovel where Isobel and her father now lived. It was little more than a rough wooden shelter, built against the rock face beside a sluggish stream. He caught his breath as the girl's slight form appeared in the doorway, a hand shading the bright sun from her eyes. She wore a faded dress of coarse brown wool and her feet were bare.

'The fine gentleman has brought you a horse to ride seemingly so think on your manners and thank him kindly. Strange that he should have truck with the likes of you since he says he's no kin of yours. Odd, that, wouldn't you say, Isobel?'

Isobel made no answer. She looked at Luke with

expressionless eyes as though they focused on a point behind him.

'Can she ride?' Luke asked.

'I doubt her's ever tried,' said the old man. 'You'd best tie her on then she'll not be able to fall off.' He laughed again, an ugly raucous sound, then spat derisively. Luke took Isobel's hand and led her towards the horse he had brought for her.

'I'll help you,' he said in a low voice and he cupped his hands for her foot. After a second's hesitation she put her foot into his hands, put a hand on his shoulder and allowed herself to be swung up on to the horse's back. She would ride side-saddle and from beneath the rough skirt her bare feet hung incongruously. 'Well done,' said Luke and he smiled at her but she stared down at him in the same unseeing way. He put the reins into her hands.

'Why, her looks every bit a lady, don't her just!'

'Aye,' said Luke. He mounted his own horse and took the leading reins from Isobel's. 'We shall be gone two days, maybe three,' he said. 'Will you be here when we return?'

'Oh aye, I'll be here,' said the old man. 'But if you lose her along the way, why, I shan't grieve overmuch. Her's no sort of company, and her'll not be missed and that's the truth.'

'I'll not lose her,' said Luke shortly and they left the man to his cooking and rode out towards St Cleer.

For a while they rode in silence. Luke was concerned to satisfy himself that she could control the horse and ride as safely and comfortably as the highway would allow. When he was sure on that score, he would talk to her and try to explain where they were going. Meanwhile, the sun shone and from time to time they passed other travellers on their way to Tavistock who gave them a 'Good morrow' and a smile. A woman with a flock of geese, an old man with a wagon load of peat and three young gallants, decked out in their finest clothes, who sang a bawdy song about a crooked parson. Isobel showed no interest in any of them, scarcely turning her head at the sight of them and making no response to their cheerful greetings.

Luke and Isobel rode side by side without speaking. Luke was at the mercy of a range of conflicting emotions and was glad to let the morning pass. The girl beside him was his wife. This strange, withdrawn woman in her tattered gown was Luke Kendal's legal wife. She was the mother of his only legitimate child. For this woman he had committed a grave sin, had betrayed Alison and had made bastards of his other four children! Because of this woman Elizabeth had sinned also. The sum total of the harm thus done was terrifyingly high. Yet here they were riding together, their horses' hooves clattering in unison over the hard-baked mud of the highway.

'You are quite safe with me,' he said suddenly and was surprised when Isobel turned her head towards him but she said nothing and he went on slowly, choosing his words carefully. 'We are going to ride together. We will ride through Gunnislake and Kelly Bray and come at last to St Cleer. You know of it, mayhap?'

Her eyes moved inquiringly as if seeking to find the answer in the air, then he fancied that she shook her head. 'St Cleer,' he repeated. 'We'll be there by night-fall. We'll rest there and eat. Aye, we shall have food and wine. You'll enjoy that. The fresh air and the exercise will give us an appetite, I warrant.'

She looked at him again and he longed to comb the tangled hair and wash her face and hands but he had vowed he would not touch her. He would do nothing that might be misconstrued by her or anyone else.

'Tomorrow we'll visit the Holy Well at St Cleer,' he

told her. "'Tis a good place – a holy place. The water in the well has magical powers to heal a sick mind.'

She stared ahead, impassively, and Luke could not judge how much, if anything, she understood of what he told her. Possibly he had said enough. He must not overburden her mind. Tomorrow would bring its own problems and he would face them then.

By six o'clock they were crowded at a long table in the small hospice enjoying a simple meal of baked mullet with fresh baked bread washed down with ale. Isobel ate ravenously but fortunately many of their fellows attacked their food with equal vigour so that her lack of manners went unnoticed. Luke watched her as the long thin arm stretched out again and again to snatch bread from the platter in the centre of the table. He noted with surprise that the blank expression had faded from her face to be replaced with one of cautious interest. Her glance travelled up and down the table and she listened intently to all that was said. However, she made no reply to the remarks addressed to her and gradually it was accepted that she was 'one of them' and left alone. There were so many in a similar condition, some better, some worse. The Holy Well of St Cleer was famed for curing just such afflictions of the mind and sunrise on 1 May was a highly propitious time for pilgrimage to the sacred waters. Supper at the hospice was thus shared by equal numbers of sane and insane and the sight of so many unfortunates sharing the meal was not a cheerful one. There were old and young, men and women. Some dribbled or had to be fed. Some rocked backward and forward on the bench, others jabbered endlessly. A man beside Luke ate clumsily so that most of his food fell into his lap. A very young girl at the far end of the table fought and swore as her parents strove to feed her.

Luke, sickened, attended to his own and Isobel's needs and tried not to see what was happening around him. His pity was mingled with disgust and he was ashamed.

'Your wife?' asked a man opposite, nodding towards Isobel.

Luke shook his head guiltily.

'Sister then?'

'Aye.'

'I can see the likeness. Been that way long, has she?'

'A few years.'

'A few years can be a lifetime, eh? Wouldn't you say so? This here's my younger brother Samuel. Eighteen, he is, and born like it, but much worse than he is now. Every year I bring him here. Every first of May, without pause, for the last five years and he's nigh on cured. Wouldn't you say so?'

Luke forced himself to look at the young man. His large mouth hung open and his eyes wore a vacant expression. 'Aye, I'd say so,' he agreed kindly.

'First time for your sister, is it?'

'That's right.'

'Thought I hadn't seen you before, leastways not on May Day. Some come on the summer solstice but I swear by the first of May. You'll bless the day you brought her here, I promise you. A new woman she'll be. But let me give you a word of advice – ' He leaned across the table confidingly, a hand cupped to his mouth to muffle his words. 'Let her drink of it. That's the secret. Let her take it in, as well as cover her body. That way the curative power is doubled. Wouldn't you say so? My brother here, when his head's under I hold it there till he splutters for help. Then I know he's taken some into him. That's the secret, you see, but that's not widely known.'

'My thanks to you, sir,' said Luke. 'I'll remember that.'

'Do that and you'll not regret it. Ah! Here comes the custard tart and not before time. He's a good old cook, is Brother Daniel. Wouldn't you say so, my brother? I say, you're a good old cook and none can beat your custard tarts.'

'If you say so, then 'tis likely true,' said the old monk, beaming at the compliment. He placed the large tart in the middle of the table and began to carve it into generous portions.

In the light of the early morning, the long straggle of people formed up along the path to the Holy Well. As the sun rose above the sky line a ragged cheer greeted its appearance and at once the first supplicant moved forward and down the steps to the water. Everyone else shuffled forward a little and resumed their patient, hopeful wait. Luke had been wondering how to explain to Isobel all that would be required of her. He had no wish to alarm her and no way of knowing if his explanation would be of any value. Finally, he sought the advice of the man who had been so forthcoming the evening before and now stood behind them in the queue.

'No need to tell her of it,' he advised. 'There's a monk by the pool. He's used to such folks and has a way with him. Very gentle and holy, he is, and that's how it should be. Wouldn't you say so? Poor souls, they're grieved enough without harsh words and rough hands to wound their spirits. Very gentle, this monk. A real holy man and no mistake. Not like some I've seen that would hurry and chivvy us poor folk like so many sheep through a sheep dip! This one's as gentle and as holy as our Lord himself. You'll see. Aye, you'll see.'

When it was Isobel's turn Luke led her forward and dropped a gold angel into the wooden bowl at the monk's feet. The young man nodded, smiled gently at

Isobel and made the sign of the cross over her.

'The Lord's will be done,' he said. 'The Lord casts out evil spirits. He has blessed the Holy Well of St Cleer. Come child. Let me help you.'

Luke watched, fascinated, as the young monk led Isobel down the steps into the water. Wonderingly, she followed him. Then Luke waited on the bottom step while the monk accompanied her into the water. When she was waist deep, he urged her to kneel. 'Close your eyes,' he told her. 'Take a breath. That's well done. Good girl.'

Lightly he ducked her head under the water and she came up spluttering slightly. Luke remembered the previous night's advice. 'Drink of it, Isobel,' he cried softly.

Immediately and without question she cupped her hand and scooped some of the water to her lips. The monk nodded and smiled, helped her to her feet then led her up the steps again.

''Tis well done,' he told her. 'The blessed St Cleer sees your plight and will be merciful.' To Luke he said: 'Change her clothes, feed her and take her home.'

Luke breathed a sigh of heartfelt relief. Isobel was in God's hands. The worst was over.

They rode home in silence. Luke watched hopefully for signs that a cure had been effected but could see no change in her manner. She did not answer his questions or acknowledge his comments. He had combed her hair and washed her face and hands. All that could be said for her was that she went home a little cleaner. But there was still time, Luke told himself. The improvements he had wished for might come gradually, day by day. He fought down his disappointment and, on their return to Tavistock, handed her over to her father with an air of assumed cheerfulness.

'She looks well, I think,' he said. 'The monk was very hopeful of her recovery. I'm well pleased.'

'Are you, then?' said the old man. He looked her over critically. 'I can't say as I see much change in her. Her's as sullen as ever, I don't doubt. Does her talk?'

'Not yet – but she will. I'm convinced on it.'

'Oh you are, are you? Well, I reckon I'll wait and see what happens 'cos I'm not at all convinced. Still, pleasant for a man to take his wife riding if nought else.'

'I've warned you!' snapped Luke, his good humour evaporating instantly. 'I've told you never to speak that way, and paid you well.'

'Ah, there's the rub, though,' he whined. 'I recall well while the money lasts then – 'tis most odd this – soon as the money's spent, my memory fails me. Sad thing to be an old man with a failing memory. Very sad thing, and awkward too for some folks.'

He waited, his eyes on Luke's unwavering, until the latter pulled the purse from his belt and tossed it to him. 'Take it, you wretch, and I'll bid you good day.'

Furiously Luke rode away, leaving the old man to count the coins gleefully. Unnoticed, Isobel stumbled after Luke, her hands outstretched. 'Luke! Luke!' she called, but there was no one to hear her.

Alison was waiting for him. She ran across the Hall and into his arms, begging for his kiss. He lifted her from the floor and held her close. He had prepared a careful selection of half-truths with which to satisfy her curiosity but she put a finger to his lips. 'No, Luke,' she said softly. 'There is no need for explanations. You have asked me to trust you and I will do so. Whatever you have done these last two days has been done with the most honourable intentions. That I know. You have no need to share your secret with me if it were best kept.'

He stared at her. 'Oh my lovely girl! My sweet Alison! If you could know how much those words mean to me – and what a burden they lift from my shoulders! I would rather not speak of it. That way 'tis soonest forgotten. Oh, what a brave little mouse you are. And how I love you, Alison.'

He held her tenderly and the doubts that had racked her faded as she felt herself safe once more in the compass of his arms.

It was late July, 1531. Jack sat against the stable wall cleaning the brass tackle and Beth swung on the lower half of the stable door, watching him critically.

'You've more grease on your clothes than you've got on the leather,' she told him. 'Just like a man. All fingers and thumbs. I could do a better job on it myself and that's the truth.'

He held it out towards her. ''Tis yours for the asking,' he said. 'If you would do it better – '

'That's right! Me do your job and who's to do mine?' she said. 'And this door creaks like old bones. A spot of grease wouldn't come amiss.'

'Seems to me you're wasted in the house,' said Jack caustically. 'You know so much about my job.'

'Aye, and could do it a sight quicker. Ten minutes you've been polishing that harness.'

'And ten minutes you've been swinging on the door doing nowt!' said Jack. 'Nice for some folks to have time to spare – and that door only creaks when you're swinging on it.'

'I've a good mind not to tell you what I heard in the market.'

'Don't tell then. I'll hear it all in good time.'

'But you'd like to hear it now. 'Tis about the Queen.'
'Oh?'
Beth abandoned her swinging and sat beside him on the dusty cobbles. 'Aye, the King's sent her away.'

'Away? Away where?'

'To Kimbolton Castle, for ever, so they say.'

'But that's miles away. I doubt you've got it straight, Beth.'

'I have then! I rode behind the master and Master Benet and heard it from their own lips so 'tis true enough. The poor soul is banished from her own husband and all for the sake of Nan Bullen who wants to be Queen in her stead.'

Jack shook his head mournfully. 'Ah! That Nan Bullen,' he said. 'They say she's bewitched the King to do her bidding.'

'But pity Catharine, the poor creature. Though the master says 'tis a just solution. Just? says Master Benet. How can that be? If a man be legally wed to a wife, how can he put her aside like a useless old animal? But the master says Catharine *may* be useless if she cannot give the King a son and if a man weds in error, why then he should be able to mend matters. Master Benet was quite affronted and I thought they'd come to blows. Such an argument they had on the matter.'

'The master said the King *should* send Catharine away?'

'Aye. I'm telling you he did. Most strong he was for Henry and wouldn't hear a word against him.'

Jack shook his head, bewildered. ''Tis a fine thing if the poor creature is so punished,' he said. 'She has given the King a fine daughter, and might yet bear a son if God's willing.'

'She'll not bear son nor daughter, banished to Kimbolton, that's certain,' said Beth. 'But how will England like Nan Bullen for Queen?'

'She'll never be Queen, that one,' said Jack.

'Well, the master thinks otherwise, clever clogs,' said Beth tartly. 'He reckons the King will get his divorce and we shall have a new queen, though I'll not raise my voice to cheer for her, nor throw petals in her path. Poor Catharine shall have my prayers.'

'Best not to let the master hear you say so,' said Jack. 'From what you say, he's the King's man though I'll warrant he'll find it a lonely state.' And Jack, speaking more prophetically than he knew, resumed his polishing while Beth took herself off to the orchard to gather up the sheets which lay bleaching in the sunshine.

CHAPTER EIGHT
September 1536

Harben Priory stood grey and compact as the rough winds of early spring sent an occasional flurry of rain against its walls and rattled the shutters. The gaunt gardens were covered with wet leaves. The courtyard was bare and rain rippled the surface of the small pond. A shivering dog leant against the closed oak door of the chapel which separated him from the chanting monks. Young Billy came out of the kitchen store with a basket of logs and whistled for him to follow but the animal barked a refusal and scratched instead at the door with his front paws.

'Here boy!' cried Billy. 'They'll not let the likes of you in so come away and I'll maybe find you a scrap or two.'

Unmoved by this, the dog persisted but Billy, hushing him sternly, seized him by the scruff of his neck and dragged him away after which the courtyard was silent again. It was mid-morning but lowering clouds hid the sun and cast a gloom over the day.

Alison reined her horse to a standstill and tied him to the Priory gate. Head bent against the elements, she hurried through the garden, across the courtyard to the kitchen and knocked on the door. Tom opened it and smiled a welcome. 'Why Mistress Kendal, come you in and stand by the fire,' he said. ''Tis a raw old day and not fit for the likes of you to be scurrying round like a drowned rat!'

Alison thanked him and moved closer to the large hearth where a fire burned under an assortment of large iron pots and a kettle. 'I come in search of Brother Andrew,' she told him, 'but by the sound of it, I am too early.'

'They'll not be long,' said Tom. 'Billy! Fetch up a stool for the lady and stop feeding that mongrel. The animal will likely burst if you go on filling its belly.'

''Tis but scrawny still,' Bill began, but Tom cut him short: 'Stool, I say!' and he hurried to bring one. Alison settled herself by the fire and smiled in its glow.

'How long have you been here?' she asked Tom and saw by his change of expression that he understood the significance of her question.

'Twenty-nine years,' he said. 'Near enough thirty.'

She nodded.

'I've been here a long time,' said Billy. 'More'n three years, I – '

'No one's asked you,' said Tom. 'So hold your tongue.'

Alison watched, amused, at the young man's acceptance of the older man's criticism. What would happen to all the Toms and Billys if the King went ahead with his plan? She sighed heavily. Like so many others, she feared change and could not begin to imagine a land in which the monasteries and priories had no part. But she heard such rumours and the King was a ruthless man, they said, and would tear out the 'sickness' which he professed to find in the religious houses. Her thoughts were interrupted as the sounds of chanting ceased and she went out to greet Brother Andrew. After the preliminaries she asked him directly: 'Andrew, have you had news of the Priory of St Nicholas? 'Tis a bad business.'

'Why none, Alison. The commissioners are due there any day.'

'They were there this morning, Andrew, and Luke tells me their visit caused quite a commotion.'

'Come into the Guest Hall,' said Andrew. 'We shall be blown away if we stand out here.'

'I fear you will all be blown away forever if the King persists,' she said and continued her story as they crossed the courtyard and went into the large room where travellers, pilgrims and other guests were made welcome. 'It seems,' she told him, 'that two of Cromwell's visitors arrived in the morning and spent several hours prying into the financial affairs of the house. They then retired to dinner, leaving one workman with orders to start demolishing the church.'

'So soon?'

She nodded. 'Aye, they waste no time, these so-called commissioners. The man was actually pulling down the rood loft when a group of poor women arrived for food at Poor Man's Parlour.'

'They give bread and meat,' said Andrew, 'or fish if it be Fridays. On St Nicholas's day they give also a penny piece each to the poor. They will be sadly missed.'

'Yet Luke will not have it so,' said Alison. 'He laughed when he told me of the women, poor souls. Hearing the noise, they went to the church door and finding it locked, broke it open! They stoned the wretched man and would have seized him and beaten him but he ran into the church tower to hide. They sought him out and would have laid hands on him but he jumped from a window and was nigh on killed!'

'Poor wretch,' said Andrew, 'What are we coming to that such things should happen?'

'He was found with a broken rib and the women locked themselves in the church shouting that 'twas God's house and the rood loft should stay. Alderman Blackaller himself arrived and forced a way in but one of them landed him a dreadful blow and sent him scurrying for safety.'

'And are they there still, these women?'

Alison shook her head. 'No. The mayor himself took a hand and they were all arrested but later freed with a caution as to their conduct. They say the commissioners asked that they be freed. Luke says they are good men doing a worthy job! Sweet Heaven! I cannot see it his way. Indeed I cannot.'

Andrew, frowning, shook his head slowly. 'More like they wanted an end to the disturbance as quickly as possible. They cannot welcome such scandals. They are unpopular already and do not relish more attention.'

'What will become of the poor?' asked Alison. 'Who will feed them if the monasteries are closed down? Who will care for the sick? Who will give hospitality to travellers? Oh Andrew, what is the King about to order such miseries? Luke will have it that the King knows best and we must trust him. I hate to disagree with him yet my conscience tells me the King is at fault.'

'Hush! Lower your voice,' urged Andrew nervously. 'There's no knowing who may be listening, even here.'

''Tis a bad business,' said Alison. 'The King's break with Rome will bring ruin on us – and all for the sake of the Bullen witch who now rots in her grave. He should have cherished his Catharine. God rest her soul, then England might have been spared this latest folly.'

'I beg you do not speak so clearly!' said Andrew. 'Times are not easy and they say the King's temper grows shorter. I pray you keep such thoughts to yourself – and do not quarrel with your beloved Luke.'

'My beloved Luke!' She sighed. 'Aye, I love the man dearer than my life yet cannot understand the workings of his mind. But what of you? What of Harben Priory? Are you like to suffer a similar fate?'

'I fear so, Alison, but we are in God's keeping. He will

provide for us.'

'Indeed I trust so and yet I fear for you all.'

'You must not fret yourself, Alison. Look to your family and your husband. We are God's children and we must put our trust in him.'

When the day arrived for Cromwell's commissioners to visit Harben Priory Luke waited for them on the highway, a mile outside the town. He had offered himself as 'escort' in view of the recent disturbances at St Nicholas's and they had accepted his offer with gratitude. He had told no one of his gesture and now greeted them conspiratorially.

'I rode earlier to the Priory,' he told them 'and saw no one unlawful there. With luck the visit may pass without incident but 'tis as well to be prepared.'

'Is the Prior known to you?' asked one of them.

'He is. He is a good man.'

'And capable?'

'I would not venture an opinion.'

The man smiled. 'Then we shall have to find out for ourselves,' he said.

John Towen, Prior, moved in his high-backed chair.His right leg grew stiff without exercise but he said nothing. The two men who sat across the table would not sympathize with his aches and pains. The chief commissioner asked the questions, his voice harsh and suspicious. The other man wrote in a large ledger.

'And you do not deny selling six ounces of plate on November 2nd of last year?'

'I do not deny it. We had many poor to feed, the harvest was a bad one and grain was dear. 'Tis in the accounts.'

'I can find no record of it.'

The Prior raised his hands helplessly. 'They may be mislaid,' he said, 'Brother Jeremy was very forgetful towards the end.'

'Then he should have been replaced.' He turned to his assistant. 'Make a note, that the proof is missing. And what of the cattle? It seems they vanish from one year to the next for out of twenty beasts three years since you now have only seven. Did the poor eat them also? They have rapacious appetites in this parish!'

Luke laughed. He sat at the door of the Prior's parlour, his sword laid across his knees. Old Towen was an incompetent idiot and had mismanaged the Priory for many years. He deserved his present discomfiture for he had allowed the buildings to fall into decay and the discipline to falter. Small wonder the King sought to put matters right. Such men as Towen should be prevented from doing further harm. Old age was no excuse for incompetence.

'We were not able to replace the beasts as often as we needed to,' said the Prior. 'The chapel roof was leaking and the cost of new timber and a workman's wages – '

'Find the entries,' said the commissioner to his assistant, 'and check them against the value of the beasts. What of the plough? There is one not accounted for.'

''Tis loaned to one Master Pringle of Manor Farm, the other side of the town.'

'Check that also. What of this silver chalice pawned for the sum of £15?'

'Ah, the chalice. Dear me,' stammered the old man. ''Tis not redeemed as I recall.'

'Not redeemed? In four years? Likely it has been sold long since. And these other holy vessels? Are they still unredeemed after six years?'

The old man shook his head wearily, then changed his mind and nodded without speaking. He shifted again in his seat, with a grimace of pain, and suggested: 'We might have a flagon of wine, gentlemen, to refresh ourselves.' But the commissioner was not to be so mellowed. 'I think you can ill afford to drink wine,' he said. 'Perhaps a jug of ale. Meanwhile we will continue. I see no mention here of two wood lecterns, a sacry bell, pair of bellows and a lamp. Can you account for them?'

'Ah, let me think.' The old man put a trembling hand to his head. 'The lecterns I recall were eaten away with worm, we burnt them in the refectory. The sacry bell was stolen.'

'Stolen? By whom?'

'We never discovered.'

'But you reported it to the justices?'

'I think so – yes, we did. The bellows, let me see, the bellows await repair –'

'Await repair? For all of six months?'

'Aye. Brother Dominic has been poorly and unable to mend them. The lamp was dropped and broke apart and we couldn't afford to buy another.'

The ale came and they all drank. The commissioner leaned back suddenly in his seat and scratched his head in pretended confusion. 'Where is Brother George?' he asked. 'Not fed to the poor, I trust?'

There was a long silence. Brother George had gone on pilgrimage five years earlier and had never returned.

'We do not know his whereabouts,' said the Prior. 'He never returned. The Bishop knows all the facts.'

'And did a certain silver bowl valued at £5 go with him?'

'It did, but without our knowledge.'

'I trust so! And this bowl is where?'

The old man shrugged despairingly. He could follow the line of the investigation and could see where the leading questions were leading. He was not clever enough to disguise his mistakes and not brave enough to lie.

'A rascally monk is no great loss. The silver bowl is a

different matter. Make another note . . .'

The investigation continued without a break and was most thorough. Tithes, loans, servants, behaviour of the monks, extent of charity and hospitality, mismanagement, sickness, acts of God, disasters dating back twenty years or more. All were held up to a merciless scrutiny by a cold, hard man who enjoyed his task.

Luke, at the door, listened with half an ear, growing bored with the catalogue of errors, until a chance remark from the commissioner startled him from his apathy. 'You perform weddings, I believe.'

For the first time John Towen was able to protest ignorance. He stared uncomprehendingly at the commissioner.

'There is mention here of a rumour that a wedding took place in this priory in the year 1518 between one Isobel Gillis and an unnamed man. Do you know ought of the matter?'

'I know 'tis a most damnable lie!' cried the old man. 'There's been no such wedding here, you have my word on the matter.'

'But 'twas widely rumoured at the time. Make a note –'

Luke turned suddenly, keeping his voice steady with an effort. 'I recall it,' he said. 'I can help you there. 'Twas a malicious rumour put about by the girl's mother who was later hanged for witchcraft.'

The commissioner looked at the Prior. 'And you had no knowledge of such a rumour?'

'He was in Galicia,' said Luke, 'at the shrine of Compostella and returned with a persistent fever. The matter was of little consequence and most likely he was not informed.'

The commissioner appeared satisfied. 'Then I think we may rest until after dinner,' he said. 'I confess to a certain hunger and food will be most welcome.'

Thankfully the old Prior got to his feet, hobbling

awkwardly as his weight rested on the right leg.

'Are you eating with us?' the commissioner asked Luke but he shook his head. He was aware that his presence at the visitation would not be welcomed by the monks, and had turned down the Prior's unwilling invitation to join him and the commissioner for dinner.

'I must away home,' he said. 'Or my wife will send out a search party.'

'Then our thanks to you for your assistance and God be with you.'

With a courteous nod Luke left them and rode home in a thoughtful frame of mind. The commissioner's question about the wedding had frightened him. The dissolution of the Priory and the dispersal of the monks could not happen soon enough for Luke Kendal.

'You want to go to sea?' cried Alison. 'Never! I won't allow it and neither will your father.'

'I've asked him, Mama. He says I may go.' Jeffery stood at the window, defiance in every line of his broad back. He faced away from the light and she could only vaguely make out his expression but the tone was firm and uncompromising. 'I will go, Mama,' he went on. ''Tis no rash decision. Paul will tell you. I have thought of nothing else these past three years and waited only to finish my schooling.'

'Paul knew of this madness and said nothing?'

'He envies me, Mama. I have been offered a place on the *Mary Rose*!'

She was silenced momentarily by the significance of the name. The *Mary Rose* was King Henry's pride and joy. 'You know what they say,' she told him. 'There are three kinds of people. The living, the dead and those at sea. You cannot want that sort of life. I don't believe it.'

'I will go.'

'Not if I can stop you, Jeffery.' She confronted him, white-faced. 'What of Heron?' she asked. 'You have a duty to –'

'Paul is welcome to it.'

The words hung strangely familiar in the air. Hadn't Stephen spoken them many years ago? Poor Stephen, God rest his soul. These Kendal men were a strange breed. She could not understand them. Loved them, aye, but could not see the workings of their minds.

'And Paul, does he wish it?'

'He loves Heron. You know that, Mama.'

'Aye – but the life at sea is so hard, Jeffery. Such terrible food and so many diseases! You are not bred to such hardships. Why does your father give his consent without speaking to me on the matter?'

''Tis settled Mama. I can join the ship next week. And I shall be an officer one day, I swear it. You shall see us when we come into port – come aboard and meet the Captain –'

'I shall do no such thing, Jeffery,' she said, her fear turning to anger. 'If you go 'twill be without my blessing, and Heaven knows you will have need of that. Would you sleep in a hammock, slung from the ceiling like a smoked ham? And the sailors are such rabble. Always fighting and stealing from each other. How will you bear to live with such men? And you are not a strong swimmer – not as strong as Paul. If you go overboard you'll drown. There'll be no turning back to look for you.'

'Mama, please! You know nothing about the King's Navy. He has built a fleet to be proud of and the *Mary Rose* has been Sir Edward Howard's flagship and has just now been rebuilt at Portsmouth. They have upgraded her to seven hundred tons and she carries more gunners. And her guns, Mama. No one will match her fire power. I couldn't sail in a stronger ship. The *Mary*

Rose has breech-loaders *and* muzzle-loaders. She can soften up the enemy at long range and –'

'Stop, stop, I tell you!' cried Alison. 'I have no wish to listen!'

'– by the time she is closed the battle is already won! How can she fail? She's superb!'

'Don't talk of fighting, Jeffery. I thought we were done with wars. Is there no end to it all?'

'She has demi-cannons, culverins, sakers –'

'Stop, I say! I'll hear no more of this folly!' Alison put her hands over her ears and ran outside in search of Luke who had taken care to be elsewhere when her eldest child broke the news of his departure. In spite of all Alison's threats and entreaties, Jeffery left a week later to join his ship.

Jack, inside the stable, was glad of the stable door between himself and his mistress. Luke's wrath he could cope with, Alison's was another matter. 'What d'you mean, you can't say?' she demanded angrily. 'Do you mean the master confides in his stable boy and not his wife? Where has he gone, Jack? I must know.'

Jack shook his head despairingly. He had passed Luke riding towards the Priory and everyone knew that today was set for the final dissolution. There would be trouble, no doubt on that score! And the master would be in the thick of it, on the wrong side, if rumour was to be relied upon.

'He's gone to the Priory, hasn't he?' she demanded.

'I daresn't say,' said Jack. Luke, passing him, had put a finger to his lips and said 'Not a word to your mistress, d'you hear?' And Jack had heard.

Alison was fast losing her temper. 'Then you can point the way,' she snapped. 'And make haste or you'll regret it.'

Jack considered carefully. He was well aware that women lay traps for men and he had no mind to fall into one of Alison's. She caught hold of his arm suddenly and shook him. 'Then answer me with a nod of your head,' she cried. 'Is Luke to be found at the priory?'

He nodded.

'Then saddle me a horse. I must go down there right away. The man is so stubborn. God knows what's gotten into him these last four weeks.'

There were seven religious men in Harben Priory including Andrew and the Prior made eight. The yearly net income was £136 and there were outstanding debts to the sum of £81.12 s. John Towen had been found guilty of neglect of the buildings; gross mismanagement of funds; inability to maintain proper discipline among the brethren; failure to observe the rules laid down for the order; the keeping of livestock other than for domestic use, namely dogs and falcons, and distributing more money to the poor than the Priory could afford. Finally, after examination, the Prior was found to be lacking in the amount of learning required by his office. It was a highly exaggerated version of the true state of affairs but it was intended to ensure the Priory's dissolution and it succeeded. On 1 November Cromwell's commission would see that the King's orders were carried out. Prior John Towen would be forcibly 'retired' on a pension of £18 per annum plus six wainloads of firewood. The monks would receive between £3 and £5, depending on age, with the alternative of an arranged transfer to another larger establishment which might or might not be dissolved in its turn. Only Brother Dominic had chosen the latter and he had departed a week earlier. The lay servants would receive nothing and must find employment elsewhere.

When Alison arrived at the Priory she was dismayed by the size of the crowd gathered outside the gates. Of Luke there was no sign.

'Are they here yet?' she asked.

'Aye. Inside this last hour.'

'And Luke Kendal?'

'Him!' The woman spat in disgust. 'He's aiding and abetting them, he is. I'd not have his conscience, I can tell you. Turning honest monks out of their home as have never done no one harm. Why can't the King leave 'em be. Nursed my son, they did, when he was near to death.'

'And fed me and mine last winter,' said a swarthy man who carried a cudgel in one hand and held a child's hand with the other. Another man, carrying a wooden mallet, said, 'Aye, and gave me a blanket for my bed and shoes for my children and a penny now and then to buy bread. Aye, and taught my father his letters, they did, and how to spell. They're holy men, they are. Blessed in God's sight and woe betide any that casts them down.' He peered shortsightedly at Alison. 'Aren't you Mistress Kendal?'

'I am.'

'Then you watch out for your husband, mistress. Aiding and abetting the King's men, he is, and he'll be punished like them on the Judgement Day.'

'Don't!' cried Alison fearfully. 'I won't listen. Each man must do as he thinks fit. My husband has his reasons.'

'Oh, he has his reasons, right enough,' said a woman with a hare lip. 'No doubt filling his purse with money from the monks' coffers like the rest of the thieving swine.'

'No, that's not true!'

The woman looked at Alison pityingly. 'How d'you know that, then?' she asked. 'In his confidence, are you?

Does he tell you all his business? Does he? I'll warrant he's got a secret or two!'

There was an embarrassed titter at this last remark to which Alison gave but scant attention for she suddenly saw Andrew, and called to him waving over the heads of the crowd. He came out to her to cries of 'God bless you, Brother Andrew.' He would not be moving away but into Heron to rejoin the family.

Alison seized his hands anxiously. 'Oh Andrew, have you seen Luke?' she whispered. 'Is he – with them?'

He nodded. 'But you should be at Heron,' he said. ''Tis no place for you here. I fear there will be a demonstration of some kind and you are best out of it.'

'No, Andrew. I must stay. I must be with Luke, whatever happens to him. Sweet Heaven! This is a sad day. A sad day. What can be done, Andrew? Is it too late?'

'Aye. Too late by far. Ah, here come the Brothers. I must bid them God speed.' He left her and hurried back. Four of the monks were leaving. Watched by the crowd they strapped bundles and baskets to their saddles and then mounted. John Towen blessed each one and they rode slowly out of the gates and through the crowd. 'God be with you all,' they cried.

One carried a bird on his wrist. A small dog ran at the heels of the fourth man's horse but the monk shooed him away. 'Go back, boy,' he told him. 'I can scarce afford to feed myself and cannot feed an animal also. Go back.' But the dog, reluctant to lose his master, continued to follow at a respectful distance.

Alison blinked back the tears in her eyes. She alone in the crowd was ashamed to meet their eyes, was unable to call a farewell or ask a last blessing. Her husband was a willing party to this tragedy and that made her guilty too.

All eyes now were on the four Brothers as they rode away. Beside her a young man watched them go. He was tall with hair the colour of corn and deep blue eyes above the prominent cheekbones and fine narrow nose. Alison found herself staring at him. He had a look of Jeffery about him, but the mouth was full and beneath the rough shirt the shoulders were broader. He became aware of her gaze and turned suddenly to look at her but someone called 'Simon! Over here!' and he moved away.

Then everything happened at once. A man was seen in the tower dismantling the bells and the crowd gave a concerted cry of anger.

'Leave them be!'

'Get down before we pull you down!'

'You'll not make old bones if you touch those bells,' cried an old woman. 'I've a silver piece in that tower bell. Watched it being cast, I did, many years ago. Take your thieving hands off it!'

While they shouted, they pushed forward and the large wooden gates, in need of repair, gave way under the pressure. With a roar, the people ran into the gardens and from there to the courtyard.

'Bring that man down!' They began to chant. 'Bring him down! Bring him down!'

Alison's horse, terrified by the commotion, lunged sideways and threw her into the crowd. Struggling to her feet, she was swept through into the courtyard, her hair dishevelled, mud and gravel clinging to her face and clothes.

The commissioner came out. Fists were raised, stones were thrown. Luke appeared beside the commissioner and a fresh howl went up against him. John Towen appeared at the window, his hands held out beseeching order, and the cries of rage changed to cheers. The man in the bell tower was forgotten as a man at the back of the crowd saw another workman crawling along the ridge of the roof, easing up the lead.

'So the King steals lead, does he?' he shouted. 'See there!'

A positive barrage of stones flew towards the roof and the unfortunate man fell out of sight uttering a hoarse scream.

'Dear God, he'll be killed!' cried Alison. 'Stop this, all of you. 'Twill do no good and the innocent will suffer. Stop it, I beg you.'

'Oh, she's for the King, is she?'

'No! I merely beg you –'

Rough hands reached out. Her hair was pulled and her face was slapped.

'Two rotten apples, that's what they are!'

'She's no better'n him!'

A violent blow across her shoulder sent Alison stumbling. Above the noise she heard Luke shouting to them to stop but he was too far away to help her. Groaning, Alison fell and would certainly have been trampled underfoot but two strong arms were suddenly round her and a young man cried 'Hold! The lady is blameless.' He pulled her on to her feet again, one arm supporting her, the other warding off blows. 'The first one who harms her shall have me to reckon with. Hold, I say!'

Something in his manner demanded obedience and to Alison's surprise and relief he fought a way through the crowd with her.

'My horse,' she stammered. 'I was thrown.'

'I see it. Wait here.' He left her for a moment and she stood dizzy and swaying until he came back.

'Can you ride?' he asked her.

She nodded and he helped her up into the saddle. 'My heartfelt thanks –' she began but he smiled briefly.

'No time for thanks,' he told her. 'Go home while you still can.'

'But my husband –'

He shrugged. 'He must look after himself,' he said.

'You must away.'

She nodded. Weary and frightened and sick from her beating, she was only too glad to obey. He slapped the horse's rump and the animal broke into a trot. Alison glanced back as she rounded the bend in the lane. There was no sign of her rescuer but his face was imprinted on her memory.

CHAPTER NINE
January, 1537

The log of the *Mary Rose* read:

'9 am. Light wind NNE. Crew prepare to sail. Midday – Pilot returned to harbour.

'6 pm. All sails set. Lizard Point bore NNW about 15 miles. Wind freshening. Four knots . . .'

The familiar roar of the ship's wake went unheeded, as did the continual groan of taut halyards and the sharp flap and flutter of sail. The long Tudor pennant streamed through the rigging, green and white against the clear blue of a cloudless sky, and the crew's spirits lifted now that they were underway. Bare feet pattered across the deck as the crew secured ropes and stowed the anchor while others went aloft, scrambling confidently among the rigging like monkeys in the branches of a familiar tree. A ship's boy, no more than eleven years old, checked the various pens of livestock – four pigs, twenty chickens, three sheep and two goats, the latter to give milk for the officers. He paused for a moment or two trying to make friends with the goats but received a painful nip for his efforts and retired discomfited and cursing.

Below decks there was further activity. Pumps were manned and the bilges slowly emptied, though not for long. The tireless waves would work the wooden hull, seeking out weaknesses in her timbers and seeping in through the smallest crack until there would be no dry spot on the whole ship. In the hold, large traps were baited for rats and food stores were re-checked against a number of lists and receipts. They had been checked on loading to deter the cheats on land, but pilfering on board ship was not unknown and further checks were made at intervals. The coopers examined the tightness of the barrels of rum, wine and water, testing for leaks. Sacks of oatmeal were counted and barrels of salt fish and beef made firm against the ship's roll. Casks of pickled cabbage nestled beside barrels of dried peas and the sailor noted enviously the half dozen pots of honey for the especial use of those fortunate enough to dine at the Captain's table.

The Captain himself sat in his cabin aft and rubbed his eyes tiredly, envying the majority of his crew who left no families. Leave taking was always a sad occasion and coloured the first few days of any trip. To distract his thoughts from home, he considered his two new midshipmen, Jeff Kendal and young Rob Miller – the first a promising young man, eager and willing with a cheerful disposition. The second, arrogant but resourceful. They would both make officer material, the latter when he mastered his seasickness! The Captain smiled as he pictured the young man, his face grey, slumped in his hammock in abject misery. Sickness was something to be reckoned with but no one had died of it.

In the cookroom the cook whistled cheerfully as he kneaded the dough. Salt beef, roughly shredded, and onions bubbled in iron pots on the stove beside him. He was a tall man with a permanent stoop from a lifetime between decks that were built without regard for a man's height so that a sailor who didn't double himself up would knock his brains out on the many beams and projections. Now he whistled but he had a vicious temper and was a match for anyone when the worse for liquor. Beside him, an hour glass swung from a beam and he watched for the last grains to trickle through, then inverted it with a practised flick of his right hand. An hour to go before supper. He began to pull the dough apart with large hands scarred by countless slips of the knife and brushes with hot ovens. The pile of dumplings grew higher and he shouted for the shifter to leave the scouring and add them to the stew.

On the gun decks men cleaned and polished the cannons in preparation for gun drill on the following day, boasting to each other of their aim and performance.

Jeffery dipped his quill in the ink and continued his letter. '– for the wind rises steadily as poor Rob will vouchsafe. 'Tis his first voyage and he suffers greatly with "mal de mer". Thank the Lord I am past such miseries. Your letter reached me yesterday for which my thanks. Be reassured, I am in good health and spirits. I wish you might all see the *Mary Rose* before too long. A fine beamy ship and strongly armed with as fine a crew as one might hope to find tho' lacking one Lascar lost overboard at first light yesterday. 'Tis said the result of a drunken brawl and no accident but who can tell. My appetite improves daily and I am thankful for an able cook, one Jempson, and will shortly sit down to beef and dumplings with a mug or two of ale. Perchance I may eat Rob's share if he is not recovered . . .'

As he wrote, the table was being set up between the rows of cannons on the deck below him and laid with pewter tankards and bowls. Half a pound of new bread was put by each plate. Tonight the Captain would dine alone in his cabin and the men would talk freely with no need to moderate their language. Large bowls of steaming stew were carried to the table and jugs of ale stood ready on the side table. The shrill call on the ship's whistle brought a stampede of hungry men from all directions. On the bridge the Captain wrote: '8 pm – wind moderating. Two knots. Course SW. The ship, pride of King Henry's navy, sailed on, her canvas white against the darkening sky.

Alison read the last few lines of the letter and then smiled at the boy who had delivered it. He was small for his eleven years, with pinched features and small dark eyes half hidden under a mop of unkempt hair.

'So you are Jonah,' she said.

'They call me Jon.'

'Do they? And you have walked all the way from Fowey?'

'I walked from Tavistock,' he said. 'I had a ride that far – in a wagon with a fine lady. Not that I rode with her but hung on the back with her not knowing.' He grinned at the memory and Alison pretended not to notice.

'My son asks that we find you work. He says you stowed away.'

'I did so,' he said, 'but they found me and sent me back on the next ship that passed.'

'And were you sorry?'

He shrugged. 'I was that queasy,' he confessed 'with the ship rolling and tossing like a mad thing.'

'And my son – he's well?' she asked.

'Oh aye, ma'am, and kindly.'

'I'll speak to my husband,' said Alison. 'Are you honest, Jon. Will you work hard?'

'That I will, ma'am. I swear on it.'

'Then I'll see what can be done when my husband returns. In the meantime you shall eat. Come.' Folding the letter, she led the way to the kitchen where Nan sat polishing silver and Izzie pressed curdled milk in a muslin cloth. 'This lad is come from Jeffery,' she began then paused in confusion as she realized the extent of silver plate which stood on the kitchen table. With a

179

guilty cry, Nan put a hand to her mouth and glanced at Izzie for help. No one spoke as Alison moved forward. 'A silver chalice,' she said wonderingly, 'and candlesticks – and four, five, no six silver goblets! And gold! A golden crucifix . . . Sweet Mother of God!' She drew back her hand and crossed herself hastily. 'How come these here?' she whispered, her voice trembling.

No one answered her. With an anguished expression, she looked at Izzie. 'I must know,' she said. 'Tell me, are they from the Priory?'

Izzie nodded reluctantly.

'Oh no,' murmured Alison, her eyes wide with dismay. 'But how can this be? The dissolution was weeks since. The Priory has stood empty this past month and yet I have not seen these pieces. Were they hidden? Is that it?'

Izzie nodded.

''Twas no fault of ours, ma'am,' broke in Beth. 'The master brought them. 'Twas he as hid them – in the stable loft they was, until Brother Andrew be gone, he said.'

Alison nodded slowly, beginning to understand. This, then, was Luke's reward from the King's commissioner. These pieces were his share of the Church's wealth that the King had declared should be redistributed! And even while Andrew lay at Heron, they were concealed in the stable. Now that Sophie had fetched him away to London Luke had judged it time to declare them. Such ill-gotten gains!

'Heaven be merciful,' Alison whispered, 'or we shall all pay for his heresy!'

'I never meant to do it,' cried Beth, greatly agitated, and she threw down the polishing cloth fearfully. 'I only did as I was bid by the master. I never meant no harm. I swear I'll not touch them again.'

'Hush, you foolish girl,' cried Izzie. 'No one's blaming you. So stop whining.'

'And what were you to do with it, when 'twas polished?' Alison asked.

''Tis to go in the Hall, ma'am.'

'Never,' said Alison as firmly as she could. 'We shall bring down God's wrath.' She saw a sack neatly folded on a stool and looked at Izzie inquiringly.

'Aÿe,' said Izzie. 'That's how it come here.'

'Then put it back into the sack,' said Alison. 'No, don't clean it further. Leave it be. I shall speak to my husband – I shall beg him –' She sighed heavily and turned to go.

'And the lad here?' prompted Izzie.

'The lad?' Alison had forgotten all about him. 'Ah, feed him Izzie, please, and treat him kindly. He's come from Jeffery and will tell us later of the *Mary Rose*.'

Leaving them, she went in search of Luke.

She found Thomas Benet busy with the household accounts, Melissa beside him solemnly watching. He told her that he expected Luke home from the mine within the hour.

'Then I'll ride down and meet him,' she said, unable to tolerate the silver under their roof a moment longer than was necessary. Within minutes she was on her way, cantering along the highway, her cloak wrapped tightly round her for the winter air was sharp with frost though no snow had fallen. As she rode she prayed for guidance, for the proper words with which to sway her husband from his intentions. Yet when she saw him the words faltered momentarily. He looked tired and his face, before he recognized her, wore an expression of great sadness.

'Luke!'

His smile when he saw her revealed his real pleasure

at the sight of her and she almost regretted the purpose
of their meeting.

'You rode to greet me,' he began but she interrupted
him, turning her horse clumsily in her haste.

'The silver, Luke,' she said and the words chased the
smile from his face instantly. 'The silver from the
Priory. Oh Luke, how could you? How can you bear to
give it houseroom after what has happened?' The first
faltering words became a veritable torrent. 'To see those
men turned out of the only home they've ever known
with nought but a pension – and Andrew, also. Your
own kin. How can you justify acceptance of such gifts?'

'They were no gifts,' he snapped, 'but bought
legally.'

'Bought!' Alison stared at him. 'With what did you
buy them, such heavy silver? Those candlesticks! Are
we become rich, then, that we can fritter our money?'

'They were bought very reasonable,' he protested.
'For my services to His Majesty's –'

'For services? Bought cheaply as a favour? Oh Luke,
what has gotten into you that you can't see the wrong
you do! Sweet husband, forgive me for speaking thus
but my heart is full of a terrible dread that God will
punish us all for this work of yours. Give it back, Luke, I
beseech you. Let them sell it elsewhere.'

''Tis too late for that, Alison.'

They had reached the outermost edge of their garden
and he reined in his horse, reluctant to be overheard if
they rode further.

'No, Luke, it is never too late,' she urged him. 'Or if
all are entered in a ledger somewhere why then, give
them back and suffer the loss if you must. Don't give
them houseroom longer. I shall have no peace of mind
while they sit under my roof.'

'My roof!' he reminded her icily and his face was as
grim as his voice. 'Heron is mine and I will decide

what's fit to sit beneath its roof. You are hysterical for no reason and argue to no purpose.'

'Oh dearest Luke, I cannot do otherwise,' she protested, tears springing to her eyes to be brushed away impatiently as she struggled to remain calm. 'The dissolution is an evil thing, Luke. All say so, except only you.'

'And the King himself,' said Luke. 'The King is wiser than his subjects.'

'How can that be, Luke?' she whispered. 'This break with Rome is well known to be for his own ends. That he might put aside his lawful queen.'

'And if that was the reason, what of it?' cried Luke. 'Is a king to be tied to a useless wife? Is a king to be dictated to by Papists? No man should suffer the indignity of a false marriage –' He stopped short, aware that he was shouting. Alison, beside him, sat her horse like a statue, white-faced. For a moment neither of them spoke. Alison broke the silence.

'I beseech you one last time, Luke,' she pleaded. 'Send back the silver plate and let us rest easy in the sight of God.'

'I will not do it,' he said angrily 'and I will hear no more on the matter. The plate is mine and come by honestly. It shall stay.'

He urged his horse forward again and she did likewise. As they neared the house, he made an effort to control his feelings and said levelly, 'What news?'

'News?' she echoed. 'Oh yes. A boy is come from the *Mary Rose*, with a letter from Jeffery.'

'A letter! I warrant that pleases you,' he said with forced cheerfulness.

Alison looked at him. She longed to say that her pleasure was now overshadowed by fear but dared not make such an answer. Instead she averted her gaze and they rode into the stableyard in silence.

A week later a servant at Buckland Abbey eyed Alison curiously. She had slid from her horse, dishevelled and out of breath but refusing all offers of hospitality, asking only to speak with the Abbot. 'The Abbot's at his meal,' the man told her. 'Would you have me disturb him? Or maybe Brother William could help you. He's fasting for the health of his soul or the ease of his conscience!' He laughed knowingly and winked at Alison who recoiled slightly. He was a rough-looking man and looked as though his own conscience might not be as clear as it should.

'Not Brother William, no,' she told him. 'I must speak with the Abbot. Go tell him Mistress Kendal is ridden from Ashburton and would speak most earnestly with him.'

The man shook his head slyly. 'More'n my life's worth to disturb the Abbot while at his meal,' he said. 'Likes his food, he does. Mind you, I reckon I might be persuaded . . .' He shrugged expressively.

'Oh, sweet Heaven!' Impatiently, she found a few groats and handed them to him. He gave the coins in his palm a disparaging look before stowing them in his purse.

'And who shall I say 'tis?' he asked.

'Mistress Kendal of Heron.'

While she waited, Alison rehearsed her speech as she stood in the courtyard holding her horse. A large sack was tied across the front of the saddle. She waited anxiously, aware that her name would be familiar to him – Luke's assistance at the dissolution was well known in the area. He might refuse to see her. Or leave her waiting in the cold as a mark of his disapproval. He would not know that she, Alison, had been no party to it. Shivering, she stamped her feet to warm them and blew on her fingers which had grown cold inside her gloves. At last the servant returned to say the Abbot would be with her directly; she waited a few moments more before his ample figure appeared at the doorway and he moved towards her with outstretched hands.

'Greetings and God's blessing,' he murmured but she felt there was little warmth in his tone – and who could blame him, she thought.

'Thank you,' she said. 'Father, I would not come to you for fear of thieves. This sack,' she pulled it, 'contains much of value.'

He looked puzzled but allowed her to continue.

''Tis obvious you know my name,' she said, 'and that of my husband, Luke Kendal. I cannot speak of – that matter.'

He nodded his understanding of the reference to Harben Priory.

'I beg your help, Father,' said Alison. 'I have brought with me such plate as my husband bought from the King's commissioner on that occasion. Know, Father, that 'twas not with my knowledge or goodwill and I fear the wrath of God. Indeed, I have spoke with my husband, beseeching him to return the plate but he turns away. In the name of Heaven I believe he intends no wrong. I do most honestly believe his conscience is clear on the matter. He is the King's true subject and most loyal.' She sighed deeply and allowed herself a glance at the Abbot's face. His expression had softened somewhat.

'I have brought the plate: candlesticks, chalices, goblets and a gold crucifix. See here.' She tugged the sack open and the startled Abbot found himself staring down at some of the spoils of Henry's dissolution. Then he shook his head.

'You mean well,' he said. 'You are an honourable woman.'

'Take them, I beg you!' cried Alison, struggling to untie the sack from the saddle. 'I dare not live with them longer. I am in such fear that God will turn away from us.'

'But your husband, madam,' he protested. 'These are his property if legally bought. You have no right to dispose of them, and I no right to accept them.'

'But give them houseroom until I can talk further with my husband,' begged Alison. 'I will convince him –'

'Indeed I doubt it, my child. I admire your spirit,' he said, 'and I sympathize with your dilemma but alas, I cannot help you. Even if I accepted them, I doubt they would find a final resting place here. Who is to say what fate awaits us here in Buckland? The King is a ruthless man and a greedy one.' He sighed. 'It may be our own plate will be changing hands. A grievous prospect but pertinent. Who can say, my child, who can say?'

'What shall I do, Father, tell me?' Alison whispered. 'I am lost without the support of my dearest husband, and fear to quarrel with him and yet I am so feared.'

'Go home, Mistress Kendal,' he advised wearily. 'Ride back before your husband discovers you are gone. Replace the plate and pray for God's guidance and forgiveness.'

'And will you pray for us also, Father?'

'I will.'

He helped her remount and she looked down at the hand that clasped her own. 'I'll pray for Buckland,' she promised. 'That you may be spared.'

The Abbot watched her go with a heavy heart. They would all pray for Buckland Abbey but he had little hope. The times were perilous and the King would have his way.

'My nose is cold,' grumbled Melissa. 'I thought you said 'twas a fine morning for a ride.'

'And it is,' said Paul, urging his horse alongside his sister's as the path widened. 'The sun shines and the wind is still. What more would you ask of the end of March?'

'A heatwave!' said Melissa, laughing.

'Why then you ask the impossible,' said Paul. He turned to Abigail. 'You don't complain, do you Princess?'

They waited for the younger girl to catch up with them. Her sorrel mare was old and docile and disinclined to hurry. The Kendal children made a handsome group as they rode on. Abigail's face still retained its childish plumpness, with rosy cheeks and clear grey eyes. Paul, approaching manhood, had the same finely shaped nose as his father but eyes that were hazel. He was sturdier, too, and lacked the tall frame of most of the Kendal males. Melissa had Alison's colouring, but at fourteen was much taller, a fact which did not please her.

Two greyhounds accompanied them, circling the horses and darting away at intervals on explorations of their own.

'Don't call me Princess,' she said, 'or I shall tell Papa. He says you are to call me Abby.'

'Then you sound like a monastery,' he teased, 'and you may soon be dissolved,' but she was not amused.

'Mama would not tolerate such a jest,' said Melissa nervously. 'It distresses her to hear folk speak so.'

Paul shrugged. 'But everyone does,' he said. 'I heard a ballad singer in the market on Monday. The crowd laughed so heartily I thought they would lose their wits altogether! The second verse –'

'Paul don't!' she begged. 'Don't listen to him, Abby.'

'I won't,' said the little girl stoutly. 'He's a pig and I shall set the dogs on him and they'll chase him away for ever.'

'How sweetly said,' he mocked. 'I swear you will make a shrewish wife one day, Princess.' Abby gave a squeal of rage and he laughed triumphantly. 'Oh, hark at the squealing,' he taunted. 'Now who's the pig?'

Melissa groaned. 'I have told you not to tease her, Paul,' she reproved him.

'Why so you have,' he said, 'but since you are my sister and not my mother, why should I pay heed?'

'Because I am older than you,' she told him earnestly, 'and nearly a woman.'

'Then why aren't you betrothed?' he challenged and the two girls exchanged exasperated looks. It was understood in the Kendal household that Melissa was still immature after her earlier problems and the matter of her marriage had been postponed. Paul, away at school in Hampshire, was unaware of this, and blundered on. 'Will no one have you?' he asked.

'I've no desire to be wed,' said Melissa and it was true. She moved through the world as a detached observer, almost unaware of her own role in it. Her large grey eyes watched friends and strangers with the same impassive expression. She registered the emotions of others but seemed untouched herself. Content to be one of life's spectators she lived in a world of her own. For a moment they rode on in silence. Under the horses' hooves blackened leaves crackled, their edges white with frost, and an occasional squirrel darted above them in the bare branches.

'Let's race,' said Paul suddenly. 'I wager I'll be home before either of you.'

'Cloud will not race,' said Melissa. 'She is far too old for such folly and we must not leave Abby to ride alone. But ride on, if you will, and we'll follow at our own pace.'

Paul dug his heels in and, hallooing loudly, gave the horse his head and was soon out of sight.

'I don't care for brothers,' said Abigail primly. 'They are noisy and they tease me.'

Melissa smiled. 'He means no harm,' she said. 'I think you do care for him – and Jeffery also. You care for Jeffery.'

'Aye,' the little girl agreed, 'but girls are sweeter. And will you truly not be wed, Lissa? Not ever?'

'Wed?' Melissa stared at her vaguely. 'I cannot say. I think not . . . oh, see there, Abby. A dog fox, on the path ahead! Too late, he has hidden himself in the bracken. Oh, such a fine brush on him – but don't fret,' she added hastily, seeing her sister's disappointment, 'keep your eyes open and you may well see another. Looking for a coney, I don't doubt, to take home for his supper.'

They rode on happily and were quite unprepared for the sight that met their eyes at the crossroads. Paul's horse, riderless, grazed unconcernedly while Paul lay crumpled and motionless beneath the hawthorn tree.

'Paul!' With a frightened cry, Melissa crossed herself then slipped from her horse. She stumbled through the long grass and tangled briars to kneel beside her brother. He lay white-faced. A thin trickle of blood oozed from his nose and another ran from the corner of his mouth. Abigail screamed then burst into a torrent of weeping. Melissa, denied the luxury of tears, fought down the despair which swam darkly in front of her eyes, blurring her vision. The boy lay on his side and Melissa rolled him over gently until she could listen to his heart. It was still beating.

'Hush!' she told Abigail. 'He's not dead but like to be if we do not bring help.' She thought hurriedly. It would be unwise to leave her younger sister with the unconscious boy. 'You must ride on to Heron,' she told Abigail, 'and tell them what has happened. Leave his horse. You will make better time alone. Go, Abby, for

God's sake. I'll wait with Paul.' And please God do not let him die, she prayed.

Tenderly she arranged the boy's limbs so that he lay more comfortably, then took his head into her lap. Not once did her eyes leave his face as she waited for signs of life in the still body. But apart from the rise and fall of his chest and the slight flutter of his eyelids, there was no sign of returning consciousness. It seemed an age before her vigil was at an end and Luke and Thomas Benet reached the crossroads with a litter in which to carry him home.

The doctor's verdict was unhelpful.

'The stars are not well placed,' he said 'but the boy is young and the life force strong. If he regains his wits, he should recover. If not –' He shrugged expressively.

When he had gone, Alison faced her husband bitterly. 'Now see what you have done!' she said. 'Did I not say your greed would bring down God's anger? This is your doing, Luke. You are to blame. Oh why did you do it, Luke? Why did you take that plate? He will die, I know it!'

'Hush-a,' he begged and moved to take her into his arms but she pushed him away fearfully.

'Don't touch me, Luke. Those hands that took the silver have brought this terrible vengeance upon us. Oh Luke, Luke! Can you not see how 'tis? Your ill-gotten silver will ruin us all! First Paul, then –'

'You speak as though the boy is dead.'

'And so he will be,' she said as the tears welled into her eyes. ''Tis only a matter of time, I know it, Luke. I feel it in my heart like a cold dark pain.'

'Alison! Let me hold you – comfort you.'

'No! Make your peace with God first, while there is still time. Beg his forgiveness Luke, and Paul may yet be spared. No, do not stay to argue, Luke. Go and pray, I beseech you, or we will lose our son.' She ran from him into the chamber and threw herself on the bed, weeping passionately. When she had recovered she splashed water over her face, composed herself and went to sit beside her son. He lay unconscious in the bed he had once shared with Jeffery, oblivious to his mother's bowed head and the lips moving feverishly in prayer.

Time passed and it grew dark. Alison lit the candles and looked at Paul in their wavering light. The long lashes lay across the pale cheeks and his mouth was partly open. His breathing was very shallow and a light perspiration stood on his skin. Gently she dabbed his face with a cloth, pushed back a lock of hair. Luke had left the house earlier and she had not heard him return. Although she still believed them to be true she regretted her bitter words and accusations. She loved the man and grieved for him.

The moon rose and still he stayed away. Alison sat beside Paul's bed until she grew cramped and weary. Then she called Izzie to watch beside her son and throwing a warm shawl over her shoulders let herself out of the house. She wanted to walk a little to ease her cramped limbs and clear her mind. The garden looked strangely unfamiliar in the eerie light and the trees and shrubs threw dense shadows across the grass. Nervously, her heart fluttering, she made her way along the path, through the orchard and down the steps to the small neglected garden beside the river. As she reached the bottom she gave a gasp of fear. A man crouched beside the water. Hearing her approach he turned.

'Alison!'

It was Luke. She held out her hands to him, pulling

him upright. 'Come into the house,' she said. 'You will take chill here.'

'It's gone,' he told her. 'All of it – into the water.'

'Gone?' she repeated, puzzled.

'The chalice, plate, even the goblets. All of it.'

She stared at him. 'You've thrown it into the water?' she said.

'Aye,' said Luke. 'Where else?' And shrugged helplessly.

Aye, thought Alison. Where else indeed.

'I'm glad of it, Luke,' she said softly. '''Twas bravely done.'

'And I prayed for Paul,' he said.

'God will hear you, I know it. Now come back to the house with me, Luke.'

Just before dawn Paul opened his eyes and smiled. Alison and Luke exchanged joyous looks. The boy could eat nothing, and did not speak, but he was conscious and Luke's heart filled with gratitude. But before the doctor's promised visit the boy slipped once more into unconsciousness and died shortly before seven. Luke's hope of salvation died with him.

CHAPTER TEN

Simon paused at the churchyard gate. It was bitterly cold and raining and his hair clung wetly to his head and dripped down his face and neck. He put up an arm to wipe the rain from his eyes. What weather for a burial, he thought, pitying the sodden mourners their dismal task. The priest's voice hurried through the meaningless Latin and the bell tolled. Curiously Simon pushed open the creaking gate. One of the mourners, a young woman, turned sharply at the sound and through her veil their eyes met briefly. She turned away again and he moved nearer to join a few villagers who stood in the rain to pay their last respects.

'Who is it?' he whispered.

A young woman answered. ''Tis Luke Kendal's youngest son and the vengeance of God, so they say.' She pulled a tattered shawl over her head and blinked to clear her wet lashes.

'How's that then?' asked Simon, his voice low.

She looked at him, surprised. 'Why, you've heard of Luke Kendal, haven't you?' she asked. 'Him as helped the King's Commissioner to close the Priory. A man as flies in the face of God must expect God's wrath.'

'I remember,' said Simon. 'His wife was there.'

'Aye, so she was, poor soul. How does she feel now, I wonder, when 'twas most likely her husband's sin killed the boy.'

'Poor wretch,' whispered Simon, but he meant the

unfortunate Luke. Now he remembered the disturbance at the Priory and the wife he had rescued. So it was their son who lay lifeless in the narrow coffin, deaf to the rain which beat a dull tattoo upon the wooden lid.

He watched silently as the earth was shovelled into the grave and his informant watched him curiously. 'You live round here?' she asked.

He shrugged. 'Looking for work,' he told her. 'Like a lot of others.'

'What do you do?'

'Anything I'm offered.'

'What's your name then?' she asked.

'Simon Betts to most folk, Simon to a few.'

She liked the firm tone and the shrewd blue eyes. 'There's a job at my father's bakery,' she said. 'Lad's died of a fit this very morning. Maggie's my name.'

'Maggie? My thanks.'

'And if you want somewhere to sleep you can have his bit of a room under the roof. We'll look after you well enough.'

The final chant said, the group of mourners turned now from the grave and walked slowly along the gravelled path out of the gate. Simon recognized Luke Kendal, his face grey and drawn with grief and beside him Alison, her face partially hidden under a thick veil.

Two daughters followed with a tall man between them. 'That's Benet, the steward,' whispered Maggie 'and the two girls are Abigail and Melissa. They've only one son left now and he's at sea.'

As Melissa passed them she lifted her veil briefly to wipe her tears and once more her eyes met Simon's. He felt strangely drawn to her as though an unspoken message leaped between them. A wordless message that he could not begin to decipher. Then she had passed by and he watched them climb into the wagons which waited in the muddy road. Some of the mourners would ride, others, hired for the occasion, would walk. Whips cracked, the loaded wagons groaned in protest and the wooden wheels sank further into the mud. Simon and several others now ran forward and pushed and tugged until finally the horses could move forward once more. The men received a few coins for their efforts and stood back impassively as the procession got underway on its doleful journey to Heron.

'Another soul on its way,' said Maggie, shaking her skirt to free it of the splatters of mud thrown up by the wheels. 'Are you coming then?' she asked.

Simon nodded. He gave one more glance at the Kendal family as they moved away up the hill, then turned reluctantly and followed Maggie down.

The river Dart flowed gently below the June sky, its smooth surface only rippled where it encountered a boulder. As it slid past Heron it cooled the feet of the two girls who sat on the two largest boulders that formed the stepping stones across the river. In winter the boulders were hidden by the deep rush of brown water but now they were half exposed and well warmed by the July sun. Melissa and Abigail sat together exchanging confidences, their bare feet in the water, their skirts tucked well up.

'Adam,' mused Melissa. 'Adam Jarman . . . Aye, 'tis a nice enough name.'

'Mistress Jarman,' said Abigail. 'I confess I like it but imagine me wed, Lissa! And mistress in my own home.'

Melissa tossed her foot, throwing a cluster of glistening drops over her sister's bare leg. Abigail screamed indignantly and splashed her in return.

'You won't be mistress just yet,' said Melissa. 'Your mother-in-law still lives and is in good health by all accounts.'

Abigail groaned. 'Don't speak of her,' she begged. 'She is the canker in my rose!'

They both laughed. Reliable rumour had it that Clarissa Jarman was a force to be reckoned with. A very large woman with a shrewish tongue who ruled her husband Alec with a will of iron yet doted on her eldest son.

'Never mind,' comforted Melissa. 'She cannot live forever no matter how healthy she may be. A sudden fever, mayhap, or a thunderbolt –'

'Lissa! Hush such talk!' said Abigail, glancing round fearfully in case they sould be overheard. 'But you are right. Someday I will be mistress and in the meantime –' She shrugged.

Melissa glanced at her mischievously. 'And no doubt father-in-law will make sheep's eyes at you,' she giggled, 'when the canker is looking the other way!'

'Lissa!' cried her sister. 'What's got into you today? You are not usually so wicked.' She stared dreamily at the weed which reached out with long green strands and tickled her toes. 'But my Adam, is he not handsome? Tell me truly, Lissa, for I swear I am so besotted I would find a mole on his skin something to rapture over!'

'Oh he's handsome, Abby,' said Melissa. 'If his miniature is anything to go by. A broad forehead, wide eyes and such a sweet mouth. You are a very fortunate girl, Abby, and I warrant the future Mistress Jarman will be very well pleased with her lot.'

'I hope so,' said Abigail earnestly. 'I shall do my utmost to please him . . . Oh Lissa, when will you wed? 'Twill be so good to write to each other of our husbands and children.'

'And you will tell me all about Rochester,' said Melissa 'and how the boats are built. You must write to Jeffery, too. The boat yard will interest him . . . You might even get to sail on a boat yourself!'

Abigail gave a scream of pretended horror at such a prospect. 'I am as near to the water as I wish to be,' she told Melissa. 'Sitting on this rock with ten inches of river below me! I do not fancy the wild sea.'

'The Medway is hardly the wild sea, you ninny,' said Melissa. ''Tis only a river like this one.'

Abigail stood up and stepped across to the next boulder, watching keenly for fish. 'That's where you're wrong,' she said. 'The Medway is a wide, wide river – an estuary Thomas calls it, and when the neap tide's coming in and the wind's blowing out to sea –'

Melissa shrieked with laughter at this nautical outburst. 'You talk already like an old sailor!' she teased. 'I shall make sure I wed a landlubber. I don't want to catch sea fever. It addles the brain seemingly!'

Abigail refused to be drawn into an argument. She would shortly be leaving for Rochester to join her new family and although she spoke lightly, she valued these last days with her sister.

'When will you wed, Lissa?' she asked, suddenly serious. 'Do make it soon.'

'And if I don't care to?' suggested Melissa.

'But you will, Lissa. Papa will find you a good man.'

'Mayhap,' said her sister, rising abruptly to her feet. 'If the stars are propitious . . . Ah, look, a fish! There, under the weed. A grey mullet, I think. I shall send Jack down with his hook and line.'

'Oh Lissa,' said Abigail. 'I shall miss you so.'

Melissa reached out a hand and touched her sister's face lightly. 'And I shall miss you,' she said.

Two weeks later, Adam and Alec Jarman arrived to escort Abigail to her new home. Melissa was disappointed with her sister's future husband. The miniature had flattered him. The eyes were smaller and the mouth larger, almost slack. He was shorter than they had imagined and his conversation lacked wit but charitable Melissa put that down to a certain natural shyness. Alec Jarman, a larger version of his son, spoke volubly to the company but rarely to his son for they had had a disagreement on the journey west. But if Abigail was at all disillusioned, she hid it very well and gave an excellent impersonation of an excited bride-to-be, smiling demurely at the two men and immediately winning both their hearts. They even argued as to which one should help her mount the grey mare Adam had brought her as a gift. Adam was successful, however, and she was soon seated. All the servants had run out to see them go and to wish them a safe journey and Abigail rode out with her two proud escorts to a chorus of heartfelt farewells and good wishes.

'Another bird flown the nest,' said Izzie mournfully, wiping away a tear with the corner of her apron.

Melissa looked anxiously at her mother. Alison, her lips trembling slightly, looked up at Luke. Tenderly he put an arm round the slight shoulders and smiled reassuringly. 'We still have our little Lissa,' he reminded her. 'And when she leaves us we will have each other.'

Alison nodded and he glanced at Izzie. 'Bring us some of the best madeira,' he told her cheerfully. 'And we will all drink a health to Abby's future happiness.'

Luke, hungry and tired, waited impatiently as the last pack-horse was loaded with ore. Nathan Bewley, the new overseer, marked the list in his hand and handed it to Luke for his approval. Luke scanned it carefully, then returned it. 'And I shall want an account of the second weighing,' he said grimly. 'A *detailed* account, tell them, or I shall ride over there myself. Once bitten, twice shy and they won't get away with it again.'

Nathan looked discomfited as well he might for the previous smelting had given rise to doubts. After weighing, the ore was melted down and the resulting ingots re-weighed. The loss of weight had seemed unnaturally high and such discrepancies were not uncommon. It was inevitable that at some stage in the process small amounts of the precious tin would find its way into the wrong hands. Such petty thieving was impossible to stop. But thieving on a larger scale was another matter and not to be tolerated.

'Tell them this,' said Luke 'that if I have any doubts I shall send my tin elsewhere – to the far side of the moor if needs be. I will not be robbed again.'

The previous dispute had left a bitter taste in everyone's mouth and it was only with great reluctance that Luke had agreed to give them another chance.

'They sacked the Witten boy,' Nathan reminded him.

Luke laughed derisively. 'Aye, they sacked the lad but that was to appease my anger. A lad of his tender years would never have the gall to steal on such a scale. If he was involved, then I warrant someone was behind him. And I told them as much but to no purpose. There's none so deaf as won't hear . . . Well, move them on or you'll not be there by dusk. And remember – a *detailed* account or they'll have me to reckon with.'

Nathan nodded and turned towards the horses. Luke moved away to where his own horse grazed, nibbling the fine grass that pushed up among the clumps of moss. To his surprise, a young boy of nine or ten years stood waiting for his attention.

'Where the devil did you spring from?' he asked.

The boy said nothing but held out his right hand. 'She said to give you this,' he said gruffly, not meeting Luke's eyes.

'She? Who is this "she"?'

'I don't know,' he said.

Luke held out his hand and the boy dropped into his palm a small gold ring. For a few seconds it meant nothing. Then Luke paled suddenly. 'She?' he whispered. 'What name did she give, lad?'

'I told you, I don't know,' said the boy. 'She said you'd give me something for –'

'What was she like, lad? Old, young, tall or short?'

His tone was harsh and the boy backed away from him warily. 'I dare not say the name,' he protested. ''Tis bad luck.'

The boy's words confirmed the growing suspicion in Luke's mind. 'What else did she say?' he asked.

The boy shook his head and looked over his shoulder for a way of escape but behind him was a wall of solid rock. He misread Luke's consternation for anger and he put up a thin arm to ward off the expected blow.

'Sweet heaven, I'm not going to beat you,' said Luke, softening his voice with a conscious effort. 'Just tell me, I beg you, what the lady said.'

The boy looked at him, twisting his fingers nervously. 'She said tell him to come to the beach – no, the cave on the beach. Aye, that was it! Bid him come to the cave on the beach.'

'Dear God!' whispered Luke.

'At sunrise,' added the boy. 'That's what she said.'

'And it was – Isobel Gillis?' he asked. 'Come, you can nod or shake your head, can't you?'

'She be the daughter of the witch woman,' cried the boy. 'I'd not say her name!'

Luke's patience was exhausted. Roughly he took the boy by the shoulder and shook him. 'But it was her, wasn't it? Tell me!'

Fearfully the boy nodded and, cursing, Luke released him. The boy seized his chance and darted a few yards away. 'She said you'd give me a shilling,' he lied.

Luke took a coin from his purse and tossed it towards

him but he dropped it. He scrabbled among the moss until he found it again then darted further away. The coin was less than he'd hoped for and he spat on it contemptuously. He put a few more yards between them then snatched up a stone and hurled it at Luke but it flew harmlessly past him while the boy sped away. Luke didn't even hear it nor did he notice the boy's disappearance. He was staring at Isobel's wedding ring, turning it over and over in the palm of his hand, while a terrible blackness welled up inside him and the palms of his hands prickled with fear. Sweat glistened on his forehead.

'Sunrise,' he muttered. 'I must be there . . .' A shout from Nathan made him start, then he raised a hand in farewell as his overseer led the three pack-horses past and down the hillside. 'Sunrise,' he said again and, slipping the ring into his purse, went home with a heavy heart and no appetite for supper.

It was cool on the beach next morning as Luke made his way down the rock face as he had done so many years before. The hand and footholds came naturally to him as though it were only weeks or months ago that he had scrambled down, his heart racing, his body eager. Was she already waiting for him? He had already searched the beach from the cliff top and seen no one. Possibly she was in the cave. Reaching the bottom of the cliff, he brushed the sand from his hands and looked around him. The tide was half way out but coming in fast as it always did across the last twenty yards of flat sand. A glow in the western sky heralded the sunrise, tingeing the small clouds with a soft coral light. The water, dark and cold, slid across the smooth sand and hissed round the rocks and into the pools left by the receding tide twelve hours earlier.

There was no sign of Isobel. The cave where they had so often lain together was empty and he wandered down to the water's edge trying to calm the panic that filled him at the thought of seeing her again. And yet if she didn't come that, too, would be unbearable. A slight movement caught his eye and he swung round. There by the rock – Isobel.

'Luke!'

She was standing in the shallow sea, holding her skirt with one hand to keep it free of the water. He went towards her slowly, straining his eyes to see her face, but the rising sun was behind her and her face dark in the eerie half-lit beach. When he was only a few feet from her she stretched out her hand, fingers outspread, as though to keep him at arm's length and he stopped. She said evenly, 'I knew you would come,' and he nodded speechlessly, confused by the sight of her and the rush of emotions that threatened to overwhelm him. She looked thin and frail silhouetted against the sun which now rose like a rosy ball behind her. His throat was dry but he managed one word: 'Isobel.'

For a long moment they stood thus, facing each other. The glow from the sun fell across his face, softening the rigid lines of his jaw and highlighting the small muscle that jumped in his right cheek. Then, as though reassured, she let her arms fall and took a step nearer to him. 'I want my son, Luke,' she said simply.

'Your son?' he echoed the words stupidly.

'My son,' she said. 'You see, I am recovered and I recall everything. Oh, have no fear, Luke. I intend you no harm.'

'Forgive me,' he said. He could not pretend the same self-control that Isobel showed. Helpless and confused, he needed time to adjust to this stranger who stood before him calmly asking for the return of a child stolen from her years ago when her mind was deranged. Her tone was matter-of-fact, her manner unemotional.

'You took me to the well,' she said 'and gave me back my sanity. Give me back my son and I'll have all I desire in the world. I ask no money, beg no favours.'

Luke shook his head. 'I don't know where he is,' he said. 'I swear it. I have not seen him since he was born.'

He expected a change in her attitude: reproaches, accusations. Instead she nodded slowly as though she had anticipated his answer. 'My mother took the child,' said Luke, 'and found a home – a good family. She wouldn't tell me where or who.' He broke off, adding lamely, 'She thought it wisest.'

Isobel nodded again. As she turned her head the sunlight outlined the hollow cheeks and he glimpsed dark shadows under the large brilliant eyes. She sighed deeply; suddenly he saw that her hand trembled as she raised it to push back a strand of the long wavy hair that fell nearly to her waist. It lacked the curls of her youth and Luke found himself wondering why that should be, then cursed himself for his foolishness. He wanted to touch her and the knowledge frightened and disarmed him.

She turned back to him. 'You killed my mother,' she said, but there was no malice in her voice. 'My father is dead too, now, of a knife wound. I have no husband. All I have is a son, Luke. I want you to find him for me. I want someone to love, Luke, and someone to love me.'

'Isobel . . .' Tears sprang into his eyes unbidden and he wept unashamedly while Isobel watched him, her face expressionless. He put up his hands to cover his face but the sobs still racked him as he stood there alone and comfortless. Then her arms were round him and she was holding him gently, patting his back as though he were a child, murmuring kind meaningless words to soothe him.

'I'm sorry,' he sobbed. 'I'm sorry. I'm so sorry . . .'

'Don't weep for me,' she said. 'It was God's will. Don't reproach yourself, for 'tis all done with so long ago. Only find me my son.'

'I will,' promised Luke. 'I swear I will. You shall have your son – Oh, Isobel, forgive me!'

She stood back from him and looked at his stricken face. 'I forgave you,' she said, 'on the way home from the well. All my hate vanished with my madness and you did that for me. You took me to St Cleer and God wrought my miracle. I still love you, Luke. Ah! Don't speak. Don't say you love me for I would hear the lie.'

Luke was silent, shaken and weary, his weeping finished. She went on. 'I love you, Luke, but I don't know you. I don't need you. I don't need a husband.'

'How do you live?' he burst out, 'and where? How do you feed yourself? I'll give you money, Isobel. Aye, that's it, I'll send you money.'

'My son, Luke,' she said simply. 'Find my son for me. That's all I ask of you.'

'I will,' he said, 'and take this, I beg you.' He took the money from the purse on his belt and thrust it into her unwilling hands. 'And I'll send you more, Isobel. Tell me where you live and you will never go cold or hungry. I swear it.'

'I'll be here at sun-up in a week's time,' she said. 'And the week after that and the next. I will be here week after week until you find him. Now, I must go before we are seen together. God be with you, Luke.' And she was gone across the beach, hurrying up the cliff path, never pausing, never looking back. For a moment he saw her outline against the sky on the cliff top, the wind tugging at her hair and skirt. Luke remembered the wedding ring and shouted to her but she had gone.

'Next week,' he told himself. 'I'll bring her son. I'll bring more money. I'll find them a home. Aye, they shall want for nothing. My wife and my son! Dear God, why does the thought bring such terrible joy?'

On the way home he turned his mount towards the old Priory. The horse's hoof-beats echoed reproachfully round the empty walls; he was glad to slip from the saddle and twist the reins over the branch of a stunted hawthorn. He stood in the deserted courtyard, dismayed at the air of desolation. Dead leaves lay sodden in every corner and floated in the rank water of the pond where no fish swam and the fountain was silent and still. A half-wild cat, skittering past, eyed him balefully before springing through a gaping window robbed long since of its lanthorn window and wooden shutters. The doors had gone and the steps, lacking their usual daily scrubbing, were stained with bird droppings from the nest above the doorway. Weeds sprouted everywhere between the flagstones. A dead decaying thrush lay beside the pond, its head twisted grotesquely, the spindly talons curled, the speckled breast rumpled. Luke glanced up at the roof, sighing heavily. He had contributed to this devastation. Part of the blame rested on his shoulders. He had acted in good faith but had he been right? Had he been wise to uphold the King against God? If he had been wrong, then the guilt he already bore was compounded. A coldness seized him as somewhere a woodpecker drilled into a tree and the cat, crouched in the window, flicked its ears at the sound. Tentatively Luke put out a hand to touch it but it took fright and jumped down inside what had once been the refectory. Luke remembered visiting it as a child and saw again the long tables loaded with food and wine and pitchers of ale and heard the cheerful babble of voices and sensed the excitement of the occasion – Brother Andrew's saint day when he, Luke, was only six years old and his uncle had given him a sip of wine and a handful of almond biscuits and had lifted him shoulder-high . . . Now the old monk had gone, the Priory, too. Luke was filled with a desperate sadness and sense of loss. Abruptly he crossed the courtyard and made his way down the steps to the crypt. There, he and Isobel had wed. 'Oh sweet heaven!' he whispered and falling to his knees, began to pray.

Alison found him there and heard his murmurings but could make little of it. 'Luke!' she called softly, reluctant to disturb him yet unable to bear the sight of his bowed head and hunched shoulders. As he turned, she ran down the rest of the steps and was pulling him to his feet, comforting him in a torrent of sweet words.

'Whatever you have done, Luke, God will forgive you,' she told him passionately. 'Don't grieve so, I cannot bear it. To see your dear face so stricken, your eyes so often brimming with tears. Tell me, Luke, what ails you and ruins your sleep. Whatever it is I will most generously forgive you. I swear it on my heart! I cannot stand aside and see you suffer.' She clung to him while he stroked her head, struggling to hold back the words which would bring him such wonderful relief and her such bitter disillusionment.

'I cannot,' he whispered. 'Believe me, I cannot tell you.'

'Then I will tell you, Luke!' she said, suddenly vehement, 'I will tell you!'

He looked at her in alarm as she stared at him, her face pale in the gloom.

'Luke,' she whispered. 'Promise me you will confess it – if I am right. Confess it, hear my forgiveness and be yourself again. Promise me, Luke. And if I am wrong, we'll speak of it no more. Will you promise?'

He hesitated, unable to believe that she knew, and finally nodded.

Alison took a deep breath and, turning her face away from him, said, 'That young man – Simon. He's your illegitimate son.'

She was so near the truth it took his breath away. 'He is,' continued Alison, her voice trembling. 'That is your secret grief, Luke. Your secret guilt. Simon is your illegitimate son.'

For a moment relief and regret struggled in Luke's mind. 'You are wrong, little mouse,' he said gently. 'I swear to God you are wrong. Now, I have kept my side of the bargain and you must keep yours. We will not speak of it again.'

She opened her mouth to protest, but he laid a finger over it. 'A bargain is a bargain,' he said lightly. 'A promise is a promise. Now, let me kiss you. Now smile for me, Alison, and take my hand. We must go home.'

CHAPTER ELEVEN

It was hot in the bakery and the air was thick with the smell of boiling mutton and onions. Simon, ladle in hand, wiped his face with his forearm as he gave the pot a quick stir. John Ball watched him critically from the far side of the room where he had sat for the past twenty-one years 'giving an eye to the lad' as he put it. He knew all there was to know about baking and no one within a ten-mile radius could make a better meat pasty but now he must sit and watch the lad do it for he had lost both his legs above the knees when he had been run down by a cart. Every morning his wife and the lad carried him into the bakery and sat him in his chair and his wife would hand him the long apron which he wore to cover his stumps.

His main topic of conversation was 'how his legs came about' and Simon had already heard the tale several times. However, the last lad's sudden death had given him another story and he was just beginning his third account of it.

'He was same age as you, the lad was,' he told Simon who glanced up occasionally to suggest his interest in the account while his hands were busy with the dough. 'Aye, same age as you but a tidy bit shorter. A nice lad,' he mused. 'A nice *willing* lad.' He emphasized the word for Simon's benefit. 'Don't lean on it lad!' he cried suddenly. 'Kneading and leaning's two different things as I told you yesterday. Don't lean!'

Simon nodded and began to slap the large mound of dough. 'And don't *go* at it like that. You've no quarrel with it – leastways not to my knowledge . . . Aye, poor lad. He was that willing but a bit shorter than you though broad in the shoulder. And ruddy looking! You'd have sworn there was no fitter lad in the whole of Ashburton. You would that. If you'd seen that lad the morning he died you'd have said that. I said it myself! A real ruddy complexion, that lad, and never idle!' he added as Simon paused to wipe his face once more. 'Oh no, he were never idle . . . Now skim the fat from the mutton – use a piece of stale bread. Pull it across the top and 'twill soak up the fat. Another five minutes and I reckon you can lift the pot off the fire . . . Oh aye, the lad. I was telling you. Well, suddenly he's staring at me strange like, as if he don't see me properly. Hello I think, he's off day-dreaming again. Proper one for day-dreaming, he was – not like the lad before him. Real little worker, that one was . . . Where was I?'

Simon pulled off lumps of dough and tossed them into the scale pan, pinching out a bit of dough or adding a knob as required.

'I say, where was I?' John repeated and Simon looked up guiltily. 'Oh, aye, staring at me strange like – you'll wreck those scales, if you don't let up! Good scales, they are, and should be treated with respect. Drop it in, lad, don't throw it and take that mutton off now or 'twill boil away to nought. Aye, very strange, he looked and then all of a sudden his eyes rolled up, so –' he demonstrated while Simon grinned, 'and then out came his tongue, so –' he poked his tongue out but unable to proceed with the story, withdrew it, 'and wallop, like, he was gone. Flat out on the floor. So quick it was I never had time to say a word. Not one word. Split his head clean open, it did. Right there, it was.' He pointed to a corner of the oven. 'Hit his head as he went down, see . . . I dunno, mayhap he was as tall as you or near enough. 'Tis hard to remember. One lad's much like another –'

Maggie appeared in the doorway and he appealed to her. 'Would you say the last lad was as tall as this one?' he asked.

She looked at Simon with a gleam in her eye. 'Oh no, father,' she said. 'Nowhere near as tall. Nor so handsome, neither.'

Simon shot her a warning glance but she giggled. 'Nor so quick,' she went on, 'nor so –' She paused, considering. 'Nor so lusty.'

The old man caught the insinuation in her voice and looked at Simon sharply. 'Oh, lusty is he?' he said. 'And how would you know that, Maggie?'

'I don't know for sure,' she said, her eyes on Simon's face, 'but I'm willing to wager on it.'

Simon said nothing as the old man looked from one to the other. Then he frowned, aware that he was allowing himself to be sidetracked. 'Where was I?' he asked petulantly. 'Oh aye. Split his head clean open, he did.'

The next evening they rode in the old cart along the track towards the mill. Simon, the reins loosely held in both hands, was aware of the girl beside him and knew that she cast sly glances in his direction and managed to fall against him whenever the cart turned even the slightest bend in the road. He whistled tunelessly and flicked at the reins from time to time but the old horse ignored him.

'Sing the words,' suggested Maggie. 'I'm grown tired of that old whistling.'

'I don't know the words,' said Simon.

'Then I'll sing 'em for you' she said with a saucy wink.

> 'My true love be a sailor –
> Fol lal de rol –
> Asail upon the sea
> When he comes home he'll like as not
> Sail upon me!
> Fol lal de rol dol day'

He grinned but said nothing and she embarked upon the next verse, her head set on one side, her dark curls bobbing cheerfully with the movement of the cart.

> 'My true love be a locksmith –
> Fol lal de rol –'

Simon laughed.

'I know lots of verses,' she said. 'My voice is none too sweet but I think you're getting my meaning!'

'Oh I am!' he agreed. ''Tis loud and clear, ringing in my ear like a bell, fit to deafen me!'

'Better'n a poke in the eye, though,' she said. 'I'll sing you the one about the archer – Oops!' The wheel of the cart fell into a deep rut and they were thrown sideways, a heaven-sent opportunity for Maggie who contrived to end up in Simon's lap, with her legs in the air. She looked up at him grinning mischievously, aware that her low cut dress showed off her rounded breasts to perfection.

'Hey, let me be!' she cried. 'You baker's lads have but one thought in your heads!'

'To get to the mill and collect the flour,' said Simon but he helped her up willingly enough and watched with obvious pleasure as she smoothed her crumpled gown and examined her neat ankles for non-existent bruises. When she was ready he coaxed the horse forward and they jolted free of the pot-hole.

'I'll make you a verse about a baker's lad,' she offered. 'Let me see now:

> "My true love is a baker's lad –
> Fol lal de rol
> As loves me more each hour.
> Er – He is the only fellow I'll
> Allow to grind my flour!
> Fol lal de rol dol day"'

Simon roared with laughter in spite of himself. 'That's very good,' he told her. 'You've hidden talents, Maggie.'

She rolled her eyes expressively. 'Oh I have,' she agreed. 'I have. Delights undreamed of. Don't you ever wonder?' she asked, 'about the other lads and me?'

'No,' he lied. 'I never so much as gave it a thought.'

Maggie hooted derisively. 'You're a poor sort of liar, Simon Betts,' she said. ''Tis writ all over your face as you're dying to know.'

He shook his head but she laughed. 'I see it in your eyes,' she said 'like writing on a page. Oh, we've had lots of lads –'

'We?' queried Simon, tongue in cheek.

She looked at him innocently. 'Whatever do you mean, Simon?' she demanded. 'I trust 'tis not what I think. As I was saying, we've had lots of different lads.' She began to count on her fingers. 'Young Eric, he was a bit slow but good at the job once he got the idea.' She glanced at Simon's face to see his reaction, but he was careful to keep his face straight and appeared to be concentrating on the road ahead. 'Then there was the lad with red hair – real carrotty he was but very keen. Keen as mustard, my father used to say and I'd second that! Then we had the tubby one from Chagford – he was a good little worker. Lardy we used to call him.' She looked at him suspiciously. 'Are you listening, Simon?'

'Aye, I'm listening,' he said 'but I'm wondering, too. What made 'em all leave, these marvellous good workers.'

She leaned towards him suddenly and put her head on his shoulder. 'My father reckons we weren't paying them enough,' she giggled, 'but he was wrong. There's more to life than money, wouldn't you say?'

He reined in the horse suddenly and the cart creaked to a standstill. He looked down at Maggie's flushed face, noting the gleam in her eye. Her curly head lay against his arm and her skin was faintly freckled. 'Aye, Maggie,' he said softly, 'there's more to life than money.'

'Such as?' she whispered.

'Such as this,' he said, kissing her hair, 'and this –' kissing her shoulder.

'And this,' she suggested, pulling up her skirt and offering a sweetly rounded knee for him to kiss. He kissed it laughing and as he bent forward she kissed the back of his neck, her tongue tracing his hair line so that his body melted delightfully.

'Maggie! Maggie!' he whispered. 'I don't know why those lads left! I swear I don't.'

'No stamina,' whispered Maggie, 'and no sense of decency. They'd make love in a cart in the middle of the highway, if I'd let 'em.'

He took the hint. 'Then where shall we go?' he asked.

'Round the next bend,' said Maggie, promptly straightening her skirt, 'there's a bit of a hedge. You can drive the cart round behind it.'

It was shady behind the hedge, under the tree. Maggie hopped out of the cart and pulled out a few empty sacks. 'They're full of flour dust,' she said, 'but I daresn't shake 'em. It flies so into the air if you so much as look at it!' She lowered her voice conspiratorially. 'And 'twould betray us!'

When the sacks were arranged to her satisfaction she turned and threw her arms round Simon's neck. 'Five months I've waited for this,' she whispered. 'You've led me a fair dance, Simon, but I'm not one to bear a grudge.'

'I'm glad of that,' he said softly.

He slid his arms round her waist and pulled her towards him. 'So they were all good workers, were they?' he asked. 'All those lads you spoke of?'

'Aye,' she said 'but I reckon you'll do better, Simon Betts.'

'You do?' He was fumbling with the buttons on her gown but impatiently she did the task for him, wriggling so that the top of her bodice slipped forward away from her full breasts. Then she put her arms round his neck. 'They're like my father's best dough,' she whispered. 'Soft to the touch but weighty in your hand. Try 'em!'

She stepped back so that they fell free of the bodice and as his hands closed gently over them their eyes closed in the beginnings of ecstasy. 'Simon Betts!' she murmured and together they sank down, their journey forgotten, each engrossed in the delights of the other's body. It was as well that no one passed that way for as their play gave way to passion the tell-tale flour dust began to rise.

Luke searched for a week without success. Many people told him that a couple named Betts had adopted a little boy many years ago but they had both since died and the boy had moved on – where no one knew. Or if they knew, they kept silent on the matter. No, the Betts had no children of their own. Yes, the Betts were very poor. Tom Betts was a turner but not a very good one and they lived very humbly. The adopted son? He had been named Sam or Simon or possibly Simeon. And that was all he could discover. He would have to greet Isobel with disappointing news. He had a surname and a choice of Christian names and that was all.

A week later, an hour before sunrise, he rode past the bakery on his way to meet Isobel. In the room under the roof Simon was woken by the sound of hoof-beats but, finding it still dark, he turned over again and went back to sleep.

Before he reached the cliff top Luke saw Isobel flitting like a wraith in the misty air. She turned at the sound and waited fearfully in case it should be someone else who rode alone through the darkness.

''Tis I, Luke,' he reassured her, reining in his horse. 'Ride behind me – here, give me your hand.' She was so light. Luke thought of plump little Alison with her softly rounded arms and the small pudgy fingers. This woman could have little spare flesh on her frame to lift so easily on to the saddle behind him. They rode on until the bare highway gave way to gorse and bracken on top of the cliff, where they dismounted. The horse grazed while Luke and Isobel stood together in the fine misty rain which hid the sea far below them.

'I hardly dare ask,' said Isobel. 'Is there any news?'

'No,' said Luke, 'at least, I haven't found him but I believe that he goes by the name of Betts and his first name is Simon or Simeon. No one agreed on that point.'

She drew a deep breath. 'So he is still alive. I feared secretly that I might be too late. What of the family – the Bettses?'

'Both dead.'

'So he is alone unless he is wed already.'

'So young? Let us hope not. I'm sorry I cannot bring him to you as I promised.'

'You tried,' she said gently. 'I can search on now. I know who I'm looking for. I shall find him.'

'And I shall help you,' he told her. 'I shall go on searching. Between us we'll find him.'

For a moment she was silent, then she said, 'Our son, Luke. 'Tis strange to be speaking of it this way after all these years.'

'Aye. I can't tell you –'

She held up a hand. 'No! No more regrets, Luke. The past is done with. 'Tis clearly not forgotten but you are forgiven. We were both so young and knew so little of life.'

'I did you a grave injustice.'

'I was partly to blame.'

'And then your madness – 'twas my fault. Even your mother –'

'Don't speak of it!' she said abruptly. 'They were evil times. The less said the better . . . And you. Are you happy, Luke?'

'Never truly so,' he said simply.

'I will be happy when I have my son. He is all I have.'

He tried to make out her features but the light was poor and she was no more than a shadow beside him. 'We are like two ghosts,' he joked, 'with no form or features. I wish it was lighter. I should like to see you clearly.'

'To see what I have become,' she said but without bitterness.

'Just to see you.'

He sensed that she smiled in the darkness.

'I'm flesh and blood,' she said.

'But so frail.'

She shrugged, pulling her shawl closer round her shoulders. 'And are you grown stout?' she asked him.

'I eat too well and drink too often.'

They listened to the sea rolling across the sand and watched the pale grey glow in the west as the sun cleared the horizon. 'Luke,' she said hesitantly. 'Will you take my hand in yours while we talk. 'Twill mean nothing to you, I know, but it would comfort me. I'm so much alone and sometimes fearful.' He took her hand and rubbed it to warm it. 'Luke, I'm so afeard.' Her composure was breaking down. 'What if my son will not know me, Luke? What if he does not care for me?' Her voice sank to a whisper. 'They call me the witch woman's daughter! What if I shame him, Luke? Oh dearest Heaven, what then!'

Impulsively, protectively, Luke pulled her towards him. His arms went round her and his lips moved in her hair. 'They will have me to deal with!' he cried. 'If any man miscalls you I shall run him through!'

'No, Luke! You must not –'

He held her closer. She was no longer a wraith beside him in the darkness but a woman in his arms. 'No one shall dare to call you names,' he insisted. 'No one, I say, Isobel. That is all over now. You shall start a new life with your son. Dearest Isobel, I swear it on my honour!'

She was crying suddenly. He felt the fierce trembling of her body as she struggled with her tears. The grief and fear had broken through the pretended calm.

'Don't weep so, I beg you,' he whispered. 'No one shall hurt you again. You are safe now. Be still. Hush these tears – they will shake you to pieces!'

'I didn't mean to,' she wept. 'I swear it. I meant to be so calm, so ladylike. So unlike the Isobel you remembered.'

'And so you are,' he assured her. 'You are different. I was impressed –'

'But not now.'

'Aye, still,' he said. 'Even a lady must weep now and then. Even a gentleman.'

She looked up at him. 'Even you, Luke?'

'Aye. I weep also.'

'But why, Luke?'

He considered his answer while he stroked her hair, noting that her sobs grew quieter. 'I weep for my mistakes,' he said at last, 'for the wrongs I do. For the grief I bring to those I love . . . And I weep for my dead son.'

'I'm sorry,' she said 'I didn't know. You mustn't blame yourself. We all make mistakes. The wrong is when we mean ill. When we mean well but it turns out ill why then we are not to blame.'

'You comfort me,' he said simply.

'We comfort each other,' she said.

A light breeze had sprung up and the mist drifted past them and out over the sea, allowing the sun to reach them. Luke turned Isobel so that it lit her face. 'Such a sad little face,' he said. 'Thin and pale and stained with tears – but still beautiful.'

'Oh Luke, don't,' she whispered.

'You are still a beautiful woman,' he told her gently. 'The same large eyes, the same wild mane!' He took a strand of her hair and put it to his lips. And then, hardly knowing what he did, he had taken her face in his hands and was kissing her forehead, her eyes, her lips. The salt of her tears was like a goad urging him on to obliterate with kisses the years of misery this woman had suffered because of him.

'Luke!' she cried and struggled to free herself until the strength of his arms and the growing passion in his kisses melted her resistance. Tremulously, she returned his kisses, wonderingly, her fingers explored the once-familiar face, and felt the firm jaw, the high cheekbones and the hair curling softly at the nape of his neck.

'Isobel! Dear God!'

'What are we doing?' she cried but for answer he held her closer until the protest died on her lips and her desire for him, dead for so long, flared into life again.

'Take me, Luke,' she begged. 'Once, only once and I

will never – what is it? What have I said? Luke, answer me for pity's sake.'

Her urgent words shocked him into awareness and he drew back a little, with a gasp of dismay. Alison's image hung in his mind's eye, loving and innocent. 'Dear God!' he whispered. 'It cannot be. It must not.'

'Please Luke,' she begged, clinging to him frantically, her fingers plucking at his arms as he tried to free himself. 'No one will ever know. Take me, for God's sake. If I am beautiful, take me this last time for all that we once meant to each other.'

'No!' His voice was harsh with desperation.

'To prove that you still love me. Oh do not refuse me Luke. Alison has known you these past years while I have suffered for her sake. I am still a woman, Luke, yet cannot wed because I have a husband – you! How is it wrong for a husband to make love to his wife? You share a bed with Alison, who is nothing to you in God's eyes, yet deny me a few moments' ecstasy. Surely Alison herself could not refuse me this. Oh Luke, don't look at me like that. Don't push me away. No, Luke, don't turn away from me. Luke! Luke!' She snatched at his sleeve but he jerked his arm away. She sprang at him wildly and tripped, to fall sprawling at his feet. Her thin cry tore at his heart and he knelt beside her. As the bracken closed over them his arms were round her, and he was lost.

The thin sunshine found its way through the bracken and warmed them. Isobel lay still, her passion exhausted. Beside her Luke covered his face with his arm, so that she might not see the expression in his eyes.

'Luke, tell me it was good.'

He made no answer.

'Luke!'

He gave a slight nod of his head.

''Twas good for me also,' she said.

He sat up slowly.

'Don't go, Luke,' she whispered. 'Not yet, I beg you.'

Slowly he stood up to meet the new day. Isobel caught his hand and pulled herself up beside him. They looked out across the sea which thrashed itself against the rocks below them. The tide was coming in and the waves, cold and green, burst into pink spray as the sun reached them.

'Tell me you love me, Luke,' said Isobel. 'Then I will go away and find my son and never trouble you again. Luke, tell me. Say it.'

'I cannot,' he said. 'We have turned back the clock and I am fearful.'

'Luke!' She moved round to look into his eyes and saw the stricken expression. In it she read the confusion and regret. With a sharp cry, she stumbled back as though he had struck her.

'Isobel!' he cried. 'Listen to me.'

'Oh no,' she whispered. 'I can see it in your face. You despise me. I am nothing to you. I can see it in your eyes –' She turned and began to run from him. She ran a few yards then stopped in mid-flight to face him once more. 'Tell me you love me,' she said desperately but Luke was silent. With a groan she threw up her arms in a gesture of despair like one drowning, then turned blindly towards the cliff edge.

'Isobel! No!' he shouted but it was too late. He saw her thin arms flung wide as she fell and heard the thin wail of her last sounds as the breeze blew them away. He reached the cliff top and looked down in time to see her shawl flutter into the sea, which lapped the crumpled body at the water's edge. Momentarily stunned, Luke could only stand and stare, his lips forming her name silently. Then the full horror of the situation seared into his brain and forced his rigid body into movement.

The familiar climb down the cliff took on a nightmarish quality. He reached Isobel and knelt beside her. She appeared uninjured: no twisted limbs, no bleeding. She lay with one leg bent over the other, and her arms were spread out across the sand while her head was slightly turned to one side. Her eyes were closed and she could have been sleeping, so peaceful did she appear, but she was dead.

Luke felt her wrist and listened to her heart. Nothing. It was all over. A terrible black despair numbed his senses. He wanted to take her in his arms and lie with her until the sea covered them both and hid them from the eyes of the world. If only he could die too . . . Wearily he shook himself out of his stupor. Only the good die young, he thought. The wicked were destined to live on. Luke Kendal was not allowed to die. He straightened her skirt, tidied her hair and kissed her forehead. It was still warm. He made the sign of the cross over her. 'Isobel,' he whispered. She made no sign that she heard. 'I love you,' he said. Could a dead woman detect the lie? He hoped not but crossed himself none the less. From his purse he took her wedding ring and slipped it on to her finger. 'It was good,' he told her. That at least was true but would it comfort her? He looked at the limp hand with its gold band and a shudder went through him. What of her soul? Her body would eventually be washed up and maybe identified. Daughter of the witch woman! They would bury her in unhallowed ground and would say no words over her. He sighed deeply. Quickly he straightened her body, setting the long legs together. He spread her arms wide, then etched a large cross in the sand below her, the upright extending above her head and past her feet. Kneeling beside her, he closed his eyes. 'This is my wife, Isobel,' he whispered. 'Be merciful, God, for I have crucified her.'

Exeter market was busier than usual. The square was thronged with people, some buying, others too poor to spend, mingling with the crowd for the enjoyment of the occasion. The warm sun encouraged the women to leave their firesides and venture out to meet and gossip with friends and neighbours. An old woman sat on an upturned barrel with a basket of eggs for sale and beside her a good-looking young man crouched among a selection of pottery – jugs, platters and bowls of all shapes and sizes.

'Pots for sale! Fine pots! Come and buy!' he shouted but his eyes were on the young girls who passed his way flouncing their skirts and tossing their heads for his benefit.

A large woman perched on a small stool plucked at a chicken with a dexterity which kept the air full of feathers and advertised her wares without words. Six more birds, ready plucked, hung from a staff beside her and she kept a fierce eye on them for fear of thieves.

A scrawny young woman held a basket of fish while with her free hand she rocked a wooden crib in which a very new baby sobbed despairingly. Further over her father rigged a primitive awning to protect his butter and cheese from the sun's heat.

Livestock added to the clamour as ducks complained about their confinement in rickety coops and squealing piglets were drawn from a sack to be inspected by prospective buyers. A nanny goat bleated irritably as her owner tried unsuccessfully to squeeze a few last ounces of milk from her teats and a donkey brayed. Only the larks maintained a resentful silence as they jostled each other on and off the perches in their large wicker cage which swayed crazily against the shoulder of its drunken bearer.

Maggie had found herself a suitable corner and leaned against the wall of the ale house with her tray of pies.

Only three remained as many of the customers of the ale house were tempted by the sight of crisply browned pastry and the glimpse of rich gravy oozing from the crust. She scanned the crowd for sight of Simon who would bring her a fresh batch. If he didn't make haste, he would be too late for already the crowd had thinned a little and one or two of the stall holders were repacking their wares in preparation for a long journey home. At last she saw him, the cloth covered tray balanced on his blond head, and her heart quickened at the sight of him.

'I thought you'd lost your way,' she chided.

'Well you thought wrong,' he said as she loosed the leather strap from his tray and fixed it to hers. 'Your father was in one of his talkative moods.'

She groaned. 'Not the tale of his missing legs!' she said.

Simon nodded. 'Then I was half way here and met a man riding from Torquay. His brother had found a woman washed up on the beach there yesterday and he must recount the gory details.'

'Poor wretch,' said Maggie. She slipped the leather strap over her head and cried 'Hot pies! Fresh mutton! Fine onions! Pies oh!'

'All broken she was and battered from the rocks and —'

'Who was she, do they know?' She handed over two pies in exchange for a pot of honey.

Simon shrugged. 'Seemingly not, nor like to for her face was —' he broke off, 'but she was wed apparently. She wore a wedding ring.'

'Poor soul,' said Maggie again. 'Heaven preserve me from a watery death — ugh!' She shuddered and crossed herself. A group of prentices shouldered a way through the crowd and besieged their favourite pie seller with saucy remarks, and not a few pinches. Elbowed aside, Simon watched laughing as the tray emptied. With any luck they would sell out and could wander round the market themselves. Glancing up suddenly, he caught the eye of a young woman on horseback. She had obviously been watching him for now she turned her head away, a slight blush colouring her cheeks. An older man rode beside her, probably in his thirties. Her husband perhaps? For some reason Simon hoped not. He saw her speak to her companion and the man urged his horse through the crowd towards Maggie. In search of a bite to eat! The woman looked his way again and he smiled and gave a small nod in deference to her obvious quality. Her riding cloak was of warm woollen cloth but the gown that showed beneath it was of heavy silk and she wore gloves to match. He had seen her before somewhere, but where? The question troubled him more than he expected. Then, the pies purchased, they turned their horses and rode out of the market square. Impulsively, Simon followed, a discreet distance behind, taking care to keep himself hidden. Maggie was busy with her wares. Before she missed him, he would be back again.

Melissa had dismounted, leaving her horse with Thomas Benet who waited for her beyond the market. She needed some lace, she told him, and wanted to find her favourite pedlar. Having found him, she inquired after a small wooden hand mirror and held it up to search the crowd behind her for the young blond man. He had followed her as she had known he would. Puzzled, she returned the mirror with a shake of her head and fingered a necklace of polished shells, holding it against the silk of her gown as though to consider the effect as her heartbeat quickened. Who was he and why were they so drawn to each other? Suddenly two dogs rolled towards her, snapping and snarling at each other, oblivious of the curses and kicks bestowed upon them by the indignant shoppers who stumbled over them. They hurled themselves against Melissa's legs, knocking her off balance, and she gasped as the shell necklace was jerked from her hand. Stumbling, she clutched at the nearest arm for support and found herself face to face with Simon. With two well aimed kicks he sent the dogs howling in opposite directions.

'Oh, the necklace!' cried Melissa. ''Tis lost.'

The pedlar shouted for its return and they searched the cobbles but in vain. Light fingers had hidden it away beneath a basket of vegetables and it was gone for ever. Abashed, Melissa began to apologize, offering to make good the pedlar's loss but he, a shrewd businessman, refused her offer declaring it 'the will of God'! Out of gratitude for his generosity she then bought the hand mirror for Nan, a yard of lace for herself and a pomander for her mother! Her purchasing done, she turned to Simon. 'My thanks,' she said, 'for your intervention. I like dogs but not such disagreeable ones.'

'I'm glad I was on hand to help you,' said Simon.

There was really no more to be said yet neither of them wanted to end the conversation. They stood irresolute, looking into each other's eyes for the answer.

'I've seen you before,' said Simon.

'At my brother's funeral,' said Melissa, then wished she had been more discreet. It would not do for him to know she had noticed him.

'Was that it?' he asked. 'My condolences on your loss.'

'Thank you.'

That said, there could be no further common ground. Melissa looked at the blue eyes and noted the high cheekbones and firm jaw. So was that it? A passing resemblance to her dead brother? At that moment Thomas Benet reached them, leading the two horses.

'I must go,' she told Simon. 'This young man was kind enough to rescue me,' she added to Thomas.

'From a dog fight,' said Simon lightly. 'I was glad to be of service. And now, farewell to you ma'am and to you, sir.' He nodded to them both and began to push his way back through the crowd.

Thomas and Melissa watched him go. 'He reminded me of Paul,' she said.

'I saw the likeness,' Thomas admitted.

They remounted and rode back to Heron. Thomas spoke cheerfully of the morning's events but Melissa, busy with her thoughts, said little in return.

'Rochester May 1537, with loving greetings from Abigail. In faith I am ashamed at my delay in answering your letter but must plead a great many distractions – so near to London and the court. My sweet Adam sends greetings and is in good health and spirits as I am also. I learn daily of winds and tides and my ears are assailed by tidings of this boat and that – enough to turn my wits. In truth I am happy with my new life and urge you Melissa with all speed to choose a husband that you may share my new found delights. My views are sought and I am treated with great courtesy. My maid, Janna, is respectful and eager to learn and I can ask no more of her.

'I do not ride as often as I would wish but Adam has given me a young hound to rear – the runt of a litter – that is my special pet and constant companion.

'And now my only regret is that Adam's mother as foretold is not an amiable woman and the sweetest of God's angels would be hard put to please her but still I hope she may like me better as the year passes. I strive to please her with my cooking as Mama advised but when that does well she must cast her eyes elsewhere and will then speak ill of my embroidering!

'All talk here is of Queen Jane who is with child and, God willing, promises to bear King Henry a male child. They say the King is beside himself with joy and the Queen has such a craving for fat quail that the King scours London for them and yet cannot satisfy her. He has cancelled his summer progress north and promises to stay within sixty miles of the Queen for fear some alarm or other may distress her in his absence and so affect the child. I trust my Adam will show me such protection when my time comes! There will be such rejoicing in the capital if a son is born and I am in hope you will visit us here that we might all travel to London to share the festivities.

'Until such times as we may meet again my prayers are with you all. I remain your affectionate sister.'

CHAPTER TWELVE

Alison dabbed at her forehead with a linen handkerchief and prayed for a breeze. The windows of the Hall were unshuttered, the doorways at either end of the room were uncurtained, yet still the humid air hung motionless. Ruefully, she anticipated another sleepless night for the small bedchamber was airless at the best of times. Tonight it would be unbearable. Perhaps she would ask Izzie for a draught of lime tea. Across the large white-walled room Thomas's head was bent over his lute and he fingered the strings with a delicate but sure touch. She studied him covertly, noting how the once-gold curls had deepened to a soft brown. The once boyish face now bore a few lines and the downy skin had coarsened. She enjoyed his company. After so many years he was familiar in a brotherly way and since Luke's departure had taken his additional duties as protector very seriously indeed. He was singing, his voice low but clear toned:

> 'My lady waits impatiently
> And frets away the livelong day
> She waits her true love for to see
> Alas she does not wait for me.
>
> 'Her own true love is far away
> But the lady she will faithful be
> Nor from the path of virtue stray
> Yet waits forever and a day.'

He paused, his head still bent so that his face was hidden from her.

'You sing mournfully tonight,' she teased, 'and yet the song pleases me. 'Tis unfamiliar, though. I haven't heard it before.'

He looked up slowly. 'I haven't sung it before tonight,' he said.

'Sing it again, then, Thomas,' she said. 'And this time I will pay better attention.'

He sang and to Alison it seemed that each word came straight from his heart. When it was done, she clapped her hands lightly in applause. 'And are they your words?' she asked.

'They are.'

'Your melody also?'

'Aye.'

'Then my congratulations, Thomas. You have proved yourself poet and composer. But why so sad a song? Must true love never be requited? Is that it?'

He smiled faintly. 'Rarely in a song, ma'am,' he told her.

She laughed, refilled her glass with wine and held the flagon up for his attention. Thomas shook his head. 'No more, ma'am,' he said. 'I have a little left in the goblet but have drunk too deeply already.'

Alison lifted her glass. 'Then join with me in a toast,' she said. 'To Luke.' She hesitated and then added 'and his salvation.'

They drank and he set down his empty goblet while Alison twirled hers in her fingers, watching the golden liquid. She frowned slightly, wondering how best to approach the subject she wished to talk about. On no account must he think her unduly concerned.

'The "own true love" in the song,' she said lightly, 'that could be Luke. He's far away.' He waited. 'Where will he be by now?' she asked.

'Nigh on Winchester,' said Thomas, 'if he left Glastonbury soon after daybreak. By this time tomorrow he should be in London, the next day Canterbury.'

'Did you ever make a pilgrimage?' asked Alison curiously.

Thomas laughed. 'I didn't,' he confessed. 'My sins have not been great enough for that.' He broke off in confusion. 'Not that your husband – indeed I intended no such thing, believe me.' The colour rushed to his face as he stammered profuse apologies for his tactless remark. Alison looked at him soberly, saying nothing to relieve his embarrassment. When at last he faltered into silence she said: 'To go so suddenly, Thomas, it troubles me.' She avoided his eyes as she spoke. She had set down the goblet and now twisted her fingers in her lap. 'I would not speak of it to any other, Thomas, and yet you know the man also. I think you love him. You are not only master and man but friends.'

'We are,' he said.

'Then tell me truly, Thomas, is it not strange that he should be so sudden in his resolve? One day to speak nothing of such an idea, the next to be packed and waving his farewells. I tell you, it troubles me. He is not gone just to London or Canterbury but to Glastonbury and Winchester! What has he done, Thomas?' She could no longer keep the fear from her eyes and as she faced him, he pitied her. 'Do you know of any cause?'

Thomas shook his head in genuine ignorance. ''Twas very sudden,' he agreed. 'I thought it so, I must confess but as to the reason –' he shrugged helplessly. 'I cannot begin to guess.'

Alison dabbed at her perspiring face, carefully refolded the small white square and patted her neck and throat. 'I cannot sleep for the matter,' she said, 'and the air is so close. I tossed and turned last night until the sun came up – I wager tonight will be no better . . . I begged him tell me why he left in such haste with scant preparation. "Do not ask me," was all he would say. "Do not ask me." Thomas, how can I help the man if he tells me nothing!'

Thomas hesitated but she caught the expression on his face and stared at him accusingly. 'You *do* know something!' she cried. 'I see it in your face.'

'No, no,' he protested. ''Twas just a thought. Jack tells me that the Gillis woman has disappeared.'

'The witch woman, you mean? But she died years ago!'

'The daughter, Isobel,' he said. 'They hanged Marion. She had a daughter, a poor mad creature. There were some called her witch also.'

Alison stared at him bewildered. 'He would not go in search of her. He fears the Gillis family.'

'I don't say that he has,' said Thomas, 'merely that there was talk of her disappearance and the next day your husband is gone. I dare say it means nothing.'

'Has she bewitched him?' cried Alison, 'or disordered his mind? Or sent him journeying to meet with an accident? Dear God!' She stared at him fearfully. 'Oh Thomas, you must go after him. You must bring him back at once – but no! He wouldn't be persuaded. He is the stubbornest of men as I know to my cost. Help me Thomas. What's to be done?'

'Pray for him,' said Thomas gently, 'and wait on his return.'

'If only you had ridden with him.'

'I wanted to but he wouldn't hear of it.'

''Tis true. Forgive me, Thomas. I didn't mean to reproach you. You are right and we must wait and pray. Ah, the Gillises! A plague on them all. If the daughter has disappeared, then we are well rid of them . . .' She took a sip of wine and made an effort to control her agitation. 'We'll speak of it no more. Sing to me again,

Thomas,' she said, smiling. 'Charm me with your tale of true love. Who knows, if it soothes me well enough I may sleep tonight.'

He picked up the lute and began to sing.

> 'My lady waits impatiently
> And frets away the livelong day
> She waits her true love for to see
> Alas, she does not wait for me –'

She watched his face as he sang and glancing up, his eyes met hers unexpectedly. Before he had time to guard his expression she read there at last the love he had hidden for so many years. 'Alas, she does not wait for me.' It was his song to her.

Heron stood on one side of the river, Melissa sat on the other. She sat alone for Abigail was in Rochester and Thomas was at the mine. Her feet and legs were bare and her long hair, free of its cap, was tied in a knot on top of her head to allow what little breeze there was to reach her neck. Her fingers were busy plucking daisies from the grass and fashioning them into a chain. Suddenly a shadow fell across her legs; she looked up, startled. 'You!' she said. One hand flew to hide her unruly hair, the other to pull her skirt down over her legs. 'What are you doing here?'

Simon smiled. 'Looking for you,' he told her. 'I've brought you a present.'

'A present?'

He nodded.

'I mustn't accept it,' said Melissa. ''Twould be unseemly.'

'And you don't want to know what it is?'

She hesitated, for she most certainly did want to know. 'Won't you tell me what it is?' she said.

Simon shook his head. 'Only if you promise to accept it,' he said lightly.

'I daren't,' she said.

'Because you're betrothed?' he suggested but she shook her head.

'You are not?' he insisted.

'Not yet,' she said defensively, 'but I believe the preliminaries are –' She stopped, for he had tossed a shell necklace into her lap. 'Oh! But I don't think –'

'They are like those you lost in the market,' he reminded her. She picked them up gingerly. 'They won't bite you,' he laughed. 'I guarantee you are quite safe.'

'Now you're mocking me,' she said.

He knelt beside her, took the necklace and fastened it round her neck. 'Very beautiful,' he said but they both knew he was not referring to the necklace. Melissa felt herself blushing.

'May I sit with you a moment?' he asked and taking her silence as consent sat on the grass beside her. Idly he pulled a few daisies and handed them to her. Without speaking, she slit them with her fingernail and added them to the chain.

He picked up one of her shoes that lay in the grass and held it up for his inspection. 'A dainty shoe,' he said, 'for a dainty lady.'

'Thank you,' she whispered and bent her head further over her daisy chain. She was unused to such talk, unused to compliments from a stranger and unsure how to react. Her mind told her to dismiss him haughtily yet her heart raced with excitement. If only she were Abigail! Abby would know what to say and do. Although older than her sister, Melissa had remained a child for so long she had looked to the younger girl for guidance. But Abigail was in Rochester and Melissa was sitting in the grass with a young man who was a stranger and yet familiar.

'My brother had blue eyes,' she said suddenly. 'Paul – the one that died. His horse threw him.'

'Do you have other brothers and sisters?'

'An older brother, Jeffery, who is gone to sea on the *Mary Rose*,' she told him proudly, 'and Abigail my sister, now gone to her betrothed at Rochester.'

'And so today you are all alone.'

She nodded. 'Except for Thomas, our steward, and Mama and Izzie and Nan, the new maid, and –'

He laughed. 'How can you be alone with such a company?'

She laughed with him. 'Oh, and Papa when he returns. He's on pilgrimage.' A slight frown crossed her face at the memory of her father's sudden departure but he was watching the river and missed the change of expression.

'Hush!' he whispered. 'Look there, further down. A kingfisher!'

'Where? I see nothing.'

'Beyond the bridge – ah, too late.'

Her face was woebegone and he glimpsed for a moment the child that remained in the young woman's body. 'I've never seen a kingfisher,' she told him.

'Then I'll snare you one.'

'Oh no! Never, I beg you.'

She was instantly distressed and he hastened to reassure her. 'I have no one,' he said, to change the subject. 'No father, mother or kin.'

'All dead?' She stared at him, her soft heart touched.

He nodded.

'But what do you do?' she asked. 'How do you live?'

'I work at the bakery and have lodgings there. They are kindly folk.'

'Then why are you sitting in the sunshine,' she

234

teased, 'and not kneading your dough?'

He flicked a grasshopper from her skirt and the slight touch of his hand against her leg thrilled her. 'I'm on my way to the mill,' he said, 'I came the long way round in hopes of seeing you.'

'Oh!'

Her initial nervousness returned and seeing it, Simon regretted his remark. 'I must go,' he said, rising easily in one lithe movement. As he stood looking down at her, his blond head silhouetted against the blue sky, Melissa thought she had never seen so handsome a youth. She scrambled up to stand beside him.

'Shall you – shall you be this way again?' she whispered.

'Indeed I shall,' he said 'for here, at this moment, the view is quite perfect.' She watched him go with a mixture of relief and regret. It was only then that she realized she still wore the shell necklace and also that she didn't know his name.

'Nan! Where are you?' cried Melissa. 'Nan!' Guiltily, Nan put her head round the stable door and Melissa stared at her in astonishment. 'What are you up to? I've been searching the garden for you. Izzie said you were gathering lavender.'

'I will be, ma'am,' cried Nan, 'but I found this apple and thought I would give it the mare. Jack said I could and it won't do no harm to –'

'You're chattering like a starling,' Melissa reproved her. 'Give her the apple and make haste. You are to ride with me into town.'

'Ride with you?' Nan's mouth fell open with surprise and alarm. She had never ridden before and was not sure she wanted to. 'But why ma'am? Where are we going?'

'I've just told you,' said Melissa. 'Into Ashburton, so

hurry, girl and don't ask questions,' she added seeing the words form on the maid's lips. She turned away to saddle the old cob. As she tightened the buckle she turned to Nan who waited anxiously beside her. 'You shall have my wooden trinket box but you are to say nothing.'

'But ma'am, Izzie will flay me alive if –'

'I have told Izzie you are to come with me.'

'But the mistress –'

'Mama won't miss you. She is gone over to Maudesley and will be away all day. Stop arguing. Here, give me your hand.'

After several unsuccessful attempts Nan finally found herself astride the cob and clinging to Melissa. She closed her eyes as Melissa urged the horse into a trot and they rode out of the yard and on to the highway.

'You are squeezing the life out of me,' Melissa complained. 'You won't fall, Nan. Hold me less tightly I beg you. I can scarcely draw breath!'

The girl relaxed her grip a little and squinted cautiously, as though by opening her eyes fully she would be more aware of her danger and more likely to fall off.

'But where are we going?' she asked again. 'Ooh, 'tis shaking my stomach something terrible. Should I not walk alongside?'

'Certainly not.'

'But I feel poorly ma'am. I swear it.'

Melissa laughed. 'You'll get used to it, Nan. I warrant you have your eyes shut. Open them and look about you. See, there's a coney in the bracken.'

'I daresn't!'

'Then you must bear with your queasy stomach. Only don't prattle so for I've an important matter to think on.'

'Important, ma'am?' echoed Nan, intrigued in spite of her discomfort. 'What way important, ma'am?'

'Private matters,' said Melissa 'and not for your ears.

236

Now, cease your chatter and let me think. We shall be there shortly.'

They rode the rest of the way in silence and soon reached the outskirts of the town which was already thronged with people busy about the day's business.

'Keep your eyes peeled,' said Melissa. 'We are looking for a baker's shop or maybe a cookhouse.'

'A baker's?' cried Nan. 'A cookhouse?'

Melissa rolled her eyes despairingly but almost immediately they came to a small bakery. The long shutter was already hinged outward and propped to form a counter. Melissa took a coin from her purse and slid to the ground.

'Don't leave me ma'am!' screamed Nan, appalled to find herself in sole charge of the old horse, but Melissa had walked to the counter and now rapped on it for attention. A large coarse-faced woman waddled to serve her; Melissa hid her disappointment.

'One of your veal pasties,' she said and received it, still warm, into her outstretched hand. She paid for it and went back to Nan.

'Eat this,' she told her.

'Eat it?' cried Nan.

'What else?' said Melissa somewhat sharply, but it was no time to be upbraiding the girl for her annoying habit. While Nan bit into the delicious pasty Melissa led the horse with its rider along the street, side-stepping the worst of the rubbish. Fortunately they had had no recent rain so the cobbles were not slippery but the midsummer heat increased the smell of rotting garbage and slops. They stopped at a small dirty-looking cookhouse where Melissa once more abandoned Nan to peer in at the door. An elderly man thrust his scarred face into hers.

'Well?' he demanded. 'What's it to be then? I haven't got all day.'

She recoiled hastily. 'Er – an apple turnover,' she suggested.

'Not until later.'

'A tart, then,' she said. 'A jam tart.'

'Only one?'

'Two,' she said and was shortly handing up two rather stale tarts to the astonished maid who had just swallowed the last of the veal pasty.

'But ma'am –' she began but was silenced by Melissa's expression.

Fortunately for her digestion, the third establishment was the one Melissa had been looking for. A young woman smiled at her inquiringly and Melissa glanced at her hand to see if she wore a wedding ring. The fingers were bare. Looking past her, Melissa could see into the bakery itself. An old man in a large apron sat on a chair, talking to someone who was out of sight.

'Two pies,' said Melissa craning her neck to see into the bakery. Someone whistled cheerfully and stopped to laugh at something the old man said. Melissa's heart pounded. It was the young man! She was sure of it.

'Mutton pie, veal pie, mince pie, vegetable pie – which is it?'

The girl was waiting, looking at her strangely. Melissa stared at her blankly. 'Which?' repeated the girl, indicating a selection of trays behind her. 'Mutton, veal, mince –'

'Oh,' said Melissa, 'the mutton pies, please. Two of them.'

As she was fumbling for the money Simon came to the doorway to speak to Maggie and saw Melissa. His words faltered and died as their eyes met fleetingly then instinctively both turned away. Melissa felt her cheeks burn. She threw down the money, snatched up the pies and ran across the road, narrowly avoiding being run down by a wagon loaded with turf.

'Take these,' said Melissa thrusting the two mutton pies into Nan's astonished hands. She mounted, snatched up the reins and urged the horse forward, her thoughts chaotic. She had seen him! He was as handsome as she remembered!

'Ma'am,' inquired Nan. 'What am I to do with these two?'

'Eat them,' said Melissa.

'But ma'am, aren't you having one?'

'No,' said Melissa. She turned a radiant face towards the little maid. 'You need fattening up so eat your fill.'

'I dunno as I can,' she protested. 'I'm that full already,' but she obediently bit into the first pie and was half way through the second before she realized they were on the way home. 'Why ma'am,' she cried. 'I thought we was going somewhere on important business.'

'That's right,' said Melissa.

'But all we've done is buy pies and such like.'

'That's right,' said Melissa and she began to laugh. When she had finished laughing, she began to sing. Not another word could Nan coax out of her and she rode home behind her young mistress in a state of great bewilderment.

The chance friendship continued through July and into August, sustaining a rare quality of innocence. Simon was attracted by Melissa the child-woman who could still delight in a daisy chain and who would ride in search of him like a naughty child seeking forbidden sweetmeats. For her part, she marvelled at Simon's physical beauty – the slim body and well-shaped limbs and head – as she would wonder at a flower or butterfly. If somewhere deep inside her the female cried out for the male, she was unaware of it. For her he was both lost sister and dead brother. A secret companion. For many weeks there was no hint of love, no sign of passion.

Luke returned from his pilgrimage exhausted but spiritually refreshed. He had confessed everything and had received absolution. The past was a closed chapter. Alison was delighted at the change in him and, welcoming it, put all doubts and questions from her mind with a resolution that in her younger days would have been impossible. Husband and wife were united as they never had been before. With only Melissa still at home, Alison was freer to devote herself to Luke's happiness and her joy showed in her eyes. They were so involved with each other that it was left to Thomas Benet to notice Melissa's frequent absences and to wonder at it. Over the years she had spent a great deal of time in his company, finding a sympathetic friend in the shy man, entrusting him with her confidences. Now he sensed a withdrawal on her part but, ignorant of the ways of women, he attributed it to the fact that she was no longer a child and had less need of his support.

The summer unrolled its long golden days, the crops ripened in the fields and in London the birth of the Queen's child drew near. Luke and Alison had decided to accept Adam and Abigail's offer of hospitality and plans were made for their journey to Rochester. Melissa declined to accompany them, and would stay at Heron with Thomas Benet and the servants. Letters were written, plans were made and Heron and the rest of England waited on the safe delivery of Henry VIII's third child.

CHAPTER THIRTEEN

The Queen's lying-in took place at Hampton Court where, in the afternoon of 9 October, she went into labour. The usual prayers for a speedy and safe delivery went unanswered and a prolonged and difficult labour lasted for three days and two nights. Luke and Alison had started their journey on the 10th and arrived in Rochester at two o'clock in the afternoon of 12 October, exactly twelve hours after the birth of Henry Tudor's son. The child, normal and in good health, meant that England at last had a legitimate male heir to the throne. The whole country went wild with delight. The highways leading to Hampton Court were thronged with riders. Royal messengers were despatched to carry the glad tidings the length and breadth of England and loyal messages of congratulations poured into the palace from every quarter both at home and abroad.

'Oh, the bells!' Abigail told them. 'They began to ring at eight o'clock this morning as soon as the news reached London. Each church trying to outring the others and they say in London two thousand rounds were fired from the Tower guns. Two thousand! Here the streets were suddenly full of people. Everyone ran outside to cheer and shake the hands of neighbours and kiss their kin folk – strangers, too. Adam was quite overcome with it all, weren't you dear?'

He grinned amiably. 'Even the old biddy from across

the way thumped me on the back,' he said, 'and that from one as can't abide me, nor my father, neither. Beside herself she was, poor old soul. Quite beside herself.'

'Been at the wine I'll wager,' said Abigail. 'Reeked of it she did and could scarcely stand!'

'I warrant she won't be the only woman in London drunk for joy,' said Luke as he raised his own glass. 'To our new Prince, God bless him!'

All four raised their glasses and sipped the fine madeira which Adam had chosen for the toast. They sat in the neat parlour in the tall house behind the boat yard. From the window they looked out over the river where every boat fluttered brilliantly as flags, and yards of bunting, were hoisted to celebrate the glad tidings and set the calm brown water aglow with colour. Adam's mother and father had travelled to London the previous day to stay with relations, leaving Adam and Abigail to wait for Luke and Alison.

'And we had such a journey!' said Alison. 'Everyone that we met must raise his hat and exclaim for the new Prince and King Henry and halloo for England and St George. Why, I believe had we fallen among thieves they would have robbed us cheerfully and spared our lives in honour of the greatness of the occasion!'

'The King is a happy man at last,' said Luke, 'and I feel for him. The man has had his share of misfortunes.'

'All this talk, Mama, of the Prince and the King!' cried Abigail. 'What of our brave Queen Jane? Does no one spare a thought for her? Three days in labour, poor wretch, and scarcely a mention.'

'She's done her duty,' said Adam. 'No more, no less.'

'Her duty!' cried Alison, rallying to Abigail's cause. 'A fine kettle of fish when a woman must risk her life to bear her husband a son and earns scarcely a "thank you" for her pains! I trust you won't treat your own wife's efforts so lightly, Adam, or Abigail will have plenty to say on the subject.'

Adam rolled his eyes in mock horror and Abigail gave him a loving look. 'He would not,' she said loyally.

'Or dare not!' said Luke behind his hand. 'But how is our daughter treating you, Adam? Does she promise well, do you think?'

He pretended to consider. 'She has not disappointed me so far,' he offered, 'though her apple tart was sadly wanting.'

'I forgot the cloves,' admitted Abigail.

'This shirt is her handiwork,' Adam went on, displaying it, 'and as you see is adequate. A hole for my head and a sleeve for each arm –'

'Oh, you impossible man!' shrieked Abigail. 'I have stitched my fingers sore these last two weeks and you make mock of all my efforts.'

Playfully, she tried to box his ears but he caught her wrists and pulled her gently towards him. 'I tease you but I love you,' he confessed.

'You do,' she whispered, 'and I know it.'

Lightly he kissed her on the tip of her nose then put aside such romantic notions. 'But now that our visitors are rested and refreshed, I think we should make all haste to London for the evening festivities. What do you say? Shall we join the rest of London in their merry-making?'

A chorus of 'Ayes' settled the matter and very shortly all four were dressed warmly and on their way to the capital.

It grew dark early and a chill wind blew but no one complained. They reached the outskirts of the town and left their horses at an inn where they would sleep later in a large communal bedchamber. It did not matter that the room was overcrowded and smelt of stale rushes. They were fortunate to find anywhere at so little notice and were thankful to know that if nothing else, a mattress and a threadbare blanket awaited their eventual return.

Once in the heart of London, they found the streets crowded with hysterical people in varying states of inebriation; little wonder, for wine and ale flowed in the street conduits and was free to all. Bonfires blazed on the street corners, each one surrounded by throngs of revellers, dancing and singing. People clung together, afraid of being separated by the press of people who roamed the narrow cobbled streets in search of fun and adventure. The mood was ecstatic and expansive. For some it was also expensive for pickpockets and tricksters of all kinds mingled with the crowds and grew rich on their carelessness. Occasionally a cry went up – 'Thief! Stop him!' but the merrymakers were loath to take action, lulled into a state of blissful euphoria.

'That bonfire!' Alison marvelled. ''Tis big enough to burn down the whole street if the wind changes. A few sparks are all that's needed.'

Even as she spoke, the tenant in the nearest house closed her shutters to with a clatter while downstairs her husband barred the windows against thieves and he and his wife prepared to leave the precarious safety of their home to join the rest of the populace in the streets. Ahead of them the bonfires sent a stream of sparks into the darkness overhead and lit up the faces of the crowd. A handful of chestnuts flung into the fire began to burst and splutter so that those nearest the blaze jumped back, stumbling backwards on to others and in no time at all there was a sprawling, giggling heap of people, their faces glowing in the firelight, their mouths open in laughter, their arms and legs waving in deliberate and exaggerated confusion. Like a scene from hell, thought Luke, strangely fascinated by the sight.

'I'd sooner avoid that unruly mob,' laughed Adam and they turned along an alley into the next street where a group of street musicians played – three fiddlers and a drummer. Another held out song sheets of a ballad newly written for the occasion.

'Buy a song for the young Prince! Sing of England's glory! Buy a song, now! You'll find none better in the whole of London – thank you, sir. A memento of a glorious day! Sing a song, now. Thank you, ma'am –'

A hogshead of wine had been set up on a trestle table – the gift of a rich man to the poor. Round it a group of men swayed cheerfully, supporting themselves and each other as best they could as they tried to read from one of the song sheets in the light of a torch which wavered in the breeze and occasionally spat tar over them. One of them glanced up and saw Alison. 'Ah, beautiful lady!' he cried. 'A kiss for a happy man, eh? One kiss will make me even happier! Look there, at the beautiful lady. One kiss, eh?' She shook her head, embarrassed but secretly flattered, and Luke tightened his grip on her waist.

'I see I must guard you from such fellows,' he whispered. ''Twould be a fine thing to gain a prince but lose a wife! Stay close, I beg you!'

She was only too pleased to do so as they made their way through the streets towards the Thames. It flowed darkly under London Bridge yet reflected a thousand flickering torches along its banks. The watermen did a roaring trade ferrying merrymakers to and fro and cursed less than usual in honour of the new Prince.

'I swear they are all cup shotten,' said Adam. 'See that – straight into the oncoming boat!'

'The passengers are too drunk to care,' laughed Abigail, 'or they would not be so brave. Don't ask me to set foot in one for I value my life too highly.'

A nearby peal of bells drowned Adam's reply and a

passing horse reared nervously, almost throwing his rider to the ground. Luke reached up and caught at the bridle, speaking soothingly to the animal until the rider regained control.

'My thanks to you sir,' he said. 'God bless England and the new Prince!'

'God bless the new Prince!' echoed Luke and the cry was suddenly taken up on all sides in a great roar of patriotic fervour.

'God bless the new Prince!'

'Well, God bless the new Prince,' said Thomas.

'God bless the little lad,' said Izzie as they all raised their mugs and sipped ale. The bonfire crackled and the smell of woodsmoke carried the promise of baked parsnips. The flames lit up the river where it flowed past Heron. From the shelter of the wood Melissa watched wistfully. 'There's Jack,' she whispered, 'he's the stableman, and beside him that's Nan, one of the maids and Jon who works in the garden and helps Jack.'

'And the round lardy one?' laughed Simon.

'Oh, poor Izzie,' said Melissa. 'She's so big now she can scarce waddle. 'Tis dropsy and there's nought to be done, the doctor says. Oh, there's Thomas. Thomas Benet, the steward, see him, very tall, refilling his mug. Oh can you smell parsnips? It makes my mouth water.'

'Are you hungry?'

'A little. I ate so sparingly at supper with thinking about you and wondering if I would be able to see you. And Nancy is there, the cook from Maudesley, and their gardener Harry and Bessie –' She shivered suddenly in the cold air and he tightened his arm round her shoulders.

'Are you warm enough?' he asked. ''Twould be a poor joke to pretend a chill and then catch one in earnest.'

'So it would,' she agreed, 'but I am not so cold.' She shivered again, admitting only to herself that it was nervousness that shook her.

'Then do you wish yourself beside the fire,' he asked gently, 'with a mug of hot ale?'

'I would rather be here with you holding your hand,' she said. 'And you – would you not rather be in Ashburton, watching the pageant?'

'I want to be with you,' he told her.

They looked at each other in the darkness. The night was cloudy and there was little light.

'Simon,' she said slowly. ''Tis bad news – for me. All England rejoices but I must mourn.'

'Your betrothal?' he asked.

'Aye. A cousin of the Adam who is wed to my sister. Papa hopes to discuss it while they are in Rochester.'

He was silent and she looked at him anxiously. 'Tell me you care,' she whispered.

'I care most deeply,' he said. 'I can't imagine life without you although we have only known each other these past few months. How certain is it, this betrothal?'

She shrugged helplessly. 'They will know more on their return,' she said.

'What will you say?'

'I don't know. It frightens me, Simon, to leave Heron and live among strangers.'

'But you must wed some day. A woman cannot live alone.'

'What will you do, Simon?' she asked. 'Will you wed?'

'I dare say – Maggie the baker's daughter is a willing lass and would have me. She served you when you came into the shop.'

'With dark tumbled curls?'

'Aye.'

'I recall . . . I wish –' She stopped, confused.

'You wish?' he prompted gently.

'I wish I were like Maggie, to wed wherever my heart takes me.'

They were both silent and then Simon sighed. 'I wish you were,' he said 'for then I would ask for your hand and we would –'

'Oh Simon!' Impulsively she threw her arms round his neck and hugged him. As his arms tightened round her, she felt the pounding in his chest that was a wild heartbeat.

'Melissa!' he whispered. 'My funny little Lissa!'

'Why funny, Simon?'

'You are such a child still,' he said gently.

Invisible, they stood in the darkness staring across the river to the celebratory bonfire and the people who clustered round it, safe in its warmth and visible in its light.

'I feel shut out,' said Melissa. 'Like an angel locked out of heaven. Why is it?'

'I don't know,' he said. 'I wish I did. I wish I knew what to say to you. What to suggest for you. I want to help you but I cannot. You're Melissa Kendal, of Heron. I'm Simon Betts of nowhere. A nothing.'

'Don't speak like that!' She was shocked.

'I love you, Lissa.'

'What is love, Simon? Do you know?'

'Love is what I feel for you.'

She smiled faintly so that her teeth showed palely in the darkness. 'And what is that?' she asked.

Simon hesitated, searching for a way to express his feelings for her. 'A need to be near you,' he said, 'and a desire for your happiness . . . a feeling that we belong together.'

'Oh – and do you feel those things for anyone else? For Maggie?'

'No-o, not in the same way. Maggie is fun to be with, but I don't feel this bond.' He shrugged again and sighed. 'I'm not saying what I want to say,' he said. 'I can't put it into words.'

'No matter,' she said. 'Do I love you, I wonder? Is it love to consider you beautiful?.' He laughed but she put a finger over his lips to silence him, 'to find life empty without you and, after so short a time, to trust you with my life? Is that love, Simon, for if 'tis, why then I love you.'

There were signs from across the river that the party was breaking up. The bonfire had faded from bright red to dull orange. The parsnips were eaten, the cask of ale empty. The Maudesley staff were making their farewells and Beth and Nan were struggling to pull Izzie into an upright position while her weight and an excess of ale combined to resist their efforts.

'I must go,' cried Melissa. 'Izzie may look into my bedchamber to see that I sleep comfortably. She has done so since I was a child.'

'But how will you cross on the stones?' he asked. 'In the light of the fire you'll be seen.'

'Oh dear!' She looked round in agitation. 'Upstream a little, where 'tis shallower. I must wade through.'

'Indeed you shan't!' cried Simon. 'Show me where 'tis shallower and I will carry you.'

He would listen to no arguments and she led him twenty yards upstream. 'Here,' she told him. ''Tis very level without hidden rocks.'

He swung her up into his arms. 'I'll shut my eyes,' she said, 'then I shan't see if you drop me!'

It was level as she had told him but the October rains had started and the current was considerable. But he carried her safely across and stepped up on the far bank. Before setting her on her feet again he kissed her lightly. 'Make haste to your chamber,' he said 'and sleep well.'

'When shall I see you again?' she asked.

'Tomorrow, God willing, at the usual time.'

'Take care, Simon.'

'I will. Now be off with you for I shan't recross the river until you are gone in.'

He watched her go, then waded back across the icy river. He ran all the way to the bakery. He climbed up the old pear tree and in at the window as quietly as he could. But Maggie lay wide awake in the room below, her eyes red with weeping.

Henry's son was named Edward and christened in the chapel of Hampton Court. Archbishop Cranmer was one of his godfathers, as were the Dukes of Suffolk and Norfolk. His godmother was Henry's daughter Mary and Elizabeth, only four years old, was also present. It was a sumptuous affair lasting nearly six hours throughout which the radiant Queen, propped up and wrapped in furs, received a succession of important guests. A few days later she sickened with a fever and no one could save her. She died on 24 October and was buried at Windsor in St George's Chapel.

'So now England must mourn,' said Luke. 'What times we live in, eh Thomas? Poor Alison wept when she heard.'

'She has a soft heart,' said Thomas.

'Aye. First it was poor Jane and now the motherless babe.'

He signed the two papers in front of him, sanded them and handed them to Thomas. At that moment, Nan appeared in the doorway, her eyes gleaming with excitement. 'There's a woman to see you,' she told Luke. 'She's in the kitchen.'

'A woman?' he said, surprised. 'What does she want?'

'She won't say,' said Nan indignantly, 'though Izzie gave her a few sharp words and threatened to send her packing. Not even her name! Just shakes her head and says she must speak with you alone else 'twill be your loss.'

'Send her to me then, Nan,' he said, 'and ask Izzie to send up a glass of hot wine and honey to your mistress. She's still distressed by the news and it might comfort her.'

Nan went away and Luke frowned. 'What can she want with me?' he muttered.

'I'll go,' said Thomas but Luke held up his hand. 'There's no need,' he said. 'She can have nothing to say which my steward cannot hear.'

They looked round as Nan came into the room with Maggie, who had brushed her hair and wore a dress of coarse blue cloth. Her manner was at once fearful and defiant and the two men looked at her curiously.

'I'll not say a word while he's here,' she began pointing accusingly at Luke.

'But that's the master,' said Nan, enjoying her error. 'The other's Master Benet and Izzie says you're to mind your manners.'

Maggie rounded on her angrily. 'Nor a word in front of her,' she said. 'And you'd best hear what I've got to tell you.'

She stared at Luke and he felt a prickle of unease at the girl's confidence. He dismissed Nan with a wave of his hand and turned apologetically to Thomas who nodded. 'The girl shall have her way,' he said. 'I'll come back later to finish our business.'

When he had gone Luke looked at Maggie. 'Well?' he said.

Maggie took a deep breath and then the words came in a rush. ''Tis your daughter Melissa as is meeting secretly with a base-born lad – not once but many times.'

'Melissa?'

'Aye, you may look surprised,' she cried, 'and her acting fey all these years like she would never grow up. Well, she's grown up now right enough and 'tis the truth I'm telling you for I've seen them with my own eyes.'

'I don't believe it,' said Luke, his composure shaken by the girl's conviction. 'Who is this lad – and where do they meet?'

A cunning look came into her eyes. 'Now that would be telling,' she said. 'That would be worth knowing, wouldn't it? I warrant you'd like to know who 'tis as is stealing kisses from –' Luke's hand struck her across the face and she stumbled back, cursing.

'I'll have no disrespectful talk of my daughter,' he warned her, 'so watch your tongue!'

'I'll maybe hold it altogether,' she began but he struck at her again and she put up a hand defensively and fell silent. With an effort Luke controlled his anger. 'I must know what you have to tell me,' he said, 'and I shall take measures to discover if 'tis true or not. If false, you will find yourself in the stocks and lucky to escape a whipping. Now tell me what you know, girl.'

'I've told you,' she muttered sullenly. 'Your daughter has a – an admirer.'

'And his name?'

'Maybe I don't know it,' she said.

Luke took her by the shoulders and shook her. 'I've warned you,' he cried. 'Don't try my patience for I have none where my daughter's honour is concerned. What is his name, this lad you speak of?'

'Simon.'

'He has another name?' Luke's voice trembled slightly.

'I don't recall,' she said but as Luke's fingers bit into her arm she added hastily, 'Betts, maybe. Aye, that's it – Betts.'

He released her arm and turned away to hide his consternation. Isobel's son! His own son – and his own daughter! Maggie stared at him as he lowered himself on to a stool, visibly distressed and with all the colour gone from his face. 'Dear God!' he whispered again and again. 'Dear God, help me!'

Unnerved by the effect of her words, Maggie edged towards the door, intent on escape. 'Wait!' he said hoarsely. 'We must speak further.'

'No!' she cried. 'I've nothing more to say.'

'You know this Simon Betts?'

'Aye. He works for my father in the bakery.'

He was recovering and she waited. 'Who else knows of the friendship?' he asked.

'None I'd reckon. They're clever and meet where none can see them. Day after day and night times.'

'Nights?' He was horrified. 'Nights, d'you say?'

'Maybe not nights,' she admitted, 'but after dusk.'

Luke put a hand to his head as though the revelation wearied him, as indeed it did. The shock had drained his energy and his heart was behaving strangely. 'I must see the lad,' he told her. ''Tis most urgent. Tell him to come here – no wait. Let me consider.'

'He won't do as I say,' said Maggie. 'If you want to see him you must come to him.'

'Then you must arrange a meeting between us, without his knowledge. I'll pay you well. See here. Take this in part payment and there'll be more.'

She gasped at the florin he offered and took it wonderingly.

'I leave it to you,' he said. 'Let me know where I am to meet him. And not a word to anyone on pain of my severest displeasure.'

'You can rely on me,' she said. 'I'll arrange a meeting.'

'And with all haste, girl. Bring me word. Come to the

253

kitchen. I'll tell Izzie to let you in. Now go and let me think on it.'

She fled thankfully; from the window he watched her running through the garden towards the river. 'Melissa and Simon!' he whispered then turned as Thomas, seeing her departure, came back into the room.

'I cannot work with you now, Thomas,' he said. 'I have had bad tidings which I must keep to myself for the present.'

'Bad tidings?' said Thomas.

'Aye. Most damnable tidings.' He sighed and rubbed his eyes tiredly. 'My life, Thomas, has been a series of bad tidings! Misfortune is my constant companion.' There was an attempt at lightness in his tone but Thomas saw the despair in his eyes and wondered at the nature of his latest problem, and hoped it would not mean further grief for Alison.

The last day of October was All Hallows' Eve and found preparations in progress for the night's activities. Beth was running to and fro between the pump and the kitchen table where a large wooden tub was gradually filling with water. A whole evening of unalloyed pleasure stretched before them for the family, taking Nan with them, had gone across to Maudesley to share the excitement with Jo and his family.

'Did you see Melissa?' Beth asked Jon.

'Aye. I saw them all, I tell you,' he said, busily cutting a face in a large turnip.

'Then what's she going as?' Beth insisted.

'A ghost, I reckon. She was all in white – sort of tatters.'

'Tatters?' She stood waiting, the empty pitcher on her hip.

'Aye. And Benet has gone as a devil, all in red with horns.'

'A devil! Oh I wish I'd seen them for meself. I've been keeping an eye open for them for hours.' She flounced out into the yard but was soon back again with another full pitcher.

'How's that?' asked Jon, holding up the turnip for her approval. 'Fierce enough for you, is it?'

''Tis fair enough,' she said. 'I like the sharp teeth. Aye, 'tis good. But where's the candle stub?'

'All in good time,' said Jon. 'I've got a few hid away but first I'll make another two faces. Three will give us enough light.'

'I wish we was going to Maudesley,' said Beth. 'Izzie says when she was a girl everyone was invited and there was a troupe of play-actors with dogs that did tricks, and a juggler.'

'We'll have more fun here,' said Jon. 'You hurry up with that water – a couple more will be enough. Then fetch the apples –' Beth grumbled but removed herself.

As she went out Jack came in with an armful of logs which he stacked against the hearth. 'I reckon the sky's just right for a witch's ride,' he told them, lowering his voice dramatically. 'A clear moon and a few clouds! The goblins are watching, little eyes everywhere! And the owls are hooting already. 'Tis a sure sign of evil, when the owls hoot.'

'Ooh don't!' cried Beth. ''Tis me who has to keep trotting out into the yard for this dratted water.'

'Then don't let the goblins even see the whites of your eyes,' he teased and she screamed and threw down the pitcher and refused to go outside again.

Izzie waddled in, a great mountain of a woman, bloated with dropsy. 'Pick that up at once and none of your tantrums,' she told Beth as she sank on to a stool, breathless, 'just 'cos 'tis Hallowe'en there's no call for everyone to neglect their work. Stoke up that fire, Jack, it's raw tonight and the cold's getting into my bones –

and put the wine on to mull and grate the nutmeg into it. There's a half left and don't grate your finger this time.'

Beth tipped an apron full of chestnuts on to the table and began to grate the nutmeg, 'And what of the mistress?' she asked.

'She's gone as a witch with a pointed hat and green fingernails.'

'Green! Ugh!' said Izzie. 'And a right unlucky colour green.' She turned to Jack. 'Ready for the nut-cracking are you?' she demanded.

'Nut-cracking?' said Jack. 'What's that, may I ask?'

'Why, to tell if your lover be true or false,' said Izzie, 'you choose a chestnut and set it by the fire to roast. If it roasts neatly, why then you've nought to worry about.

'And if it don't roast neat?'

'If it bursts or rolls away then your lover's unfaithful,' she told him.

'I haven't got a lover,' said Beth.

'How about me?' said Jon, grinning. 'I'll be your lover if you fancy me. I'm a man and a half – feel these muscles.' He raised his arm, clenching his fist to tense his bicep, and Beth shrieked. 'Call them muscles!' she cried. 'Why they're no bigger than the chestnuts!' and she laughed at his pretended dismay.

At last all the preparations were completed. The three hollow turnips were lit and hung from a beam and the apples floated in readiness in the tub.

'Right,' said Izzie, taking charge from her 'throne' at the end of the table. 'We're all ready. Gather round the table and we'll say the rhyme.'

They all closed their eyes and muttered the incantation.

> 'The thirty-first be full of woe
> Answer "aye" or answer "noe".

Flying fiend and evil eye
Wait upon you ere you die.
Devil's King and hellions Queen
Banished be from this our Hallowe'en.'

They all reached forward, dipped a forefinger in the tub and, turning to their right, 'anointed' their neighbour with the sign of the cross. Beth gave a little shudder.

'Oh, it's scary,' she said. 'I'm going all goosey.'

They watched in silence as Jack blew out the first turnip-light. By the light of the remaining two they took it in turn to bob for the apples. With hands tied behind their backs they leaned over the tub and tried to seize an apple in their teeth. It was harder than it looked, causing great hilarity and not a few wet chins and noses.

'Go on Jack!' screeched Beth. 'You have it – ah, no 'tis gone again. Try for a smaller one that you can get your teeth round.'

'He's got a big enough mouth,' said Jon. 'He should be bobbing for pumpkins!'

As soon as Jack had caught his apple he offered it to Izzie who, twisting her neck, managed to take a bite from it. Then it was Jon's turn.

'I'll tie your hands,' cried Beth 'then there'll be no cheating. Now let's see how clever you are, Master Jon.'

Jon reached forward, his mouth open, but his nose touched the apple, sending it spinning slowly away across the tub.

'Let me help you, my duck!' cried Beth and she pushed his head under the water amid shrieks of laughter from Izzie and a protest from Jack. Jon emerged spluttering and blinking the water from his eyes.

'Ooh, your chin's all wet!' she said innocently. 'Dribbling at your age. You should be ashamed!' and ran screaming to escape his wrath.

Then Izzie produced wine, cinnamon biscuits and baked apples stuffed with currants and the four of them sat in the firelight telling ghost stories until the midnight bells were heard. The first of November had arrived and it was safe to go to their respective beds.

CHAPTER FOURTEEN

They met in a wood. Simon came on foot; seeing the man on horseback, he walked straight up to him. Luke looked down into his face for a few moments without speaking.

'Your mother would have been proud of you,' he said at last.

It was the last thing Simon expected to hear. 'My mother?'

'Your real mother,' said Luke. 'You have the look of her, about the mouth and jaw – and something in your voice . . .'

'You knew my real mother?'

'Aye and wronged her grievously. I had to talk to you. There is much to be said.'

A suspicion sprang into Simon's mind. 'What of my real father?' he asked. 'Do you know him also?'

'You're *my* son.'

Hardly a flicker crossed Simon's face. 'Your bastard son!' he said with no trace of bitterness. 'A bastard Kendal, is that it?'

Luke nodded. The whole truth would put his family at risk. The boy must share the same illusions as Alison.

'I'm sorry,' said Luke but Simon laughed harshly.

'Don't be,' he said. 'To be a bastard Kendal is better than to be nobody.'

'You have a right to feel bitter,' said Luke.

'I'm not –' Simon stopped in mid-sentence. 'God's wounds! Then Melissa –'

'Your half-sister.'

'No! I don't want to hear it!'

Luke nodded. It was much harder than he had anticipated because he liked the boy. He was drawn to this son that Isobel had given him.

Simon's face was haggard. 'Now I know why you must see me so urgently,' he said, 'and Maggie has done this to hurt me.'

'She didn't know,' said Luke. 'Not everything. She knew only of your liaison, not the relationship.'

'Dear God! What a betrayal!'

'I want you to know –' Luke began.

'– that you're sorry, is that it?' said Simon. Anger replaced the hurt in his eyes and they blazed suddenly against the pallor of his face. 'Sorry that I am born out of wedlock and sorry that I may not have your daughter for my wife! You are sorry!'

'You surely never hoped to wed her!' cried Luke.

Simon shook his head. 'Desired it most passionately,' he whispered, 'but no, I never presumed to hope.'

'I wish it were otherwise,' said Luke.

'Have you told Melissa?'

'Not yet but I will. Poor child!'

Simon smiled faintly. 'She is not a child,' he said. 'Not a woman yet, 'tis true, but on the brink of it. Don't look at me that way. I read the question in your eyes and the answer is no. Melissa is a virgin still.'

Luke could only nod his head.

'I should like to tell her,' said Simon.

Luke would not hear of it. 'You must go away,' he said, 'right away. I will provide for you; you shall learn to read and write; a good position with a good family. If you truly love Melissa, do as I ask and leave Ashburton. Go away and make a new life. She can never be your wife, Simon, but you will find another woman to share your future.'

For a moment Simon bowed his head then he looked up at Luke. 'You talk so glibly,' said Simon. 'You don't begin to understand my feelings.' He paused. 'I will leave tomorrow morning,' he went on. 'My few possessions are soon packed. You will bring a name or an address?'

'And a mount,' said Luke. 'You shall have a horse and this ring. Take it. It was your grandfather's.'

'My grandfather!' Simon looked at it wonderingly. A gold ring heavily inscribed and set with a garnet.

'Until tomorrow then,' said Luke. He was already turning his horse when Simon stopped him with outstretched arms.

'My mother!' he cried. 'Who was my mother?'

There was a terrible silence. 'Your mother was a very beautiful woman,' Luke said finally, 'and I loved her. Lately she tried to find you but now she's dead. Don't ask me her name, Simon.'

''Twas Gillis, wasn't it?' Simon's voice was very level. 'Isobel Gillis, daughter of Marion.'

'How did you know?'

'Tongues wag,' said Simon. 'Rumours fly like birds! I went in search of her once, to discover the truth. Her father said she was mad and gone to be cured.'

'He spoke the truth,' said Luke. 'I took her to the holy well at St Cleer. Until tomorrow then,' he repeated and slapped the horse's rump. Simon watched him until he disappeared among the trees then made his own way home.

Luke was waiting with the newly purchased horse, a chestnut cob with good legs and a sturdy frame.

'But a wild look in his eye,' Luke warned Simon as the

latter inspected the animal. 'You don't want them timid or they'll shy at the sight of a rabbit, nor too independent. This one promises well and has stamina.'

'My thanks,' said Simon briefly. He slung his pack on to the saddle and lashed it with cord. His possessions were few – a change of clothes, a wooden bowl and mug and a flute which he played indifferently. When the pack was secure, Luke handed him a roughly drawn map.

'The name of a man where you will lodge,' he told Simon. 'An acquaintance of mine who knows nothing of our relationship. He has frequently asked if I will look out for an honest lad and now I send you.'

Simon nodded and glanced at the map.

''Tis Porthleven in Cornwall,' said Luke. 'The man, Wicklow, is a ship owner.'

Simon smiled faintly. 'Am I to be a sailor, then?' he asked.

'No, no,' said Luke. 'A clerk with prospects. You will work in the office once you can read and write. Until then, and while you are learning, you will do general work, loading and unloading the ships, and preparing them for sea again. You will learn the trade thoroughly. I have told Wicklow you are a good cheerful worker as I believe you are.'

'My thanks,' said Simon. 'I have a question.'

'Ask it.'

'About my mother. Was she truly mad as they say?'

'No. I think 'twas the shock of your birth and my desertion. Later she recovered her wits and was as you or I. You have my word on it.'

'I see.'

'Here is money,' said Luke, putting a leather purse into Simon's hand, 'and here is the name of a tutor. Wicklow will tell you where he lives. I don't know the address, only that he is the best in the area. With your permission, I shall visit you from time to time and if you need further help you can send to me secretly.'

Simon nodded, adding the purse and folded paper to his pack.

'One thing more,' said Luke nervously. 'I have a favour to ask of you – that for Melissa's sake I do not tell her of your relationship. To lose you as a loved one will be hard enough. To know you as a brother and lose that also –' He left the rest to Simon's imagination.

'What will you say then,' he asked slowly, 'to explain my disappearance?'

Luke looked at him steadily. 'I'll say nothing,' he said. 'I will pretend ignorance of your existence and she will discover you gone. If she tells me, I will comfort her. If she hides her grief, I will pretend not to see it and she will have to bear the shock alone.'

'She will feel herself betrayed.'

'Aye, but 'tis I who betray her, not you,' said Luke.

'How will she know that?'

'She won't. It will be very hard for her – but what other way is there?' said Luke. 'If I confide in her I must beg her to keep the knowledge from her mother for she too is innocent and does not deserve such grief. 'Tis a heavy burden for one so young.'

The boy nodded. 'She may go in search of me.'

'Then she must not find you! You must vanish from her life without trace.'

'Maggie will wonder, and the old man.'

'They too must remain in ignorance. All must be done for Melissa's good. She loves you now but in time she must wed, and love another. How can she do that if she knows of your whereabouts and believes you still love her? 'Twill be impossible.'

'You are right, I know, yet I shrink from the deceit.' He sighed. 'But we have agreed it must be done. Words will not alter circumstances. I'll go now.' He sprang lightly into the saddle and held out a hand to Luke, who grasped it. 'Will you ever love *me*?' Simon asked suddenly.

Luke made no answer and the boy turned his horse abruptly and dug in his heels so that it sprang forward, scattering the crisp autumn leaves with its flailing hooves.

'I love you!' called Luke. 'Simon! D'you hear?'

But the boy had gone.

Thomas Benet was a heavy sleeper and as soon as he opened his eyes he knew something must have disturbed him. He lit his candle, pulled on a woollen nightshirt and went out into the passage and listened. Another sound, though very slight, came from the children's bedchamber where now only Melissa slept. He moved quietly to the door and waited. It came again – the sound of muffled weeping. He was distressed but not surprised. There had been talk in the kitchen and Luke's strange visitor a day or two earlier. Somehow Melissa was concerned but he didn't ask for details and no one had furnished them. What ailed the child? To Thomas she was still the withdrawn little girl who followed him like a shadow for so many years, watching him, listening to him, content only to be with him. On occasions she had crept into his room at night and slept beside him on the rushes wrapped only in a blanket. The childish trust had moved the shy man to a kind of love. He had no woman in his life – his undeclared love for Alison prevented that. He had no physical contact with anyone. From time to time the passions of Heron erupted round him like a battle round an impartial observer. He remained aware but mainly unscathed. It was happening again. Secret moves were being made and secret words spoken. The servants gossiped among themselves, hardly bothering to moderate their voices when he walked in unexpectedly; they paid him so little heed. At times he felt almost invisible as though he had no part in life except to watch and ponder on the lives of others. Snippets of conversation intrigued him but he never felt able to ask for explanations. It would be unseemly for one in his position to ply the servants with questions. Possibly they thought him in the confidence of master and mistress and often this was so. Occasionally his advice was sought. But on occasions he was not in touch with events. Now he must guess at the cause of Melissa's grief, the reason for Luke's distracted air and Alison's growing anxiety that all was not well.

Was anyone aware, he wondered, that Melissa wept? Should anyone be told or should she be left to her sorrow? He listened but the sound continued. She would cry herself to sleep perhaps. He went back into his room but left the door ajar. From the warmth of his bed he strained his ears for a sign that she had fallen asleep and was, for the moment at least, out of her misery. Unable to sleep while she grieved, he searched his memory for images of her childhood when she had needed him. Then, to her, he had been important. He had a role as her protector . . .

He saw her as a little girl, paddling in the river where it was shallow below the stepping stones, calling to him that she had found a fish for his supper. But in her excitement, she had dropped the net and it had floated out of reach. He had retrieved it for her and the round grey eyes had looked into his with admiration and girlish adoration that went to his head like wine . . . With a smile, he recalled the piteous look she would later turn to him in an unspoken plea for rescue from a scolding from Alison or a tiresome session with the singing tutor. Then he sometimes pretended a summons for her and she would skip off delighted with the deceit, her eyes gleaming with mischief, escaping to the freedom of the herb garden or the orchard where he would join her . . . Then she was holding out her hand to him as he transferred the sparrowhawk from his wrist to hers – the bird he had trapped and trained for her. Their secret enterprise, so she would have it! Thomas could trap a bird. Thomas could find the first primrose. Thomas could take away the sting of a nettle with his 'magic' dock leaves. Could comb her hair when Beth tangled it. Or feed her with gruel when she was sickly and would take no nourishment from anyone else. Melissa's beloved Thomas could move mountains – yet here he lay, helpless, while she wept in the next room.

With a sigh, he got up again and stood at her door. All was quiet. She was asleep. He would take a look at her to reassure himself. Pushing open the door, he stepped inside the room. Her bed was empty! He hurried back to his room to dress. Taking a blanket from the bed he went downstairs and out into the garden. With luck she would be in the lower garden by the river and he made his way there. As he reached the top of the steps, a low growl told him he had guessed correctly. Melissa sat huddled on the bottom step, her arms round one of the dogs which now sprang up, wagging his tail as he recognized the newcomer.

'Hush boy!' cried Thomas as the dog yelped excitedly.

Melissa didn't turn round. She sat in her nightgown, her elbows on her knees, her chin in her hands, the picture of despair. Thomas sat beside her and draped the blanket round both of them. 'This reminds me of times past,' he joked tentatively.

She gave a long shuddering sigh and turned suddenly towards him to lay her head on his shoulder. He drew the blanket closer, tucking it in around the narrow shoulders and slim neck, then patted her back. For a long time neither spoke. Thomas didn't know what to say and waited hopefully for a clue to her distress. Melissa's emotions were so raw she could scarcely bear to express them in words for fear of reviving the anguish she now struggled so desperately to suppress. At last she said, 'He's gone – without a word, without even a hint. Oh Thomas, help me!' and began to sob again, deep painful sobs that shook her body and made further speech impossible. He took her in his arms, murmuring comfort and love. So that was it. She had a lover and now he was gone. No doubt Luke's preoccupation was also explained – and the girl's visit. Had she betrayed them, perhaps? Gradually Melissa's tears lessened once more.

'To go so suddenly,' she said brokenly, 'without a farewell? I can't believe it, Thomas. He wouldn't treat me so unkindly. I'm afeared that he is not gone but taken – or else –' her voice dropped to a whisper, 'dead mayhap and none will tell me. Oh Thomas, how can I bear it? He was my life, my secret happiness! How can I tell you? You will never understand. You have never loved in this way. The pain of losing him is not just in my heart. I feel it everywhere and my body aches with a terrible grief. What shall I do without him, Thomas? How shall I live?'

'Tell me about him,' he suggested. 'Who is the man who wrongs you this way?'

'Oh he doesn't wrong me,' she cried. ''Tis not of his doing. That much I know. He would never hurt me. No, someone has spirited him away. Someone jealous of our love has robbed me. I tell you he would not go so suddenly. He loved me.'

'I'm certain he did,' said Thomas, 'for how could anyone not love you. But tell me his name, I beg you.'

'Simon. His name was Simon.' Slowly at first and then more coherently, she told him of their early meetings and the way their feelings had deepened from friendship into love. He listened without interruption, amazed that matters had gone so far without detection.

'When he didn't meet me as usual, I went into the town to ask after him. I did it most discreetly, for fear he was sick. But they were none the wiser! They knew nothing. The girl Maggie had wept also for him. She didn't tell me but her eyes were red-rimmed and her cheeks blotched. The old man was angry at his sudden departure. They have been good to him, Thomas. He was happy there. Don't you see that he would never leave us this way? Oh, I'm so fearful for his safety. What has become of him? An accident mayhap, or murdered by cut-throats. I cannot bear to dwell on it. What can be done, Thomas? Tell me what I must do to find him.'

He shook his head. 'I will make inquiries,' he said carefully. 'I'll help all I can but I doubt there is much that can be done. If he is dead, which I doubt, there is nothing to be done for finding him cannot bring him alive again. If he has gone willingly then he will not thank us for our investigations. Perhaps he has done someone an injury and needs to go into hiding.'

'He would do no man harm,' she said firmly. 'Not Simon. You are wrong there, Thomas.' She sighed deeply. Only an occasional violent sigh racked her now and her mind was occupied with more practical aspects of his disappearance. Thomas shivered as the cold mist from the river penetrated the thin blanket and chilled his bones. If Melissa noticed, she gave no sign and he wished he had dressed more warmly. He sat silent, letting her talk on, but nodded once or twice to show that he grasped her meaning.

'He loved me Thomas,' she said earnestly. 'Of that I am quite certain. He touched me so tenderly, and spoke so disarmingly. And I loved him – love him,' she corrected hastily and crossed herself as though by the use of the past tense she might somehow bring about his death. 'Last time we met we were like lovers, Thomas. He held me in his arms and stroked my skin saying it was like silk. Can you imagine, Thomas, our joy in one another? Do you know aught of love?'

He nodded but she rushed on regardless. 'We were sweet together, Thomas. That's how it was for us. He looked at me and thought me beautiful.'

'You *are* beautiful,' said Thomas.

'Oh no, not beautiful of face but through and through! Beautiful to my very soul . . . And when he touched me, when his lips met mine – oh yes, he kissed me. Not once but many times, that last time we met.'

Thomas sighed. 'I envy you,' he said and she looked at him in surprise.

'Do you?' she asked. 'Do you envy me such joy if now 'tis taken from me? Do you envy me this terrible grief? Suppose I never see him again. Suppose these meetings are all I ever have. Then do you envy me?'

'Aye. The world is full of love and pain but some know only the pain. You have known both and I count you richer than most.'

She considered his words breathlessly. 'That is true,' she said at last, 'but it doesn't make the pain easier to bear.'

'No, but when the pain is past, you will still remember the love.' He went on. 'Mayhap there is a price to pay for love and a time to pay it. A woman loves a child for many years and it brings her joy and then it dies. The time is up and she must pay for those years of love. A beautiful woman grows old and grieves for the loss of her beauty. The homely woman has no such price to pay. Consider, Lissa. If you had known your love would end this way, would you have wanted it still? Or would you have said "No! The price is too high. I won't meet him. I won't love him." If your grief is but slight, then your love was slight. Your grief is as deep as your love.

'Tis as simple as that . . . Now you know why I envy you.'

They sat for a while longer until he shivered again.

'You are cold,' she said. 'We must go in.'

'Aye.'

'Thomas, we were not –' she faltered. 'Simon did not –'

'I understand,' he said.

'But he did find my body beautiful.'

'I don't doubt it,' he said. Her lips trembled and he said hastily, 'Come, we must go in,' and helped her to her feet. The dog woke from his dozing and scampered ahead of them as they walked slowly back to the house.

Nan wrinkled her nose as she strained the contents of the pan which hung over the fire. 'What have you put in this?' she asked Beth. 'It smells most vile. I'm thankful I shan't be tasting it.'

'Only what the doctor prescribed,' said Beth. She left the apples she was peeling and came across to sniff the pot for herself. 'Ugh!' she agreed. 'Let me see – 'tis lily of the valley, twice as many broom tops and dandelion root. Aye, that was it. But 'tis boiling and should only be simmering. Pull it off the heat for a little, that's better. We'll stir some honey in if it tastes as bad as it smells. Poor old Izzie. I've a nasty feeling in my bones she'll not get up again.'

Nan stared at her. 'What, not ever?' she said.

Beth shook her head grimly. 'Dropsy is a sad complaint for there's no cure. Still, she's in good hands and better off than many for she'll not be thrown out to fend for herself. Oh, don't stand there like a wounded hare. None of us lives for ever. That'll be ready now so take it down and set it on the hearth. Here, peel this apple and let's see who'll be your true love – poor man!'

Ignoring this last comment, Nan took the large apple and peeled it carefully so that the peel remained in one piece. Jon looked at her over the harness he was polishing. 'Let's hope 'tis not a J,' he remarked.

'I hope so too,' snapped Nan. 'What have I done to deserve such a fate?' Gingerly she picked up the peel, closed her eyes and swung it round her head three times. She let it fly out of her hand and it landed beside the wood pile. Hands on hips, she studied the curling peel. 'Well, 'tis not a J thank the Lord!' she told them. 'More like a curly E. E for Edgar.'

'Poor fellow,' said Jon.

'She doesn't know any Edgars,' said Beth. 'Perhaps 'tis E for Edward. Going to marry the Prince, mayhap, when he comes of age!'

Laughing, Beth crossed to Nan's side and looked at the peel. 'Look at it from here,' she suggested. 'Then 'tis either a W or an M, depending on where you stand.'

Nan frowned. 'M for Melissa.'

'What ails Melissa?' said Jon. 'These last three days she's taken the palfrey as soon as the sun's up and ridden off, hell for leather. Brings the poor beast back in a proper lather. You should hear Jack rant on. And her face – 'tis longer'n a yard of pump water!'

'Where's she go then?' asked Beth.

'Don't ask me,' said Jon. 'Jack's told the master. Let her be, Jack, that's all he says. I reckon he knows.'

'Aye, there's something going on,' said Beth. 'Thomas knows more than he'll say. He's a quiet one but he doesn't miss much. Still if the master knows, there's nowt for us to worry about. She'll give up if she doesn't find whatever it is she seeks.'

'The sooner the better then,' grumbled Jon, 'for all our sakes.'

'If 'tis W,' said Nan, 'then could be Walter or William. The miller's called William. Do I want to wed a miller?'

'I hope not for he's wed already,' said Jon. 'That funny old crow with one ear missing – that's his wife.'

Beth snatched up the peel and tossed it into the fire. 'Reckon you'll have to stay an old maid,' she grinned. 'Now add a dollop of honey to that brew and stir it well. Then ladle it into the pitcher and take it up to Izzie. A glassful three times daily, the doctor said and don't stay tittle-tattling . . . Now Jon, are you nearly finished with that polishing because I'd like another bucket of apples from the loft. If I don't get these apples done soon, they'll be spoiling.'

Nan turned at the door, the pitcher in her hand. 'Mayhap 'twas an E after all,' she said. 'There's Eric over at Maudesley, as digs the garden. Maybe 'tis him.'

'And maybe 'twas a W for wallop,' said Beth, 'for that's what you'll get if you dawdle any longer.' And she winked at Jon as Nan, muttering rebelliously, fled upstairs on her errand.

CHAPTER FIFTEEN

Melissa did not find her beloved Simon nor, as the years passed, did she agree to marry any of the suitors put forward for her. She withdrew once more into a world of her own where no one could disturb her memories. She walked or rode with Thomas or her parents and watched approvingly as Abigail married Adam and later produced three children, two boys and a girl. All the excitements in Melissa's life were second hand but she appeared content to help Alison with the management of Heron. When Izzie died she spent every morning in the kitchen training Beth to take her place as cook and when Thomas fell ill with jaundice she nursed him efficiently until he recovered. Alison's health was failing rapidly and she left more and more to her daughter. Luke immersed himself in the affairs of Heron, the miners and the new land and properties he was acquiring, attending auctions whenever monastic lands and buildings were offered for sale in the neighbourhood. If Alison knew of his dealings, she pretended otherwise. In 1540 she fell prey to the common scourge of consumption and her lungs were seriously affected. Her once-plump body dwindled, her sweet round face grew thin and tell-tale spots of colour glowed in her cheeks while her eyes darkened with the unnatural lustre of sickness.

Five years later Henry Tudor declared war on France

and crossed the Channel with his troops to besiege and capture Boulogne. Such a loss could clearly not go unavenged and on 6 July 1545 the entire French fleet, under the command of Admiral d'Annebault, set sail for England. A string of beacons burned along the south coast as the King prepared to meet the largest French invasion fleet ever sent against him. As soon as the news reached Heron, Luke determined to ride to Portsmouth where the English fleet was assembling.

'I shall ride all night,' he told Alison, 'and Benet shall come with me. With any luck we shall see the *Mary Rose*. 'Tis possible I shall speak with Jeffery.' He reached for a travelling bag. 'Fetch me clean linen, little mouse, and ask Beth to prepare food for two for the journey. It will save time –' He looked at her in surprise as she made no attempt to comply.

'I shall come with you,' she said.

'Come with us?' he echoed. 'To Portsmouth? Have you lost your wits, woman? Consider your health. I tell you we are riding through the night and 'twill be hazardous.'

'And I tell you I shall come,' she said. ''Tis of no use arguing, Luke. If you will not take me, I shall ride alone. He is my son, also, and if there is to be a battle –' She broke off, reluctant to think of the possible outcome.

'Alison, are you mad?' said Luke. 'We must ride fast and furious. Aye, and sleep rough if we sleep at all. 'Tis no trip for a woman, leastways a frail one.'

'I am not too frail to travel.'

'You are sick,' said Luke 'and you are forty-six. The physician will forbid it.'

'Physician or no,' said Alison, 'I want to see my son, Luke, and I have made up my mind. Melissa shall manage Heron and I shall come with you to Portsmouth.'

Luke argued in vain and finally gave in to her. There was little time to be lost. Already the French fleet had skirmished at Newhaven and was moving west towards the Isle of Wight. Thomas Benet was found and preparations set in hand for the journey.

Weary but triumphant, the three of them rode into Portsmouth early on the morning of 20 July. Passing a wagoner with a load of driftwood, they hailed him and exchanged greetings.

'What news?' Luke asked him. 'Are the fleets engaged?'

The old man shook his head. 'Nor like to be,' he said, 'if the wind don't change for 'tis blowing scarcely at all and our ships are still in the harbour.'

'Our son sails in the *Mary Rose*,' said Alison.

The old man smiled at her. 'Does he now,' he said. 'Then you may rest easy ma'am. A fine ship, that one. A very fine ship. And the damned Frenchies shall find out to their cost!'

'They shall indeed,' said Luke with a grim nod of his head. 'And where is the army?'

'Where?' laughed the old man. 'You may well ask! I swear they are everywhere – the town is crawling with military and the Grand Parade is fair bristling with cannon and the like. Southsea Castle looks like a pin cushion, there's that many gun muzzles poking from it. But the pavilions are set up in the plain behind the castle – you'll see it for yourselves. If you can get near enough for all the other folks has had the same idea.'

'We'll be on our way,' said Luke, 'and God go with you.' He spoke cheerfully and they turned their mounts and rode into the town.

The tents and pavilions of Suffolk's troops sprouted from Southsea plain like a crop of gaudy toadstools, patterned blue and white, red and yellow, white and red in a great confusion of colour. Commands rang out, men shouted and cursed and above it all the drums rolled and men sang to keep their spirits high.

'We'll look for Jeffery's ship first,' said Luke and they made their way to the waterfront. The sight made Alison gasp and the two men shake their heads in wonder. The cream of King Henry's navy lay at anchor in the narrow stretch of water, their masts and rigging criss-crossing the clear blue sky.

'So beautiful,' whispered Alison, 'and yet so deadly. 'Tis a fearsome sight. How shall we know the *Mary Rose*, Luke? What are her colours?'

Luke shook his head. 'I cannot say,' he admitted. 'And in that tangle I wager we never should pick her out.'

'How then shall we see Jeffery?' said Alison but he turned away exasperated for she had plagued him with the same question throughout the journey and would not believe that they might not.

''Tis likely we shall see him later,' said Thomas taking pity on her, 'when 'tis all done, why, then we'll search him out and find an inn where we can drink the King's health together. How d'you like that idea?'

'I like it well,' she said.

They spent half an hour longer watching the activities on board the ships, which fluttered with floats and streamers. The decks were crowded with mariners, the fore and aft castles with soldiers in the King's white and green colours. There was an air of expectancy and all was bustle and excitement as they prepared for the coming confrontation. Alison strained her eyes in a desperate attempt to single out the *Mary Rose* but gave up in despair. 'Let's ride on further,' she suggested. 'We'll have a better view of the ships when they finally leave the harbour.'

The sun shone as they made their way across the short springy turf. Wagons rumbled past loaded with ammunition for the guns and food for the men. A large band of pikemen awaited orders, their tall weapons glinting in the sunshine. Beyond them a contingent of gunners squatted on their heels, playing dice to pass the time and distract their attention from the battle ahead. Several fires burned and sheep and pigs turned on the spits, filling the air with woodsmoke and the promise of food. The King knew well that a man fights best on a full stomach.

Suddenly Thomas pointed excitedly. 'There goes the King himself!' he cried. 'See, in the black bonnet and white feather and surcoat of brown. I swear 'tis he.'

'He's right,' said Alison, 'for see the royal pages walking beside him, caps in their hands! Oh, Luke! And you would have me stay at home! What fine little lads.'

The two men exchanged amused glances and Luke slapped his forehead. 'Will a mere man ever understand a woman's mind?' he asked. 'Here we have the cream of England's navy and the Duke of Suffolk's army and you extol the virtues of the King's pages!'

Thomas laughed at the expression on her face. 'A woman's mind is a wondrous thing,' he told her. 'In faith, I would not have it any other way!'

On board the *Mary Rose* there was no confusion. The second largest ship in the King's navy now carried a vice-admiral, Sir George Carew who had recently dined on board the *Great Harry* with the King and Admiral Lisle. Sir George now wore the King's gold whistle and chain round his neck as a mark of his master's confidence and love. On board the *Mary Rose* mariners and soldiers had eaten their fill of fish stew, new bread and a piece of cheese. Now the trestles were stowed away and

277

the decks cleared for action. On the lower deck the magazine was unlocked and the powder monkeys filled their leather pouches. Partitions were taken down and all objects unnecessary to the action were removed. The surgeon set out his instruments, ointments, bandages and salt. The cook damped down the fires.

'Rig the hoses,' shouted Jeffery 'and sand the decks.'

Men sped away to carry out his instructions. A small boy staggered past, a bundle of rolled hammocks in his arms.

'When they are stowed, check the cookhouse,' cried Jeffery. 'See that the fires are out and report back.'

'Aye, sir.'

Pausing, Jeffery squinted along the barrel of the nearest cannon and out through the gun port. He could see the masts of the enemy only miles away off Bembridge Point. Rob joined him.

'I doubt they'll come any closer,' he said. 'They are cleverer than we'll admit.'

'Aye,' said Jeffery. 'More's the pity. I'd like to see those fine ships aground on Hamilton Bank and see the surprise on their captains' faces!'

Rob laughed. 'And if they use the deep water channel, they'll be right under Southsea Castle,' he said, 'and will take a pounding from shore batteries. No, they'll wait for us to go out and meet them. What a fleet, eh? Nearly two hundred ships, they say. And here they come! Look! Four-oared galleys. I think the French mean business!'

Jeffery grinned. 'They're displeased with us, I fear. They did not like losing Boulogne last year and want it back!'

'They will lose more than Boulogne before we are done with them,' said Rob. 'Ah, the first shots! I'm wanted forrard.' He disappeared.

Above them orders rang out and feet pattered across

the decks like heavy rain.

'Prepare to hoist sails!'

'Run out your guns!'

'Man the braces, there!'

It was dark on the gun deck, the only light coming in at the gun ports and down the hatchways where scramble nets served as ladders. The boy ran back to Jeffery, panting, his eyes bright with the excitement of his first engagement. 'Fires out, sir,' he gasped and received a nod and smile.

On the fore and stern castles the soldiers were crowded together, a mass of bow tops visible above the green and white tunics.

'Remove tompions!' came from the gun decks.

'Keep her close to the wind!' came from the main deck.

'We're moving,' Jeffery told himself and could not repress a shiver of apprehension at whatever lay ahead. The guns were run out to the middle of the decks prior to priming, the crews chattering like magpies as they waited for the next command. Under sail, the ship began to move and all hearts quickened with the sound of water below them and sail above. The flagship, the *Great Harry*, would lead the fleet towards the French. Jeffery felt a thrill of pride as he looked around him. On the main deck Sir George Carew lifted a hand in salute as their sister ship drew past.

'Bring her round!'

Jeffery steadied himself as the deck tilted and the boat heeled slightly to starboard with the change of direction.

'Point your guns!'

He watched the nearest crew as the slow match was held ready for the word 'fire'.

The deck tilted further and the men cursed. Alongside a cry came from another ship. 'You're heeling!'

They were indeed. The open gun ports on the starboard side were level with the water which lapped in, wetting the deck. The men looked uneasily towards Jeffery for reassurance but he could give none. Suddenly they were all struggling to keep their balance, slipping and sliding on the sand.

'God's blood!'

'Hell and damnation!'

'What are they doing?'

One of the powder boys lost his footing and rolled down the deck, the powder spilling from his pouch. Water began to pour in along the whole length of the deck. Christ! Would they never right it? Jeffery clung to the nearest beam for support, shouting to the crews to 'hold fast', but it was impossible. He heard the Captain's voice: 'I have such knaves as I cannot rule –' And then, the daylight was suddenly diminished as water blotted out the starboard gun ports. On the larboard side the horizon had vanished and the masts and rigging of the ship alongside sank out of sight to be replaced by empty blue sky.

Jeffery crossed himself hastily, searching his mind for the words of a prayer, but none came.

Men slithered helplessly, tumbling over each other and screaming as the water gushed over them. Sponges, rakes, shot, all were swept along the deck which now lay at about fifty degrees. There were screams and oaths as one of the heavy cannons broke free of its breeching ropes and slid into the tangle of bodies. Jeffery's fingers scrabbled desperately but finally lost their hold and he too fell backwards into the churning mass of water and men. Everywhere despairing arms reached upwards towards the only remaining light but even that was finally extinguished as the *Mary Rose* slid under the water, taking nearly seven hundred men to the sea bed and their souls to eternity.

On shore the cries of horror faltered and a murmur of disbelief spread through the crowds. Even as they watched, the green sea rushed foaming to hide the hull of its latest victim. Soon only the two mastheads showed above the water to mark the disaster. The cries of the trapped and drowning men carried thinly on the clear air. A few fortunates swam in the water or clung to what little debris floated on the calm surface. More swam to the protruding masts and clung there. Boats put out to rescue them and a hush fell on those that watched.

'He will be among them,' said Luke, holding a near-fainting Alison in his arms. 'Pray for him, little mouse.'

'I do. I do,' she whispered.

The two men watched as though hypnotized, never taking their eyes from the dreadful scene, oblivious to the commotion that now sprang up all around them. In silence they watched the survivors being brought ashore.

'Stay with your mistress,' Luke told Thomas. 'I'll go down and see –' He left the sentence unfinished but Thomas nodded and put an arm round Alison. Her face was grey with shock and her eyes dark with unexpressed fears.

'All will be well,' he told her, yet he knew the chances to be slight.

'Poor wretches,' she whispered and the tears which sprang to her eyes gave some relief to her anguish.

The battle continued almost unheeded as the wind increased and the tide turned in the defenders' favour. An hour passed and another before Luke returned. One look at his face told them all there was to say. The survivors were pitifully few and Jeffery Kendal was not among them. It was time to go home.

Thomas came so quietly into the room that Alison thought she was still alone. She sat with her hands resting on the keys but she did not play. Idly, she traced round the keys, her head bent, her eyes unseeing. In her mind's eye she saw Jeffery at seven, his small earnest face upturned, listening as she played. As a treat, he was allowed to stay up occasionally to share their music and Luke would sing in his fine tenor voice. Thomas would play the lute and sing his own compositions and she would play the virginals . . . She saw Jeffery swimming in the river, thrashing his legs and arms, his eyes tight closed against the water . . . and riding his first pony. She had made so many plans for her son and had watched him grow to manhood. She had adored him. Of all her children he had given her the fewest worries and the most affection. Paul had been a willing child but lacked the warmth of his elder brother. Melissa had been withdrawn for so many years they had missed her childhood. Abigail had been bold and resolute as a boy with the looks of an angel but no time for anyone but her beloved Melissa. But Jeffery . . .

A sound startled her and she looked up to see Thomas watching her. 'You're thinking of him,' he said and she nodded, tears trembling in her eyes.

'Less than a week ago,' she said. 'I can still scarcely believe it.'

'He loved you dearly,' said Thomas.

'If only he had stayed at Heron,' she said. '*Mary Rose*! I wish to God I had never heard the name!'

'You mustn't think that way,' he said gently. 'He loved life at sea. His letters were so full of pride. He loved the ship.'

'I know . . . I know. But it has taken him to his grave!'

'We all have to die, Alison. No doubt he would have wanted to die at sea.'

'But so young, Thomas!' she protested and he was silent.

He said again, 'He loved you dearly.'

She dared not speak but nodded again. If she said one word her fragile composure would shatter.

'We all love you,' he whispered and she sensed that he longed to say more but never would. 'I haven't spoken of – the disaster,' he said. 'I feared to distress you further but my heart ached for you. I want you to know how much I feel for you in your loss.'

'Thank you, Thomas,' she said.

'I haven't heard you play for so long.'

'I haven't the heart for it.'

'Nor sing.'

'No.' She sighed deeply. 'The world is become a grey place for me. I wait and wait for the colours to return.'

'I wish I could colour it for you,' he said softly.

'Oh Thomas, you are such a good man. Heron wouldn't be the same without you.'

'Do you mean that?' he asked.

'I do.'

'Is there anything I can do to help?' he said. 'You only have to ask.'

'I know. But there is nothing anyone can do. No one can bring him back.' She stood up and turned towards the window afraid to read the message in his eyes. He followed her and put a hand on her arm. He was shaking with nervousness and his voice was hoarse.

'Alison –'

'Oh my dearest Thomas,' she cried, 'don't, I beg you! Not now.'

'But I cannot bear to see you like this.'

'Please, please –!'

He was silent and she suddenly regretted her outburst. She was afraid of what he might say and yet she knew in her heart the agony it was for him to keep silent. She turned to face him. 'Forgive me,' she said. 'Please say what it is you feel for me.'

'That I love you,' he whispered. 'You must have guessed.'

'Oh Thomas . . .'

'You needn't answer,' he said, panic in his voice. 'I know you don't love me.'

'Thomas, listen to me,' she said softly. 'I love so many, my parents, my children, Luke. For other people I feel a great affection. For you I feel more than mere affection. You are part of my life – part of all our lives, and I feel a – a kind of love for you.' She took his hands in hers and looked at him levelly. 'Luke is my dear husband and he is the only man I can love, in that way.' He began to speak but she put a finger against his lips. 'You deserve a love of your own. You need a woman of your own. 'Twill not do for you to love me, Thomas.'

'But I do!' he protested. 'I want to make you happy. Luke –'

'No! Don't say it, Thomas. Luke loves me in his own way. He has his griefs – his secret fears. Poor Luke . . .'

'I cannot bear to see you so unhappy,' he said wretchedly. 'I want to comfort you.'

'Thomas –'

'Let me hold you in my arms,' he begged. 'Only once. Let me kiss you.'

'Oh dear God –' she couldn't bear the anguish in his eyes. Slowly, trembling, he put his arms round her and drew her towards him. Then she turned her face up to his. He kissed her then reluctantly released her.

'I love you, Alison,' he said.

'I know.'

'The kiss was very sweet,' he said.

'And for me.'

For a full minute they looked at each other.

'Don't send me away,' he said with an attempt at

lightness. 'Don't find a wife for me. Only let me stay near you and I swear I will never speak this way again.'

'If that is what you want.'

'I swear it is.'

'Then 'tis a bargain, Thomas?'

'Aye. 'Tis a bargain.' His smile was radiant. He had told her what was in his heart and she had not scorned him. She had spoken kindly and she would let him stay.

'So will you play for me now?' he asked.

'Certainly,' she said. She crossed the room again, sat down at the keyboard and, with Thomas beside her, began to play.

A few days later the door burst open and Jon tumbled into the room, his young face flushed with excitement. Alison looked up slowly from the linen which she hemmed listlessly.

''Tis Master Miller!' burst out the boy. 'In the stable yard this very moment!'

Alison eyed him wearily. 'And what were you doing in the stable yard?' she asked, 'when your work lies in the garden?'

'But ma'am. 'Tis Master Miller himself!' The boy stared at her, irritated by her lack of comprehension.

'Master Miller?' she repeated. 'Do we know him?'

'Why no, ma'am, but almost,' he protested. 'Do you recall that letter I brought from Master Jeffery – he spoke of his friend.'

At the sound of Jeffery's name, Alison's mind raced.

The boy went on. 'Master Robert Miller of the *Mary Rose*, ma'am! He's come with news of the –'

'Robert Miller!'

Alison jumped to her feet. The linen fell to the floor and lay forgotten among the rushes.

'Bring him to me,' she said, 'in the Great Hall, and then run find your master and Thomas Benet. Make haste boy! Move yourself, you slow coach.'

He sped away and she followed him downstairs, tucking strands of hair under her head-dress, and smoothing the creases from her gown. Her heart beat so loudly that she chided herself, muttering, ''Tis not Jeffery who comes, but a friend. Calm yourself, Alison.' She took deep breaths in an attempt to steady herself.

Robert Miller followed Jon into the Hall and seeing her, bowed generously.

Alison made a small curtsey and held out her hands to him. 'You are most welcome,' she said. 'Jon tells me you have news. He has gone in search of my husband but will you tell me your news while we wait and then tell it again.'

'Indeed I will ma'am,' he said and sat in the chair which Alison indicated while she sat opposite, her eyes never leaving his face.

'I did not know you were among the survivors,' she told him. 'My husband had ears only for Kendal. You will understand.'

'I do ma'am,' he said 'and would like to express my sorrow at your loss. Jeffery was a fine man – but you do not need me to tell you that.'

Her lips trembled as she nodded, unable to trust herself to words. It was three weeks since the *Mary Rose* had gone down and her grief was still a physical pain that never left her. It burned up her energy, she had lost weight and had no appetite. Seeing her distress, he hurried on.

'I thank God daily for my deliverance for, in faith, I cannot guess how I reached the surface. The last I remember was striking my head as I fell against one of the cannons. I cannot even swim! Yet I found myself drifted up against the main mast and young Alan, one of the

286

ship's boys, reaching out to grab me.'

'You were most fortunate,' said Alison and reproached herself instantly for wishing it had been
Jeffery saved in his stead. 'But tell me in your own
words – what news? Will they ever raise her?'

He shrugged. ''Tis hard to say ma'am,' he said. 'They
are still trying. They have two experts working on the
salvage, two men from Venice.'

'I want him here,' Alison interrupted him. 'I want his
body to lie in Ashburton Church where we can tend it
. . . 'tis a sad thing to lie on the sea bed with so many
others.'

'Aye. 'Tis natural to think that way.'

At that moment there came a hasty knocking on the
door and Jon was with them again to say he had not
found either Luke or Thomas.

'Mayhap they are somewhere together,' he suggested
in an agony to hear the news.

'Doubtless they are,' said Alison. 'Go look again.
Take the little mare if need be. They may be at the
mine.'

'But ma'am, I –' He looked appealingly at Robert who
grinned but said nothing.

'Be off,' said Alison. 'You shall hear it later, I promise. And if you pass Melissa bid her come to the Hall.'
She turned to Robert as the boy disappeared once more.
'My daughter is visiting in the town,' she said. 'Since
the closing of the Priory we have many in need and we
must do what we can to help.'

She did not add that her own guilt over Luke's parti-
cipation in the matter made her rather more generous
than she could afford. 'But continue, I beg you,' she
said. 'How do they hope to raise her?'

He sighed. ''Tis a devilish tricky problem,' he admitted. 'In theory their salvage method should prove
successful but in practice it fails. Firstly they tried to lift

her. They had two large ships alongside – *Samson* and
the *Jesus of Lubeck*. Cables were attached to the *Mary
Rose* at low tide and winched tight. As the tide came in
the *Samson* and the *Jesus* lifted with it and *Mary Rose*
should have surfaced.'

'But she didn't.'

'No. The cables broke under the strain and the idea
was abandoned.'

Alison sighed. 'She likes her watery grave,' she said.

Robert shrugged. 'At low tide she lies very shallow in
only six fathoms,' he told her. 'On the southern edge of
Spit Sand. They tried to drag her into shallower water
but she will not give an inch and no wonder when you
reckon the weight of cannon she has in her. I wager she
is fast in the mud by now.'

Alison was silent, seeing once more in her mind's eye
the interior of the ship as she imagined it to be, its
pathetic cargo of dead men piled one upon another,
oblivious to the dark cold water and the occasional in-
quisitive fish.

'I shall never see him again,' she said heavily and a
fierce sigh shook her.

Robert took something from the purse at his wrist and
held it out to her. 'The purpose of my visit was to bring
you this,' he said. ''Twas Jeffery's and I thought you
would value it.'

In his palm lay a small wooden thimble. Alison stared
at it wonderingly then took it with fingers that shook.

'He lent it to me,' said Robert 'that very morning.
Mine had gone missing – stolen no doubt. They were a
light-fingered lot! See, it's stained by the sea water.'

Tears fell gently on to the small brown object and
then she lifted it to her lips. Robert's own eyes filled
with tears of pity but footsteps approached and he
blinked them away. Alison handed the thimble back to
him. 'Give it to his father,' she said. 'He is here now and

I will order refreshment for you.'

Luke came into the room with Thomas and Jon and Alison turned to her husband and took his hand briefly.

'No doubt Jon has told you,' she said. 'I'll leave you to talk and will ask Beth to prepare some food.'

She found Melissa in the kitchen and told her of their visitor; the girl hurried to join her father and hear all that Robert had to tell them. While Beth found pasties, soft cheese and ale, Alison spoke bravely of the *Mary Rose*, and the wooden thimble.

'Now that's a precious thing to have,' said Beth kindly, 'Master Jeffery's own thimble. Bless his heart, I can just see the lad stitching away –' she stopped abruptly as Alison sank on to a stool and covered her face. Her shoulders shook and tears trickled from beneath her spread fingers. Beth hurried to her and put a comforting arm round her shoulder.

'Oh Beth!' cried Alison. 'Twenty-six years of caring and loving and all we have left is a thimble!'

Hester allowed four weeks to pass before deciding the time was ripe for a visit to Heron. She sent no message of her intention and Luke, busy with business matters, was taken completely by surprise. He stared at Nan as she stood breathless in the doorway.

'Hester here?' he repeated. 'Is her husband with her?'

'No, sir. She's come alone except for her stable lad who rode as escort.'

A frown settled on his face as he stood up. 'Then I must come down –' he began.

'No need to come down,' said Hester, sweeping past Nan into the room. 'I don't want to disturb you, Luke, but felt the very least I could do was come and pay my respects for your terrible loss.'

She drew off her riding gloves and slipped off her

cloak. Handing them to Nan, she gave the girl a nod of dismissal and turned back to Luke. 'You'll forgive me, I know,' she said 'but I had to come.'

To Luke's surprise, she gave him a brief kiss.

'I'll order you some refreshment,' he said.

'No need,' said Hester. 'I saw Izzie as I came in and took the liberty to ask for camomile tea and three biscuits. You look pale, Luke, and your face is thinner – but that's to be expected. Tragedy leaves its mark on us all. And poor Alison! Izzie tells me she's at Maudesley at present. Oh, what a journey I've had. I must sit down before my legs give way beneath me. I swear the roads have been untouched since I rode out of Heron all those years ago. Alison was such a comfort to me then, when poor Stephen died. I leaned on her for support – and who, I said to my husband, will *she* lean on! Oh, what a cruel loss. That dear lad! And not even to have his body! If there's no body, there's no funeral and how does one pay one's last respects? I said to my husband I *must* ride over when the first shock has lessened. I didn't wish to intrude on your grief but – ah, thank you Izzie. Bring it here.'

Luke watched as she took the tray, set it on the table and busied herself with the tea. He had never liked Hester and the speed with which she remarried had not endeared her to him. Stephen, for all his faults, had been her husband and the short mourning period had affronted the family. He studied her surreptitiously as she poured the tea. The years had not been particularly kind to her. The body was more angular and the round shoulders now almost a stoop. Her face wore a pinched look and he thought that the small features that had once looked so dainty now looked mean; the nose reminded him of a small beak. She gave him a brittle smile and he thought that under the torrent of words and assumed manner she was nervous. It puzzled him.

'And how are you faring,' he asked, 'the children and your husband? All in good spirits, I trust.'

She considered, her head on one side, her eyes bright. 'Well enough,' she said, 'though my husband suffers with his stomach. Always has done, poor man. It keeps him from his sleep at times and that's a tiresome nuisance. What are we without our rest? It saps the energy and dulls the mind. Poor man.'

He nodded. She seemed distracted as though her mind was on something else, unaware of his lack of response.

'Poor dear Alison,' she said again. 'And Abby – no doubt you have informed everyone. To die at sea, poor lad. Is there any news? Any hope of salvaging *Mary Rose*? Though mayhap you don't relish the idea now. I said to my husband, would I want them to bring them up, all those brave souls, or should they rest in their watery grave? He's with his companions, if that's any comfort, and died nobly in a good cause. You can be proud of him. My poor Stephen, hacked down by those evil men. There's a life thrown away if you like. Such waste! Such wicked, wicked –' She stopped in midsentence to examine the tea she was drinking, sniffing at it suspiciously. 'The water wasn't boiling when she made this tea,' she declared. 'I can always tell. My own woman does it. I've taken her to task for it, of course, but she will not listen. The leaves don't give out their full flavour and with a keen nose you can smell it.' She sniffed at it again. 'Alison should speak to her about it. Poor Alison,' she added. 'How is she? I was sorry to learn that she was ill. Is there no hope of recovery?' 'None at all,' said Luke, 'although she does not know it. She grows weaker and the cough troubles her.' He waited for her comment but none was forthcoming. 'Are you staying long?' asked Luke.

'I'm not certain,' said Hester. 'Expect me when you

see me, I told my husband. If Alison needs me, I shall stay. That poor girl. I couldn't stay at home knowing what she must be suffering. Family is family, with or without a funeral.'

'We had a small memorial service,' said Luke. 'Close family and friends. We felt it was enough in the circumstances. If they do recover his body we'll bury him in our church and –'

'And have the funeral then. How sensible you are. I swear I couldn't think straight when I lost Stephen. I wasn't at all sensible, I'm afraid. I left it all to you and Alison I recall but there. That's all over and done and you'll find time heals.'

Luke nodded. She didn't catch his eye, he noticed. Not once. She's uneasy, he thought, almost guilty. Was that the word? He gave her a long, straight look and fancied that the colour rose in her cheeks. He sat down opposite her and waited curiously.

'And your children?' he asked.

'All well, thanks be to God!' she said. 'The girls are obedient and Sarah is betrothed and gone to London these last two months. Such a charming family and well-connected. The father is a silversmith; I wondered if he might know the Lessors.'

'He was a goldsmith,' said Luke.

'I know he was but 'tis the same thing, near enough. I said to my husband 'twould be strange if they knew the Lessors – or Matthew, of course. Poor Matt, last time I saw him he was very bent, and his sight was troubling him. All that close work. Give it up, I told him, you're a wealthy man but he laughed, "A goldsmith can't give up," he said. There's always one piece he wants to make. One piece more beautiful than any he's done before. His crowning achievement! They seem very happy, he and Blanche. Such an unhappy start and yet –' She spread her hands helplessly and smiled.

'I hardly knew Matt,' said Luke. 'The difference in our ages was so great.'

'Of course,' she agreed, 'but he's family and blood's thicker than water. I said to my husband, the Kendal family is losing all its sons. There's only Hugo left now.'

'Hugo?'

'Of the next generation. Matt has only Sophie and you have Abby and Lissa. Hugo is the only Kendal left to carry on the name.'

So that was it! The only male Kendal! He was careful to let nothing show in his face as she hurried on, eyes averted.

'Who's to inherit Heron, I asked my husband, and he could only shrug. The girls cannot inherit, I said. Luke must be quite distracted. To lose a son is bad enough, God knows, but to lose one's only heir!'

'The problem has not distracted me,' said Luke. 'I have given it no thought at all.'

'Then 'tis time you did!' cried Hester. 'Hugo is the only Kendal left.' Now that her mission was declared, she gave up all pretence at subtlety.

'I'm not dead yet,' said Luke, and she had the grace to look abashed.

'But you've no sons, Luke,' she said, 'and when you *do* die, what then? Alison is too old to give you any more children.'

'Is she?' said Luke. 'My mother was well past forty when I was born.'

She looked at him, taken aback.

'I doubt we shall have any more children,' said Luke with a faint smile, 'but 'tis still possible.'

'That's as may be then,' said Hester, recovering her composure now that he had reassured her on that point. 'The fact remains, Luke, that if Stephen hadn't been killed, *we* would still be at Heron and you would be at

Maudesley. There'd be no question of the inheritance going to anyone but Hugo.'

'That's very true,' he said 'but you chose not to return to Heron after Stephen's death. You chose to marry a Papist – and speedily.'

This last barb went home and she coloured angrily. ''Twas no speedier than many others,' she cried, 'and what else was I to do with a young son to rear and being with child again.'

'Heron was your home but –'

'A home that was no home!' she protested. 'Stephen never wanted Heron, you know that! He hated the mine and we were none of us truly happy there. When Stephen died, if you must know, I never wanted to set eyes on the place again!'

He raised his eyebrows coolly at this outburst. 'So you hated Heron,' he said. 'How strange, then, that you now consider Hugo has some claim to it.'

There was a long silence.

'Nothing alters the fact,' she said at last, 'that Hugo is the only Kendal son still alive. Stephen's son has as much right to Heron as your son – and now you have no son.'

'Not quite, I think. Heron belonged to my mother from her first husband Daniel who died without heirs. John wed her and gave her his name. The property became his but it came through her. Stephen and Matt are John's sons by his first wife. *I* am my mother's only child. I think, therefore, that my sons have the greater claim.'

They looked at each other – Hester burning with anger and Luke calm and cold as ice.

'But you *have* no sons!' she hissed.

He continued to look at her steadily until suddenly he smiled.

'And you,' he said, 'have no son named Kendal. You

changed his name when you remarried. For your husband is a rich man. Richer than Stephen ever was.'

For a moment she looked baffled, defeated even. What he said was true.

'But he is still Stephen's son,' she said. 'He is the last of the Kendal line. A changed name can be changed again.'

'No, Hester,' said Luke. 'It won't be necessary. You have had your say. My answer is no. Hugo will never inherit Heron.'

'We can fight you,' she said.

'A costly business and you would be wasting your time.'

She stood up, swallowed hard and moved towards the door but at that moment Alison came hurrying in. To her surprise, Hester made no move to greet her but stared at Luke, her expression grim.

'I had thought you a reasonable man,' she said.

'I had thought you what you are,' said Luke, 'a very greedy woman.'

'Luke!' cried Alison. 'Hester! Whatever –'

But Hester pushed past her without a word and called to Beth for her gloves and cloak.

'Luke!' cried Alison. 'What has happened?'

'We will speak of it later,' said Luke grimly. 'Hester is leaving.'

CHAPTER SIXTEEN

'Hold him still, damn you, or your own nose shall feel the feathers!'

The girl, perched on an upturned tub, tightened her grip on the horse's head, lifting it so that Rube could force the goose feathers further up the nostrils. Dipped in garlic and sneezing powder, they would soon produce the desired effect. They waited and the animal began to sneeze violently, shaking its head wildly and rolling its eyes in great distress.

'That's it! Stand away!' shouted the old man and she was only too willing to duck away from the large head that swayed and jerked above her. 'Fetch the pot and look quick about it. I've no wish to be late with three to barter.'

The pot, encrusted with the dirt of ages, contained a mixture of garlic, mustard and strong ale, well shaken. The horse's head was thrust up once more and with the help of a horn both nostrils were filled with the obnoxious liquid. Rube flattened his hand over the nostrils, keeping them closed until he judged it time enough, then released the horse.

'Out of there now,' Rube ordered and the girl clambered over the stable door and stood beside him to await results. The horse, a four-year-old piebald, began to sneeze once more and rapidly emptied its head. The accumulation of mucus was a symptom of glanders. The animal's head would now stay clear until the sale was concluded and the luckless purchaser would discover his mistake too late.

'Wipe it down,' said Rube, 'and then clean up the colt. I'll fetch the Punch.'

From the far end of the lean-to that served as stable, he led out the twenty-year-old Suffolk Punch and looked at it critically. He had done his best with it, God knows, but it was long past its prime – 'If it ever had one!' thought Rube sourly – its back-bone showed through the dull chestnut coat and the once sturdy legs were rickety and covered in sores. The worst of these he had hidden with splashes of mud and the long teeth had been filed down to disguise its age. Rube eyed it truculently, his small mean eyes glittering under the scraggy eyebrows. His lips moved soundlessly in a stream of invective and he raised a clenched fist to strike it, then thought better of it. A lifetime as a horse thief and jingler had left its mark on his already base nature and his daughter's recent death now left him with a grandchild to care for and a girl at that! The situation had increased his resentment and he drank more ale to cheer his spirits.

He looked at the girl as she led out the colt and his mood worsened. She was ten years old and skinny as a reed, her body discoloured by countless flea bites, many of them scratched and bleeding. Her short tufty hair was matted, her feet were bare, and her gown faded. Her small face wore its usual sullen expression which was a mixture of defiance and despair. Why was he burdened with such a feckless child. The image of her father and with even less common sense! Transferring his gaze to the colt, his face brightened slightly. It was dapple grey – a nice looking animal and a fashionable colour. Let's hope the real owner doesn't show his face, he thought. The horse had been stolen in Somerset two months earlier and kept out of sight until the inevitable hue and cry had died away. It should command a very fair price, he thought.

'Ah, you've done the mare. That's a sight better,' he said grudgingly, seeing the row of neat plaits. 'And is it still lame? Walk it a bit . . . that's right . . . A pox on it! The shoe'll have to come off. As if we're not late enough. Fetch me a knife and stir yourself.' He gave her a kick to speed her on her way. 'You move like an old woman. Tut! What ails the child?'

She came back with a knife and put it into his outstretched hand, darting quickly out of reach for fear he should further vent his ill temper on her. She watched as he lifted the animal's leg, eased the shoe and tossed it aside. Then he straightened up.

'That's not a bad bit of horseflesh,' he told her. 'Not bad at all. Spirited but biddable and that's how they like 'em. If I don't do well out of that one, my name's not Reuben Pick. No, that's not bad at all. Well, don't stand there with your eyes on stalks! Get the blanket out here.'

She struggled out with it and he slung it over the colt's back. He sprang up on its back and looked down into the peaky face. 'Up with you, then,' he said.

Reaching down, he hoisted her up behind him and, taking up the halters of the other two horses, led his cavalcade on to the highway and turned east.

The Horse Fair was already under way. Held on the common, it reached as far as the eye could see in a sprawling mass of caravans, wagons, horses and men and the sounds of man and beast competed in the crisp December air. Luke paused on the fringe of it to survey the scene and Jack, beside him, looked about without enthusiasm. The fairs were notorious as a meeting place for thieves and tricksters of all types and a man and his money were easily parted by the swindler's smooth tongue or the cutpurse's sly fingers. Here was a collection of the lowest of mankind, beggars, cheats, prostitutes, thieves – the list was frightening. Rich gentlemen came to buy horses and they brought their wealth with them. The poor man's part was to relieve them of it as quickly as possible and they played their parts in a variety of ingenious ways. The jingler could deceive only the gullible and unwary. The thief robbed indiscriminately and the most astute and intelligent of men could fall victim to their activities. Jack's purse was hidden for extra security inside his shirt. He watched keenly anyone who came within five yards of them and anyone nearer than that was treated with deep suspicion.

On the far side of the area, gipsy caravans lent colour to the occasion while the gipsies themselves, the most famous horse dealers of them all, paraded a bewildering succession of horses before the huge audience of would-be purchasers.

The women had made pegs and baskets and now hawked their wares among the crowds who gathered to buy and sell or merely to watch the day's dealing. Their dark-skinned, sloe-eyed children slipped among the crowds on errands best known to themselves while their many dogs roamed freely, snapping at the legs of the horses and scrapping among themselves.

'No friars,' said Jack. 'No indulgences for sale – and no sermons to prick our consciences.'

'We are well rid of them,' said Luke tersely and Jack cursed himself for a fool and changed the subject.

'At least the weather is set fair,' he said hastily. 'A horse fair in the rain is a sorry affair.'

'Aye.'

At that moment Luke was hailed by a friend and doffed his hat by way of greeting.

' 'Tis Gordon Manning,' he said, surprised. 'I thought him still on pilgrimage. I'll have a word with him while you ferret out two or three likely looking animals for me to consider.'

Luke had decided to buy Melissa a new mount. Her own was twenty years old and slow and would serve ideally for Abigail's children when they made their promised visit in the spring. Jack rode off, delighted at the chance to be on his own. Though in his thirties he was still a good-looking man with a square bearded face set on a bull-like neck above broad shoulders. He walked with an almost arrogant swagger and the women would eye him as he passed, some winking, some whistling and others, bolder than most, offering their wares with a jerk of the head and a come-hither look, all of which did wonders for his morale and greatly increased his enjoyment of the expedition.

'What tidings, then, Gordon?' cried Luke, leading his horse as he moved towards his friend. 'When did you return to England's cold clime? I thought you still abroad.'

Gordon shivered extravagantly. 'How I wish I were!' he laughed. 'But I returned two days ago to find my poor Eleanor in tears and her little mare dead. Poisoned seemingly, though how, none can say. So here I am in search of a dappled grey to take the place of the other.'

'I'm on a similar errand,' said Luke 'but for my daughter, though she's set on a black.'

They began to walk as they talked, pushing a way through the crowd, scanning the horses and fending off the beggars as best they could, turning deaf ears to the coarse language that assailed their ears on every side.

'So what news since I went away?' asked Gordon. 'Has the King beheaded his latest queen? I thought it probable some weeks ago.'

'Ah, Henry Tudor is a true giant!' said Luke. 'They call him an old fox but in truth he has the heart of a lion. I can't help but admire the man. Speak how you will of him but he's a king and a half and none can deny that. I warrant England will never see his like again.' Admiration gleamed in his eyes as he spoke and Gordon noted it with impatience. Everyone knew that Henry was a bully and a tyrant. He had dealt the church a fatal blow and his marital exploits were marvelled at on both sides of the Channel. Yet still Kendal extolled the man.

'But his health is failing,' Luke went on. 'They say the doctors fear for him. A lesser man would be dead by now.'

'Is it the fever still?'

'Aye, that and the constant pain in his leg. Some say 'tis an ulcer, others an infection in the bone.' He shrugged. 'But he fights on and the doctors marvel at such strength of purpose. He has an iron will. He'll cheat death a little longer if the stars are favourable.'

Gordon stepped over a baby who crawled unattended among the careless feet. 'So we shall soon have a new king – Edward Tudor. The name has a fine ring to it, wouldn't you say?'

Luke considered it. 'Well enough,' he said, 'but I like Henry better! And what will England do with a nine-year-old boy for a king. Who's to be Regent, I wonder. Rumour has it that the King refuses to sign his will. That's set the cat among the pigeons!' He laughed grimly. 'I warrant they'll be bickering like hounds over a bone and who's to stop them?'

Gordon shook his head and stopped to inspect a dappled grey. He ran his hand over the shoulders and along its back to the haunches. Opening its mouth, he satisfied himself that the teeth had not been tampered with. 'How old?' he asked the girl who held it.

She shrugged. 'Ask him,' she said.

The old man was busy with another sale but he turned to them briefly and said, 'Three years and in fine fettle. That's a bargain, is that. A real bargain. You won't find a prettier horse here today. Walk it for the gentleman, the way I told you.'

He gave the child a push and she stumbled forward.

'The way I told you!' he roared. He had given her careful instructions to lead it in a circle to disguise the uneven gait. The girl gave him a look of intense dislike and, ducking his outstretched hand, ran straight forward, urging it into a trot. Gordon and Luke exchanged looks as the old man cursed under his breath.

'Is it lame?' asked Gordon suspiciously.

The old man, anticipating the question, busied himself with his other customer.

'Walk it again, child,' said Luke. 'Take it further.'

She looked anxiously at her grandfather. She was already due for a beating.

'Here, give it to me,' said Luke.

He took the horse and led it forward, urging it into a trot while Gordon watched.

'Aye. Lame in the right foreleg,' he said. 'Pity, for it's a nice looking beast, as he says.'

'Lame?' said the old man turning indignantly. 'There's nothing wrong with that horse that a shoe won't put right. See –' He lifted the foreleg and showed the missing shoe. 'A bit hoppity, that's all. Needs a new shoe. I'd have done it myself but there wasn't time. Only collected her yesterday because I knew there'd be someone here today as wanted a pretty little horse like that. Last owner just lost his wife, poor wretch, and couldn't abide to see her horse. Brought back memories, you see. There were tears in his eyes, he was so loath to part with the beast. No, you won't find one prettier, believe me.'

'Hmm,' said Gordon and the old man, seeing him

half-decided, turned abruptly away to a man who was eyeing the old Punch.

'Beautiful horse, that,' he told him. 'But I won't lie to you. Fourteen years old, he is. Suffolk Punch. Aye, fourteen. I see you look surprised and no wonder. He's a game old boy, this one. Pulls five times his own weight and he weighs near on a ton. And handsome, too. Handsome as they come. Look at those shoulders and that neck. Beautiful lines.' He patted it with a show of affection. 'I tell you, this is a handsome animal. I'd like to keep him myself. 'Tis not often I can say that about a horse but this one . . .'

Gordon conferred with Luke who looked hopefully round for a glimpse of Jack whose knowledge of horse-flesh was far superior to his own. The girl watched them sullenly. Luke went in search of Jack and found him with a gipsy girl. Watching unnoticed, he was astonished at the animation in his face as he flirted. Glancing up, Jack saw his master and made his farewell, albeit reluctantly. He had seen nothing promising, so far, he told Luke, but was still looking. He had asked the girl if she knew of a superior black but she –. Luke interrupted him, and sent him hurrying back to lend his expertise to Gordon. As the crowd swallowed him up Luke turned and saw a familiar face not twenty yards away. It was Simon. Luke saw him clearly, first side face and then for a second or two full face. For a moment he was frozen with shock. His son, here! His only surviving son. He had thought of him constantly since that terrible day in Portsmouth but had firmly rejected the urge to claim him. He had not visited him since nor made contact of any kind. Now he *had* seen him and was filled with a wild longing to speak with him again. The boy was his own flesh and blood. His legitimate heir. With a choked cry, he began to force a way through the crowd, pushing and elbowing in a frantic effort to clear the mass of humanity that now conspired to keep them apart.

'Let me pass! Let me through, I say! Out of my way, I beg you!' He caught another glimpse of the blond head, then a large Shire passed between them and Luke lost him again. He searched unsuccessfully for another hour before giving up but the brief glimpse had revived a longing that he knew he must satisfy. He must have Simon with him at Heron. Alison would have to be told. The family and the world would have to know the truth. It would not be easy. But Luke's mind was suddenly made up. At whatever cost to himself or others, now was the time to claim his son!

A mile out from the common Jack turned sharply and glanced behind him.

'What is it?' asked Luke irritably, his mind elsewhere.

'I don't know. My fancy mayhap . . . I keep thinking I hear footsteps but I see nothing.'

He shrugged and they rode on. Jack relapsed into silence, letting his thoughts dwell on the gipsy girl. She had invited him to meet her later. He knew he daren't accept. If her family found out they would kill him as soon as look at him. Four brothers, she had! They would make mincemeat of him! He grinned as he thought with relish of the fight he'd put up first. It might even be worth it for an hour with such a woman. He sighed. In his heart he knew he was better off as stable man at Heron, but it was pleasurable to consider the alternatives. If he put up a brave enough fight they might even accept him into their 'family' – make him a blood brother. Did he want to be a wanderer? Most likely not, he admitted, grinning to himself. It was good to come into the kitchen at Heron after a long hard day and idle an hour or so away in friendly chatter with Beth and Nan. And Jon was a decent lad though inclined to be lazy. He sighed. But then, on the other hand, to be a gipsy was to have no master. There was a thought to conjure with! No master to bid you go or stay. No one to say 'Rise' in the morning – except a wife. Damnation, he had almost forgotten the wife . . .

They were almost at Heron when the horse dealer's child allowed herself to be spotted. She sprang out of the hedge a few yards behind them and stood glaring defiantly as they turned at the sound.

'Mother of God!' exclaimed Jack.

''Tis the child! What in heaven is she about?'

Nonplussed, they looked at her. She looked smaller than ever and the day among the horses and dust had left a film of grime over her face which did nothing to improve her appearance.

'I'm coming with you,' she announced loudly, her black button eyes on Luke's face.

Luke shook his head. 'Oh no you're not,' he told her. 'Get off home, back to your father – or grandfather, whoever he is. Be off with you.' He was trying not to laugh. The child looked so ridiculous, small face screwed up in a fierce expression, her fists doubled, like an angry goblin!

'I'm coming with you,' she insisted.

Jack spurred his horse towards her, his hand up-raised, pretending to strike her, but she stood her ground firmly though her eyes rolled with fright. He pulled up suddenly, lowered his arm and smiled down at her with a disarming change of approach.

'Be a good girl now,' he said, 'and run off back to your home. We've no use for a snippet like you. None at all.'

Ignoring him, she stared at Luke, her face set in a scowl. 'Take me with you,' she said. 'I'll be good and mind my manners. I'm strong.'

'You don't look it,' said Luke gently. 'You look very

young and not at all strong. There is nothing you can do for us and there's an end to it. Your father will be anxious for you.'

'He's my grandfather.'

'Then your grandfather will be anxious. Now if you don't start back right away 'twill be dark before you are there.'

The two men rode on but the child still followed, trudging determinedly in their tracks but careful to keep a few yards behind the horses. Luke turned on her angrily. 'I'll not tell you again,' he shouted. 'Be off home to your grandfather or I'll come down from my horse and tan you!'

'I've been beat before,' she answered 'and I never weep. Not once did I weep. Beat me all you can, you shall see for yourself. Not one tear will I shed though you beat me black and blue! Not one, d'you hear me!' Her small face blazed with rage and, baffled, the two men surveyed her helplessly.

'What's to be done with the wretched creature?' said Luke. 'I swear I'm in no mood for this nonsense.'

The girl drew nearer. 'I showed you the horse was lame, didn't I? Take it round, he told me, in a circle, but I never. So take me with you.'

'Damnation!' muttered Luke. 'I think you had best take her back for we'll not be rid of her otherwise and the daylight's fading.'

Jack slid from his horse and before she realized what was happening he caught her by the arm. With a quick movement of her head she bit his hand and, as he released her, cursing, she returned to stand at Luke's stirrup. 'I'll work hard,' she told him, 'and never back answer, I swear it, and I'll soon grow, you'll see. I'll be eleven next year. Eleven! I'll be bigger when I'm eleven!'

'I'll be damned,' said Luke slowly, shaking his head.

'I almost think I'll take her. I wonder . . .'

His mind raced. Soon, within a day or two, he must take his courage in both hands and confide in Alison, an ordeal he dreaded. At one stroke he would shatter her peace of mind forever and try as he would, he could see no way to lessen the blow. His gentle, loving wife who had done no wrong would soon share his torment. And then he must go in search of Simon and she would be left alone with her thoughts. Perhaps this urchin would occupy her mind. They could do with another maid now that Izzie was dead. Beth had taken her place and Nan was hard put to care for Melissa as well as Alison. Nan should stay with Melissa, and he would take the child for Alison. She would have a full time job on her hands to tame the wretch . . .

He looked at her again and she saw that he wavered. A glimmer of hope shone in the small dark eyes but speech suddenly deserted her and she could only gaze imploringly into his eyes and cross her fingers in an effort to influence his decision.

'Let her be, Jack,' he said at last. 'I've a mind to take her. Ride back alone and find the old man.' He tossed a purse into Jack's astonished hands. 'Tell him what's happened and say there's a place for her at Heron if he's agreeable. Give him the money. If he's not, then he must fetch her back.'

Jack nodded and rode off, inwardly despairing of Luke's sanity. Luke held out a hand to help the girl up. 'And if I ever see you bite anyone again,' he said grimly, 'I'll draw out every tooth in your head!'

Her name was Minnie. Her grandfather was thankful to be rid of her and within a day or two everyone at Heron knew why. In the encouraging atmosphere she shed her sullen manner and became wilful, mischievous and entirely incorrigible. Minnie did not keep her promise to 'be good and mind her manners'. Or perhaps she had no manners. She did, however, have an excess of energy, an inquiring mind and a vocabulary that shocked the entire household. As a maid in training, she left much to be desired. As a distraction for Alison she was perfect.

'What am I to do with her?' she wailed. 'She is not at all biddable, indeed I feel fortunate if she stands still long enough for me to tell her what it is she should do. Before the sentence is half said she has darted off again. She will not call me "ma'am", has trod on Melissa's foot, torments the dogs, back answers Beth and Nan – and she spat at poor Thomas. I won't repeat what she called him and the poor man trying to be kind to her.' She paused for breath and Luke hid a smile. It was a long time since he had seen his wife so excited. 'And she eats like a horse,' she went on, 'and steals food from the larder. A whole loaf and a raw mullet. Raw, Luke! D'you hear what I'm saying? The child is a savage. There's no other word for her.' Luke opened his mouth to speak but she rushed on. 'And smell! She is disgustingly dirty with all those horrible bites all over her. She won't let anyone near enough to look at them, let alone treat them. Her head must be full of lice! Oh Luke, whatever possessed you to bring me such a God-forsaken creature?'

She ran out of breath at last and allowed herself to be gathered into his outstretched arms. Gently he kissed the top of her head.

'Mayhap because she is God-forsaken,' he said. 'What a life, eh? A poor little savage. Wild, like an untamed horse. You are quite right, little mouse. She is a barbarian – but greatly to be pitied. You, if anyone, can make something of her. You can help her, teach her, care for her.'

Alison looked up at him. 'Care for her?' she repeated incredulously. 'Oh Luke, don't ask that of me for I know I shall disappoint you.'

'You have never disappointed me, Alison,' said Luke, 'and I doubt you will do so now.'

Alison looked doubtful. 'Dearest Luke, I'll try. Indeed I will but in truth I hardly know where to start!'

He kissed the tip of her nose. 'Start by giving her a bath,' he said.

'Clear the decks!' cried Jon as he struggled into the kitchen with the large wooden tub that served as a bath if and when it was needed. 'All ashore that's going ashore!'

Despite the brevity of Jon's stay on board the *Mary Rose* he still sustained an image of himself as a seafaring man, which he fondly believed set him apart from, and a little above, the 'landlubbers' around him. He dumped the tub in front of the hearth and grinned at Nan who stood waiting with a large kettle of water in her hand, and two others hanging ready over the fire.

'You can grin,' Nan protested. 'You don't have to live with the little wretch. You can sneak off to the stable and hide away with Jack. I've to share a room with her. Not a wink of sleep did I get last night for her chatter. Then when she fell asleep, it was snore, snore, fit to wake the dead. Tossing and turning she was and that bed always did creak.'

'I'll put some oil on it for you,' he offered. 'That'll quieten it.'

'I'd like some oil put on her!' said Nan. ''Tis her that needs quietening.' She emptied the kettle into the tub and added a pail of cold water, then handed it to Jon. 'Fetch me another, there's a dear,' she said and he trotted off willingly enough. She scooped out a few leaves and a dead spider that now floated on the water, then emptied the second kettle into the first. Jon returned with the full pail in time to hear a bloodcurdling scream from Minnie as she was hauled into the kitchen by Alison and Beth. They held her arms but she wriggled and kicked while a stream of oaths bombarded their ears and sent the colour rushing into Alison's scandalized face.

'– and you'll not get me into that damned stuff!' shrieked Minnie. 'I'd rather die, by God's blood, than be boiled alive in a hot tub.' Her foot shot out and kicked the pail from Jon's hands while the other sent a stool flying across the room to fall against a crock of scalded milk and smashed it. ''Tis poxy stuff, water,' she went on. 'My ma said so and her ma before her! Harm can come to you – Ah! Take that, you devils!' She lashed out and with a final wrench loosed herself, and shot out of the kitchen with a shriek of triumph to the accompaniment of footsteps clattering up the steps.

Wearily Alison put a hand to her head and tried to recover her breath. Beth rubbed at her injured shin.

'She's a right little spit-cat!' she said. 'I wish I had half her energy. Where's she gone now, I wonder. Lordy! What was that?'

There was a crash from overhead and with one accord Alison fled upstairs followed by a grim-faced Beth.

Giggling, Nan added the third kettle of water to the tub and fetched the soft soap. Then purposefully she rolled up her sleeves. 'Now we shall see the sparks fly,' she grinned. 'Are you staying, Jon, to see the fun?'

'Am I staying? What a question!' he said. 'I'd not miss this little treat – not for half a sovereign!'

He was not disappointed. It took all four of them to undress Minnie and get her into the water. Once in there, her screams were shattering to ears and nerves alike. She flailed her arms and thrashed about with her legs until Nan put the soapy flannel into her mouth to silence her. Water went all over the kitchen. It pattered on to the big table like drops of rain and fell hissing into the fire, making it smoke. Jon and Nan held her down while Alison plied a soapy flannel to her face and neck and Beth poured jugfuls of soapy water over her hair. The noise was so incredible it woke the dogs who were sleeping in the Hall. Barking furiously, they rushed into the kitchen to add their contribution to the general confusion. Minnie's countless bites stung painfully as the soap was applied to arms, legs and body and her screams of rage gave way to howls of pain.

Surprisingly few actual words were spoken because no one but Minnie had energy to spare on opinions they wished to express. The same thought was in all their minds – to finish the job as quickly as possible and retire from the fray with a minimum of injuries! For the first five minutes such an outcome seemed unlikely but as the minutes passed their joint efforts and the child's own emotions proved too much and she gradually surrendered to her fate. Her agonized howls faltered into whimpering and she was finally hauled out in front of the fire, a subdued shadow of her former self. With a deep sigh, she closed her eyes and allowed herself to be towelled dry. The four adults looked at each other hopefully. The first battle was over and Heron had won.

Luke delayed telling Alison as long as he could but at last his mind was clear on the matter and his plans were made. First, he would break the news to Alison and with time, secure her acceptance of the situation. Then together they must decide how best to break the news to Abigail and Melissa and after that the households of Heron and Maudesley. It was a daunting, even frightening prospect and there were times when Luke's courage was low, when he felt he would never be able to utter the first sentence that would bring the world tumbling about his own ears, and shatter the security and peace of his loved ones for ever. He had argued with himself interminably in the grey hours between night and day, examining his motives and evaluating the probable results of his decision. Wasn't it a purely selfish desire to expiate his guilt? Was it, perhaps, a loyalty to Isobel and an attempt to right the wrong he had done to her? Was that how Alison would interpret it? Perhaps it was none of these but an instinctive love for Simon, his child, and a fierce pride in the young man who so resembled his father. Simon had Kendal blood in his veins and Heron was his by right. Now that Jeffery and Paul were dead, should no one inherit Heron? His resolve veered with each fresh attempt to discover the instincts that governed his reasoning. At last his resolve hardened. Rightly or wrongly, he would declare his son.

One morning, before the sun was up, he woke Alison and told her that they must talk. He tried to keep his tone as normal as possible but the words were brittle and, instantly alert, Alison rolled over to face him and propped herself on one elbow.

'Talk?' she echoed. 'Talk of what? What is it?' She peered at his face, trying to read his expression in the half light. 'Luke, what is it that is so important you must wake me at this hour?'

'Don't look at me that way,' he chided. 'Don't alarm yourself.'

She was immediately alarmed. 'Luke!' she cried. 'Are you sick? Is that it and you fear to tell me? Oh dearest Luke –'

'I am not sick, Alison.'

'Alison? Why do you call me Alison? You never do Luke. 'Tis always little mouse!'

'I beg you, calm yourself,' he said. 'Come, lie in my

arms. The air is cold and you will catch a chill. No, don't speak. Lie down, that's the way.'

He tucked the sheets around her neck and held her close.

'Your heart!' she cried. ''Tis beating fit to burst.'

'Hush!' he insisted. 'I have something to tell you but I must crave your silence. 'Tis no easy matter –' He fell suddenly silent, appalled now that the moment had come. There was no drawing back now – he had said too much already.

'Luke!'

He could hear the panic in her voice. Dear God, he thought, I'm tormenting her with my cowardice. Tell her, for pity's sake. Say it and be done. He swallowed hard and took a deep breath.

''Tis the boy you spoke of,' he said. 'You asked me in the Priory, many years ago, if the boy Simon was my bastard. I told you he was not.'

'And you lied?' she whispered.

'I spoke truly, little mouse. The boy is not a bastard but my son and only true heir.'

'Your only *true* heir? I don't understand, Luke. What are you trying to tell me?'

She had not grasped his meaning. He cursed his folly. He was prolonging her distress. Out with it in plain speech – and let the hurting start.

'His mother was my wife. My legal wife in the eyes of God.'

There was a long silence. 'Your wife, Luke?' she said at last and her voice was strangely normal. 'But I'm your wife.'

'No, Alison. I wed Simon's mother before I wed you.' His voice dropped to a whisper. 'You were never my true wife.'

Her senses reeled. 'Oh . . . Oh Luke . . . but the children! Jeffery, Paul –'

313

'Not my true heirs.'

'Jeffery and Paul not your heirs?'

The room grew lighter and he could make out her face. He opened his mouth to explain but she stopped him.

'No, wait,' she said. 'Let me speak, Luke. You are saying that I was never your wife and the children were born out of wedlock. Have your wits deserted you, Luke? You expect me to believe that?'

'I hope you will for 'tis the truth.'

She looked at him, wide-eyed. ''Tis nonsense,' she whispered. 'Do you realize what it would mean, if it *were* true? What it would do to Lissa and Abby – and to me.'

He sighed heavily. 'Do you think I haven't considered that?' he said. 'Why would I pretend such things? You must know I wouldn't willingly inflict such pain on my girls or on you. Alison, believe me, I beg you. 'Tis monstrous I know but I swear 'tis the truth.'

Alison sat up in bed. She tried to speak calmly but he saw that her lips trembled. 'I know why you are doing this,' she said. 'You want a son, Luke, that's it. You have lost the only boys I gave you and so you think to adopt your baseborn son. Is that the truth of it? But I'll not be party to such a tale. Just think on the disgrace if you spoke truly. Poor little Abby. What would the Jarmans think – their eldest son wed to a love-child. And Melissa! Who would ever wed *her* believing her illegitimate?' He was silent. 'Would you ruin them, Luke? Your own daughters!'

'What more can I say, then. 'Tis the truth, Alison,' he said.

'I won't believe it,' she cried. 'Tell the world of your baseborn son if you must but tell it truly. He is the bastard! I am your true wife and the girls are your true daughters, born in holy wedlock. I cannot accept anything else.'

Luke could only shake his head helplessly. Her reaction was so unexpected he hardly knew how to handle it. He had expected shock, tears, hysterics and recriminations. This refusal to accept the true state of affairs dismayed him.

'Alison,' he began but she interrupted. She sat up abruptly, hugging her knees, her face turned from him. When she spoke, her voice was quiet but resolute.

'Tell me about her,' she said.

'Her name was Isobel – Isobel Gillis.' He waited for an outburst but none came. 'I met her before my betrothal to you was arranged. Because of her lowly background I knew she and I could never wed but I loved her. At least I believed myself in love and she said she loved me.' There was still no response from Alison and her silence unnerved him. He was silent for a moment seeking the right words, then continued. 'When you arrived at Maudesley I knew I must give her up and made up my mind to tell her –'

'Tell her what?' said Alison sharply.

'That I must be faithful to you.'

'That you loved me?'

'No. I did not love you then . . .'

'Was she very beautiful?'

Luke hesitated, reluctant to hurt her more than was necessary, but his hesitation spoke for him.

'I see,' she said. 'Go on.'

'I made up my mind to tell her but before I could do so she told me that she was with child.'

Imperceptibly Alison had begun to rock backwards and forwards. The movement soothed her but disconcerted Luke.

'Go on,' she said again.

'She was desperate to be wed and at last I agreed . . . When the child was born the birth was difficult and her mind was deranged. I confided in my mother and she

315

had the child taken away and put with another family. I didn't know where. Isobel grew worse, much worse . . . Alison, I –'

'Go on!'

'You and I were wed, at least we –'

Alison stopped rocking. 'We were wed,' she said flatly. 'Who married you to Isobel?'

'A monk at the Priory.'

'With the Abbot's knowledge?'

'No, but –'

'With anyone's knowledge, save the monk himself?'

'There was one witness, one of the lay servants.'

She was silent, thinking.

'Listen to me,' begged Luke. 'Do you not see that I could have made this matter easier by pretending that Simon was born out of wedlock? Why should I antagonize you needlessly by pretending that Isobel and I were wed if 'twere not so? I wanted to tell you the truth after all these years of secrecy and guilt.'

'You wanted an heir, Luke. That is why you've spoken after all these years. You may have *believed* the wedding in the Priory was legal. Isobel may have believed it but I don't . . .'

He shook his head, unable to marshal his thoughts further.

'Isobel,' said Alison. 'They found her body, I recall. How did she die, Luke? You did not –'

'Kill her?' he said bitterly. 'No, I am no murderer. 'Tis one crime I haven't committed. She fell, it was an accident.'

'But you were with her?'

'Aye. She came to ask me to find Simon. She had no one – nothing. Her father had died also. Her sanity was all she possessed in the whole world. I didn't know where the boy was then. I couldn't help her.'

'And she fell over the cliff?' There was the faintest

316

emphasis on the word 'fell'.

'Aye.'

He hoped desperately she would not press him further. The horror and shame of that last meeting still haunted him. She said nothing, thinking desperately.

'Alison, I cannot ask you to forgive –' he began.

'I do forgive you, Luke,' she said. 'And I pity you with all my heart. To have suffered such a burden all these years! And I sympathize with you in your longing for a son. But unless you bring me proof of the legality of that ceremony,' she looked at him and he saw the terrible misery in her eyes, 'I shall never believe it.'

CHAPTER SEVENTEEN

The wood was very dark and the trees dripped moisture although the cold January rain had ceased earlier in the day. Underfoot, bracken and bramble combined to trip his stumbling feet which, wrapped in rags, were already sodden and throbbing with the cold. Overhead a few birds sang and a squirrel making his way among the branches paused to chatter at the old man who disturbed their peace with his rambling. The old man looked up at it, screwing up his eyes short-sightedly.

'God provides for the likes of you,' he said sourly. 'Nuts on the trees and berries in the hedgerows. 'Tis fine for you but a man must fend for himself. You stay out of my reach, d'you hear, 'cos you'll end up as my supper if I catch you.' The squirrel still lingered and the old man waved his arms to frighten it. Muttering, the old man continued. Under one arm he carried several sticks of wood and the pocket of his shabby coat bulged with fir cones. His hair was long and grey as was his beard. The frame under the shapeless garment was emaciated, his knees swollen with rheumatism. He was hungry and chilled to the bone but eight years on the road had hardened him to his harsh existence and his wits, sharpened by circumstances, had served him well. He prided himself on his survival in a hostile, unsympathetic world. He had learned to beg only food and clothes. Money was too great a responsibility since a more aggressive vagrant would probably steal it from him; it was scarcely worth a beating.

Searching around at the foot of a large oak, he discovered a rabbit caught in the snare he had set two days earlier. He disentangled it and looked at the limp body critically. It was a young one but plump enough and he had a turnip to go with it. Heartened by this find he straightened up, grimacing at the genuine pain in his knees. Not all his pains were genuine. He had long since mastered the art of deception in such matters. He prided himself on his very convincing fits which had served him well on many occasions. Or his raw and bleeding 'sores' painstakingly created and perfected over many weeks.

'A coney and a turnip,' he muttered 'and a crust of bread! I shall dine well tonight.' And in solitary splendour, he thought and the idea pleased him as much as the prospect of the meal itself. He had grown weary of the company of other unfortunates and the constant harassment of constables who moved them on from town to town or threw them into the stocks whenever they could find just or unjust cause. No, he was better off alone. Easier to go undetected when the need arose and less likely to fall foul of the law. A short spell in prison had taught him the value of freedom, no matter how spartan the existence.

He left the shelter of the wood and cut across open country, bent double to avoid being seen. As the Priory came into view, he allowed himself a small sigh for the life he had once had. A servant in the Priory had a place in the scheme of things. His day was ordered, he ate well enough and could boast a bed and a roof over his head. Now there was no roof. The Priory buildings stood open to the elements, windowless and doorless – except for the crypt. It was this area that Henry Bell had finally made his own. Turned out at the dissolution, his wanderings had taken him across Devon, into Cornwall and back again. It was, he told himself, the will of God for unseen hands had guided him back. Harben Priory was no more but he had found refuge beneath it. Like an animal, he ventured out daily in search of food and wood for his fire, returning to it each evening like a fox returning to its earth. He counted himself fortunate and was well content, revelling in his solitude. If his lonely existence affected his mind, he was not aware of it. If he mumbled incoherently or sang wheezily, there were none to mock him.

At the entrance to the crypt he paused, suddenly alerted by the sound of hoof-beats. They passed by at a distance and he nodded.

'Aye, pass on, whoever you are,' he muttered. 'Leave me be and pass on.' He couldn't know that it was Luke Kendal who thundered by in search of him.

Alison's eyes were on Minnie's small fingers as they pushed and pulled the needle through the pale fabric. They sat together by the fire in the Hall with two of the dogs on the hearth in front of them. Opposite, Melissa plied her own needle and thread, her face glowing in the firelight, her expression calm. Minnie's needle strayed from its path and Alison's sharp eyes detected the error.

'No, no, Minnie,' she said. 'That stitch is too long. See? Let me have it and I'll pull it back for you. Oh, what a face! Don't look so black, child.'

Minnie scowled and swung her legs angrily. 'I'm tired of stitching,' she said, 'and my fingers ache.'

Melissa caught her eye and smiled. ''Tis only your first lesson,' she said. 'You will find it grows easier.'

'I don't like to stitch,' said Minnie. 'I don't want it to grow easier. My back aches and the needle pricks my thumb.'

Alison looked at her severely. 'I warrant it should be your conscience that pricks you,' she said, 'for I told you to wash your hands before you started. See here – 'tis soiled already. Show me your hands. Hold them out I say.'

Minnie promptly sat on her offending hands, for she had not washed them. Alison's voice sharpened. 'Show me, I say! Ah, I thought so. Such grimy fingers. Look at them. You should be ashamed. Now go to the kitchen at once and ask Beth for soap and a cloth. Do as I say now and hurry back for you shan't have any supper until you have finished the row.'

'I don't want to,' cried Minnie rebelliously. 'I don't care to stitch. I hate it.'

Melissa hid her own amusement and Alison struggled to keep her face straight as Minnie's small features settled themselves into the familiar expression. The child made it her business to hate everything with the exception of food. She was used to fighting and secretly enjoyed the conflict with authority; the occasional blow, earned by her difficult behaviour, was counted proof of its effectiveness. Minnie felt that if no one was driven to box her ears then her existence was largely passing unnoticed and that thought was anathema to her. She slid to the floor stepping on the tail of one of the dogs as she did so. The animal leaped up growling his reproaches, and Alison made an effort to keep her temper.

'Minnie!'

'He doesn't like me,' said Minnie sulkily. 'He always growls at me. I hate him.'

'He doesn't like you because you torment him,' said Alison. 'Now leave him be and go to the kitchen. Come back when those hands are as clean as mine. See?'

She held up her own hands and Minnie glared at them balefully.

'I don't like washing,' she said.

'Seemingly there's nothing in the whole of Heron that you like,' said Alison.

'I like Luke,' said the little girl.

Alison sighed. 'How many times must I tell you,' she scolded. 'Don't call him Luke but "the master".'

'I like the master,' said Minnie. 'Why is he gone away?'

'He's gone to buy land,' Alison lied 'but 'tis none of your business.'

She spoke glibly enough but Melissa detected the shadow that passed over her mother's face and wondered anew at the suddenness of her father's departure.

'Out!' said Alison, pointing. 'Not another word or there'll be no supper for you. You shall come back with clean hands and finish this row of cross-stitch. Now make haste. My patience is nigh exhausted with your shilly-shallying.'

Minnie walked slowly across the Hall, scuffing the rushes as she went in an effort to provoke Alison further but she refused to be drawn.

'Oh that child!' lamented Alison when she had gone. 'Whatever provoked Luke to bring her into this house I'll never know. She's as stubborn as a mule.'

'Mayhap you should put her into Jack's hands,' laughed Melissa. 'He's used to breaking in horses and might have more success.'

'He's welcome to try,' said Alison. She put a hand to her chest as a fit of coughing racked her and Melissa looked at her anxiously. The consumption was telling on her more rapidly now and the doctor was a regular visitor.

'Are you tired, Mama?' she asked. 'I'll finish Minnie's lesson if you want to rest.'

Alison shook her head. ''Tis over now,' she said as the pain subsided. 'Don't concern yourself.'

While she waited for Minnie to reappear, her thoughts returned to Luke and his quest. The old monk must surely be dead by now, she thought, but what of the servant who acted as witness? Henry, was it? Was he still alive and, if he was, would Luke be able to find him? She allowed herself to dwell on the young man who might one day take his place at Heron. She had a clear picture of him as she remembered him when he had come to her assistance. A strange awareness had sparked between them then. Was the part of him that was Luke reaching out to her? In her heart she longed for a son but could she ever love Isobel's son? And what of Melissa? Luke had told her of Melissa's love for the young man and Alison wondered afresh how the girl would react to the knowledge that Simon was her half-brother.

And if Simon was part Luke, he was also part Isobel. How much of that unfortunate creature was in the boy? And what of Marion Gillis, the witch woman? Dear God! It wasn't possible that such blood should mix with Kendal blood – and yet it had! Simon was proof of that if proof were needed . . . She rubbed her eyes wearily, picked up Minnie's sampler and put it down again.

Melissa laughed gently. 'Do you think you will make a needle-woman of her?' she asked.

'I can but try,' said Alison. 'Where is the minx? She's taking her time.'

'No doubt wheedling a few currants out of Beth,' said Melissa but time passed and the child did not appear.

'Now what mischief is she up to?' muttered Alison and, sighing resignedly, followed her to the kitchen.

Minnie was not in the kitchen eating currants and Beth had not seen her at all. They looked all over the house and Jon was despatched to search the stable, all without results. It soon became evident that the recalcitrant Minnie had run away and Alison, already greatly distressed by other matters, flared suddenly into anger at the betrayal. Despite warnings about the state of her health, she ignored all their entreaties and insisted on riding out in search of the missing servant. She did not find her. Instead she found her way to the ruined Priory where she went down into the crypt to investigate some wisps of smoke. At the foot of the steps she discovered a ragged old man crouched beside a fire. In his hands he held a bowl and a dripping spoon was halfway to his lips as he looked up fearfully at his intruder. In his shock he dropped the spoon and spilt the stew into the flames of his modest fire. He huddled back against the wall of the crypt, now darkened with soot and green with the damp. He stared up at Alison like a cornered animal, his lips moving soundlessly. She had expected to find Minnie and now, taken aback, she stared at the old man.

'What are you doing here?' she asked, her surprise sharpening her tone.

He didn't answer but slowly rose to his feet, flattening himself against the wall while his eyes darted to one side and then the other in search of escape. Alison's face softened. Poor wretch. He was one of so many helpless and homeless and it seemed nothing could be done for them.

'There's no need to be afeard old man,' she said softly. 'I don't mean you any harm.'

He uttered a little cry, incomprehensible, almost a moan, and looked from Alison to his spoilt stew and back again.

'What is your name?' she asked.

He shook his head fearfully.

'You don't know your own name?'

He shook his head violently, then nodded.

Alison sighed. The poor creature was witless, no

doubt. 'Your name,' she said clearly. 'Is it John? William? What do they call you? Your name, man?'

Suddenly he found his voice. 'Henry,' he said. 'My name's Henry, but don't hurt me! I'm doing no harm, I swear it in the name of Good King Henry!'

'The King is dead,' said Alison.

Her gaze took in his makeshift bed: a layer of straw and heather roughly covered by a frayed blanket and beside it the pile of wood, upended to drain and dry.

'Dead, is he?' said the old man. 'Why then the Lord have mercy on his soul.'

'How long have you been here?' asked Alison.

He shook his head vaguely. 'But not long,' he said hastily. 'No, not long at all. A day or two, mebbe three.'

She did not venture further in for the smell was abominable. 'Who are you?' she said again.

'Bell,' he said. 'Henry Bell – late of this parish!' He giggled foolishly at his attempt at humour and failed to note the change of expression on Alison's face and the indrawn breath.

'Late of this Priory also,' he went on, his grin revealing two rotting teeth, 'for I spent many a good year here before the King saw fit to send us all packing! Aye, many a good year –' He broke off, peering through the gloom. 'I seen your face afore,' he said. 'Aren't you from up the big house at Heron? I seen you some place, that I do know.'

'I'm – I'm Mistress Kendal,' stammered Alison. Her mind was racing as she stared at the grotesque old man who now hobbled closer like an animated scarecrow.

'I'm doing no harm here,' he said again, 'and I've nowhere else to go and no strength, neither, to roam the highways with a gang of villains. I'm a God-fearing man, and this is only a rabbit. Surely a man's got to eat, ma'am, and 'tis little enough when all is said and done. An empty belly is no good to man or beast.'

She nodded distractedly. So this was Henry Bell! This pathetic scrap of humanity was the man her husband was looking for because he alone might be able to prove her marriage invalid and her daughters bastards! This was the man and she had found him. This wretch might hold the key to the future happiness and prosperity of those she loved. It was incredible that he should be here, virtually on their doorstep, while Luke scoured the country for a clue to his whereabouts. She, Alison, had found him. Was it the hand of God, she wondered? Had some divine intervention guided her to the spot and if so, then to what purpose? She regarded him through narrowed eyes and he grew anxious under her scrutiny.

'I've done no harm, I tell you,' he repeated feebly. 'Be merciful I beseech you. Have pity on an old man.'

'Do you recall my husband?' she asked, interrupting him. 'My husband is Luke Kendal. D'you recall him?'

'I do, aye,' he said. 'A fine gentleman.'

'Did you ever speak with him?'

'Oh I dare say I did,' he said cautiously. 'I served the Priory for many years and I spoke with many gentle folk as came to visit or passed through on pilgrimage. They were good days . . .' He sighed tremulously. 'So the King is dead,' he said, trying to hide his satisfaction at the news. 'Ah well, it comes to all of us . . .'

Alison came to a sudden decision. She would find out what, if anything, this old man remembered. Maybe her fears were groundless and God intended her reassurance. She took a few steps towards him and forced a smile to her lips.

'Tell me,' she began. 'Think back, I beg you. Do you know aught of a woman called Gillis? 'Twas many years ago.'

His eyes widened fearfully at the name. 'Gillis! Don't breathe that name to me,' he implored her. 'Witch woman she was – but they hanged her, didn't they?'

'Not the witch,' said Alison. 'I speak of the witch woman's daughter, Isobel. D'you recall her? There's money in it for you, if you do.'

The old man considered, unwilling to fall into a trap. 'I might,' he said at last.

'Tell me what you recall,' said Alison, her tone hardening in spite of her efforts to remain calm. She stepped forward again and caught at his arm. 'Tell me everything you recall!'

The old man did not care for the vehemence in her tone and was alarmed. 'I don't recall anything –' he began hastily, but it was too late to withdraw. The fingers holding his arm increased their pressure.

'Tell me, I beg you,' she cried. 'All that you recall. For God's sake, old man!'

Her fears overwhelmed her and she found herself shaking him with all her strength. 'Tell me, I say! What of Isobel Gillis? What do you know of her – and my husband?'

'I – know – nought,' he lied but the truth was written in his averted eyes.

She shook him again, and he struggled with her in a futile effort to extricate himself from the situation which now frightened him.

'I recall nought,' he began again. 'Let me be for pity's sake. I've done no harm, I swear it.'

'Isobel Gillis,' cried Alison, 'and Luke Kendal. Think, old man! You were here. You saw them, heard them. You did, didn't you? Tell me, for God's sake.'

'Aye, I did,' he mumbled terrified. 'I saw them wed. Brother Eustace, it was. Come, he tells me. You're a witness, Henry. Aye, to the wedding. Oh aye –'

No sooner were the words out than he wished them unsaid for Alison's face went white with shock. At last she had heard what she feared to hear but she had never

327

anticipated the effect such a revelation would have on her. The passionate despair which filled her as the old man spoke of Luke's betrayal gave way to a black anger. She screamed, 'Luke! Dear God! Luke! What have you done?'

With a shriek of fear the old man pulled himself free but stumbled backwards, tripped over the pitcher and fell heavily. As he went down, he struck his head against the stone wall of the crypt. He lay half across the makeshift bed, his limbs awkwardly sprawled, his eyes staring. Alison, frozen with horror, watched him die. Then she crossed herself and whispered a brief prayer for his soul. She threw the pitcher of water over the remains of his fire and went slowly back up the steps to find her horse. On the way home she began to cough painfully and was soon vomiting the blood that filled her diseased lungs. She arrived back at Heron in a state of physical and mental collapse from which she never recovered. By the time Luke came home, she was dead and her secret, gained at such a high cost, died with her.

In the summer of 1548 the shocked family were told of Luke's illegitimate son. Luke told them that for natural reasons of discretion he preferred to keep the identity of the boy's mother to himself, but said that she was dead. For Melissa the revelation was doubly shattering. The memory of their stolen meetings returned to accuse her. They had been so close to consummating their love! So close to disaster! Only Thomas Benet fully understood the implications for her and he gave what comfort and support he could throughout the weeks that followed. Slowly, painfully, Melissa came to terms with the idea and only then were arrangements made for Simon to move into Heron.

Melissa asked only that she might greet him alone

and this was granted willingly. She therefore waited for him in the riverside garden well away from prying eyes. She sat on the steps and watched the river. The water was low – it had been a dry summer to date – and the smell of almond blossom hung in the warm air.

Looking across the water, she saw the chestnut tree where she and Simon had stood while they watched the rest of Heron enjoy the bonfire. And she saw herself and Abigail sitting on the stepping stones, their bare feet dabbling the water, talking of girlish matters . . .

Once at the age of eight she had slipped on the stones and fallen in. Thomas had waded in to her rescue and she had thought him the most courageous man she had ever met. Jeffery had made her a fishing rod from bamboo with a bramble tied to it and a bent pin for a hook. She had caught a small roach and had been so proud of it until Paul told her later that Jeffery had fastened it on to the hook while her attention was distracted elsewhere. It had hurt, that small betrayal. She smiled faintly at the memory and then sighed. Two brothers and she had lost them both. But Simon was her half-brother and she didn't know how to react. Her heart cried out for his love and that could be warm and brotherly. But would her body still cry out for his after so many years had passed? Such love was now forbidden her.

Had he changed much, she wondered. He had not wed, for which she was thankful. To greet him as a brother and smile upon his wife! She doubted she could do that. One day perhaps. He would have to wed or Heron would pass to Hugo, her cousin, in Sampford Courtenay. Where would she, Melissa, go when Simon brought a wife to Heron? To Maudesley, perhaps. One thing was certain: she could not live under the same roof with Simon's wife no matter how sweet-natured she might be. To see them together would be an agony she could not endure. But that was all in the future.

Today she must greet her lover as a brother and that was ordeal enough.

Her sharp ears caught the sound of approaching hooves and the frenzied barking as the dogs ran out. He had arrived! She imagined the excitement in the house. The servants would be peeping from every window with Minnie bobbing up and down like a cork and the others striving to keep her still. Thomas, still mourning Alison's death, would be polite but say little, seeing Simon as living proof of Luke's infidelity.

Resisting the sudden urge to run across the stepping stones and away from Heron, she stood up, smoothed her skirt and went down to stand beside the water. How should she greet him, she wondered? With dignity and a few kind words? Perhaps she should not speak of the past but greet him as a stranger. No, that would be impossible. She would calmly suggest that they put the past from their minds. Tossing a small pebble into the river, she composed her features into a semblance of serenity. She would welcome him to Heron, to the Kendal family – graciously. Aye, that was the key. A mature and gracious woman, a new Melissa. If only he did not speak to her of love for then she would be undone and her resolve would vanish like melting snow! 'Don't speak to me of love,' she whispered. 'Don't look at me the way you did before.'

She wore the blue damask gown but wondered suddenly if the green suited her better. And surely she should have met him in the house with everyone else. How strange it would appear to the servants. They would whisper among themselves that she resented his coming and wished to insult him by her non-appearance . . . Above the water tiny flies hung in the air and a silver fish leapt from the water to snap them up, falling back with an almost soundless splash that sent up no spray. She would say that she forgave him his abrupt departure

330

so many years ago, that it had hurt her but now she understood the reason. She would hold out a hand in greeting or nod her head courteously . . . Oh sweet heaven. Why didn't he come? How much longer must she wait, fretting by the riverside? What could he be doing?

There was a flurry of feet as the two dogs hurtled down the steps announcing Simon's arrival. Melissa heard his feet on the steps and turned slowly. At the sight of him, her intended speeches fled from her mind and the control she had striven for almost deserted her. He reached the bottom of the steps and paused uncertainly. Dear God! If he held out his arms she would run into them! She longed for the touch of his hand or the feel of his lips on hers. Neither of them spoke, each searching for appropriate words. At last Melissa gave a nod of greeting and he bowed slightly. 'Greetings,' she said, 'and welcome to Heron. I trust your journey was a pleasant one.'

'Aye, very pleasant.'

To hide her confusion she bent to pat the dogs and bid them calm themselves. Simon saw her fine slim neck above the pale shoulders and longed to reach out and touch her. Instead he picked up a piece of bark and tossed it into the water, laughing as the two dogs plunged in to retrieve it.

'They are pleased to see you,' said Melissa watching them as they squabbled boisterously over the bark on the far side of the river.

'And you?' said Simon. 'I had the gravest misgivings but your father assured me –'

'He spoke truly,' she said. Finally she met his eyes with a calm expression, but her voice trembled. 'I could not refuse you your birthright and my father was adamant. 'Twas unthinkable for him that Heron should pass to a cousin.'

331

'But you, Melissa – do you truly welcome me?' he persisted, 'for if not then I have made up my mind to renounce Heron.'

'Oh no!' she cried. 'This is where you belong. If Mama had lived, it would have been different. But she's dead and Heron lacks an heir. 'Tis proper that you should come into your own.'

'And the past?' he asked gently. 'We must speak of it this once and then put it out of our minds. Do you forgive me the hurt I caused you?'

'I do.'

'Melissa, I would never presume to try and replace your brothers in your affections. They were most dear to you, I know. But say that I may care for you as a brother.'

'I hope you will, Simon.'

'And what of your feelings for me?'

'I shall always think on you fondly,' she said and was glad that the dogs returned to interrupt them. Together they walked back to the house. Melissa was outwardly composed but her body was on fire and her senses reeled. Whatever Simon's feelings for her and in spite of her brave words, she knew that she could never live with him as sister and brother. Since he must stay, then she would have to go.

CHAPTER EIGHTEEN

Months passed and spring came again to an England uneasy under the ministrations of Prince Edward's Protector, the Duke of Somerset. Various religious innovations being introduced by his government were seen as the insidious spread of Protestantism and deeply resented. This resentment was rife in the West Country where the old religion still flourished under the Catholic clergy. The new Book of Common Prayer was being duly circulated to all churches and on Whit Sunday in every church in the land the service would be largely conducted in English instead of Latin. This struck deep into the heart of Cornish tradition for they had previously enjoyed the privileged use of their native Cornish tongue for the Lord's Prayer, Creed and Commandments. Trouble finally erupted on 5 April when William Body, an unscrupulous and unpopular commissioner, arrived in Helston. An angry crowd, led by Martin Jeffrey, a priest from St Keverne, marched into Helston, dragged Body from a house where he had taken refuge, and stabbed him to death. By the time the magistrates arrived, the small crowd had grown considerably as word spread throughout the town. They resisted demands to 'deliver up the murderers' and the magistrates withdrew to confer. Men from neighbouring towns poured into Helston and the original band of discontented parishioners from St Keverne had become a mob, nearly three thousand strong.

Thoroughly alarmed, the authorities acted swiftly and men were enlisted from the eastern parts of the county to suppress the agitation before it became a full-scale rebellion. In May a general pardon was announced but it excluded the ringleaders who were later executed. A week later Simon rode back to Cornwall to speak with his many friends and learn for himself the strength of feeling which remained.

It was the first time he had been absent from Heron since his adoption, and his absence gave Melissa an opportunity to take stock of her feelings and position. In the morning she went riding alone for nearly three hours. After dinner she walked out into the garden to find Thomas who practised dutifully, albeit unsuccessfully, at the butts. She watched quietly. He drew back his arm, sighted along the arrow and released it. It winged harmlessly wide of the target and he turned ruefully towards her. 'Let's hope the safety of the realm is never in my hands,' he laughed. 'I fear I should be more use to the enemy than to England! So far I have scored twice and have lost three arrows into the bushes.'

'Perhaps your bow is warped,' said Melissa. 'You can pretend it is. Who's to know?'

He looked at it critically. 'I shall know,' he said. 'I can't deceive even myself. 'Tis one of my failings.'

He pulled a fresh arrow from the grass beside him and slid the notch against the string. Raising it to eye level, he pressed the bow forward steadily and let it fly.

Melissa clapped her hands in mock admiration. 'Well done, Thomas!' she cried. 'You have missed the target completely. 'Tis well for you King Henry is dead.'

He flushed slightly, mortified by his lack of skill. 'I need practice,' he said.

'Or else the arrow is faulty.'

He held one out for her inspection. 'Fletched to perfection,' he admitted. 'The best peacock feathers and trimmed to a hair's breadth! No, a good craftsman doesn't blame his tools. My eye is not as true as it once was. I'm growing old, I fear.'

Melissa studied him as he spoke. Over forty now, he was still slim and his hair still curled over his head. His face retained its boyish eagerness, although he smiled less since Alison's death and Melissa knew that Simon's presence disturbed him.

'On the white!' cried Melissa as an arrow found its mark at last. 'You must stop now while you are at your peak!'

'Aye, that's good advice,' he agreed, 'and I can scarce afford to lose any more arrows.'

He pulled the last three arrows from the grass, wiped the tips free of soil and replaced them in his quiver. Together they walked over to retrieve the arrow and he glanced at her thoughtfully. 'You have dark shadows under your eyes,' he observed gently. 'Do you not sleep well?'

'No.'

He sighed. 'Nor me, I confess. Your Simon is –'

'He's not mine, Thomas,' she corrected him sharply. 'He belongs to Heron – and is my half-brother. Nothing more.'

'Then why do you lie awake at night?' he asked. He pulled the arrow free and twirled it absentmindedly, fingering the browny-grey feathers and smooth shaft. Melissa considered carefully before answering him.

'I lie awake at night,' she said slowly, 'because I am a woman with no man of my own. Suddenly I am twenty-three and unwed. Simon, as is right and proper, speaks no more to me of love nor do I read it in his face. But his very presence here has woken me to – to a certain awareness. I don't want to die a spinster, Thomas.' Her voice shook and there was misery in her eyes. 'I can't stay here much longer, Thomas, but where in heaven am I to go?'

'I'm sorry,' he said helplessly. 'Indeed I am. I had no idea.' He took her hand and squeezed it. 'My poor little Lissa,' he said gently. 'I have been so wrapt in my own griefs –'

'I know,' she said. 'You loved my mother and now she's gone. We're two lost souls, Thomas.'

'I wonder how long Simon will be away?' said Thomas. 'Luke did not relish his going. I heard raised voices.'

'Aye. Papa is obsessed with his new son.' She tried to keep the bitterness out of her voice. 'He has thoughts for no one else these days. 'Tis natural, I suppose, and yet it hurts me.'

'Simon will have his own way,' said Thomas. 'He is a true Kendal in that respect. He made up his mind to go to Cornwall and there was no gainsaying him.'

'I dare say his sympathies are with the rioters. He has lived in the area for many years and had good friends there. He spoke of Martin Jeffrey several times and now he is dead. Simon was greatly angered by his execution.'

'They say his head is still displayed on London Bridge,' said Thomas.

'Ugh! Don't speak of it,' she begged. 'These are troubled times and like to worsen.'

'I trust not,' he said.

She smiled faintly. 'Mayhap you should practise your archery,' she said. 'England may yet have need of you!'

He shook his head. 'What use am I to anyone?' he asked. 'I shall be old soon and put out to graze like the horses. And yet it seems only yesterday I was a boy. Somehow my life has slipped away . . .' He shook his head and Melissa glanced at him surreptitiously. She had something to say and this might be the time to say it.

'Mayhap you should wed,' she suggested.

He laughed, genuinely surprised. 'Who would wed me?' he said.

'Mayhap *I* would,' she said and was afraid to look at him. It seemed an eternity before he spoke again.

'I doubt I'd make a good husband,' he said, choosing his words carefully, 'but I'll think on your most generous offer. Indeed I will.'

The next afternoon he sought her out and found her in the Hall busy with her tapestry. Her fingers trembled as he approached but he was far too nervous to notice it. She looked up and smiled and there was a faint blush in her cheeks.

'May I sit with you?' he asked and Melissa nodded. Then holding up her tapestry, she said, 'Would you say Thomas, that I am improving? I don't tangle the thread as often as I did.'

Disconcerted he said, 'Improving? Oh – aye, I think you have improved. Indeed I'm certain of it.'

Almost imperceptibly he shook his head in wonder. Was she really twenty-three years old and a grown woman? Always he had thought of her as a child but he could see her clearly now, for the first time. The soft grey eyes that for so many years had stared out blankly at the world while her personality remained locked away. Once they had called her a 'fey' child but she had escaped from the prison of her closed mind. 'Twenty-three,' he marvelled aloud. 'I can scarce believe it.'

'Old enough and wise enough,' she said.

He was silent, once more taken aback by her directness which surprised him. Yet he admired her for it. He was by nature a modest man and saw little in himself that a woman might find attractive.

'Old enough and wise enough, Thomas,' she said, 'to know where my happiness lies.'

'Your happiness?'

'Aye.'

'But your heart lies with Simon. I know it must.'

'A small part of my heart, mayhap,' she said gently, 'but my happiness. Ah! That is a different matter.'

'You do me a great honour,' said Thomas, 'but I – I dare not allow myself –' He broke off, confused and embarrassed, and sighed helplessly as he moved to the window to hide his agitation. Melissa put down her tapestry and followed him. She stood beside him and slipped her hand into his. 'How often we have stood so,' she said. 'Ever since I was a child, almost since you first came to Heron, yours was the hand I clung to. Do you remember?'

He nodded. She lifted the hand to her lips and kissed each finger. 'And one for the thumb!' she laughed. 'Every night before I would settle to sleep Thomas must needs come and kiss my fingers, and thumbs. I never needed to ask for you, you were always there, standing in the doorway, rather like a heron yourself on those long thin legs!'

'Now you're mocking me,' he said, smiling.

'Oh no, dearest Thomas. I would never mock you unless 'twas done lovingly . . . Where would I be now without you, Thomas?'

'Who can say what might have been,' he began but she laid a finger across his lips to silence him.

'If I am a whole person,' she said ''tis thanks mainly to you. My family loved me, I know, but you were my rock, Thomas, and if I should give myself to you now why then, 'tis only what is yours by right.'

'Oh, my dearest girl, what can I say? I am so clumsy with words.' He drew her into his arms and she looked up at him.

'Those mild blue eyes, Thomas, are more familiar to me than any others. Your arms rocked me to sleep when I was afraid of the dark and your long legs strode in search

338

of me when I was lost. Don't desert me now, Thomas.'

By way of an answer he held her tight, kissing the top of her head. 'I've been so blind,' he said 'not to see you as you are. You know I loved your mother, but God didn't intend her for me. But through her he sent me my own little Lissa.'

They stared into each other's eyes, dazed by the prospect ahead of them, half afraid to believe their good fortune.

'So you accept my proposal,' she whispered, her tone serious behind the teasing words.

'With all my heart and soul!' he said fervently and drew her once more into the haven of his arms where she most properly belonged.

That same evening Melissa approached her father. If he was surprised by her request he did not show it, but he did ask the questions that any father would ask in such circumstances. Did Melissa feel that the difference in their ages would be a bar to their happiness? She did not, she told him firmly. Was she not throwing herself away on the family's steward? Melissa did not for one moment see it in that light. Did they love each other? She answered simply that they had always done so.

Luke allowed himself to be convinced of the wisdom of the idea. His unmarried daughter had been a source of worry for many years and he was genuinely pleased that she had finally chosen to marry. A more ambitious union would have pleased him better but he was in the throes of negotiating a suitable wife for Simon and, as heir to Heron, his future was of greater concern. If Melissa were happy, Luke was also and he gave his blessing and promised Melissa a reasonable dowry. He would set them up in a small household only four miles away on the very edge of Dartmoor and the wedding would take place as soon as possible. Meanwhile he must turn his attention to Simon, whose continued absence annoyed him more than he would admit. Luke was unaware of the seriousness of the affair at Helston but he had planned to ride over to Crediton to introduce Simon to other members of the family living there. Later he and Simon would journey to Rochester and London. Letters concerning Simon had gone out to all branches of the Kendal family and Luke was now all eagerness to show off his newly acknowledged 'son'. The legal aspects of his adoption were currently being considered and no expense would be spared to ensure a satisfactory outcome to the proceedngs when it reached the courts. Unaware of the depth of Simon's involvement with the Cornish dissidents, Luke waited impatiently for his return while the unrest in the West Country smouldered dangerously.

Whit Sunday morning dawned clear and bright and the sun glowed warmly on the orange lichen that covered the west tower of St Andrew's church. William Harper, the parson, waited nervously while his little flock filtered into the church. The attendance would be even higher than usual for everyone in Sampford Courtenay was curious to hear the old man read the new service. They would not, he feared, approve. Nor would they fail to observe that several pictures and ornaments had been discreetly removed from view and the priest's own 'Popish attire' abandoned in favour of more sober clothing considered suitable for the revised form of worship. The bell ceased tolling and hundreds of pairs of eyes watched as William Harper appeared, the new Prayer Book in his hand. William Segar, a labourer and Will Underhill, a tailor, were among the congregation on that fateful morning . . .

The service itself passed peacefully enough and the old man breathed a sigh of relief. He was seventy years old and wished to spend his remaining days peacefully tending his small Devon flock of five hundred souls. It was not to be. The following morning, as he busied himself in the vestry preparing for Morning Prayers, two men asked to speak with him. They were Underhill and Segar and instinctively the old priest knew that the trouble he had anticipated was about to begin.

Apparently the two men did not approve of the new form of worship nor, they assured him, did anyone else. But, argued the old priest, it was the law and he was liable to certain penalties if he did not comply. They were unimpressed. Other parishioners arrived on the scene to add weight to the two men's argument. Henry VIII himself had written in his will that no changes should be made to the religion of the country until Edward was of age. By what right, then, did Somerset and his government make this new law? The young Edward was only eleven years old and it was Henry's intention that the religion should continue unadulterated for at least another thirteen years! The old priest shook his head helplessly in the face of their determination. He was one voice against the whole congregation. They were unanimous in their demands. The old man donned his familiar vestments and restored the banished ornaments. The satisfied congregation settled down to worship and the old Mass was celebrated in the usual way.

Within hours, rumours of the incident had spread to nearby villages and small groups rode into Sampford to learn at first hand what had actually happened. The streets were full of people discussing the morning's events and excitement grew into an exhilaration that once more the ordinary people had dared to make a stand against the authority of an unpopular government. It wasn't long before the news reached magistrate Sir Hugh Pollard at King's Nympton and he took three colleagues and rode out immediately to try and pacify the small unrest before it flared into rebellion. He arrived to find the road to Sampford barricaded with tree trunks and the villagers united under the leadership of Segar and Underhill. After lengthy negotiations, Pollard and his men were forced to ride away to report his complete lack of success and within days the village was crowded with men from neighbouring towns and villages. The situation was already out of hand when a certain gentleman named William Hellyons rashly decided to try and end the riot single-handed. He therefore rode to Sampford and demanded to see the rebels' leaders. They talked in the church house but his hectoring, almost hostile manner frayed tempers rapidly. He finally admitted defeat and abandoned his lone mission but as he attempted to leave, someone struck him a blow that sent him tumbling down the steps. He fell screaming into the crowd where he was hacked to pieces.

The whole of Devonshire was now alerted and men began to move into the area. A few hundreds came also from Cornwall, Simon among them.

Melissa stared at Luke as his face darkened with anger. 'Look at this!' he cried, thrusting the letter towards her. 'See for yourself! The boy's half-witted! After all I've done for him, all I've planned for him. To join a rebellious, illiterate rabble! What games does he think he's playing, eh?'

Before Melissa could read the letter he snatched it back and scanned its contents once more, his lips moving furiously as he read the hastily written words. 'And Hugo, also!' he burst out. 'Is there no end to their folly? What is his father about to allow such a thing?' He screwed the letter up and tossed it to the ground in one angry gesture while Melissa waited anxiously for him to draw breath. As soon as he did, she said, 'What is happening, Papa? I pray you speak calmly and tell me what's wrong? Where is he – and what is Hugo to do with it?'

'Hugo has everything to do with it!' roared Luke. 'The young fool lives at Crediton and that is where Simon has gone. That's where half the West Country is gone, if there is any truth in the rumours, and if the rumours be bad, why, then you can be sure they're true enough! The county is up in arms against the New Prayer Book, seemingly, and Simon and that young fool of a nephew are intent on joining!'

'I thought Simon was in Cornwall,' faltered Melissa.

'He *was* in Cornwall,' cried Luke, 'but now he's in Crediton with thousands like him, all set to confront the government and as like as not get himself killed! God's wounds, but I have no patience with them. Rebellion solves nothing. I've already lost one brother that way, years ago before you were born. Am I to lose my only remaining son now – or a nephew? I won't tolerate it, I say.'

'But what can you do?' she asked fearfully.

'Do? I can stop them,' he cried angrily. 'I shall ride down there and bring him back to Heron – and to his senses. I shall knock their heads together if needs be to let a little sense in! Find Jack and tell him to saddle me the cob. Fetch Thomas for I'd speak with him before I go. And ask Beth for a pasty and some wine. I'll take it with me.'

Melissa hurried off as directed. The idea of rebellion was alien to her. England had been peaceable for many years; the only news of fighting came from abroad and did not intrude on her way of life. A small prickle of fear touched her but she gave it no heed, except to mutter a prayer inwardly for the young man she must now call 'brother'. In the kitchen she was surprised to see Beth standing over a red-eyed Nan who sniffed tearfully. They looked up guiltily at her entrance.

'What's wrong?' asked Melissa, distracted immediately from her original errand.

'Oh ma'am!' cried Nan, her tears flowing afresh. ''Tis Jon. Run away, he has, to join the rebels and Jack says he'll be killed like as not.'

'Jon too!' cried Melissa and the prickle of fear became a cold sick feeling in her stomach.

Beth took up the tale. 'Coming back from the town he was and sees all these men. Carrying bows some of them and others bill-hooks and the like. Off to Crediton, they say, to fight against the Duke of Somerset!'

'That's enough!' said Melissa. 'If he's gone then we must pray for him, but Papa mustn't know. He is worried enough already.'

'That letter?' queried Beth and Melissa nodded.

'Aye, Simon's gone too and Hugo. Papa is off in hopes of bringing him home. He wants meat and wine, Beth, and a horse. Stop crying, Nan, run to the stable. Ask Jack to saddle the big cob. And where's Thomas?' She was directed to the garden where she found him asleep in the shade of the large chestnut, the book of accounts open in his lap. Kissing him lightly, she woke him and in a few words roused him to the seriousness of the situation.

'I'll go with Luke,' he said at once but Luke declined his offer, believing privately that he could ride faster without his steward who was a poor horseman. Within a quarter of an hour he was saddled and ready to go and Melissa watched him ride off towards Crediton.

Hugo Kendal had his mother's dark looks, the same swarthy skin and brown eyes. He was shorter than Simon by two or three inches but his shoulders were broader. Simon had introduced himself and the two men had taken an instant liking to each other. The fact of Simon's lowly birth had proved insignificant. Hugo welcomed another male Kendal. His own household, he told Simon, was 'so full of petticoats a man might smother in them!' His father was in London most of the time with Simon's stepbrother Walter which left Hugo, his half-sisters Sarah and Catherine and his mother, Hester.

Although Hugo and Simon had known each other only three days the circumstances of their meeting had thrown them close together and they now sat on a pile of straw in a barn on the edge of Crediton, their weapons beside them. Each owned the harness which was currently issued to men of fighting age so that in times of a national emergency they might be armed and ready for enlistment at very short notice. This consisted of a helmet and a reinforced canvas jacket. As archers, they dispensed with the forearm splints and wore only a bracer on the left wrist. Both men carried swords, and since neither had seen any real action before, were hoping to remedy the situation. Around them men sprawled at ease, talking, eating, drinking or dozing while others sat astride the rafters which formed the loft, watching hopefully from the windows for any sign of the government's forces approaching from the direction of Exeter. Hester had pleaded with them not to go, inwardly cursing Simon's appearance at such a time, but once reconciled to their intention she bustled about providing food and drink in generous quantity so that 'whatever else might befall you shan't starve to death!' Watching them go she had marvelled at Simon's likeness to the Kendals and, sighing, thanked the Lord that Alison had not lived to witness Hugo and his bastard cousin riding out in friendship while her own two sons lay cold in their graves. Then she went back into the house and called for parchment and quill to write to her husband of the day's happenings.

'So this Martin Jeffrey – you knew him?' Hugo asked.

Simon nodded. 'He was parish priest at St Keverne. Hot-headed mayhap, but likeable enough. I met him some years back when I visited friends in Keverne and attended Mass with them.'

'Some say 'twas a priest who killed Body,' said Hugo.

Simon shrugged. 'Who can say whose blow was responsible,' he said. 'Kylter was certainly involved and Trevian also. I never met them but Jeffrey spoke of Trevian. Pyes, of course, you've seen for yourself here.'

'They pardoned him, didn't they?' Hugo asked.

'Aye. He was very fortunate.' He took a drink from the flagon beside him and handed it to Hugo who finished it off.

'Somerset is sending Sir Peter Carew,' said Hugo, 'though God knows what he hopes to achieve.'

Simon laughed. 'He'll be lucky if he gets past the barricade,' he said, 'and there's no other way into Crediton for mounted men. Still, he can say his piece. No doubt he's been told to pacify the wicked Cornish rabble!'

'Not forgetting the Devon malcontents!' said Hugo, a rare smile softening his lean face. At that moment a man stepped into the barn and shouted to attract everyone's attention.

'We've had word that they're nearly here,' he yelled. 'We're using this barn and the one opposite,' he went on. 'Knock holes in the walls at loft level so the archers can shoot down if necessary. Half of you up top, half on ground level but keep out of sight until we give the signal. Those with bills, scythes or pitchforks will be outside manning the barricade or in the trenches. You'll be in full view so they'll get a good view of our strength. If you've no harness or weapon, find yourself a pocketful of stones and keep to the rear. Any questions?'

'How soon before they get here?'

'An hour, maybe less, so go to it.'

His departure was the signal for frenzied activity. When Sir Peter Carew arrived with his company they would be waiting.

Luke, almost within sight of Crediton, reined in his horse suddenly as he saw the highway ahead of him blocked with a company of mounted men. He wanted no trouble – only to find his son and persuade him to come home. Shading his eyes, he studied the men for clues to their identity and purpose, and recognized the Carew livery and one of blue which was unfamiliar. They wore little or no armour over their harness – doubtless prepared for negotiation and not for battle. 'Thanks be to God,' muttered Luke. Somerset's Council must try to avoid civil war at all costs. They had a new war with Scotland to contend with and most of their troops were north of London. This group ahead of him could only be locally raised. But one of the near riders had seen him and called on him to halt, spurring his horse back towards Luke who waited for him.

'State your name and the purpose of your journey,' snapped the man, one of Carew's retainers.

'Luke Kendal of Heron on my way to Crediton,' replied Luke.

'For what reason?'

Luke dared not hesitate. Nor did he wish to announce to this company that his son and nephew were among the rebels.

'To visit relations,' he said.

'Are you aware that the town is taken by agitators?'

'Aye. I hoped to satisfy myself of the welfare of my family.'

So far he had not lied except by omission.

'Follow me.'

Luke rode after him. They pushed a way through the company, now halted, until they reached the top of the column where Luke recognized Sir Peter Carew.

'Kendal of Heron,' reported Luke's companion, 'headed for Crediton to visit relations, sire.'

Carew nodded a dismissal and the man returned to his position at the rear of the riders.

'Kendal?' said Carew. 'The name's familiar.'

'The *Mary Rose*,' Luke reminded him. 'You lost Sir George Carew on the *Mary Rose*. My son served under him and was lost also.'

'So that's it. A fine captain, George. A great loss to the King's navy.'

'He was. My son was Jeffery Kendal.'

'Jeffery Kendal? Ah, that's it. Very tragic indeed.'

'Aye.'

'Kendal,' he mused again. 'Wasn't it a Kendal who helped the commissioners at Harben Priory during the dissolution? Was that you?'

Luke nodded.

'Ah, that's it, then. I rarely forget a name. You'd best join us, Kendal. We have need of men loyal to the Crown. Ah, I wonder what George would have made of this rabble.'

He waved a deprecating hand in the direction of Crediton and Luke said nothing. 'What do they expect, eh? To turn back the clock? This country will never be great without a good many changes. When Edward comes of age he will be England's first Protestant king and we must be ready for him. England has no need now of Popish tricks – we are well rid of them!'

The two gentlemen to his right exchanged looks as he promised to launch once more into a familiar tirade but Carew, seeing it, laughed suddenly. 'But that can wait,' he admitted. 'Introductions first and then we must ride on. I want this matter done with by nightfall. My uncle Gawen Carew and Piers Courtenay – Sheriff. Luke Kendal of Heron.'

The men exchanged polite greetings as Carew, with a wave of his hand, signalled the ride to continue.

Sir Peter Carew's tone was irascible and Luke sensed his impatience as he continued to outline the case against the rising.

'I blame Pollard,' he was saying. 'The man bungled Sampford. He should have been much firmer! These rabble don't understand logic and they've little enough commonsense. The Protector urges conciliation. They don't know the meaning of the word. All they know is what they want and God knows we've tried to make their lot easier. The government's proclamation against enclosures will be issued shortly. What more do they want? I think they must needs have something to talk against. First 'twas the enclosures and trouble here and there on that score.'

'The June proclamation put an end to that!' said Courtenay grimly.

'Aye, it damped their ardour for a time,' Carew admitted 'but now they find a new cause. Prayer books! God's wounds! I think they'd fly to arms for a change in the weather if they had nothing else to quarrel with!'

Two riders sent on to reconnoitre now returned to describe the road block and Carew cursed angrily.

'It was to be expected,' said Courtenay.

'Expected or not, 'tis a confounded nuisance,' snapped Carew and without further consultation he urged his horse forward at a gallop so that he finally slithered to an abrupt halt in a rattle of stones.

'I come in the name of the King's Council,' he declared loudly, 'and I demand to speak with your leader.'

His voice carried clearly the twenty yards to the barricade.

349

'Keep back!' came the answer. 'We've nothing to say that's not been said before.'

'I come in the King's name –' Carew began again.

'The King knows our demands. Keep your distance or you'll regret it. Crediton is in the hands of the people.'

Luke searched the faces that showed above and beside the barricade but Simon was not among them.

'The King demands that we negotiate,' shouted Carew. Already his face darkened with anger at their resistance to his command. 'He wants no bloodshed but a peaceable solution.'

Behind him the horses fidgeted, the metal of their bridles glinting in the sunshine, their restless hooves raising a fine white dust from the brittle clay road.

'Let me through,' shouted Carew, 'or take the consequences of your folly!'

A man behind the barricade stood up suddenly, his arm raised in a hard fist. 'King Henry's laws were good enough for us,' he shouted and there was a roar of approval from the men around him. 'We want the old Mass as was good enough for our fathers and their fathers! We want our babes baptized any day of the week! We like our palms on Palm Sunday!'

'Aye!' they roared, and a mass of clenched fists and bows and other weapons were raised on high in a disconcerting show of strength.

'Damned knaves!' muttered Carew. 'Do they think I'll stand here all day bandying words?'

More voices were raised now as the rebels grew bolder, several leaping on to the barricade, the better to be heard.

'We don't care for your English service,' they shouted, 'we want our Latins back. We want our chantries –'

'Prayers for the dead –'

'Sacraments over the high altar –'

'Down with Somerset and a pox on the likes of you!'

'To hell with the Council!'

'We want free passage to parley with the King himself!'

Carew's eyes blazed with anger but he persisted for the best part of an hour. It proved a useless exercise. The men of Crediton, with no real leadership, were fearful of the consequences should they allow these smooth-talking representatives of the Council to pass their barricade. At length Carew withdrew his troop a further distance and the three leaders conversed in heated tones. Finally word was passed among the weary company to close up ranks. They would, Carew told them, advance up the street towards the barricade. If the men did not allow them through, then they would force an entry into the town. Luke was helpless to do anything but join them. To decline would have looked suspicious at best. He drew his sword and stationed himself along the right hand side of the cavalcade as the signal was given to move forward at a canter, unaware of the presence of armed men within the barns on either side of the road. All eyes were on the men behind and beside the barricade. These suddenly rose up with a great shout and a hail of stones whistled through the air. Carew urged his horse to a gallop but as the horsemen swept within range of the barns a hail of arrows met them from two directions. Several men died instantly, others, wounded, struggled to retain their seats as the horses maddened by the din reared frantically. Luke, an arrow through his neck, fell to the ground and his horse trampled on him as he fell. A cry went up from the defenders and the brief fierce battle that ensued only ended when the attackers set fire to the barns. The rebels streamed out, some beating the flames from their hair and clothing and screaming in agony. Suddenly demoralized, the resistance at the barricade wavered and collapsed and a retreat set in. The rebels withdrew, joined by most of the townsfolk, and when Carew's men found themselves inside the town, Crediton proved a hollow victory in more ways than one. The only people who remained to witness it were the very old and those too infirm to travel.

CHAPTER NINETEEN

Nan closed her eyes and inhaled the warm scents of the herb garden, thyme, sage and rosemary and the tangy smell of mint. Sniffing her fingers, she could detect traces of them all. The basket beside her was full and the pocket of her apron bulged with bay leaves. Gathering the herbs was one of her favourite tasks and the warm June sun made it perfect. Beth was busy ironing the linen, a tiresome chore on such a warm day and one which she would rather have passed on to Nan except for the girl's habit of scorching collars! Nan had long ago decided that ironing was not for her and now, basking in the scented garden, she knew she had made a wise decision. Suddenly she heard voices coming from the lawn and ran to the hedge to peer through. Thomas Benet and Melissa were walking in the garden, hand in hand! Nan's eyes widened and her face wrinkled with a satisfied smile. This would be something to tell them later in the kitchen. It was generally known that the shy steward was to wed the daughter of the house but they had all watched in vain for signs of affection between them. Nan giggled. Had he taken Melissa's hand or she his? Beth had called Thomas 'a dry old stick' declaring him 'not much use for a lovely girl like her', but Jack had smiled knowingly. 'Wait and see,' he'd urged them. 'The dry old stick might surprise you yet. Many a fine tune played on an old fiddle.' And he'd given Nan a

353

naughty wink which made her think maybe *he* was not over the hill either!

The voices were low and Nan couldn't catch the words but they looked happy enough with each other, Thomas still in his black since the mistress's death and Melissa in her second best with the lacy sleeves, the one Nan coveted, hoping to inherit it when Melissa grew tired of it.

'If she ever does,' Nan grumbled to herself. 'If I had all that money, I'd hand my gowns on a sight faster, that I would – saints be praised, he's kissing her now, though not much of a kiss. More a peck, I'd say, still 'tis a start. The poor man's probably new to kissing. Not like Jack.' Jack had taken to recounting his romantic exploits, both real and imagined, to while away the summer evenings and in Nan's eyes, at least, he was a veteran. Nan craned forward, straining her neck uncomfortably, for they were moving further away. Her bare feet moved cautiously among the clumps of lavender as she balanced herself against the hedge. She watched Melissa pluck a daisy from the grass and present it to her betrothed with an elaborate curtsey.

'She's making fun of him,' muttered Nan, 'or maybe leading him on a bit. Oh Lissa, you'll never get Thomas Benet to play love games if that's what you're after. Good at sums and a fair scribe but not well tutored in the art of – ooh, look at that! *He's* picked a daisy now – do I believe my eyes! Popped it down the front of her second best! Just wait until I tell Beth. She'll – ouch!' Her glee gave way suddenly to pain as she lost her balance and fell sideways into the lavender with a shriek of dismay that could be heard all over the house, and garden. Seconds later Melissa arrived to offer a hand and she had just pulled the embarrassed servant to her feet when a rider appeared in the drive with the limp body of Luke across his saddle.

'Sweet mother of Christ!' whispered Melissa running to meet him. 'Not dead?' she begged. 'Not dead, for pity's sake?'

'Not dead ma'am,' said the soldier, 'but near to it.'

She saw the broken arrow still protruding from his neck and would have fallen without Thomas's support.

'We've trouble enough,' the man told them, 'for the rebels are everywhere and arming fast. We've no doctor among us so Sir Peter bade us bring him home. Once the arrow's out he'll bleed like a pig, I warn you. My master sends his sympathies. Now I must go.'

While he talked he had lain Luke on the gravelled path and now remounted. With a brief salute, he was cantering away to rejoin his company and Nan, Melissa and Thomas were left stricken with shock, beside Luke who lay unconscious between them.

Thomas rallied himself first and sent Nan to find Jack. Melissa came to her senses again and knelt beside her father. She took his head in her lap, shuddering at the sight of the broken arrow shaft which projected to a length of six inches. Jack ran up from the stables and with Thomas, carried Luke to his bedchamber and laid him on the bed. Then Jack was sent to ride for the physician, and Beth was ordered to blow up the fire and heat water. Melissa loosed his clothing as best she could but with each small movement Luke moaned in pain and she finally gave up. The arrow had entered from the right just above the shoulder, narrowly missing both spine and the main artery from the heart. Luke's unconscious state seemed to result from a severe blow on the back of his head probably caused by the hoof of his horse. Three of his ribs were also cracked but none appeared broken. Nan tiptoed into the room with a clean linen cloth and bowl of warm water and Melissa began to wipe the dust from Luke's face. Another man's blood had congealed on his right arm and hand and she washed it away with eyes blurred with tears. Fearfully she looked up at Thomas.

'He won't die, Thomas, will he?' she asked. 'Not Papa. Tell me he won't die.'

'He stands a chance,' said Thomas, honestly able to say no more and reluctant to raise her hopes. 'He's lost little or no blood and if the doctor can retrieve the arrow head safely – '

They both knew that the fight for Luke's life would only start there. The real danger was the infection that might set in after, with the fever that accompanied it. But they did not speak of it and Thomas took her hand and squeezed it reassuringly.

She looked up at him, her face dark with despair. 'First the boys,' she said, 'then Mama. If Papa dies . . .'

'We must pray for him,' said Thomas, 'but if 'tis God's will, why then you still have Abby – and me,' he added humbly. 'I'll take care of you, have no fear.'

'I know you will, Thomas,' she said softly. 'Ah, here comes Jack back.' She flew to the window. 'And alone! Where is the physician? Doesn't he realize how urgent the matter is?'

She ran downstairs to learn that the physician was away on private business of his own and was not expected back until the following day.

'Tomorrow?' cried Melissa. 'But that will be too late.'

Jack gestured helplessly. 'I spoke to his neighbour who told me he was away and told him also of the arrow in the master's neck. He said he saw many such wounds when he was a lad and that the arrow should be drawn out in the same direction. Never pull it backwards for the barb will do greater damage.'

'Pull it out ourselves?' cried Melissa horrified. 'Dear God, I swear I couldn't do it! Oh no!'

Thomas looked startled. 'I think we may well do more

harm than good,' he agreed hastily. "Tis best left until the doctor comes.'

'But that'll be the days, like as not!' protested Beth who had arrived with the first kettle of hot water in time to hear Jack's suggestion. 'You can't leave the poor man in that state. Someone must take it out.'

'But if we do,' said Melissa 'what then? How do we stop the bleeding? Oh, I dare not.'

'Push the arrow through, he said,' said Jack, 'then wash the wound with vinegar and plug it with honey. He said he'd seen it done – scores of times.'

Luke's face was pale, his eyes were shut and he breathed quickly with a harsh rasping sound. Melissa looked at him and willed her body to stop trembling. Beth was absolutely right and someone must remove the arrow. She, Melissa, was mistress of Heron now that Alison was dead. It would be unfair to put such a responsibility on to someone else.

'I'll do it,' she said shakily. 'I'll need some help – and all your prayers for Papa's recovery.'

They looked at her with a new respect but she was too distracted to see it. 'Beth, bring up clean rags, honey and vinegar,' she instructed 'and Nan some towels to put under him. Thomas,' she looked up at him, 'I'll need you and Jack to hold him down. If he recovers consciousness, he will be in great agony and may struggle.'

Gently she turned her father's head but there was no sign of the arrow point. Somehow she must force the arrow until it pierced the flesh. Thomas might be able to pull on it. The short length of splintered wood was just about long enough for her to grasp with one hand.

'Dear God,' she whispered, 'help me, I beseech you. Show me what to do.'

Beth returned and Nan brought the towels. Carefully, they lifted Luke while the towels were spread under the upper part of his body. The oak chest was moved round

357

to the side of the bed to form a table where Melissa put a bowl of hot water, the cloths, honey and vinegar. Still Luke remained oblivious to what was happening and Melissa hoped that he would continue so until the worst was over. She had no clear idea of the shape of the arrow head. It might be smooth or it might be dangerously wide at the base. Forcing the wider end through the neck was going to be the greatest hazard for it meant inflicting a greater wound than Luke had already.

When all was ready, the others stood back to give her space.

'Roll him on to his side, Thomas.' For the first time she touched the arrow shaft, feeling the wood warm and hard against her fingers.

'When I say "Now" brace his head and shoulders for the push,' she said and Jack and Thomas, holding him securely, prepared for her signal.

'Now!' she said and thrust her weight against the arrow with as much strength as she could muster. She felt the flesh yield slightly and saw the flesh close further along the shaft. Only five inches remained. The sensation had sickened her momentarily and she put a hand to her mouth while her stomach churned horribly.

Thomas watched her anxiously but she straightened up. 'It's harder than I expected,' she said. 'I've moved it an inch or more. Maybe next time – are you ready? Now!'

This time the tip of the arrow was forced out and blood began to flow from the new wound. Melissa closed her eyes.

"Twill soon be through,' said Jack. 'Don't give up, ma'am. You make a fine surgeon!'

The attempt at humour helped her compose herself once more.

'If it comes through far enough I'll take hold of it,' said Thomas.

Melissa drew a deep breath and leaned once more against the splintered shaft which slowly gave way to the pressure.

'I have it!' cried Thomas and with a last effort, the bloodied arrow head was drawn out, leaving a wide deep hole which oozed blood, slowly and then faster until it flowed. Transfixed, they watched it soak into the towels below Luke's head. Then Melissa drew a sharp breath.

'The vinegar!' she said and sprinkled it liberally into the open wound. The acid burned into the raw tissue so that Luke cried out in pain. 'Hold him fast, for pity's sake!' cried Melissa. 'Please God he doesn't recover his senses too soon.'

She dabbed the mixture of blood and vinegar from the wound as thoroughly as she could then laid a fresh cloth saturated with honey against Luke's neck. A similar application went on the other side where the arrow had entered.

'Will it staunch the flow?' asked Thomas.

Melissa watched anxiously for the tell-tale signs but for the moment there were none.

'Now I'll bandage the neck,' she said. 'Oh Papa! I hope I've done all that I should.'

She wound strips of linen round his neck to keep the honeyed pads in place.

''Tis very healing for the skin, is honey,' said Beth, who had been struck dumb throughout the operation but now found her voice again. 'And the vinegar does cleanse a wound marvellously well.'

'I hope so, Beth.' She looked at Luke critically. He still wore his riding clothes and looked incongruous laid out on the bed. 'I think we must leave him as he is,' she said. 'We'll take his boots off then cover him with a sheet. He has suffered enough for one day and I feel we should keep him as still as possible.'

When all was done to her satisfaction, she drew a deep

shuddering sigh and Thomas put his arms around her. 'He is in God's hands now' he said gently, 'we must pray.'

Rumours of the affray at Crediton reached Clyst St Mary but made little immediate impact. Saturday morning brought the devout villagers to church as usual. An old woman hurried on her way, uncomfortably aware by the emptiness of the road, that she was late and would have to tiptoe into church to avoid too much attention. She kept her eyes on the uneven ground for fear of stumbling. She did not bother to glance up as a rider approached. If he was an honest traveller she had nothing to fear. If he were not, he would hardly bother to attack and rob a poor old woman who carried only a rosary.

She was surprised, therefore, when he halted his horse and pointed at her accusingly. 'What, still carrying that bauble!' he demanded irritably. 'They are playthings for idle fingers. Throw it aside, there's a good woman.'

The old woman held up the rosary. 'This?' she asked. 'Throw it aside?'

'Aye, forget such popery. England has a bright new future and such old fangled gewgaws are out of place. The King bids all his subjects put away such toys. 'Tis the law of the land.'

'The law?' Her expression registered a growing anxiety. The King and the law were forces to be reckoned with.

'The new law forbids these,' he tapped the rosary with the toe of his boot and she recoiled hastily, 'and such like knick-knacks. The new religion has no need – '

'I know nought of new religion,' she quavered, a touch of defiance creeping into her voice. 'I'm just a poor old woman on my way to church and late enough already. I mind my own business.'

'The King's law is your business,' he cried, his tone sharpening. He had not expected such a reaction from so humble a soul and now regretted putting himself to so much trouble. However, he did not intend to let her have the last word on the subject. She should no longer be able to claim ignorance.

'The law states quite clearly,' he began but to his extreme annoyance she put her hands to her ears and shook her head.

'I've no time to listen,' she told him. 'I'm late, I tell you.'

'Late or no,' he shouted, 'you'll hear me out!' He spurred his horse and it sprang forward, blocking the old woman's way.

''Tis for your own good, the new law,' he insisted. 'Would you not rather hear the words in English and understand them?'

'Let me by!' she cried fearfully. 'You've no call to stop me.'

'The Act of Uniformity – '

'I don't wish to know of it!'

'– is intended to help the likes of you. To make a religion simpler and – '

''Tis simple enough for me.'

She tried to pass him but he manoeuvred his horse to prevent her.

'If you don't abide by the law,' he shouted, 'you must be prepared for the consequences. You can be punished, you know.'

The old woman had finally taken fright. She opened her mouth and began to scream for help.

'There's no need for that,' he urged hastily but she had dodged past him and was running towards the church as though her life depended on it. She burst inside, interrupting the service.

'They're after me!' she told them, clutching her side and gasping for breath. 'The King's men!'

The outraged eyes of the congregation were on her as she recounted her experience with a few exaggerations. Two men ran outside but reported no one in sight.

'Throw away that bauble, he says to me. Bauble, he called it.' She held up her rosary and there were loud murmurings. ''Tis a plaything, he says, and you'll be punished – '

The people exchanged nervous glances. They had heard the rumours lately of attacks on villages. Some said Crediton was burned to the ground by the King's men. Were they now harrying innocent folk? Was anybody safe?

'Forget such popery, he says, 'tis against the law. I begged him let me pass but he wouldn't. Kicked out at me he did!'

'Kicked you? And was he armed?'

'He carried a sword, aye, and threatened to punish me. I thought my end had come and that's the truth! They'll be after all of us. They'll kill us all afore they're done!'

She collapsed into comforting arms as the rest of the congregation streamed outside. Their lives and liberties were threatened; they knew what they had to do. The alarm was raised throughout the town and a defence was organized immediately. Trenches were dug across the roads leading into the village and trees were felled. Word spread and once more men rallied to the aid of the defenders.

Clyst St Mary was only a few miles from the harbour at Topsham and it was decided to ask for cannon from some of the ships moored there. In view of the gravity of the situation, this was granted and the guns hauled back to Clyst. By nightfall the town was snugly dug in behind impressive defences. The cannons covered the road from Exeter where it crossed the river from which direction reprisals might be expected. It took only a few hours for news to filter into Exeter and Sir Peter Carew was soon acquainted with details of the latest emergency.

The following morning brought Simon and Hugo to Heron. They had ridden furiously to reassure Luke of their whereabouts and safety and were appalled to find him unconscious and possibly near to death.

'The doctor came this morning,' said Melissa. 'We pray now that he will regain consciousness, for there is nothing more we can do.'

'Does he lose much blood?' asked Simon, seeing the fresh stains upon the bandages and towel.

'Not a great deal,' said Melissa, 'but we fear he may be taking some blood deeper into his body. The wound goes right through from one side to the other.'

The same thought was in the two young men's minds. Had the arrow that struck Luke been fired by either of them?

'From which side did it enter?' asked Simon.

'From the right.'

He breathed a sigh of relief. 'Thanks be to the Lord!' he said. 'Hugo and I were on the left of the road.'

'If he dies, that will be of little comfort,' said Melissa sharply. 'I have no sympathy for a cause that injures innocent men.'

Simon looked at her steadily. 'Do we know that?' he asked. 'He was riding with the Council's men – with the Carews and Courtenay.'

'He was riding to find you,' she retorted. 'He was distressed for your well-being and wanted to persuade you to come home and have no part in it.'

'Then how does he come to ride with an armed com-

pany of the King's men?' cried Simon. 'Hugo will bear
me out, that 'twas they who attacked – we who de-
fended.'

'He speaks truly,' said Hugo.

Melissa turned to him. 'If he recovers, we may learn
how he came to be with them but for the present I care
only for his life. Leave us again, if you must. Play your
games and fight your battles. But don't expect my admiration.'

She spoke more vehemently than she had intended
and they fell silent, embarrassed.

'We must go back,' said Simon quietly. 'We will talk
of it another time.'

'If you are spared,' she said coldly.

'If we are spared,' he agreed, casting a look at Hugo,
'but until then, we have comrades who risk their lives
for the people of the West. We should be branded
cowards if we stayed home while they fight on. Before
many days have passed the whole of Devon will be in a
state of rebellion. Clyst is being harassed and is de-
fended with guns. We hear on good advice that the
Cornishmen are marching towards London with a peti-
tion for the King. They will take Exeter – '

'Take Exeter!' echoed Thomas. ''Tis as simple as
that?'

'Exeter will come over to us,' said Hugo earnestly. 'We
mean to join the rebel forces when they reach Exeter.'

'They did not go over to the rebels in ninety-seven,'
said Thomas.

'This is not ninety-seven,' said Simon brusquely.
''Tis forty-nine and I believe Exeter will join us. We
have a just cause and your father – '

'Your father also,' Melissa reminded him.

'*Our* father is misguided if he takes sides against the
common people,' said Simon.

'And I tell you he did not take sides,' she said. 'He

didn't intend to ride with Carew.'

'He rode with the King's commissioners against the Priory,' said Simon, 'and nearly cost your mother her life.'

Melissa's face was white with anger and Thomas took her hand. 'We quarrel to no purpose,' he said quietly. ''Tis obvious Simon and Hugo are sincere in their beliefs and must do as they see fit. They must have refreshment before they go.'

Simon hesitated but Hugo's set face relaxed into the ghost of a smile. 'That would be most welcome,' he said.

'I'll tell Beth to see to it,' said Thomas and hurried out before Melissa could argue further or Simon could say things he might later regret.

Simon knelt suddenly beside the bed and, taking Luke's limp hand, put it to his mouth. His lips moved silently and Melissa's anger faded. Hugo also bowed his head in silent prayer. Simon stood up and looked at Melissa. 'I crave your understanding,' he said softly, 'or if not that, then the benefit of doubt. I believe we do what must be done.' She nodded without answering. 'He is in good hands,' he said.

'I trust so. I pray God go with you and Hugo.'

'Amen to that,' said Simon.

Later, watching them ride away, her eyes were bright with unshed tears.

'We shall see them again, never fear,' said Thomas, reading her expression correctly but for once, she did not share his optimism.

Exeter did not go over to the rebel cause. Alerted by the events at Clyst St Mary, Mayor Blackaller and the city council had voted their allegiance to the government although there were a great many in the town including

Blackaller who still favoured the old religion and sympathized with the aims of the revolt. But they saw their first loyalty towards the town and the maintenance of law and order. The message from Arundell, the rebels' leader, asking him to throw open the city gates was refused. A second demand that they offer aid and hospitality to the rebels was also rejected and Arundell's threat of a siege became a reality. Exeter was a wealthy town and contained vast numbers of men and munitions, both vital for the success of the rebel cause. The two thousand Cornishmen prepared to wait for their prize and the eight thousand inhabitants of the town resigned themselves to a state of siege until the King's forces arrived in sufficient numbers to rescue them. Hugo and Simon were camped out to the west of the city and lay in the darkness beside the camp fire, talking together, while they waited for the meal being prepared for them by one of the many women who had come from the outlying villages to cook and care for the rebels as best they could in the hopes of generous rewards when the town finally surrendered. Some of them were wives accompanying their husbands, some were mothers caring for their sons. Others were camp followers – single women who embraced the cause and offered the men home comforts of various kinds, earning themselves a little money in the process. Foraging parties were not necessary yet for the surrounding populace, their imagination fired, saw them as a liberating army and gave bread, eggs, fish and vegetables as generously as their limited resources would allow. The meal would precede the attack timed for the early hours of the morning.

Under cover of darkness, tinners were at work quarrying under the town wall to one side of the West Gate. The plan was to drive a gallery under the wall, fill it with gunpowder and blast out a gap. With the defences thus breached, the rebels would force an entry and the defenders, hopefully taken by surprise, would capitulate.

'My belly tells me 'tis supper time,' said Hugo. 'I don't know what they're cooking but it smells good to a starving man.'

'A stew of sorts,' said Simon, 'and fish baked in a paste.'

'I'll eat it bones and all!' said Hugo. 'I wonder what time we'll go through the wall. I hope these tinners don't dig too fast or 'twill be breached before we've eaten.'

'My pretty Margaret's a fine cook,' he mused. 'Her venison pasty has to be tasted to be believed. Better than my mother's though I daren't say so for they are so jealous of each other. You should find yourself a suitable woman, Simon. 'Tis a rare pleasure to be fought over by two doting women!'

Simon laughed. 'I'll think on it,' he promised. 'What other charms does Margaret possess?'

'Oh, mousey hair but a good smooth complexion. She's bonny enough though skinny with it tho' I'm in hopes to fatten her up as soon as we're wed!'

'I don't doubt it,' grinned Simon. 'But is she obedient?'

'As a dog.'

'Soft and loving?'

'As a kitten.'

'She sounds more like a menagerie than a wife! How came you by this paragon of yours – and does she have a sister who is not yet spoken for?'

'She fell into my lap like a ripe plum,' said Hugo. 'I was in London visiting the Lessors – you won't have met them yet – '

'The name is familiar.'

'Mark Lessor, the London goldsmith, was a good friend and tutor of John Kendal, your grandfather.'

Simon nodded in the darkness. 'Melissa spoke of

him,' he said. 'And you are truly happy with your bride to be?'

'I am,' said Hugo suddenly serious. 'Pray God I come through the next weeks unscathed. We are due to wed in a few months' time.'

The arrival of their cook interrupted their chatter and they sat up gratefully as the hot vegetable stew was ladled into each bowl by the plump, cheerful woman who had prepared it.

'I wager that'll put fire in your bellies,' she promised, 'and God be with you tonight.'

They heard her wishing everyone the same protection as she made her way to the groups of men huddled in the light of countless fires which lit their faces with a ruddy glow. The stew was richly spiced with cinnamon and the pieces of parsnip, carrot and onion were large and firm.

Simon glanced up at the West Gate where small lanterns carried by the defending watch glowed fitfully.

'By this time tomorrow,' he told Hugo, 'those little flames will be extinguished and Exeter will be ours.'

CHAPTER TWENTY

For nearly a week Luke's condition remained fairly steady. He was still unconscious, but the wound in his neck bled a little less each day and there was no fever. Towards the end of the sixth day however Melissa was startled by the appearance of Beth bursting into the Hall without warning. ''Tis the master, ma'am,' she cried. 'He spoke! I was passing and I heard him. The words were jumbled, but he spoke. Will he recover?' But Melissa was already racing up the stairs, anxious to see the miracle for herself. What she saw, however, did not reassure her. He had moved – for the first time since the accident – and lay on his side. His fingers plucked feebly at the cloth that bandaged his neck and he mumbled incoherently.

'What's he saying, ma'am? Can you tell?'

Melissa put a hand to his forehead and frowned. 'I fear he's rambling in his mind,' she said. 'It comes with the fever. See, his forehead is beaded with perspiration. I hope there's no poison forming in the wound. You had best ask Jack to ride to the doctor and tell him of the changes. Meanwhile we'll cool him with damp towels – ah, don't touch your bandage!' Gently she moved Luke's fumbling fingers but as soon as she released him, his hand returned to his neck and the finger scrabbled ineffectively at the binding.

'Such bony fingers,' Melissa mourned. 'Poor Papa,

369

you are wasting away. If only he could take a little gruel.' She glanced up and saw that Beth still lingered. 'Go quickly, Beth,' she said. 'Fetch towels and cool water and tell Jack to make haste to fetch the doctor. I can't believe this change is for the better.'

The doctor, when he came, endorsed her opinion. He examined the wound and shook his head soberly. 'It has a fiery look and see, how puffed the skin. A poison has set in, I fear, and with it a fever. He will ramble on and may open his eyes but without recognition. Have you sassafras root?'

Melissa nodded.

'Make a strong infusion and encourage him to take a little. Slip the spoon between his lips. 'Tis the only way. As for the wound – the honey has done well enough but now grate comfrey root or bruise it well and apply to both sides of the neck where the arrow entered and left the flesh. Reapply it freshly every six hours. 'Tis not called the healing herb for no reason. It makes the flesh multiply. You'll see.'

She nodded again.

'If he fingers the bandage, then bind his arms against his side, or tie his wrists together. We must not allow him to do further damage. With the partial return of his senses, the pain will tell.'

He promised to make another call the next day and left them to carry out his instructions. They changed the dressing on Luke's neck and managed to coax a few spoonfuls of the sassafras infusion down his throat. But by this time the fever was already establishing itself. Luke's temperature began to rise and fall so that at one moment his body was drenched with perspiration, the next shivering violently.

Melissa sat by him all night, watching him by the light of a candle. She held his two hands in her own so that he couldn't interfere with the bandage round his neck. His ramblings grew louder and his mind was obviously disordered.

'Ah, there she goes,' he muttered, 'like a leaf on the water, drifting, drifting . . . No! Don't look at me that way, no, no no . . . ' He tried to lift his head, staring wildly with eyes that glittered with fever. 'See how those knees bleed, Father. See the blood. 'Tis mine, I swear. I swear it . . . swear it. Father . . . Aah!' With a sudden cry of pain, he pulled his hands free and tore at the bandage, clawing fiercely at his neck. Melissa fought to gain control of his hands, shouting to Beth for assistance. She was sleeping temporarily in a bed at the far end of the room and was quickly at Melissa's side.

'Take his other hand!' cried Melissa. 'Oh, dear God, he undoes all our work!'

The scrabbling fingers had broken apart the loosely knitting flesh so that blood streamed on to the towels.

'They shan't take me,' he insisted hazily. 'They shan't find me. No one shall . . . no one . . . Oh, keep well back from the fire. It burns! Back, I say . . . back . . . Ah, she comes again, drifting, turning in the dark water . . . her hair floating . . . Forgive me . . . Here comes the rain . . . cold, cold rain.'

He began to shiver once more and fell suddenly still, his arms limp at his sides. Carefully they rebound the wound with fresh comfrey root. 'Shall I watch awhile?' offered Beth. 'You must be tired, ma'am.'

'No thank you, Beth, but 'twas a kindly thought. I'll stay with him until the fever breaks.'

It rose steadily throughout the night and by the morning was so high that Luke began to hallucinate. He sat up without warning, holding his hands out protectively as though to ward off an invisible danger.

'Stay away from me, damn you,' he muttered, his expression fearful. 'You shan't touch me, d'you hear. Never touch me or mine. I'll see you hanging yet for this day's work . . . Keep back!' He struck out wildly and Melissa and Thomas struggled to hold down the flailing arms. 'Don't point that finger, d'you hear. Such evil must die . . . die . . .' He fell to shivering violently until his teeth chattered and the bright colour faded from his face. His lips were cracked and dry with the heat of the fever and his hair clung damply to his head. 'Go away,' he pleaded, 'leave us be, for pity's sake . . . Ah, there she is, swaying in the breeze, her heels tap, tapping together, head on one side . . . head . . . on one side . . .'

Thomas looked at Melissa. ''Tis the witch he sees,' he whispered.

'Aye, poor man. To relive all that horror! I trust the doctor will come early.'

They tried to feed him more sassafras but he resisted violently and they gave up the attempt. By late afternoon the doctor had been again, shaken his head helplessly and departed, referring the matter to God. Luke's colour rose again with his temperature and several hallucinations occurred so that he screamed in fear and fought wildly to rid himself of snakes sent by 'the Gillis woman to plague and strangle me to death'. In desperation they tied him hand and foot to the bed where he writhed violently but to no purpose. Melissa turned away, sick at heart, and looked into Thomas's face. 'I think he'll die,' she said. 'I want to believe otherwise but no, I think he'll die.'

He was silent. He agreed and did not want to encourage her hopes.

'Should we send word to Simon?' she suggested. 'And what of Abby, and Sophie in London?'

'I doubt they would reach Heron in time,' said Thomas. 'Your father is at the crisis now. If he lives there'll be no cause to alarm them. If he dies –'

'Aye, there will be no time. You speak truly. And yet I

372

fear they might reproach me later.' She shrugged help-lessly.

'You must eat a little and take some wine,' said Thomas. 'Go downstairs. I will stay with him until you return.'

She hesitated then said, 'Thomas, Papa speaks wildly of many things. I think we must forget what we hear.'

He nodded gently. ''Tis all best forgotten,' he said. 'Never fear. Ramblings are the darker secrets of a man's soul and I pay no heed to what I hear.'

She went down to the kitchen and sank on to a stool while Nan hurried to pour her a goblet of wine. Minnie, scouring the cooking pots, watched her keenly and Melissa gave her a brief smile.

'I've neglected you, little one,' she said 'but before long –'

'Is Luke going to get –'

'The master!' said Nan crossly. 'How many times must you be told!'

'The master, then,' said Minnie, scowling. 'Is he going to get well again?'

'I trust so, Minnie. I believe he will. Did you pray for him?'

'Aye, twice over and once more for luck. And threw salt over my shoulder and crossed all my fingers and my toes!'

'And your toes?' Melissa laughed. 'Then he must surely recover.'

The child's face darkened. 'I wanted to see him but they refuse me. Later, they tell me. Always later.'

'Hush!' said Nan. 'You keep a civil tongue in your head and hustle yourself with that scouring. The mis-tress is too weary to listen to your cheek.'

Melissa sipped her wine. 'Is there news of Jon yet?' she asked.

Nan shook her head. 'But there have been few casualties. I doubt he'll come to any harm. Jack says they are all encamped round Exeter and like to stay there. The government chooses not to hurry, Jack says. But I'm rambling on. What will you eat ma'am? There's a soft cheese, newly made, or cold soused mackerel or I can coddle an egg or two.'

Melissa chose the fish and had almost finished it when the back door was flung open and Jon tumbled into the kitchen. He was weary and his face was grimy. On seeing Melissa, his face registered almost comic dismay but she was too distracted by Luke's sickness to concern herself over much with a runaway servant.

'So you're back,' she said. 'Are you so quickly wearied of fighting?'

'No ma'am,' he said. 'That is, aye ma'am. That is, there *is* no fighting ma'am.'

'Do you know anything of Simon or Hugo? Have you seen them? And what news of Hugo's family since Crediton is evacuated?'

His eyes lit up. 'Seen them, aye, and talked with them. Simon bade me tell you they are well and in good spirits and like to come home tomorrow but will return again. Hugo's family are fled to Dorset to stay with friends. Exeter shows no sign of surrendering.'

'I scarcely thought it would,' she said drily, 'but continue.'

Revelling in the attention Jon described some of his adventures, telling them of the spartan life, frugal food and the cheerful companionship of camp life. Their existence was an orderly one, he insisted, and morale among the rebels was high. But it did appear the siege might be protracted, which was not to the rebels' advantage.

"Twill take time for the Council to send down an army,' he explained, 'for when it comes it must be sizeable. We number nigh on five thousand. Some

374

say more! So they must be superior in number or in weaponry. At present they have Russell with Carew at Honiton but their men together would be no more than three hundred.' He shrugged. 'Either way 'twill take time and the Council seeks first to sweeten us with words and persuade us into good behaviour! Our leaders hope the city will come over to us before the army reaches us for then we would be hard-pressed. We surround Exeter but they would surround us.' He shrugged again. 'Apart from Crediton we have seen no action. One night a plan was made to blast our way into the town.'

'Blast a way?' cried Minnie, her eyes gleaming, a half-scoured pan in her hands. 'With gunpowder?'

'Aye, little fire brand,' he laughed, 'with gunpowder. The mine was dug and the charges and powder all ready. Simon and Hugo were to go in with the first assault. There was enough powder to bring down the wall – by the West Gate it was –'

'But what happened?' cried Nan.

His face fell. 'None can tell,' he said bitterly, 'but that the defenders got wind of the affair and flooded the shaft. Barely minutes before the time allotted.'

Melissa, secretly relieved by the outcome of the plan, stood up declaring her intention of returning to Luke's sickbed and she left Jon recounting his adventures while Nan found him food and drink.

Upstairs she found the room very quiet. Thomas looked up as she entered. 'There is a change,' he said wonderingly. 'He is calmer in his speech and less violent in his movements. See, his face is paler.'

Melissa looked at Luke. 'When did this change take place?' she asked. 'I have been gone less than an hour.'

'Soon after you left. At first I heard the breathing soften and feared 'twas failing strength. I almost called you but then I sensed it was a change for the better.'

'I believe it, also,' she said 'if I dare trust my own eyes.' Lightly she touched his face with her hand. 'He is cooler,' she said. 'Oh Thomas! I think God has answered our prayers. The worst is over.' And she fell to her knees beside the bed and gave thanks for her father's deliverance.

On 20 July, while the fate of the Cornish rebellion still hung in the balance, Melissa married Thomas Benet. They invited no guests to the simple ceremony which was conducted entirely in English by a priest too fearful of retribution to consider any alternative. Hugo and Simon were still outside Exeter with the rebel encampment but Melissa did not choose to risk a rebuff by inviting them to attend a service which so obviously conflicted with their principles. Luke was not fully recovered from his neck wound and was thus unable to be present but his dowry for Melissa included a farmhouse which had once belonged to Harben Priory. It had stood empty since the dissolution and was in dire need of attention before it could be made habitable.

Beth and Jack attended the wedding to act as witnesses and Minnie was a bridesmaid, resplendent in a new gown cut from Melissa's old blue silk. Melissa wore a simple white silk under muslin and carried three pink roses tied with white ribbon. Reluctant to arouse any outside interest which might inspire hostility, the service was set for ten o'clock in the morning when fewer people would be in the vicinity and they duly rode up to the church with Jon who was to hold the horses at the churchyard entrance. At the appointed time the wedding party walked up the path to the porch door and were met by the priest. He smiled nervously and began immediately to rush through the words of the ceremony as though his life depended on it. He was, in fact, breaking no laws but in the present confusions religious services were a sensitive area. He was prepared for the worst and only wanted to reach its conclusion without attracting any unwarranted attention from passers-by who might somehow construe the matter in a different light and regard his actions as suspect. Men were hanged for less if rumour was to be believed!

The couple made their vows, received their blessings and exchanged rings. No mass would be said and no bride cake broken. Uncertain of the exact letter of the new law, the priest erred on the side of simplicity. The vital and necessary vows were made and Melissa and Thomas must be satisfied. They might be disappointed but times were hard, even dangerous, and every man must look to his own safety.

When the ceremony was over, Minnie threw a few handfuls of petals which she had collected earlier. Jack kissed the bride and Beth received a peck on the cheek from Thomas. Smiling, they thanked the priest and then walked back to the horses.

'God be with you both!' cried Jon. 'Long life and happiness!' He had been prevailed upon to act as 'liaison officer' between Heron, Hugo and Simon and now divided his time quite cheerfully between war and peace, scurrying to and fro with rebel messages, letters, home-baked pies and other necessities of life to the advantage of all concerned.

'Thank you, Jon,' said Melissa.

'You take care of her now, Thomas,' he added boldly. 'You're a most fortunate man to have such a bonny wife! Don't I get to kiss the bride, then, as has waited here for the past quarter of an hour with only dumb beasts as company?'

'You'll have to kiss him ma'am,' laughed Beth, 'but 'twill be easier if you shut your eyes first. That face is a gruesome thing but at close quarters –!'

'Nobody's kissing me,' complained Minnie, 'and me in my best gown!'

'Kiss you?' teased Jon. 'Why, we'd have to draw lots and the winner is excused the pleasure!'

She gave a shrill squeal of pretended rage but Jack swung her off the ground and kissed her soundly. Then he tossed her to Jon who pretended to drop her. But her honour was satisfied and soon everyone was mounted. Minnie rode behind Jon and the little procession set off back to Heron. Beth had prepared a simple breakfast of cold meats, fruit flans and custards and all at Maudesley were invited. Toasts were drunk to the newly weds and as the wine flowed, the usual jokes were made, much to Thomas's dismay and Melissa's secret amusement.

Jo Tucker raised his hands for silence. 'Speech from the groom!' he cried. 'Speech, Thomas.'

Thomas looked appealingly at Melissa but she nodded encouragingly.

'Just a few words, Thomas,' she said.

'On the bench Thomas, where we can all see you!' cried Jo and he was helped up. He stood for a moment paralyzed with nervousness as the room seemed to swim before his eyes. The upturned faces blended into a mass and he thought the Hall had never looked so large and uncompromising. He swallowed hard.

'Er –' His mind became a total blank and he looked for Melissa in the sea of faces. As soon as he found it, his panic vanished. She was looking up at him with her large calm eyes, her face a little flushed with excitement, her lips parted in a smile. Not a smile that mocked his predicament but one that sympathized. There was understanding in the smile, even love.

'Ladies and gentlemen,' he began haltingly and his voice sounded strange to him, like that of a stranger. 'Today 'tis my pleasure –'

'That will be tonight!' roared someone at the back of

the crowd and there was loud laughter.

'Er – my pleasure,' he began again. More laughter and he saw that Melissa was laughing too. 'To welcome you all here to eat and drink and be merry –'

'Not too merry!' called Jack and was shouted down indignantly.

'Um – to be merry this day and to celebrate our wedding er – with all cheer –'

'Hurrah! Hurrah!'

Thomas frowned in an effort to concentrate. 'I consider myself a very fortunate man and shall do my utmost –'

'Ooh! There's a fine boast! His utmost, no less!'

There was another roar of laughter at Thomas's discomfiture.

'To make her happy.'

He climbed down hastily, shaking his head as Jo Tucker demanded 'More!' and was heartily patted on the back for his efforts.

Melissa took his hands and kissed him lightly on the cheek. 'A fine speech,' she said gently. 'I was proud of you.'

Slowly, almost clumsily, Melissa unfastened her gown and let it fall to the floor. She stepped out of it and unfastened her kirtle with fingers that trembled. How can you be so foolish, she chided herself. You are not a child and your husband is no monster.

The marriage bed is not to be feared, nor Thomas. She folded her clothes while her heart hammered. This was her own familiar room, the bedchamber she had shared with brothers and sisters. She had slept alone since Abby had left home but before that had shared a bed comfortably enough. Pulling her robe down over her head and shoulders, she thought of the two boys, recalling their tousled heads on the pillows of the opposite bed, their morning faces hazy still with sleep and their eagerness to start the day. She saw Jeffery, his oval face and large serious eyes, his head full of learning and high ideals. Now he lay under the water off Spithead, limbs sprawled, eyes blank – no, she would not think of it. Nor of Paul, cold and still in the churchyard. But on Abby she could allow her thoughts to dwell for Abby was happily wed and had her own family. Would she, Melissa, conceive and bear a son for Thomas? Was that what he wanted? Wasn't it every man's desire to boast of a son? She was still young enough. The sheets were cool to her skin and she sat very straight, her legs stretched before her, wriggling her toes among the pot pourri Nan had sprinkled so lavishly. One day they would ride out to Ladyford Farm to see the house though it would be weeks before they could move into it. But that was convenient for Luke still needed her ministrations and she would not leave Heron until Simon returned. Glancing round the familiar room, she saw the pomander which still swung in the window. It was dry and withered now but Jeffery had made it for her years ago. She would take it to Ladyford. She saw the sampler Abby had stitched so carefully as a present for Melissa's twelfth birthday. On the shelf a wooden ship that Jeffery had carved for her. Their 'little Lissa', trapped in her own world for so many years. And now she was wed! She sighed. Abby would grieve that she had missed the wedding but she would understand. The uprising affected so many aspects of their lives. The door opened and Thomas stood in his nightshirt.

'Come in, Thomas, and close the door,' she said smiling. Was he as reluctant as she was to share a bed?

He closed the door and crossed to the bed, setting down the candle on the chest beside it. Melissa threw back the sheet on his side of the bed and he slid awkwardly between the sheets.

'Do we need the candle?' he asked.

'No,' she said and he blew it out thankfully. They sat in the fading light of the July evening.

'I think our guests enjoyed themselves,' he said awkwardly. 'Jack drank too much as usual. His head will ache in the morning.'

'But he was very happy. They all were.'

'Aye. And my little Lissa looked very beautiful.'

'Thank you.' She laughed suddenly. 'I must learn to call you "my love" and "dearest husband". "Thomas" will not do. 'Tis too formal.'

'I shall look forward to it!' He still stared straight ahead, not looking at her. She took his hand in hers but he made no acknowledgement.

''Tis a very pleasant room,' he remarked conversationally.

'Aye.'

'And the bed most comfortable.'

His own bed was a single one while Melissa had shared her larger bed with Abigail so they had decided to share hers. Yawning, he put a hand to his mouth. 'An eventful day,' he said. 'A long and eventful day.'

Melissa glanced sideways at him, resisting a smile. His obvious shyness gave her more confidence. 'Are you tired, Thomas – my love!' she corrected hastily and they both laughed.

'How improper it sounds,' he said. 'I swear I shall never get used to it.'

'Nor I! But will you not call me "my love"? Try it and see how it sounds.'

'Oh . . . er . . . Are *you* tired, my love?'

'No.'

He looked at her in alarm. 'You're not?'

'No.'

'Ah!'

'Won't you lie down with me?' she said. 'We can scarce sit up all night.' They slid under the sheets; Thomas pulled out a handful of petals and tossed them to the floor.

'Is there a flower left in the entire garden with any petals?' he laughed.

'Minnie has been buzzing from bloom to bloom like a bee.'

There was a long silence as they lay very straight side by side and both searched for something to say to ease the tension. The silence lengthened until it became painful.

'Thomas –'

'Aye.'

'When I was a child you readily took me into your arms. I wish you would do so now.'

He turned to her immediately.

'Lissa! Oh, sweet girl. Forgive me. Come, let me put my arms around you – so. Is that better?'

'Much better.' She turned her head slightly so that she could kiss his chest. Thin and hairless – but his gentle heart beat within.

'I hear your heart,' she said, 'pounding like the hooves of a horse! Slow down, little horse.'

He laughed ruefully. 'My heart beats fit to burst,' he confessed. ''Tis your body in my arms. So close. Touching my skin! I have never known it . . . You are my first wife. My first woman.'

'That pleases me.'

'Does it? Does it truly please you?'

'Aye . . . You are my first man.'

'But – Simon,' he whispered.

She shook her head in the darkness. 'I told you once that we were never lovers. Why do we speak of Simon? He is nothing to me. A half-brother, no more, no less.

You are my beloved Thomas, my dear husband, my sweet lord.'

'Oh Lissa –'

She kissed his chest again then, raising herself, kissed his shoulder, arm, neck then his face, ear, hair and was aware of his reaction to her caresses. Then she stopped. 'This is a one-sided wooing,' she teased him. 'You will call me minx or baggage if I am so forward.'

He pulled her suddenly into his arms and kissed her. 'Forgive me,' he said. 'I have a lot to learn.'

'We both have a lot to learn – and many years to practise what we learn!'

'Oh what a sweet soft back!' His hands passed gently over her back and down to her thighs. 'So sweet and rounded and soft to the touch –.'

'I did not think 'twould be so sweet,' she whispered.

'Nor I.'

Moments passed as their caresses grew more intimate, more revealing – and more loving. His passion outstripped hers and at last she felt his body reach inside her, hard and eager. 'Alison,' he murmured. 'I love you . . . love you.'

The words were like a blow but Melissa kissed him. 'I love you, Thomas,' she said gently. She would not tell him what he had said. He had loved Alison for so long without possessing her. She thought of her mother. There was so much unrequited love in the world. 'That was for you, Mama,' she thought. 'Mayhap next time, or the time after, 'twill be for me.' She lay quietly hearing her husband's breathing change, knowing that he drifted into sleep. After a while, she smiled tremulously into the darkness. He would learn to love her. There was plenty of time . . .

CHAPTER TWENTY-ONE

July was nearly over and still the two armies had not met. Arundell, outside Exeter, waited with his Cornishmen for the confrontation with the government forces. Exeter waited also, to be released from the siege. At last the reinforcements promised to Russell were actually on their way and news of this reached Arundell to his great alarm. Russell was to receive considerable reinforcements including West Country levies – local men still willing to fight for the King. In addition, there would be a large contingent of foreign mercenaries – Italian infantry armed with arquebuses and cavalry under Jacques Jermigry, some of them carrying wheel lock pistols. The English cavalry would carry lances and battle axes and would be well protected. The crucial question was – in what numbers would they come? The only way to find out was to engage the enemy and Arundell decided to send a detachment of Devonshire rebels to challenge the government at Honiton. Simon and Hugo, to their extreme disappointment, were not among those sent. The battle took place at Fenny Bridges and proved disastrous for Arundell's men. After fierce fighting, they were driven back and a late arrival of two hundred Cornishmen only served to delay the government's final victory. When it was all over, the rebels had lost around three hundred dead and Russell only one third of that number.

Several days passed during which both sides reassessed their positions and prepared for a more decisive engagement. Arundell knew that the government would thrust towards Exeter. Clyst St Mary, through which they must pass, was heavily reinforced. Hugo and Simon found themselves 'digging in' behind the first line of defence which crossed the road east of the town.

'They take their time,' grumbled Hugo, peering over the hastily thrown up ramparts to the north of the road. 'Where the devil are they?'

Simon grinned at his impatience. 'You're in a mighty hurry to get killed!' he said. 'Be patient and all will be revealed. They're probably still listening to speeches from their wordy leaders!'

'Aye, prayers and a sermon from old Coverdale, a rabble-rousing word from the commander, not to mention a harangue for the mercenaries!'

Simon frowned. 'Those mercenaries,' he said. 'I don't care for the sound of them. Men who fight for the pleasure of killing –'

'And the looting that follows. No doubt being promised a fat bonus,' said Hugo. He looked along to his right where on the other side of the road a high hedge formed a natural barrier between the men and the enemy. 'If they send in pikemen,' he said, 'they'll lose speed breaking through the bushes . . .'

A cry from the lookouts on the high ground made them turn. The enemy had been seen less than a mile away. Within minutes, they could make out the colourful ranks approaching through the green fields and along the road. Simon took out his first arrow and kissed the head of it for luck. On either side of him men did likewise until the earthworks behind which they sheltered bristled with a deadly array of arrows. A hush fell on the waiting ranks as the ground quivered under the weight of the approaching army and the air was filled with the jingle of harness and the muffled but distinctive myriad sounds made by thousands of armed men.

'Here they come!' whispered Hugo. He turned suddenly and gripped Simon's hand in a gesture of friendship. Simon had time to wink cheerfully and then the enemy was upon them. The air hummed with arrows and was rent with hoarse cries as the missiles found their marks and the men went down, to sprawl and writhe helplessly in the rain-soaked grass to be trampled by their comrades and the wave of Grey's cavalry which followed. The mounted men, however, heavily armoured, resisted the arrows and soon took the advantage. The bowmen were helpless against an enemy at close range and rather than abandon their bows so early in the battle, they fled back to take up positions in the town itself. Hugo and Simon somehow managed to stay together, and found themselves at the upstairs window of a small cottage overlooking the main road. They were out of breath but in good spirits and eager to continue.

'Only four arrows gone,' said Hugo fitting a fifth. 'I must do better this time. Did we lose many?'

'A fair number,' said Simon. 'And to our right there I heard Italian. It sounded like musket fire.'

'Did you see what happened at the lane, by the hedge?'

'No – ah, they're forming up again.'

But the expected second charge was suddenly aborted. The air was filled with a furious drumming and a bugle sounded. The two men looked at each other.

''Tis coming from behind the enemy,' said a man next to Hugo. 'What does it mean?'

Hugo shook his head. Simon, watching out of the window, saw the troops outside hesitate, looking at each other in confusion. A fresh hail of arrows from the nearest cottages added to their disorder and a panic developed. Word spread among them that the rebels were behind them and the cry went up to retreat. The Germans and Italians, thoroughly alarmed, turned tail and many of them dropped their weapons as they went.

'They're retreating!' exclaimed Simon. 'Look, ground pikes, pistols, swords galore! Let's harass their retreat. Come!'

Before Hugo could remonstrate with him, he had run down the stairs and was picking his way among the discarded weapons. More followed his example and, hallooing triumphantly, several hundred of them persued the fleeing troops with a hail of stones to hasten their departure. Then they set to among the trophies that littered the roadway. Hugo joined them and found himself a finely marked dagger of Italian origin which he tucked into his belt.

'To show my grandson – when I have one!' he laughed.

'And an exaggerated tale of your exploits to go with it, no doubt,' said Simon. 'I've taken a liking to this little toy. What d'you think of this?'

He held out a wheel lock pistol and Hugo took it from him, turning it over in his hands. 'A toy, as you say,' he said as he handed it back. 'But I warrant 'twill never replace the longbow.'

For a while the rebels rejoiced in their unexpected victory and hastily gathered up the scattered possessions of the government's army. The Lord Privy Seal's war chest was among the prizes and there was a large selection of valuable weapons and ammunition. Unfortunately, the rebels were so zealous in the scavenging that they failed to realize that the enemy had reorganized and were making a second assault on Clyst.

'To arms!' went up the cry from a horrified watcher at an upstairs window. 'Here they come! To arms!'

There was a near-panic as the rebels ran to reestablish themselves and make good their positions but already Sir William Francis was leading his men in another charge, straight up the main street. As they poured into the town he was struck on the head by a rock which crushed his skull. He died instantly and fell but the attack continued.

'Their leader's down!' cried Simon.

'They've lost Sir William!'

'We've killed their leader!'

The rebels' jubilation was short-lived. Methodically, the attackers began to fire the thatches while the rest of the battle continued, raging inside and out.

'Christ's blood!' exclaimed Hugo. 'The house will be down about our ears if we don't move! Come.'

Even as he spoke the roof creaked ominously, weakened by the flames. Around them men lay dead or dying while above them the flames gained a fierce hold and threatened to engulf the rest of the building.

'Outside!' cried Hugo.

'But these men –' began Simon, reluctant to abandon them.

'Outside, I say!' Hugo repeated and was half out of the door when, with a splintering rending sound, most of the roof gave way and the room was filled with burning wood and straw as the sky appeared clear and blue above them. There were agonized screams as the flames licked first at the clothes and hair of the injured men and then at their flesh. Smoke billowed into the air and sparks hung glittering in the orange air. A burning brand had caught Simon across the left shoulder and the cloth of his jerkin smouldered, scorching his skin painfully. His face contorted with pain, he brushed frantically at it but a larger beam dislodged itself from the wall and fell across him, pinning him face downward to the floor. The fall had robbed him of breath; for a few seconds he lay helpless, weak with shock and pain. Beside him, the eyes of a dead man stared sightlessly into his and he saw with a shudder that the hair above the eyes had been reduced to a few blackened tufts. The clamour of other men's pain drowned his senses and his eyes felt heavy with an unnatural drowsiness.

'Christ's blood! Open your eyes, man!'

It was Hugo's voice. Simon tried to open his eyes but a blackness swept over him.

'Simon! For pity's sake, man. Are you alive? Give me a hand, someone.' But those that could move had already made good their escape and Hugo was thrown on his own resources. He pulled and tugged at the beam until it rolled free of Simon's inert body, then shook him violently.

'Simon! You must open your eyes and listen to me. We must leave this building. They are going to overrun us and they'll show no mercy. You must stand up! Help me, Simon. Help me. I can't move you unaided – ah, that's the way. Well done. Put an arm round my shoulder –' A fresh fall of burning thatch narrowly missed them and smoke and sparks once more filled the room. Slowly Hugo dragged the unwilling Simon to the doorway and down the stairs. Outside smoke drifted above the combatants as Russell's pikemen charged the rebels' rear guard which had been hastily formed to allow the withdrawal of the remainder. Vicious hand to hand fighting followed and metal rang against metal, interspersed with screams of agony and the moans of the dying while the smell of scorched flesh drifted in the air. Cottages crashed into ruins as the battle raged on but Hugo was able to take no further part in it. He dragged Simon clear of the cottage, then abandoned his bow so as to hoist his unconscious friend over his shoulder and staggered after his comrades across the bridge. But Arundell had not despaired of saving the situation although with the heavy casualties they had suffered he knew his chances were slipping away. During the night he rounded up all his troops and they quietly set about preparing a new position from which they would launch a counter-attack in the morning. When they were secured, sentries were posted, and the faithful women brought out food and drink for the encampments outside the town. Simon pulled the rabbit from the bone and sighed deeply. Hugo looked at him sharply.

'What ails you?' he asked.

'I can't rightly say,' said Simon. 'I'm filled with a deep unease. Someone is walking over my grave.'

'Superstitious nonsense,' said Hugo firmly. He tossed a crust to the mongrel dog who trotted among them on the lookout for scraps. 'Don't talk so mournfully. Your time's not up yet.'

'Thanks to you!' said Simon. He looked up, his face serious in the light of the fire. 'I owe my life to you. It was bravely done and I am in your debt.'

'Don't speak of it,' said Hugo, embarrassed.

'But I must,' persisted Simon. 'I would be dead now, but for your timely assistance. If I can ever serve you that way –'

'Next time I'm trapped in a burning house I'll call on you!' Hugo laughed. 'Would you have left *me* to die?'

'Indeed not!'

'Then we have said it all. I did not care to lose a cousin so soon after finding him! Eat up. You will need your strength for tomorrow. Is the hand still sore?'

''Tis bearable,' said Simon.

'Good – and this stew! I swear food never tasted so good. Those women are worth their weight in gold.'

'Then Ellen is worth a tidy sum.' He lowered his voice. 'What of tomorrow, Hugo? Do we have a chance?'

His cousin shrugged. 'A chance? Aye, I think we do. Our cause is just and I cannot believe God will let us fail.'

'But if you should die what would you miss most?'

Hugo put the empty bowl in the grass beside him and lay back with his hands behind his head. 'What would I miss? Mm . . . A good bottle of wine mayhap. Or a song.'

'Why do you leave out the women?' asked Simon.

'I can't miss what I haven't yet sampled,' said Hugo. 'But I'd miss being able to miss it . . . I have an idea! When we are done with fighting, we might ride together sometimes? Come over to Sampford or Crediton and stay a few days. We'll hunt deer or go fishing.'

'I'd like that,' said Simon.

'We'll escape from the womenfolk, bless them. We might go hawking.'

They were both silent, suddenly aware how vulnerable they were. How near to never again enjoying any of these delights.

'Aye, I'll look forward to that,' said Simon quietly. 'I pray tomorrow turns in our favour. There is much to be done at Heron and I have great plans . . .' He took a mouthful of ale from the flagon. 'Do you know my father well, Hugo?'

'Well enough,' said Hugo. 'He's not an easy man to know, I'm told. I see him very rarely – family occasions, funerals, weddings. That's all.'

'But your father, Stephen, spoke of him?'

'My father died when I was a child. My mother speaks of him sometimes as a difficult man. There was no love lost between them.'

Simon sighed. 'Pray God, I don't disappoint him. He has such plans for me.'

'There's much that's good in him. He has a soft heart. My aunt Blanche tells this story –' He broke off. 'You are not too tired to talk?'

'After my escape?' he laughed. 'No. My burnt shoulder stings a little and I swear I'm black and blue but go on. I want this night to last. We may not see another.'

'Hush!' Hugo reproached him. 'Such talk is treasonable! Yet I know how you feel. I don't doubt that both armies will talk tonight away . . . But the story. Let me see: they had taken him to London for the first time to stay with the Lessors. Your father was about seven I believe, or maybe eight. They showed him the river and London Bridge and the Palace of Westminster and such like – all the sights of England's greatest city. When he went home the cook asked him if he'd enjoyed his visit to London. No, he told her, 'twas a cruel place. How is it cruel, she asks him. They beat donkeys he says and he didn't care to go there again!'

'Beat donkeys?'

'Aye. It seems he saw a donkey being beaten in the street. No one else could recall the incident and yet on him it made a great impression.'

They were silent, thinking their own thoughts.

'I wonder,' mused Hugo, 'how our children will think of us.'

'With respect, I hope. And affection . . . What does your mother think of me, Hugo? Of my sudden appearance, I mean?'

Hugo considered for a moment before answering. 'She was surprisingly calm,' he said. 'Mama is quite robust. Not easily shocked. My stepfather –' he shrugged. 'I think he feels far enough removed from the Kendals not to let it disturb him.'

'And your Margaret-to-be?'

He laughed loudly. 'Now, *she* was shocked. Scandalized! But enjoyed every moment of the revelation. She sees you as wickedly different. I was almost jealous!'

As they laughed, Ellen's large frame loomed up in the darkness. 'Still laughing?' she teased. 'I never heard so many cheerful folks as there are tonight in this camp.

And friendly. I've had that many kisses and hugs and me like a bladder full of lard and a face full of pock marks. But tonight I feel like the Queen of England, that I do!'

'You'd best watch out for your head then!' said Hugo.

'Now don't you talk all night,' she warned them. 'You boys need your beauty sleep the same as anyone else. Get some sleep and God be with you both tomorrow.'

'Bless you, Ellen,' said Hugo.

'Save me some stew for tomorrow night, Ellen,' said Simon but not trusting herself to speak, she could only nod and move hurriedly on to the next group.

'How do you get on with your stepfather?' asked Simon curiously.

Hugo shrugged. 'Well enough now,' he said. 'But not so happily when I was young. I think he envied me my place in Mama's affection. Mama loved my father and no one could wholly replace him. I was a visible reminder of another love in my mother's life.'

'So he chose not to encourage ties with the Kendals,' said Simon and Hugo nodded.

'Will our friendship disturb him?' asked Simon.

'It may do but I care not. If we survive tomorrow, I'll think on it again. In the meantime mayhap Ellen is right. We must sleep.'

'Tomorrow we will win the day,' said Simon. 'I feel it most strongly.'

'I believe you,' said Hugo. 'Now I'll bid you goodnight.'

'Goodnight to you,' said Simon. For a while the friends lay side by side, pressed close for warmth and comfort. As the last of the day faded the small sounds of a night camp reached them; the snores of those already asleep, the moans of the wounded and the subdued chatter of those too nervous to sleep. Here and there a dog barked or someone laughed. There were the soft sounds of a sword being lovingly polished, the occasional grunting of a man with a woman and the rustle and whinnying of horses. The fires of Clyst had died down to a mere glow but the crackle of the remaining flames and the crunch of falling woodwork carried clearly in the cool night air. Separately the sounds were ordinary enough. Together they made a kind of music.

How, thought Simon, could a thousand men at war sound so beautiful? He was still pondering the answer as he slipped into a fitful doze that lasted until the dawn.

The government forces woke to find themselves under fire but there was no confusion. The night before they had made careful plans; each man knew what he had to do and the fighting machine swung quickly into action. They worked a flanking movement until the rebels found themselves caught in a trap with the enemy before and behind them. The battle degenerated into fierce hand to hand fighting as the encircled rebels tried desperately to fight their way out and struggle back to the base below the walls of Exeter. Nearly a thousand men were lost to the rebel cause and Humphrey Arundell tasted the bitterness of final defeat. The cost was too high. He and his depleted army struck camp and withdrew into Cornwall.

Between them Cornwall and Devon lost twelve hundred men in the worst fighting the area had ever known. Russell entered Exeter in triumph taking most of the rebel leaders with him as prisoners. These were later taken to London. The western rebellion was virtually over. Those who survived the slaughter, and that included the two Kendal cousins, gave thanks to God and went sadly, wearily to their homes.

Ladyford was a small gaunt farmhouse set on the very edge of the moors. No trees sheltered it from the wind and weather for any that presumed to take root and grow were immediately bowed by the prevailing wind and generally discouraged from achieving normal height. Thus the garden boasted only a few dwarfed and twisted hawthorns and an apple tree. Melissa drew her cloak round her and Thomas put an arm round her protectively. They had tied up their horses and now stood at the gate surveying the house that was to be their home as soon as it could be made habitable. A rough stone wall enclosed the garden, which was sadly overgrown and full of tangled shrubs and long waving grasses. They opened the creaking gate and went inside. Melissa looked down.

'See here, Thomas,' she said. 'Flagstones! I warrant there's a path laid under this – this –' Words failed her and she threw out her hands expressively: 'this apology for a garden!' laughed Thomas, finishing the sentence for her. 'But we'll soon have it in good order.' He looked determinedly round, refusing to be discouraged by the sight of the dead plants and decaying leaves.

'What a sad old house,' said Melissa. 'To be neglected for so long. Once it must have stood proud and new and now 'tis reduced to this.'

'Don't grieve for it,' said Thomas. 'You're too tender-hearted, Lissa. A house has no feelings.'

'Can we be certain?' she said smiling and he laughed again.

'I've brought a bill hook,' he told her. 'I'll make a start right now and you shall see your path. Wait here.'

He retrieved the bill hook from the saddle and began to cut back the vegetation which concealed the path. As Melissa had guessed, the flagstones led up to the front door and ten minutes later she was skipping along the path, delightedly.

'Oh Thomas! Our first path!' she teased. 'Why, at the end here we could set our hives. And over there in the middle, what d'you say to an aviary – in time that is,' she said hastily, seeing the look in Thomas's eyes. 'I wonder what else we shall discover. A fishpond, mayhap.'

'If not I will build you one.'

'Or a sundial or statuette!' cried Melissa.

'We will buy a sundial if you wish.'

'Or a stone seat – or stone steps!'

'And a herb garden!' cried Thomas, infected by her excitement. 'If we plant some herbs shortly they will be ready by the summer. Oh Lissa!'

'Thomas! Thomas! We are such fools!'

'Not so,' said Thomas gently. 'We are happy and we deserve our happiness. There is nothing foolish in a husband and wife finding joy in their first home.'

Lissa kissed him then darted back along the path to the gate, examining the plants on either side.

'There's a gorse bush here and heather,' she cried. 'Oh, Thomas shall we have a rowan tree – those bonny orange berries – and an elderberry, of course. And foxgloves,' she went on eagerly, 'and lavender, Thomas, growing against the wall there – and bluebells. They would look well along the edge of the path. Oh, and the tiny red poppies –'

'You shall have whatever you wish,' laughed Thomas if you will allow me to go inside out of this biting wind.'

She was all contrition. 'Why, so you shall, poor man! Let's hustle those dry old bones of yours out of the cold.'

'Not *so* old,' he protested and producing the key, opened up the door and they went inside. They had visited briefly once before but then the rain had poured down, giving the old house a grimness that was belied today for although the wind was keen, the sun shone brilliantly. Thomas flung open the shutters and it lit up the large low room, the ceiling blackened with soot.

'This will be a bonny room,' said Melissa, 'when the benches and trestles are set up, sweet rushes on the floor, torches burning on the walls! I can picture a dog sleeping beside the fire –'

' – as near as he dare get without singeing his nose and paws! When are the cleaners coming from the village, tomorrow?'

'The day after. I shall be here, of course, to keep an eye on them and the terrible Minnie shall come, too. There'll be plenty for her to do and that way I shall keep her out of mischief.'

'Are you wise to bring her with you?' asked Thomas. 'You could easily find a new girl.'

'I know,' said Melissa, 'but I'm fond of the little wretch for all her bad ways. I truly do believe she means well but by her nature she is a wild thing.'

'She hates the idea of leaving Heron.'

'Aye, but Papa wishes her to come with us. He says rightly that she needs a womanly influence to "soften her rough edges". I'll send her frequently with messages and the like and loan her when they need extra help with the washing or salting.'

They glanced in at the kitchen and were dismayed by its neglected state.

'But 'twill look fine when we clean it up,' said Melissa. 'Gleaming pans and a scrubbed table board – and hams smoking over the fire and strings of onions hanging from the ceiling. Let's look upstairs.'

The wooden stairs creaked under their weight as they went up and Thomas, going first, brushed away the cobwebs. There were two bedchambers and, at the far end, a low attic above the kitchen which would be Minnie's room.

''Twill need a great deal of work,' said Thomas doubtfully. 'There are even cracks where the daylight comes through the thatch! Mayhap she can have the smaller bedchamber instead.'

Melissa hesitated. ''Tis an idea,' she said 'but later we

shall need it – for your son.'

She followed him into the larger of the two upper rooms as Thomas nodded absently. 'I was at Maudesley yesterday,' he told her. 'Joseph is giving us a chest as a wedding gift.'

'A chest? How very generous.'

'And Matthew is sending a table clock direct from London.'

'Aren't we fortunate, Thomas?'

'We are indeed. And Ladyford will be a charming house when the work is –' He looked at Melissa. 'Our son?' he exclaimed.

She nodded, her eyes shining with the excitement she could no longer hide. 'Our son,' she repeated, 'or mayhap a daughter.'

'Melissa! So soon!'

'Are you pleased?'

'My dearest girl, of course I'm pleased,' he gasped. 'I'm pleased and astonished and – and proud.'

'As well you might be,' she laughed. 'They will tease us for our indecent haste.'

'I care not! A son!'

'Another Benet!' she laughed. 'So you had best start to think on a name for him. What was your father's name?'

'Oliver – and my mother's name was Rachel.'

'Then we need think no more,' said Melissa softly. 'Will you not kiss me and tell me how clever I am.'

She held out her arms and they clung together in the dim room, patterned by the light which came through the shutters.

'I have everything I want in the world,' whispered Melissa. 'You, our child and Ladyford.'

They kissed again and Thomas stroked her hair. As he looked into the face of his wife and mother of his child, he realized for the first time that the ghost of Alison had left him.

CHAPTER TWENTY-TWO

'Eight priests at least,' said Luke. 'Several mayors and the port-reeve of St Ives. The arrests go on and so does the looting.' He sighed heavily and Simon, watching him, wondered again which side his father would have fought on if he had been truly involved. The wound in his neck had kept him out of the rebellion. Yet Luke was known to be a man for the King. Simon himself had seen him ride with the King's Commissioners. Would it matter which king? Was it possible that he and Simon could have fought knowingly on opposite sides? Mercifully for their relationship, it had not been fully put to the test and now it never would be. The Cornish rebellion was crushed, the leaders about to be hanged. Goods, properties and lands of the ringleaders were to be confiscated. 'Examples' would be made among the rank and file and severe punishments meted out.

'All those good men,' said Simon, 'and we have gained nothing. Nothing has been granted, no allowance made, not the smallest pretence to consider our grievances. So many good men dead . . .'

They walked in the garden at Heron where the October trees had turned red and gold and falling leaves fluttered about them in the light breeze.

'Some say more than ten thousand,' said Luke, 'on both sides, that is. And now Somerset himself is out of favour if the rumours have any truth in them.'

'What difference will it make?' asked Simon. 'Arundell, Pomeroy and Winslade are still in custody. A change in power won't even save their necks.'

'No,' said Luke. 'There is no turning back the clock. People come and go, but England has a Protestant king now. The new religion is here to stay, Simon. We must either bend or go under. All of us,' he said, a slight emphasis on the word 'all'. He whistled the dogs who had treed a cat and were making a great deal of noise about it. They came unwillingly, resentful of the loss of their quarry.

'Leave that cat alone,' Luke told them. 'She has done you no harm and is twice your age. Respect her grey hairs, for she deserves a little peace. We all do,' he added grimly.

'A little peace?' said Simon and his tone was bitter. 'Is that all it means to you? Our friends are dead or maimed and the West Country has lost everything.'

'You exaggerate,' said Luke.

'Do I?' said Simon. 'Of the sixteen articles we set before the Council in London, what did they grant us? Nothing! Sacrament over the altar, the mass in Latin, prayers for the souls in purgatory, daily baptism –' he paused for breath ' – and our own language. The Cornish tongue.'

'You are not Cornish,' said Luke mildly.

'But why should those that are speak English? The Council has mutilated the Catholic religion.'

'In the name of God!' cried Luke sharply. 'Your tongue is much too free. That damned Hugo has infected you with his Popish views!'

'He is my friend,' said Simon.

'He is a hot-head and a dangerous ally.'

'No father. He is young, like me, with ideals, like me.'

'I tell you he is dangerous,' said Luke, 'and your

400

friendship troubles me. The country is governed by Protestants and 'tis dangerous to be a Roman Catholic. He speaks too loudly for his own good, you mark my words – even his bride-to-be is a Catholic and a French Catholic at that!'

'She is only part French and is by all accounts a charming girl.'

'I tell you, Hugo is unwise to wed her,' said Luke. 'He stands in greater danger now than ever he did during the last few months.'

'I trust you are wrong,' said Simon.

'I trust so,' said Luke.

But even as he said it, he knew he lied. Hugo was a threat to his peace of mind. His dangerous convictions would reflect on Heron. Thank God, the boy had changed his name although the family connections were well enough known. Hester had seen to that! And the inheritance troubled him more than he cared to admit to anyone else. By blood, Hugo was a Kendal yet so was Simon. But Simon was illegitimate in the eyes of the world and Luke could never prove him otherwise. Which boy had the stronger claim? It would be a close decision if it ever went to court, which, please God, it never would do. Damned Hugo with his Papist views and his French Margaret! What was Hester about to let the boy flaunt his opinions the way he did.

'I'm sorry,' he said suddenly. 'There is no call for us to quarrel. I speak the way I do for your own good.'

'I understand that,' said Simon, 'but you wrong Hugo.'

'Mayhap.'

'I owe him my life, father.'

'Then I am in his debt also. Let us speak no more of him.' He searched his mind for a less controversial subject. 'So what do you think of this bride I have found for you?' asked Luke.

'I know so little of this Hannah,' said Simon cautiously.

'Then let me tell you,' said Luke, 'for her father has written at length on the subject. You shall see the letter later. Hannah Wenbury is sixteen years old and plump as a partridge. Not *too* plump they tell me,' he said hastily, 'and with a sweetness of expression rare in one so young. Serenity is a better word, I think. A serenity of expression.'

'You speak of her expression, but what of her face?'

'Er – homely,' said Luke, 'a homely face with a pleasing and serene expression. You'll be charmed by her, Simon, I promise you. Her father says she is an expert needlewoman, is thrifty –'

'How homely?' asked Simon.

Luke shrugged. 'You must decide that for yourself when you see her,' he said. 'She sings most prettily, I have heard that for myself from an old friend. Cooks, spins, can speak in French and reads a little Latin.'

Simon's heart sank. Plump and homely! She did not sound too great a catch but beggars couldn't be choosers. Her dowry was large, her family well connected and he, Simon, was born out of wedlock and must think himself fortunate. Indeed he did, he insisted silently. But plump and homely!

'Looks are not everything,' said Luke, noticing Simon's reluctance. 'A pretty wife can be tiresome and a great expense. Not to mention vain and easily flattered by other men.'

'She is very young,' said Simon.

'The difference in your ages is of no consequence,' said Luke. 'Look at Melissa and Thomas. Twenty years or more between them yet they are very happy.'

'They seem to be,' Simon admitted. He was pleased to see the visible affection growing between the newly weds after so inauspicious a start. Yet he himself was strangely eager to be wed. Hugo's wedding to Margaret was due in three months' time and he, too, wished to be a husband. The friendship between himself and Hugo had been cemented on the battlefield and they now spent as much time as they could together. If Hannah was rejected it might take six more months to negotiate another possible bride by which time Hugo might well be a prospective father!

'Say you'll think it over,' urged Luke. 'I would like to see you wed before I die and I may not have much more time.'

'Father. Don't speak that way,' said Simon.

'It may grieve you, yet 'tis true,' said Luke. 'I'm recovered from the arrow but have lost my former strength. I doubt I shall live to see my grandchildren but a daughter-in-law! That would make me very happy.'

Simon looked at his father and was forced to admit there had been a marked deterioration in his health since the accidental wounding at Crediton. Luke's neck was healed but badly puckered and his face was thinner with an unhealthy pallor. His walk was laboured and his breathing was permanently impaired. He had aged suddenly and nothing would undo the damage.

Simon smiled. 'I'll do more than think on it,' he said. 'I'll take the wench. A plump body is a comforting thing and I can close my eyes while she sings!'

Luke laughed as Simon had hoped he would. 'You won't regret it, Simon,' he said. 'I promise you, she will make you happy. You are dearer to me than anyone else in the world and I want your happiness above all things. And remember Simon, beauty is in the eye of the beholder. A man sees what he wants to see.'

It was Simon's turn to laugh. 'I'll try, Father,' he said. 'I'll try.'

Hugo was out hawking with his stepfather when the government's men arrived to arrest him. They waited, still mounted, in the courtyard of the house. Hugo saw them as he rounded the bend in the drive and guessed at once the purpose of the visit. His first thought was one of incredulity. The second was anger. His stepfather thought only of flight! They slowed their horses a little and debated what should be done while the grim-faced men ahead waited for them to draw level.

'You could elude them,' muttered his stepfather. 'You could be a mile away before they gathered their wits about them.'

'And give them the pleasure of a hunt? No thank you. If I'm to be arrested, I shall give them no sport.'

'But you could go right away – to France, mayhap – though what your mother will say –'

It was too late. The leader of the group now rode forward and saluted briskly. He took a parchment from his coat and began to read in a dull monotone. 'I am hereby authorized in the name of Edward Tudor, your rightful sovereign, to inform you of certain complaints made against you and the charges laid which do amount to treason against King and country and I am hereby authorized in the name of His Majesty to place you under arrest until such time as you be brought to trial on the said charges.'

Hugo opened his mouth to protest but the man held up a peremptory hand and continued. 'Are you Hugo Bannerman born Kendal?'

'I am,' said Hugo.

'Then 'tis my duty to escort you to Exeter to be imprisoned there until further notice.'

Hugo nodded but his stepfather intervened, white-faced. 'I protest,' he said, 'in the strongest terms. My son has committed no treason and this accusation is falsely made, I will stand surety for his good faith and loyal –'

'You waste your breath, sir,' said the man coldly. 'Your son took part in the recent disturbances, did he not?'

'He did,' he agreed reluctantly, 'but so did –'

'And took arms against the King at Exeter, Crediton and Clyst St Mary?'

'I – I know not exactly.'

'And more recently has spoken provocatively against the new religion and protested adherence to the Popish faith?'

Hugo made a gesture to his stepfather to silence him. 'I am not on trial yet,' he said. 'We have no need to answer these charges or to speak on such matters. I'll accompany you.'

'You most certainly will!' he sneered. 'Take him away.'

'But,' stammered Bannerman, 'when can I visit him? He'll need clean clothes and food.'

'See the gaoler,' he said curtly.

The four men wheeled their horses and Hugo called, 'Tell Mama not to fret. They have no case against me.'

But Bannerman, watching him ride away under escort, knew that they had a very strong case. And if he were found guilty of the charge of treason, he might well hang.

The first Luke knew of the arrest was when Hester was shown into the Hall, her eyes red and swollen, her hands nervously twisting and fumbling with her handkerchief. He stared at her in astonishment and, in spite of his dislike for her, felt a certain amount of pity for her obvious distress.

'Hester! What brings you here?' he asked, indicating a chair. To his surprise she made no move to sit down but stared at him beseechingly while fresh tears gathered in her eyes.

'What's happened?' he asked. 'Is it your husband? Is he ill?'

She drew a deep shuddering sigh and dabbed at her eyes.

''Tis Hugo!' she gasped at last. 'My son! They've taken him away and they mean to hang him. They mean to kill Hugo and you must stop them. They'll listen to you, Luke.'

'Taken him away?' said Luke. 'Arrested him, do you mean? On what charge, for heaven's sake?'

'On a charge of treason,' she cried and she seized his coat desperately. 'Don't let him die, Luke, I beg you. Whatever our differences in the past I beg you to save my son.'

'I cannot save him,' said Luke, detaching her fingers from his coat. 'Please control yourself, Hester, and sit down.'

'No one can save him except you!' she burst out, springing up from the chair as soon as she had sat down. 'My husband says you have friends who will help him – influential friends.'

'Protestant friends,' said Luke coldly.

'I care not what they are if they will but speak for him. Intercede for him, Luke, I beseech you. He did no more than many others, no more than your boy. Why should Hugo die and not Simon? 'Tis so unfair.'

'You think my boy should die also, is that it?'

'Don't speak of dying!' she cried, falling to her knees, her body shaking with the violence of her sobbing. 'In God's name, Luke, be merciful. I confess we have disagreed in the past, you and I.'

'We have indeed,' said Luke evenly but his mind raced. So Hugo was likely to hang. What neater way to rid Simon of his only possible rival to Heron! He felt no compassion for the lad. How could he: they were little more than acquaintances. Since his quarrel with Hester

406

he felt no kinship. What were the Bannermans to a Kendal? If Hugo was alienated from the family, then Hester was to blame and she should take the consequences of her actions.

'But Hugo has no quarrel with you!' she cried. 'Don't punish him for our quarrels, I beg you!'

'The boy is a fool,' said Luke brusquely. 'He escapes from the rebellion with his life and instead of thanking God and lying low, he must needs rant on about injustice and reiterate his Popish sympathies. I warrant he deserves his downfall. And you are at fault for not restraining him – oh, get up, woman. Do you think your pleas carry more weight while you grovel on the floor? Here, take my hand.' He pulled her roughly to her feet and then walked to the window preferring the view of the moor to that of Hester. 'If I lifted a finger to help your son,' he went on, 'I should likely put my own son's liberty at risk. I have no desire to draw attention to the fact that they were friends nor that they were together throughout the campaign.'

'But Hugo saved Simon's life!'

'So I'm told but to my mind the facts are wildly exaggerated.'

'Exaggerated! How can you say that? Simon was trapped under a roof beam in a burning house that was shortly to be overrun by the King's troops! Had Simon stayed there he would have burned to death or been slaughtered by the enemy! Exaggerated! How dare you twist the truth –' She broke off, suddenly aware that her indignant attitude was not furthering Hugo's cause.

'I do dare,' said Luke 'but you are not here to recount old tales. You came to inform me of Hugo's arrest and to ask my help. I'm sorry I don't feel it would be wise. The Bannermans are Papists and make no secret of it – no, not even now when discretion on such matters is vital.'

'If he were a Kendal?'

'He is not a Kendal.'

'I can change his name again.'

''Tis too late. He must abide by your mistakes.'

'Oh sweet heaven! You are enjoying this!' she screamed. 'If Alison were alive now she would scarce believe her ears! You revel in my grief and gloat over Hugo's misfortune. Don't deny it, for I hear it in your voice even if you cannot bear to face me while you utter the words.'

Incensed, he turned to face her. 'You want me to face you, is that it?' he asked. 'Very well. I am facing you. And I repeat. If Hugo hangs 'twill be his own fault – I will not jeopardize Simon's life to save a Bannerman.'

With a strangled scream she flew at him, punching and tearing at his hair and clothing. She was like a woman possessed and Luke, fending off her blows, found the look in her eyes distinctly unnerving.

'If he dies, you'll die also!' she screamed, 'for I swear I will kill you with my own two hands!'

Beth, coming into the room with a tray of wine, immediately froze with shock at the sight which greeted her. Then, with a cry, she set down the tray and ran to Luke's aid. She struggled to pull Hester away from her master but in doing so turned the hysterical woman's wrath upon herself.

'Your master is a murdering swine!' screamed Hester and even her voice was distorted by the hate she felt for Luke.

'Don't you miscall the master!' cried Beth loyally, but Hester lunged forward and tried to strike her too. Nimbly, Beth side-stepped and Hester, losing her balance, fell sprawling among the rushes.

'Oh ma'am,' stammered Beth and looked to Luke for guidance for the situation was quite beyond her experience.

'Don't fret, Beth,' said Luke. His expression was grim and yet his voice betrayed him. He was more shaken than he would admit. 'Pour her a glass of wine, then help her up,' he said. 'If I lay hands on her I swear I shall do her harm.'

Beth pulled Hester to her feet and guided her on to the bench beside the table.

'When she has drunk,' said Luke, 'send her home. Thomas had best go with her to make sure she doesn't return.'

He gave Hester one last look and strode from the room. Nervously, Beth held out the wine. 'Here ma'am, drink this,' she said kindly. ''Twill soothe you.'

Hester looked at her wonderingly.

'The wine,' said Beth. 'Just a sip, ma'am. 'Twill comfort you.'

Hester looked at her with the beginning of comprehension. Her rage had vanished, leaving her dejected and tired. A few straws clung to her hair adding to her dishevelled appearance. Obediently, she sipped the wine which Beth offered. 'They're going to hang my son,' she said tremulously.

Beth's eyes widened with horror. 'Hang your son?' she repeated. 'Hang Hugo? Oh, no ma'am. They mustn't!'

'They will,' said Hester dully. 'Only Luke can save him and he refuses.'

'The master?' cried Beth indignantly. 'He wouldn't do such a thing.'

'He does,' said Hester, all the emotion drained from her voice. 'He refuses.'

Now Beth understood the spectacle she had witnessed. 'But why, ma'am? I don't understand.'

Hester shook her head without answering and Beth remembered the wine. She put it into Hester's hand and made sure that she held it safely. 'I'll be away to find

Master Bennet,' she said. 'You wait here, ma'am. And don't despair, ma'am. Your Hugo is a fine man and God won't let him die. We must pray for him.'

She hurried in search of Thomas and Hester took another sip of wine. ''Twill take more than prayers to save my son,' she said and gave herself up once more to grief.

Luke sat beside the river watching the shadows lengthen across the water. It was cold but he was not aware of it. His fingers picked at a twig, stripping the bark, and a phrase of Isobel's came into his head. 'Shrieding the brambles,' she had called stripping off the outer layer. Poor Isobel. He hoped she was at peace at last. On the far side of the river a water rat slipped into the water with barely a sound and he watched the surface ripple as it swam across. It emerged almost at his feet, and, sensing danger, turned instantly and dived back into the water. Luke sighed. Everyone else was over at Maudesley celebrating someone's birthday – he couldn't remember whose but he had pretended a backlog of work and remained behind to be alone with his thoughts.

Hugo's trial was fixed and would be held in a week's time. The evidence was heavy against him and there was little chance of a sympathetic verdict. The boy was a young fool. A hot-head . . . Once, long ago, Luke Kendal had been young and foolish. He had loved unwisely and had been alone and frightened. He shook his head. He would not dwell on the past. Isobel was dead and Alison also. The rat emerged once more on the far side of the water and vanished into a small hole in the river bank. Luke glanced round. Not even the dogs kept him company! He was truly alone and had wanted it that way but the idea troubled him. Everyone was at Maudesley. They were all united in celebration but he,

Luke, was sitting by the river without even a dog for company. He frowned, snapped the twig and tossed it into the water. It floated a yard or so and then became entangled on the edge of a patch of weed.

Damn Hugo! Why did the name haunt his dreams, waking and sleeping? Hugo – he was tired of the very word. He tried to imagine Simon trapped under a beam but the image remained elusive. Did Simon owe his life to Hugo? Sophie's letter had arrived that morning asking him to reconsider. Simon argued constantly on the boy's behalf. Hester had written after their meeting, apologizing for her hysterical behaviour and urging him to save her son, for Stephen's sake if not for hers. Poor Stephen. He had been an unhappy discontented man and by all accounts an unhappy boy. Only Catherine had ever been close to him and she was dead, too. He smiled faintly. No doubt if she had lived, she would have written also! Was he wrong? The question surfaced in his mind, shocking him. Damnation! Why hadn't Hugo died nobly during the fighting? That way the threat to Simon's inheritance would have been removed with no ill will. Hester would have mourned a hero and all would be fair. Was he, Luke, being strong now, or stubborn as Simon alleged? The servants whispered about him behind his back, he knew, no doubt calling him a monster.

His doubts multiplied. Was he making yet another mistake in a life full of mistakes? Had the dissolution of the monasteries been progress after all, or merely desecration, as some said? Certainly now the poor went largely uncared for and travellers were hard put to find decent lodgings. He looked down into the brown water and fancied he saw the glint of silver. The Priory plate lay where he had thrown it. Alison had been so pleased. But Paul had died. And Jeffery. His two fine sons . . .

With a jolt he faced another thought, that losing two

sons he envied Hester hers. Was he jealous of the fact
that her son lived while his were gone from him? The
idea persisted and he groaned suddenly. He threw himself backwards and lay staring up at the grey sky. Was he
to have no peace of mind! Was he wrong? Dear God, was
he wrong? He sighed wearily and covered his eyes. The
earth struck coldly through his clothes and he shivered,
then with a cry of desperation he sat up. 'God's blood!'
he cried. 'My head spins and my mind is in a turmoil. I
shall have no peace! No peace! Let me be, dear God, and
I will try to save him!'

The decision made, he wasted no time. Telling no one
about his intention, he saddled a horse and rode towards
Exeter. That very night he spoke with Blackaller, Mayor
of Exeter and the next day with Piers Courtenay, Sheriff.
The next day found him with Sir Peter Carew who
promised to do what he could. Wheels were set in
motion, legal advice sought and experts consulted. The
trial was a brief one at which Luke stood surety for
Hugo's future good behaviour. In spite of all their efforts, the death sentence was only narrowly averted. But
it *was* averted. Instead Hugo was heavily fined and
ordered into exile. His father would pay the fine. He
would once more take the name of Kendal and he and
Margaret would be quickly wed and leave England.
They would settle in Figeac, in the South of France,
where Margaret's grandparents would keep a watchful
eye on them. All in all, it was a bitter price to pay – but it
was a great deal better than a hanging.

The ale house was full to overflowing for the night's
drinking was nearly over. Many had drifted in during
the evening but few had drifted out. Men sat on the

benches, sprawled across the tables and lay on the floor in a variety of ungainly positions. Some, still sober enough, rolled dice and squabbled happily over the results. Another group played cards, peering blearily at each hand and finding it difficult to extract one card at a time from the fan of five. A fat man, propped in the corner for his own safety, belched loudly and frequently and with each belch the remaining ale splashed out of his tankard and on to his clothing. An old woman sat at the table, her head on her arms, oblivious to those around her who in turn ignored her snores. The air in the small room was foul with sour breath and the smell of cheap ale. A continuous stream of drinks were handed up from the cellar below as empty tankards were passed down to be refilled. On a bench against the wall sat Simon, his empty tankard hanging from one finger, out of sight and out of mind. Simon was too wretched to care. His head was spinning and his stomach heaved ominously. He would have to get out. He dropped the tankard and pushed himself to his feet. There was an immediate outcry as he tripped over one pair of feet and stepped on another.

'Forgive me,' he muttered.

He reached the fresh air outside and the January air chilled his body so that he shivered violently. He took a few steps along the road then slipped on the frosty cobbles. As he fell, his stomach gave a final lurch and he vomited the evening's ale.

His misery was complete but almost at once he began to recover. The sour ale was gone and with it the queasy bloated feeling of too much to drink on an empty stomach.

'Well,' said a familiar voice. 'You're a sight for sore eyes, Simon Betts – or should I say Kendal!'

Slowly he raised his head, which still throbbed abominably. 'Maggie!'

'Aye, 'tis Maggie,' she said. 'Here, give me your hand. We'll get you on your feet. I never thought to see you again, nor in such straits. You stink, Simon Betts, and that's the truth.'

He shook his head. 'Leave me be,' he said. 'I don't want to get up.'

''Tis not a case of what you want,' she said tartly, ''tis a case of me leaving you littering up the street so on your feet I say. Up!'

Too depressed to argue, Simon allowed himself to be hauled to his feet. He swayed uncertainly as soon as Maggie released his arm and she took hold of him again to stop him falling.

'You're coming home with me Simon Betts,' she told him, 'and don't give me any nonsense. What would your father think to see you this way. A bowl of goat's milk is what you need.'

'Ugh.'

'Aye, you may well pull a face but 'tis a certain cure. It soothes the stomach wonderfully and clears the brain. Now don't cross me, Simon. I say you're coming with me.'

She jerked him off balance and dragged him, mumbling and protesting, along the street to the bakery.

'Your father,' he began.

'Taken his usual draught,' she said, 'and won't stir until sun-up.'

'Maggie, I'm sorry –'

'Aye and so you should be,' she said but the sharpness had left her voice and there was concern in her eyes. 'Now you go into the kitchen.'

'What about the lad?' said Simon. 'He'll see me.'

'There's no lad,' said Maggie. 'The one we've got now only lives at the end of the street so he doesn't live in. Your bed's still empty.'

He stumbled into the kitchen and sank on to a stool.

The goat's milk was cool and bland after the ale and when he had drunk a large bowlful, Maggie wiped his face with a damp towel.

'You're too good to me,' he said.

She smiled. 'You look better,' she told him. 'More like a Kendal than a Betts. Oh, I know now what happened. It was a kind of justice, wasn't it? I told Luke Kendal about his daughter to be rid of her and instead 'twas you that disappeared.'

'Why, Maggie?' he asked. 'Why did you do that?'

'I was jealous. I loved you – didn't you know?'

He shook his head. 'There were so many of us,' he said with an attempt at a smile. 'So many baker's lads!'

'Aye, many lads,' she said softly, 'but only one Simon Betts. But that's enough talking. Here's me chattering like a starling and you with a sore head! Up to bed with you.'

In the little room under the roof she helped him undress. It seemed strange to Simon to be once more in the familiar room, sleeping on blankets on the straw. He stretched out thankfully and Maggie threw two more blankets over him. He closed his eyes then opened them again. Maggie was slipping out of her clothes.

'There's no call to stare,' she said. ''Tisn't often I get the chance to sleep with young Master Kendal from Heron! Oh, don't gawp at me, you ninny. I'll let you sleep. You have my word on it.'

She snuggled down beside him and blew out the candle. 'Kiss me good night,' she said, 'and I'll die happy.'

He grinned faintly as he kissed her. 'You haven't changed,' he said.

'Nor have you,' she said. 'Call it Betts or call it Kendal – I'd know that body anywhere!'

In the morning he woke to find her propped on one elbow, watching him. 'Are you recovered?' she asked.

He felt his head gingerly. 'Aye,' he said. 'That goat's milk did all that you claimed. The hammering in my head has stopped.'

'Then hold me in your arms,' she said 'while you tell me what you were about last night. Cup shotten outside an alehouse! And you a gentleman!'

He sighed. 'I've no wish to think on it,' he said.

'Tell Maggie!' she demanded. 'To drink that way, and alone. You were unhappy?'

'I was in low spirits,' he confessed. 'Hugo – he's my cousin and a good friend – he saved my life.'

'I heard all about that. But why the long face? He wasn't hanged after all. He was exiled.'

'Aye, exiled! I shall miss him.'

'Better an exile than a corpse,' she said. 'He might have been hanged. Many were, God rest their souls. He can count himself fortunate that your father spoke up for him. They say the young fool argued most rashly against the government while in prison!'

'He's a brave man, Maggie.'

'Some say otherwise and call him a hot-head. But I'll take your word on it,' she said. 'So because your cousin's life is saved you drink too much bad ale and make a spectacle of yourself.'

She kissed his shoulder lightly and he sighed. 'My bride is coming tomorrow,' he said.

'Ah!' she said, 'now *that* is a reason for drinking bad ale! What is she like, this bride-to-be?'

'Homely,' he said, 'and plump and very young.'

'Why look so gloomy? She will adore you. What more can a man ask of his wife?'

He smiled wryly. 'She cooks, spins, can read French, sings –'

'Ah, that makes two of us – "My true love is a miller – Fol lal de rol –"'

Simon laughed aloud. 'I doubt she will know *that* song,' he said.

'Then you must teach it to her,' said Maggie. 'Do you remember the first time, Simon, on the way to the mill, and my father ranted that we were so late.'

'And I said a wheel had come off!'

'He didn't believe you! You never were a good liar, Simon . . . So now you are to be wed. I shall come to the wedding and throw petals.'

'Do you forgive me the hurt I gave you?' he asked.

'I do willingly for 'twas not of your choosing – and before that you gave me such joy.'

'Kiss me, sweet kind Maggie.'

They kissed and she knew at once that when he left her the familiar heartache would remain.

'Won't you marry, Maggie?' he asked her.

'No.'

'Because of me?'

'Aye,' she said. 'I spoke truly when I said you were not one of the lads. For me, you are the one, Simon. Yet I know we cannot wed. 'Twould be improper for a Kendal to wed a baker's daughter.'

'But what will you do?'

'I'll have the lads, bless 'em!' she laughed. 'Love them and leave them. I'm a whore at heart, Simon, you know that . . . You wed your homely girl and live in your fine house but if you ever need Maggie, I'll be here waiting with a loving kiss, and a warm body.'

'Maggie! What can I say?'

'Say that you'll come to me sometimes.'

A shadow crossed his face and he sighed. ''Tis a fine offer, Maggie,' he said, 'and I swear I'm sorely tempted. Any man would be.'

'Then why the long face suddenly?'

'Because I'd be doing what my father did. I'd be making his mistake. He caused my mother great unhappiness. She wanted to be wed, wanted to be his wife. And she wanted a father for her child.'

'He told you all this?'

'Aye. But he was betrothed already to Alison, as I am to Hannah. I couldn't bear to see you suffer, Maggie.'

'Bless you!' cried Maggie 'but 'tis not the same thing at all – for I've no wish to be Mistress Kendal and I know better than to get with child. Why, I'd have a whole brood of 'em by now if I was so inclined. There's ways and means, Simon, that likely your mother didn't know. Or didn't want to know. If a woman wants a man, then a swollen belly is a fine spur to a wedding! No offence meant and none taken, I trust, but I'm Maggie and I'm happy the way I am. When my father goes, God bless him, the shop's mine so I'm well provided for.'

'You have a very persuasive tongue,' he said.

'Oh I have!' she cried wickedly and thrust it out. 'I've persuasive hands, too, and some say my breasts are –'

'Maggie! Maggie!' he laughed. 'You wicked woman! You should be sitting on a rock luring ships to their doom. You'd make a good siren.'

'I'd sooner lure the sailors to theirs!' she told him. 'So come on, Simon. Take a chance on me, won't you? If you're happy sleep alongside your lawful wedded wife but if you're not getting enough – to eat – come to the bakery for a nibble at the cake!'

He grinned.

''Tis a bargain, then?' she asked.

'Aye.' He held out his hand palm upwards and she slapped it with hers.

'Done!' she declared. 'So what say you to a breakfast of good ale and a veal pasty as melts in your mouth. Made, last night, they were, and I'd just delivered a half dozen to the butcher's wife when I saw this drunken oaf sprawled in my path.'

He groaned. 'Don't speak of it,' he begged, 'but the ale and the pasty sound perfect.'

'Then you shall have it, my dear. But first you have to earn it,' she said her eyes sparkling. 'And my veal pasties don't come cheap.'

''Twill be my pleasure,' he said.

'My true love be a gentleman,' sang Maggie between kisses.

'I'll not be gentle long,' grinned Simon. 'Keep still, you baggage!'

'Fol lal de rol,' she sang, 'and rides a fast horse – ah, that's sweet, that is! But two can play at that game!'

Her unruly curls brushed his chest as she returned his kisses. Then he felt them softly on his thighs and legs until he took the curly head in his hands and drew her gently back to look into her sensuous brown eyes that glowed with amusement and pleasure. She sighed voluptuously and gave herself up to their mutual pleasure. Later, when she lay in his arms drowsy and satisfied, she said, 'You have earned *two* veal pasties, Master Kendal Sir!'

He was still laughing when she went downstairs to fetch his breakfast singing 'Fol lal de rol dol day!'

CHAPTER TWENTY-THREE

The horse stumbled and Hannah cursed under her breath. The road, pitted and deeply rutted by the autumn rains, had now suffered a severe frost and the irregularities of its surface had hardened, making their progress slow and uncomfortable. Her brother glanced at her sullen face but said nothing. They had ridden for three days in drenching rain and bitter cold; he had been thrown once from his horse and now nursed a painfully swollen knee. His original attempts at cheerfulness had long since faltered into an aggrieved silence broken only by exclamations of discomfort from Hannah and an occasional comment from Lettice, the maid. There was no love lost between brother and sister and he would have much preferred to have stayed at home in comparative comfort. But Horace Wenbury, his father, suffered from gout which was particularly bad at present and no one could pretend he was fit enough to undertake the long journey from Rye to Ashburton.

Hannah's horse stumbled again and this time her curse was loud and clear. 'God's blood! These damned roads!' she exploded, glaring accusingly at Gregory as though he was personally responsible for them. He looked at her coldly.

'How becoming,' he said sarcastically. 'How very lady-like.'

'Is that all you can say?' she asked furiously. 'Do you

offer no help, no sympathy? Is that how you see your task as my escort – to *watch* my sufferings? Nothing more? Not a word of regret or a kindly smile?'

'Would kind words mend the road?' he asked in mock surprise. 'I had no idea. Will a smile from me guide your horse to smoother ground? Amazing!'

Behind them Lettice rolled her eyes despairingly and prayed that they would reach their destination before one of them killed the other! Fortunately, engrossed in their own disagreements, they left her to her own resources and she allowed her horse to fall back a little so that she could hum or sing to herself to keep her spirits up. She was a cheerful girl and had looked forward to the change in her life with great optimism. Gregory and Hannah might spit words at each other and their looks might wound but she, Lettice, would enjoy the adventure in spite of the discomforts of a long January ride.

Hannah, speechless with rage, reined in her horse. 'One more word from you,' she spluttered, 'and I swear I shall turn round and go home. Aye, ride home again to civilization. I shall tell Papa the journey was impossible and your behaviour matched it to perfection! I can't imagine what persuaded me to agree to such a scheme! I should have waited for spring and Papa might have accompanied me.'

'I wish you had done so!' he said. 'I find no pleasure in riding through this God-forsaken land with a shrew at my side.'

'Shrew, am I?' she shouted. 'So 'tis shrew, now, is it? A fine way to speak to your sister. A fine word to choose for your own flesh and blood!'

'An apt word!' he said. 'And you prove it each time you open your mouth. I pity the man who waits for you, indeed I do.'

'Pity *him*?' cried Hannah. 'Oh, you go far to pity *him*!

What of me, then? D'you not pity me, betrothed to a man no one has seen, a bastard son adopted with indecent haste, who has driven his half-sister out of the house – but I shall tame the wretch!'

'The sister is wed,' he protested. 'She's moved out of her own accord to live with her husband.'

'That's what they say,' said Hannah, 'but to me it sounds unlikely. If you ask my opinion –'

'I don't,' he said.

'– this Melina probably hates him –'

'Melissa,' he corrected her. 'And you have no reason to think so. You are determined to think ill of them all because you cannot wed the man you wish. Oh don't bother to deny it! You have never recovered from that disappointment and likely never will.'

'I don't deny it,' she countered. 'Vincent Cawley comes from a rich and powerful family and aye, I hoped to wed him.' She sighed heavily and a tinge of conscience smote him. Hannah's dowry had been insufficient and the long negotiations had come to nothing. By comparison, Simon Kendal was a poor match and her disappointment was understandable.

'At least he was a Protestant,' said Hannah. 'I have my doubts about the Kendals.'

'They fought in the recent troubles,' Gregory protested.

'Aye, but on which side?' she demanded. 'They did not say in so many words. The whole country is riddled with Papists if we are to believe all we hear. I shall ask him outright.'

Gregory looked at her, alarmed. 'Papa warned you not to speak of it,' he reminded her. 'It would be most foolish to do so.'

'Nevertheless I shall ask,' she said with more assurance than she actually felt. 'Do you mumble your prayers in Latin, I shall say. Do you worship wall paint-

422

ings and wave palm leaves?'

'Hannah! In the name of God, talk sensibly, I beg you. Luke Kendal was wounded by a Cornish arrow and was at death's door. How much more proof do you need? The rebellion is too recent, too painful a subject. You must not speak of it. Papa was most insistent.'

'Papa is not betrothed to the son,' she said sharply, 'and I am.'

He sighed wearily. 'Then save your inquisition until I am gone,' he said. 'I have no wish to see it. 'Tis enough for me that I know you as ill-tempered. Now, d'you intend to remain here, ride home or go forward to Heron? For my part I care little but it will be dark before long.'

Lettice, listening, crossed her fingers for luck and the charm worked. After a brief hesitation, Hannah urged her horse forward in the direction of Ashburton and the little party moved on towards Heron.

Melissa gave the Hall a cursory glance. The fire was well stocked with logs, fresh lavender had been added to the rushes underfoot and the food stood ready on the table. Upstairs fires were burning in the bedchambers and a few herbs had been sprinkled onto the flames to sweeten the air for the windows were shuttered to keep out the cold and the air grew stale. Jack and Jon had ridden out along the Exeter road to meet the visitors and Jon had returned home with an approximate time of their arrival at Heron. Jack stayed with them as guide for the last few miles of their journey.

Melissa put a hand to her heart which beat faster than usual. 'Stop thumping, heart!' she told it. 'Why are you so upset? 'Tis only Simon's betrothed and what is that to me? Anyone would think the young King Edward was making a call on me. There's no panic, little heart. Pray calm yourself.'

But her heart did not slow down. She put a hand to her face, smoothing her eyebrows, resetting her head-dress for the third time and then tucked back a stray hair that dared to show itself. If only Thomas was with her, she would not feel so ridiculously afraid but he had business in Chagford and would not be back until the morning. Where was Simon? He had made an appearance in the dark plum colour that suited him so well and had now disappeared again. She sighed with exasperation and checked the table once more. The salmon was cold and glazed and decorated. The bride-to-be had arrived at Heron and she, Melissa, who had once loved him so deeply, must go smiling to welcome her . . .

Hannah allowed herself to be helped down by Jon, whom she recognized from the meeting earlier. Gregory was dismounting and Lettice was waiting for attention. Jack dismounted and helped her to the ground. Dogs leaped around them and were scolded good-humouredly. Her mood had mellowed slightly by this time. She had been flattered that Jon and Jack were sent out to intercept them and Jack had treated her courteously and with a deference which impressed Gregory. The house, at first glance, had proved better than she expected. Rambling under a thick thatch, with well kept lawn and shrubs.

A man came down the steps towards them – probably Luke, she guessed correctly. Behind him a woman, obviously with child, Melissa no doubt, and almost a beauty. A slight frown passed over Hannah's face. She was aware of her own shortcomings – the too-plump figure and lack of grace – and was easily discomfited. But at least they had arrived and there would be warmth and food and a bed to sleep in, hopefully free of fleas. They had suffered at the various overnight stops and her body was covered with tiny red bites. But where was Simon?

'Welcome to Heron, my dear. I hope the journey has not proved too distressing.' It was Luke: her future father-in-law.

She smiled, held out her hand and he put her fingers to his lips. 'A wretched journey,' she said, 'but by the grace of God, we are arrived safely.'

'This is my daughter, Melissa.'

The two women eyed each other curiously.

'Welcome to Heron,' said Melissa and was surprised to hear her voice sounding quite normal in spite of the sudden dryness of her throat. They clasped hands briefly.

'You must be weary and cold,' said Melissa. 'Come straightaway in and we will warm you up. A glass of mulled wine, mayhap, to chase out the cold.'

Hannah looked round expectantly as she allowed Luke to take her arm and lead her into the house. The baggage was unloaded and carried upstairs to her room by Jon while Jack attended to the horses.

Gregory watched while Melissa and Lettice followed wide-eyed with excitement. Still Simon did not appear and Hannah's impatience gave way to the beginning of resentment. So this baseborn Kendal lacked the common courtesies! She caught Gregory's eye and he raised his eyebrows questioningly. The wretch could no doubt gloat over her discomfiture! Hannah forced a smile in answer to a question by Luke concerning her father's health.

'He is making some progress,' she said, 'but he is still in pain and cannot sleep without a sleeping draught.'

Once inside the house Beth came forward, dropped a small curtsey, and was introduced to the young woman who would shortly be mistress of Heron.

'Serve the wine now please Beth,' said Melissa, 'and bring the venison to the table when I ring – oh, and this is Lettice. Please ask Nan to look after her kindly.'

She gave Lettice an encouraging smile and then turned back to her guests. Luke was apologizing for Simon's absence, suggesting that perhaps he had been delayed at the mine. Hannah appeared unconvinced and a slight frown settled over her face, making her plainer than ever. Melissa, seeing it, was thankful that she herself was no longer living at Heron but could retire to the peace of Ladyford when the evening was at an end. Hannah turned to Melissa.

'My brother's knee is troubling him,' she said abruptly. 'He was thrown by his horse. I wonder if a cold compress –'

Gregory protested that it was bearable but Melissa insisted on applying a cold compress and he followed her willingly enough. Luke and Hannah thus left alone considered each other warily.

'My son was impressed with your miniature,' he told her.

'And I with his,' she said. She was aware that her own miniature flattered her. Doubtless Simon's artist had done the same for him. She was prepared for possible disillusionment.

'So what are your first impressions of Heron?' he asked. 'I trust all your expectations are justified.'

'Indeed they are.' She kept her answer short and her smile brief. This man must understand that she, Hannah Wenbury, did not take kindly to a reception which lacked the presence of her betrothed.

'My mother, Elizabeth, devoted her life to Heron,' he told her. 'It is unthinkable that it should ever pass out of the Kendal family. Simon is her most direct descendant.'

He made no mention of Hugo. For the time being the young man safely exiled posed no real threat to Simon's inheritance. 'I hope I shall be worthy of the honour you do me,' said Hannah and resisted the impulse to add

426

'and you the honour I do your son.'

He looked at her anxiously. 'We shall try to make you happy here,' he told her.

'I appreciate your kindness,' she said. 'I pray you forgive my poor spirits. It has been a long and uncomfortable journey.'

He turned away from her suddenly and walked to the window. She waited dejectedly, in no mood for formalities. She was exhausted from her ride, and every bone in her body ached. She was demoralized by her disagreement with Gregory during the journey and felt slighted by Simon's absence. She was also hungry. Tears pricked her eyelids but she willed them back, biting her lip in her anxiety not to disgrace herself before these strangers by giving way to the luxury of weeping.

'Life is never easy,' said Luke. 'Simon's life has not been easy. You know most of his background and no doubt he will tell you more if you wish it. But he has risen above his earlier misfortunes. He is a fine man. I am proud of my son, Hannah, and I love him. I want you to know that.'

She nodded, moved by his words but not trusting herself to speak. At that moment the door opened and Simon himself appeared, breathless from his haste, his hands outstretched to greet her. 'Hannah! Forgive me!' he cried. 'I must be delayed this day of all days! 'Tis quite unpardonable.'

Luke made the introductions and watched as the two young people exchanged a polite kiss. He saw with satisfaction how Hannah's expression changed as she looked at her future husband, seeing the blond head and arrogant blue eyes above the lithe body.

'Greetings, my lord,' she said. At the sight of Simon the weariness left her and her despair faded. So she, Hannah, was to take this proud Kendal for her wedded

427

husband and Dartmoor's Heron was to be her home. The latter suited her well enough. But the man? She doubted she could tame such a man but would try. And deep within herself a small voice whispered that in so doing she might love him also.

CASTLE CARNACK

A passionate romance on
the wild Cornish moors

Mary
Williams

When Sabrina, daughter of Sir Martin Penderrick,
deserted her fiancé in the middle of their wedding, she
expected the consequent uproar in the strict Edwardian
society of the day. What she did not expect was her
meeting with handsome Oliver Cavanagh, a rich
businessman whose forbears had made a fortune from
tea. Their unpredictable marriage sets off a pattern of
dramatic events, leading to tragedy as well as
passionate fulfilment . . .

HISTORICAL ROMANCE   0 7221 9103 0   £1.95

Don't miss Mary Williams' other enthralling novels in Sphere
paperback:

TRENHAWK
THE TREGALLIS INHERITANCE
THE GRANITE KING

FROM A FORGOTTEN AGE OF ELEGANCE – A STORY
OF GLAMOUR, PASSION AND WILD EXCITEMENT

ORIENTAL HOTEL

Janet Tanner

Just the mention of his name . . . and for Elise
Sanderson the years simply rolled away, taking her
back on a sea of bittersweet memories to those heady,
dangerous days before the flames of war had ravaged
the East.

Then, in the golden days of her youth, she had swept
through the doors of the Orient's great hotels, into a
world where bell-boys ran to answer every whim, where
the champagne was permanently on ice, where elegant
men in tails and women in exclusive *haute couture*
danced to the endless music of orchestras.

It was then, she recalled, that she had first seen him,
lounging languidly in a rattan chair, already in uniform,
cigarette smoke curling lazily around half-closed hazel
eyes. It was a dangerous face, she had thought in that
first startled moment. A face to be reckoned with . . .

GENERAL FICTION   0 7221 83372   £2.50

Caroline Gray

Alix Wantage was born into nobility, wealth, opulence . . .
and the stale prospect of an arranged marriage to someone
she could never love. But when she was thrown from her
horse while out hunting, Clark Hale, a brash, young
American photographer was there to lift her spirits and,
with outrageous forwardness, steal her heart.

So begins Alix's remarkable story. Banished from the
country by her aristocratic parents, she and her lover arrive
in the exotic and dangerous wilderness of Malaya to seek
their fortune in rubber. And throughout a life of hope and
passion, despair and tragedy, Alix proves again and again
that she is a woman with the courage to turn her dreams into
sparkling reality . . .

Also by Caroline Gray in Sphere Books:
FIRST CLASS
HOTEL DE LUXE

0 7221 6342 8   GENERAL FICTION   £2.95

A selection of bestsellers from Sphere

FICTION

CYCLOPS	Clive Cussler	£3.50☐
THE SEVENTH SECRET	Irving Wallace	£2.95☐
CARIBBEE	Thomas Hoover	£3.50☐
THE GLORY GAME	Janet Dailey	£3.50☐
NIGHT WARRIORS	Graham Masterton	£2.95☐

FILM & TV TIE-IN

INTIMATE CONTACT	Jacqueline Osborne	£2.50☐
BEST OF BRITISH	Maurice Sellar	£8.95☐
SEX WITH PAULA YATES	Paula Yates	£2.95☐
RAW DEAL	Walter Wager	£2.50☐
INSIDE STORY	Jack Ramsay	£2.50☐

NON-FICTION

A TASTE OF LIFE	Julie Stafford	£3.50☐
HOLLYWOOD A' GO-GO	Andrew Yule	£3.50☐
THE OXFORD CHILDREN'S THESAURUS		£3.95☐
THE MAUL AND THE PEAR TREE	T.A. Critchley & P.D. James	£3.50☐
WHITEHALL: TRAGEDY AND FARCE	Clive Ponting	£4.95☐

Cash sales form:

All Sphere books are available at your local bookshop or newsagent, or can be ordered direct from the publisher. Just tick the titles you want and fill in the form below.

Name_____

Address_____

_____

Write to Sphere Books, Cash Sales Department, P.O. Box 11, Falmouth, Cornwall TR10 9EN

Please enclose a cheque or postal order to the value price plus:
UK: 60p for the first book, 25p for the second book and 15p for each additional book ordered to a maximum charge of £1.90.

OVERSEAS & EIRE: £1.25 for the first book, 75p for the second book and 28p for each subsequent title ordered.

BFPO: 60p for the first book, 25p for the second book plus 15p per copy for the next 7 books, thereafter 9p per book.

Sphere Books reserve the right to show new retail prices on covers which may differ from those previously advertised in the text elsewhere, and to increase postal rates in accordance with the P.O.